The Stranger Under a Distant Sun

Written by

George Orchanian

Dedications

This book is dedicated to those who encouraged me to follow my passion for writing despite the challenges. To my family, who nurtured my storytelling abilities: my uncle, the minister, my aunt, and my mother, who all shared their love for writing with me. A special thanks to the Almighty for answering my prayers and giving me the strength to complete this book. To my readers for embarking on this journey with me, and to my fellow servicemembers, whose camaraderie and experiences have deeply influenced my perspective. This is also for those who have felt out of place, as I once did, adapting to a new country and culture. May this work inspire others to find their voice and share their stories.

Table of Contents

Dedications i

CHAPTER 1 1

CHAPTER 2 6

CHAPTER 3 14

CHAPTER 4 27

CHAPTER 5 35

CHAPTER 6 45

CHAPTER 7 57

CHAPTER 8 65

CHAPTER 9 75

CHAPTER 10 88

CHAPTER 11 113

CHAPTER 12 130

CHAPTER 13 146

CHAPTER 14 156

CHAPTER 15 165

CHAPTER 16 172

CHAPTER 17 181

CHAPTER 18 196

CHAPTER 19 207

CHAPTER 20 217

CHAPTER 21 222

CHAPTER 22 228

CHAPTER 23 241

CHAPTER 24 250

CHAPTER 25 260

CHAPTER 26 284

CHAPTER 27 292

CHAPTER 28 300

CHAPTER 29 315

CHAPTER 30 328

CHAPTER 31 345

CHAPTER 32 349

CHAPTER 33 376

CHAPTER 34 382

CHAPTER 35 393

CHAPTER 36 406

CHAPTER 37 420

About The Author 428

CHAPTER 1

There was an overwhelming expanse of ink blackness. There were also innumerable bright and coruscating distant dots each being a star, a planet, a galaxy that peppered in the dimness of the void everywhere.

It appeared that there was something huge and unknown object moving in this dark realm of space. As it came close enough for scrutiny by a hovering satellite, it seemed huge was not the word to describe the object; it was enormous in size. This thing was changing direction. Certainly, it was not an asteroid nor a meteor, for they don't have tendencies to change their course in mid-flight, so then, it must have been a spaceship of some kind.

This vessel was mystifying in appearance. It had huge and intimidating diametrical rod-like projections and was moving slowly in the eternal night.

These cylindrical projections came with various sizes, lengths, and girths, and they protruded forth in an omni direction. They must have served as either antennas or weapons of some sort.

This starcraft must have been an interplanetary vessel. It occupied massive spatial real estate and was intricate in design, and possibly, it was designed for colonization purposes. It had sundry nooks and crannies with odd geometrical shapes and sizes that embodied the entire exterior of this vessel. It stretched approximately six football fields in length, two football fields in width, and one and a half football fields in depth.

The occupants of this mammoth machine must have numbered in thousands. The new generation of the inhabitants who lived in the world down below had no clue of this enormous ship's previous existence. This behemoth of metal was now hovering approximately two city street blocks above the atmosphere of the planet called Eranduh and was moving silently through the stillness of space at a snail's pace.

"Eranduh" is the name given to this planet by its earlier denizens and it meant "colorful beauty." This planet is much like Earth in most of its aspects and is the fifth planet from the giant star called "Rottat."

There are thirteen planets in this solar system. These planets are in one of the arms of the Andromeda galaxy. The Eranduh planet is not the only life-sustaining planet in this solar system called Tnam; the second planet from the sun is called Ekuoroo, and the eighth Planet from the sun, called Eegroag, also sustains life.

The comparison of the planet Eranduh in reference to Earth, this planet happened to be 2.5 times larger than that of the Earth, and this planet enveloped approximately the same kind of atmosphere that of the Earth, but it contained one extra inert gas, and that was unknown to the earth people. However, there are two distinct races on this giant orb, and they are called Darkans and Eponans.

Darkans are the autochthonous race of this planet. They are physically lofty. They tower between nine and ten feet in height. They are also svelte in body, but possess muscular frames with smooth and purplish-gray skin. Their craniums are glabrous, small, and ovate. They have two large, almond-like eyes. They are in front of their faces. Their eyes are comprised of a red iris and a black pupil surrounded by a white sclera. They have no outer ears, but only a sound canal located on either side of their heads. They have arms more like a human, but their hands have four elongated and pointed digits instead of five. Their legs have thighs that protrude forward. The knees recessed backward, having cannon fetlock joints like horses. The pastern is complemented by a foot with four short digits.

Eponans, on the other hand, are aggressive and orgulous in their demeanor. They are the occupying force on this planet, which is called Eranduh. They come from the eighth planet, which is approximately three times the size of the Earth, it is called Eegroag, and it is in the same solar system where Eranduh is found, and it is called Tnam.

In the planet Eegroag's history, an alien vessel entered the Tnam in search of a metal called "Iridium." They found the planet Eegroag possessed a plethora of Iridium metal, in result, these encroaching aliens did send their emissaries to the planet's surface to negotiate the mining operation that they intended to conduct, but the Eegroag's federation committee rejected their proposal and advised them to leave their hemisphere immediately.

The aliens who inquired about the element Iridium have introduced themselves as the Onguma race from a solar system called Enambue, located approximately two billion miles from the planet Eegroag in the Andromeda galaxy.

The Onguma population were tall beings. They stood nearly ten feet in height and had a gray-green hued skin. Their craniums were wide and bald at the top. Their faces appeared curved having a pointed chin. They had an inch-long slit for a mouth and gill-like apparatus on each side of their faces used for breathing. They had large and bulging eyes, with blue iris and red pupils.

The Ongumas did not receive the mining rejection of the Eponans very well, in result, a war broke out. The Ongumas attacked the planet Eegroag with their devastating weapons, and consequently, the planet Eegroag incurred a great deal of devastation in life and in resources. Hence, after the war ended with Ongumas, the remnants of the Eponan civilization journeyed through space in great numbers to find a new home for themselves, and they chose to colonize the planet Eranduh.

In the initial weeks of the Eponan's landing on the planet Eranduh, Darkans receive them with alacrity. The Eponans brought technology, medicine, and friendship to the inhabitants of the planet Eranduh, but as time progressed, some of the Darkan tribes initiated prejudice, hostilities, and kerfuffles. This type of hostility was still an ongoing phenomenon between the two civilizations.

Eponans are inherently brawn in structure. They have wide shoulders and huge upper arms. They are also a towering race. When they stand erect, they measure approximately eight to ten feet in height. However, their females measure approximately six feet in stature. Their heads are oval and smooth without hair. Their eyes are large and ovoid, with purple irises and brown pupils located in front of their faces. The rest of their bodies are like humans, except their hands have three thin and long digits, and their feet have three toes. The color of their skin is charcoal brown.

The Eponans are the main governing body of the planet Eranduh. They maintain the planet's security forces (PSF) comprised of air and ground units. Their military bases are in the wilderness and are approximately one-half football field below the surface.

There are a few Eponan military bases situated in the northern region of this planet and some in the southern hemisphere. The ones that are in the northern hemisphere—denizens name the region Jatan. This sector of the land is comprised of hundreds of thousands of square miles of mostly heathland.

In Jatan province, there was an underground military installation that housed more than a few thousand ground troops, a few hundred land vehicles, and over four hundred fighting spacecrafts. The front entrance had a large pair of camouflaged gates simulating a verdant hill.

There was no presence of guards outside the gates or writing of some sort to identify that this was an Eponan military base. The gates contained sensitive sensors, electronic countermeasures, and explosive ordinances for area denial from outside hostile elements. There were many such headquarters around this planet, which housed thousands more troops and military hardware.

CHAPTER 2

This huge and unidentified vessel that was hovering above the planet Eranduh has suddenly come to life on the space communication and security monitors of the planet. Lieutenant Knbeh's eyes were heavy from many sleepless nights; despite his condition, he was monitoring the screens for any aberrancies.

Suddenly Knbeh's eyes widened in an utter surprise and acquired a befuddled expression laced with dread on his face. He moved his head close to the monitor screen expeditiously, glaring at the screen attentively in disbelief. He rubbed his eyes violently to confirm that his eyes were not betraying him.

"Hey Captain, come. You need to look at this. This--this thing just popped on my screen just now out of nowhere," said the lieutenant, raising his eyebrows in astonishment.

"What—what is it," asked the captain, glaring at Knbeh with absent stares.

"You won't believe this captain, but there is a strange-looking spaceship above our atmosphere. This thing just appeared on my screen, and it—it is not one of ours," said Lieutenant Knbeh in accentuated haste.

"A spaceship!" asked the captain, scowling his face in consternation.

"Yes captain—a spaceship!" said the lieutenant with his eyes still glued to the screen and monitoring its every move. The captain dropped what he was doing and walked hastily toward the lieutenant to have a look at the monitor screen.

"What—the heck is this ship doing in our atmosphere?

"That's what I want to know captain," said Lieutenant Knbeh

"That is a huge mother-load. This thing looks freaking ominous, for sure. And I would say, from the looks of this thing, it does not look friendly at all. I haven't seen anything like this— all these years that I have been working here. However, this beast is beautiful," said Captain Pumok with a bewildered expression laced with dreadful eyes. *"I wonder what are the things coming out of its surface. They look like shafts."*

"Yes sir, I wonder that too," said Lieutenant Knbeh, having eyes full of trepidation.

"Lieutenant, I want you to open a line of communication. Let's see if we're going to get anywhere with this behemoth," asked Captain Pumok, the communication officer in command. The computer at their disposal had a unique universal language translator program to communicate with aliens.

"Yes sir!" responded Lieutenant Knbeh with alacrity. He pushed a few buttons on the console and glared at the huge screen along with Captain Pumok while they both marveled at the ship's enormity.

"It is ready sir. Speak to this piece!" said the lieutenant with excitement.

"Very well." The captain took a deep breath, then sighed slowly and said, *"This is Captain Pumok, the communications officer. We have you on our screens. What is the nature of your visit? Please identify yourself,"* the captain waited silently for a response of some sort, but there was a total silence, no respond? *"Lieutenant, did you do everything right? Did the signal go through?"*

"Yes, sir. I am very well versed with these equipments. I know what I am doing, captain!

"Very well Lieutenant. I was just checking. In that case, open all frequency channels to see if we can get anywhere with this unwelcomed guest," said the captain in anticipated expression.

"Yes sir—right away sir!" replied the lieutenant. His fingers went swiftly on the keyboard and the levers.

"Is it ready, lieutenant?" asked the captain.

"Yes sir, it is all yours. All channels are now open for communication. We should have a dialog as soon as I push this button—sir," said the lieutenant.

"Very well, then do it now!" said the captain vehemently.

"Yes sir," said the lieutenant. He pushed the button and beckoned him with his hand to speak.

"I repeat, this is Captain Pumok. We are observing your vessel on our screens. Please identify yourselves and state your mission?" asked the captain and waited for a respond, but still, there was no response from this outlandish ship, and it remained enigmatic.

"Lieutenant, we're not getting any response yet. Are you sure you have all the channels open?" asked the captain, feeling dubious.

"Yes sir. However, you have asked me this question a second time. I got a feeling that you have no faith in me sir. Captain, I assure you that I have much more expertise on these machines than anyone else who is trained on these gadgets, and that is why they have placed me here to maintain these instruments. I know

perfectly well what I am doing sir. All channels were open for communication sir when you began utter," said the lieutenant.

"Fine then. In this case, we need to notify General Rawa immediately. This may be an emergency at a global scale, and who knows, this vessel may not be the only one in this sector of the universe. There may be more of them on their way here," said the captain with an anxious expression on his face, and he began to sweat from fear and anxiety.

"Lieutenant! Connect me with General Rawa immediately!" said the captain in a loud voice.

"Yes sir!" said the lieutenant and pushed a few more buttons on the consul.

General Rawa suddenly opened his eyes at least halfway up. He became startled and annoyed by the ringing of his communicator that was next to his bed and staired at it for a few seconds in disbelief. The room was dark, and the general was expecting a good and peaceful night's sleep.

"Now, who could be calling me this time an hour? This may not be a good omen," thought General Rawa, acquiring an obfuscated expression.

He reached for his lamp that was on his nightstand and fumbled with his fingers for the on button to turn the light on, then when he turned on the light, he picked up the communication device that was lying next to the lamp and pushed a few buttons then said *"hello."*

"Sir, this is Captain Pumok, the communication officer in charge of Space Traffic Coordination, speaking to you from the space traffic monitoring room. I am sorry to have to bother you at this time an hour, but we have encountered a grave situation

here, and we need you to be informed," said the captain in assertive accentuation and haste.

"All right, I see you're very concerned about something. What's seems to be the urgency you are talking about?" asked the wizened General with an expression of apprehension in his eyes and in his voice. He was going to retire from the service within a month and did not desire to entertain any trouble.

"Sir, at 0200 hours, we have encountered a huge and unknown spaceship hovering just above our atmosphere, and it is still there as we speak, sir. We have attempted to communicate with the alien vessel a few times. We even opened all the channels of communication, and yet, we have received no response from the alien ship.

Sir this ship appears enormous and ominous, and I don't know if there are any more of them on their way here. I am afraid that their intention may not be friendly sir. This is my take on the issue at hand—please advise," said the captain while staring attentively at the screen.

"Is the president aware of this situation you have described so far?" asked the General as calmly as he could manage.

"I don't know sir, but with all due respect sir, it is your duty to inform the president, sir—not I and no one else sir."

"Yes! Yes! Yes! It is late at night and I wasn't thinking. You're right; I must inform the president right away, as a matter of fact, as soon as I get off the comm line with you, but go on," said the General.

"As I was saying sir, it just popped up on our screen, and you are the very first that I have contacted sir. That is my directive *sir, to inform you of anomalies that I encounter,"* said the captain.

"Very well captain, you did well by informing me of this matter. Please open a video line to my screen so that I may witness the ship you are talking about. Here is the address, now let me think for a minute, oh yes I remember—It is "AHR259," said the General. The captain conveyed the address to the lieutenant, and by pushing a few buttons on the console, the General had access to the video.

The General took a few steps back. He became unsteady and almost lost his balance. His eyes were now wide open, surprised and baffled. He said, *"Wow, really! I see what you mean. You're right. This ship is huge! I have never seen this ship before. There must be thousands of them on this ship. You said you have attempted to communicate with that thing, and you haven't had a responded yet. Isn't that right?"* asked the General with concern on his face.

"Yes sir, that's right sir," said the captain, arching his eyebrows in an expression of affirmation.

"This thing definitely looks hostile. I must notify the President immediately," said the general.

"Very well sir. The captain is over and out sir!"

*"S**t! —I hope this is not going to be the end of this world as we know it,"* said the captain in a frustrated expression.

"Sir, I hope not sir," said the lieutenant.

The General stood in his jammies next to his lit-up console with one large red button in the middle that connects directly to the president. There were many smaller, lit-up white buttons surrounding the red one. He reached forward and laid his finger on top of the red button but hesitated for a few seconds to collect his thoughts, then pressed on it.

The president opened his eyes to the reverberating sound of his communicator. The room was dark. The only thing that was lit was the pulsating red button that rested on the fixture on his lamp stand.

The president stood erect. Wiped his eyes and glared at the red button for a second or two, then pressed on it with the palm of his hand.

"Hello, this is the president speaking. What's the nature of this call at this time an hour, and it better be good?" asked President Ganabon.

"Mr. President, this is General Rawa. I know this is an inopportune time to call on you sir, but the nature of my call is of extreme urgency. It involves an unknown and huge vessel hovering just above our atmosphere as we speak, Mr. President," said the General.

"How many ships are there, General?" asked the President.

"So far, only one sir, but there could be more on their way here, Mr. President," said the General.

"Did you attempt to communicate with the alien ship, General?" asked the President.

"Yes sir, there were many attempts made to communicate with the alien ship sir, but they haven't landed a response yet, sir. We really have no idea what their true intention is, or what they are capable of doing sir," said the General.

"In that case, we can't just sit and wait for their reaction, can we, General?" said the president with some concern in his voice.

"No sir we can't," said the general.

"In that case general, galvanize the military immediately. Do not waste any further time, and do what's necessary, then inform me of the progress. God's speed, General Rawa," said the president with resolve.

"Yes sir!" said the General emphatically.

"I would say this conversation is over. Have a good day General," said the President, *"and may the good lord be with us."* He pressed the button and ended the call. General Rawa pressed a button on his console and opened a line of communication with Colonel Vacha. The communication devise pulsated with sound on the other end.

"This is Colonel Vacha. How I may address this call?" asked the Colonel.

"Colonel, this is General Rawa. Gather the war committee to the war room immediately. I'll be there in five minutes. This is urgent, very urgent. Do it now! That's an order!" said the general as if there was an urgency in his voice.

"Yes sir! Right away sir!" said the colonel.

CHAPTER 3

An Eponan soldier with the rank of Second Lieutenant, a Darkan in race. He went by the name of Odeoh. Odeoh has been serving in the Eponan's military ground force for two years. He has gained the respect and honor of the Eponan's military officials through his unmatched skills, performances, attributes, and manners.

Odeoh is a slender build, one-hundred-eight pounds in weight and eight and a half feet in height. It is considered an average height for a Darkan race. However, he gimped slightly as he sauntered —a military accident, he claimed.

Odeoh sashayed into the cyber operation center and went straight into his office, which he shared with an Eponan soldier, then he shut the door behind him. The room was austere and somewhat aphotic.

"Oh! It's about the time you showed up. It is two-thirty in the morning, pointing his finger at his watch. What took you so long? You know you were supposed to be here by twelve in the morning. You are two and a half hours late. I didn't think you were going to show up for work", said First Lieutenant Emoak, an Eponan Soldier with disgust on his face.

"Why do you say I am late? For your information, I am not late, in fact, I am half an hour early. I am supposed to start at three in the morning, didn't you know that? There was a temporary change in my schedule. I thought I had told you that last week. As I have said before, you should have known that by now. You must have forgotten it," said Odeoh with contempt.

Lieutenant Emoak remained silent with a displeased expression on his face.

"However, I am not like you—getting here half an hour late most of the time. You should feel lucky I don't report you," said Odeoh vehemently.

"All right, all right, you've made your point, but no, I don't remember you telling me your new schedule," said Emoak with a slight case of discontentment, then turned around and faced his screen.

"Never mind what I have said, but You know—I am detecting displeasure or fear in your eyes what's troubling you, Lieutenant Emoak. Look—if it is about reporting you to the supervisor for you being late, don't worry, I won't be reporting you. That should ease your mind, now I hope. I want to keep the peace. You understand that don't you?" said Odeoh broodingly.

"It is all well. Thanks for your generous response and for your concern, but no, it's not that I am being late and that you will be reporting me to the management that's troubling me," said Emoak.

"Then—what seems to be eating you? I want to help," asked Odeoh anxiously.

"How about, when you settle down, check your computer monitor and select 'On video'. You are going to be surprised as to what you will be witnessing," said Emoak.

"What—what am I supposed to see, another video of a slaughtered Darkan by your race as it does usually happen?" asked Odeoh dolefully.

"No, no, don't be a racist Odeoh! You know darn well your tribe, 'Nakrue,' and our race have been coexisting peacefully for some time now, thanks to god Moqua, but the Yojy tribe hasn't learned that yet. We provide them with everything: food, clothing, medicine, and education, but they remain barbarians.

"The Yojies attempt to challenge us. They murder our people. They steal our weapons and technologies, and then they use them against us to destroy us. However, as far as the slaughter you have mentioned, no, it is worse than that," said Emoak.

"What!---Really! What could be worse than that?" said Odeoh.

"Well—as I have said, just check it out and find out for yourself. You will see why I am looking so freaking concerned," said Emoak.

"All right then, you've made your point, Lieutenant. You have gotten my attention now. I will see the video as you have suggested," said Odeoh.

"You do that, and let me know your thoughts," said Emoak.

Odeoh sat on his unassuming chair, placed his personal belongings in one of the drawers, and set the backpack under his table. And, when he settled down, he turned his computer on, then selected "On video," and then began to gaze at the screen.

Suddenly, Odeoh's eyes widened in sheer amazement. He froze his sight on the screen for a few seconds in bewilderment. Soon, his chin dropped in trepidation. He couldn't believe what his eyes were witnessing.

Odeoh immediately bolted out of his seat with a perplexed look on his face, and his eyes were still glued to the screen. The chair bolted back at least a few feet. He appeared consumed by the frightening scene on his screen and became perplexed. Odeoh grimaced his face in dread and choler, but he maintained his silence with a look of stupor for a moment or two, thinking, *"This can't be right! This can't be happening! Damnit! The computer can not lie. this is the time to die."* Emoak couldn't stop glaring at Odeoh and uttered, *"What's wrong with you Odeoh, you found out, didn't you? You have become more emotional than I ever expected, as if you are almost going to have a breakdown. Is the situation as bad as I thought it would be?"*

Odeoh turned his head with an anxious look on his face toward Emoak's direction and said: *"It's worse than I have ever imagined. I know I am not all right after seeing this video! However, I do see your point. You have good reason to be concerned. When I entered the room, I saw your face. You appeared dumbstruck. Now that I know the reason, I wouldn't blame you.*

You should be more than worried right now. I don't know if we are going to be alive to see tomorrow," said Odeoh. He pushed his chair towards the table and sat on it, then embraced his face with the palms of his hands in total angst and dismay.

"What the hell are you talking about? It's just an unknown vessel. Yes, it may pose a danger. That is what it concerns me, but we will deal with it," said Emoak.

"Yes, we'll have to deal with it soon, very soon for sure—by our lives perhaps," said Odeoh.

Odeoh knew all about this ship the moment he witnessed its presence in the video. He reckoned that this ship had been here before. He remembered the archived videos that he saw of this ship a few years in the past that made an indelible and frightening impression in his mind.   The chronicled video he observed about this ship belonged to his grandfather Ruhbak, passed on to him from his predecessors.   The video depicted this vessel in mind and the horrid depictions of major destruction of life and resources.

Odeoh thought the arrival of this ship did bode possible eradication of the inhabitants and the resources of this planet on a mammoth scale.   His worst nightmare has just materialized right before his eyes.

Odeoh managed to gather his composure then suddenly blurted out, *"I must address my findings to the war committee as soon as possible.   I hope it is not too late by now.   The brass ranks, and everyone else is clueless about this vessel.   They have no idea what is about to explode in everyone's life. Trust me, it is going to be soon, very soon,"* said Odeoh, having much concern in his expression and in his voice.

"What—what the hell are you talking about Odeoh? You are scaring me!" asked Emoak.

"Look, I don't have much time to explain it all to you right now.   You will find out soon how scary it's going to get.   Summon the war committee to the war room immediately," said Odeoh.

"Is it really that urgent?" asked Emoak.

"Yesssss! —it is that urgent! Time is of the essence! Do as I say while we have time! I must address my findings A.S.A.P. As I have said before, they have absolutely no clue as to with whom they are going to deal very shortly," said Odeoh with intensity in his voice.

"But they're already in the war room contemplating their next move about this freaking vessel that you are so concerned about," said Emoak.

"Excellent, so they do already know about this vessel, and they have seen it on their screens obviously. This is great, and then I will join them right now!" exclaimed Odeoh vehemently. He exited the room expeditiously, meandered through the well-lit but narrow corridors, and when he reached the war room, he faced its large and closed door.

Odeoh held on to the cold doorknob, paused for a few seconds, and ruminated as to what he had to convey as a message to the committee. He quickly gathered his thoughts, made a slight twist at his wrist, and realized the door was unlocked. He pushed and opened the door, then entered the war room; it was dark, illuminated only by a giant video screen that hung on the wall.

There were full of high-ranking Eponan military personnel, and some Darkan officers in the room. They were watching the video of this mammoth ship. The light from the video screen was partially lighting up the faces of the committee members, and Odeoh realized that their expressions were that of a dread. Some were quietly exchanging conversation among themselves and others were silently attempting to absorb the contents displayed on the screen.

Odeoh boldly stepped up on the podium, grabbed the microphone then said, *"Greetings to you all. May I have your attention please!"* Suddenly, the entities in the room quieted themselves, and their eyes became glued on Odeoh, having surprised expressions on their faces.

"Great, now that I have your attention, my name is Odeoh. I am sure most of you are familiar with that name and face but for some of you who don't—I oversee cyber operations. Of course, many of you know that already, but when it comes to this starship on your screen that you are witnessing before your eyes, I am sure all of you are clueless about the nature and intention of this ship. However, don't be dismayed; I have all the answers you are looking for, and that is why I am here at this moment, yes you heard me right, and some of you are already wondering how is it that I should know a thing or two about this vessel you are looking at." Many of the room occupants began to murmur among themselves, asking this same question as to, how be it that he knows a thing or two about this spaceship and we don't.

"May I have quiet here please. I am just about to start if you allow me!" said Odeoh. Everyone suddenly stopped talking and glared at him with unsettled expressions on their faces.

"That's better! —yes, as I have said before, you have heard me right. I have the answers you are looking for. However, I must inform you that the occupants of this enormous ship that you are looking at on the screen are called 'Grolz'.

"The Grolz are grotesque in appearance. They have a huge round head, large bulging eyes, vertical slit in the middle of their faces used for breathing only, and a large mouth with Larna-like teeth (Larna is a flying predator, which has teeth like Parana)."

"How do you know all that, and where are you getting your information from, lieutenant?" blurted an Eponan commanding officer, Colonel Vacha, aloud. He is short in stature, measuring approximately six feet in height, and slightly stocky.

"Well sir that is a good question. I am glad you have asked. You see, colonel, according to my ancestor, they have kept a video Journal, which was well kept and passed on to my grandfather Ruhbak, these species who are called 'Grolz'. They have been here before with the same spaceship and with the same scenario. At first, there was one ship; then, many more followed. You are now looking at the same ship that was in the video of my grandfather. Of course—that was way before your time here on this planet. Heck, I wasn't even born then.

According to the video records, these aliens have caused a great deal of mayhem to our civilization. They destroyed approximately one-third of our population, amounting to approximately 500 million of us, with their devastating weapons, but for your information, we also fought them well. We managed to destroy much of their troops and their military hardware by our wits and fortitude," said Odeoh.

"But there are two things that you haven't told us yet. Why did they come here in the first place, and what were they looking for?" asked Colonel Vacha, the commanding officer.

"I can't answer that question for certain. However, the video archives displayed that Grolz was excavating the northern part of the 'Zarket' region, to be exact. This area happened to be a flat and marshy land. It extends miles and miles in every direction. Surely you are familiar with that area, aren't you, commander?

"Yes, as a matter of fact, I am. I still see remnants of some sort of technology there, and it is rotting. However, the Zarket region is cordoned off to this day. A huge fence runs around about it with a stern warning placed every one hundred feet or so, but many thrill seekers have violated the posted signs and

entered the area by their own discretion and never came out alive. To this day, we have lost more than a million thrill seekers and adventurers in that region. Once they enter, no one comes out alive.

"It looks like no Darkans nor Eponans have been able to investigate the technology that has been left there all along," said the commander Vacha.

"You are absolutely right sir, and for a good reason. At this moment, I don't really have the exact coordinates of their excavation sites. However, to this day, we don't really know what they were looking for. It was apparent that they found what mattered to them, but amazing as it seemed, they suddenly left the planet and, in a hurry, mind you.

"The video archives depicted there were many; I would say many Grolz were in that area. I would also say maybe numbering in thousands. However, they were all found dead at the excavation site. Some of them had half of their faces bitten off and half of their bodies eaten up. Some had their limbs missing by something that we still have no idea or knowledge of to this day.

"An interesting thing I found in all this—is that, everyone who had their faces still attached to their bodies had their mouths agape, and their eyes were bulging out as if in pure horror. Maybe there were ghostly or nonvisible to the naked eye creatures that were calamitous and devouring in their nature, and as we are the denizens of this planet, we haven't been able to witness their presence for we haven't seen their physical attributes at any given time.

"*The unseen creatures must come off the ground to consume the bodies of their prey and immediately take their prey down with them right back under the ground, but not all follow the same. Some leave their prayers where they lay, and who knows how many are taken down below the ground. However, some Grolz attempted to escape, but lost their limbs in the process.*

"*Who knows, these elusive creatures might have colonies that are in millions strong and they are living and cherishing right beneath our feet as we speak. One day, we might have to contend with them just as we did with Grolz.*

"*Grolz must have been powerless against them, whoever or whatever they were. The cause of their death doesn't seem to make any sense to us. But I would say this: we as a race are very grateful that they have left in such a hurry. Otherwise, I wouldn't be standing here and talking to you about them today.*

"*Here is the disturbing factor, according to my forefathers' writings about the Grolz, they have vowed to return one day and make this planet their own, and as you see, they are already here now. They have arrived folks, perhaps with more technology and with more devastating weapons than they had before.*

Right now, we see the Grolz on our screens. It wouldn't be long before we know their possible motive. This time, it could be nothing more than total extermination of our civilization, and that includes your race too—mind you," said Odeoh.

"*The situation with Grolz is sad and very disturbing information that you have conveyed to us Odeoh. We didn't know anything about them until now. Thanks for all your input. The president is well informed about the spaceship that we are witnessing on the screen, and he has given us the green light to neutralize any threat to our society,"* said Commander Vacha.

"I am glad the president knows about this event. But, when it comes to the point where you have said I don't know what they were looking for—do you have your own conjecture or hunch as to what that thing must have been that they were so anxious to obtain?" asked the Eponan Colonel Todar.

"No sir, I don't really know for sure. It doesn't come to mind now," There was a pause for about three to five seconds, and Odeoh seemed to be in a state of muse.

"Wait a minute. I just remembered. The place that they excavated was full of Zhearmak. This object is translucent, green in color, and crystalline in nature. They are just about a foot long and a half a foot wide. You have seen the crystals I am referring to, haven't you?" said Odeoh.

"Yes, as a matter of fact, I have," said Colonel Todar.

"That is all I know. However, I also want to add this of their character: according to the archival information, Grolz were ruthless pillagers. They took what they wanted whenever they desired. They had no respect for any life form, or any regrets in destroying anything in plain sight.

"The Grolz have no capability to extend compassion, love, care, or compunction for anyone or anything. They are pure evil. They are also very intelligent creatures make no mistake about them.

"I think their main motivation is to conquer and dominate weaker races and utilize their resources for their own good. In other words, I would say, maybe they are the biggest and the most

aggressive predators in this corner of the universe," said Odeoh vehemently.

"This all is good information. Thank you, Lieutenant Odeoh. I think I know the reason they were excavating these Zhearmak crystals. However, we can't, and we will not just sit and wait here and let them have their destructive way with us," said Colonel Vacha. Just then, his personal phone wrapped around his wrist made an alerting sound. He glared at the screen and noticed it was General Rawa.

"Oh! It's General Rawa. I must take this call. It must be important," said Colonel Vacha to Odeoh.

"Yes General, go right ahead. I am listening," said Colonel Vacha.

"Colonel Vacha, this is General Rawa. I've just received a call from the president. He doesn't want to wait any longer for them to respond. He said we must attack first as soon as possible. So, mobilize your forces immediately. Do not waste time. We must take that ship down at any cost. This is an order. Is that clear?" said General Rawa.

"Yes sir, it's clear sir!" said the colonel.

"Very well then, this conversation is over. General Rawa is out."

"Well, I have just received a call from General Rawa. We have the green light to attack these bastards. We are going to hit them fast and hard. I am sure if we respond first, they will be greatly surprised.

"However, I don't think we have much time to find out about their real intentions, nor their weak points. It would have been a

great asset for us if we had known, but regardless, we are going to deal with them head-on. I would say sooner, the better."

"*Ok captain Vlernyk, how fast can you muster up your squadron for battle?"* asked Colonel Vacha.

"*In ten minutes, sir,"* said Captain Vlernyk.

"*Excellent, I want you to sound the alarm now and be ready to take off in five minutes, God's speed,"* said Colonel Vacha.

"*Yes sir,"* said Captain Vlernyk and executed a firm solute.

"*You are dismissed, Captain,"* said the Colonel. Captain Vlernyk made an about-face and left the war room expeditiously.

"*Lieutenant Odeoh, I want you to gather as much information about Grolz as you can and report back to me as soon as you have it, and I would like to look at your grandfather's video archives as soon as possible. In addition, Major Lorapy alerts the ground forces for a possible ground attack and has them be ready with their full fighting gears and mechanized equipment and be mobilized in fifteen minutes.*

"*Yes sir,"* replied Major Lorapy.

"*You're excused,"* said Colonel Vacha.

"*Yes sir,"* said Major Lorapy and delivered a firm salute, made an about face, and walked briskly out of the war room with firm steps.

"*For the rest of you, get back to your stations, keep your eyes on the monitors, and immediately inform me of any further changes or events that you may witness,"* said the Colonel.

CHAPTER 4

The two huge apposing doors that comprised of camouflaged gates have slowly parted with a gentle humming noise—one to the left and the other to the right. Within minutes, the Eponan pilots were ready to fly out of the gates. They wore their flight uniforms and their headgear, bustled through the well-lit underground tarmac towards their Starfighters, jumped into their cockpits, fired their ion-propelled engines, and took off one by one in tandem through the exit gate.

There were hundreds of Eponan flying war crafts. They were leaving the planet's brilliant blue atmosphere behind and embracing the vast blackness of the immense void. From a distance, one could have likened them to a bunch of fireflies moving in unison and exiting the planet's atmosphere.

The pilots of the Eponan Starfighters were heading towards the imposing mammoth ship and were anticipating an immense challenge. Despite all the danger, they were anticipating victory in conquering the Grolz Mother Ship. The Eponan fighters were well-trained in air combat. They also had the celerity and the great resolve to meet their objectives.

Suddenly, hundreds of Grolz fighting crafts jettisoned out of the belly of the Mother Ship with great momentum to confront and engage the Eponan Starfighters. The intention of the mother ship had become unmistakably clear, for it had displayed its true and nefarious intention. Now, it was obvious that its presence here portended death and destruction for the inhabitants down below.

The space surrounding this behemoth ship was rife with fast-moving, fast-maneuvering fighting crafts. The space in the near proximity of the large ship was likened to observing hundreds of gnats hovering above one's head.

Both sides, the Eponans and the Grolz, were rapidly exchanging their deadly arsenals and briefly illuminating the ink-black space with their crimson-red Ion charged projectiles, hence destroying each other's crafts and creating short-lived plumes of fireballs in the space.

Both fighting forces sustained a considerable amount of damage, destruction, and casualties of life, but a few hundred Grolz "Troop Transport Pods" (TTP), each carrying approximately 60 heavily armed Grolz infantrymen, managed to escape the war in space and entered the planet's atmosphere unharmed to start their ground assault operation. Autonomous Flying Gunships (AFGs) accompanied the (TTPs) to protect the troops when TTPs have landed on the ground.

Soon, four more of the same class mother ships arrived above the planet's atmosphere, and each hovered at a different hemisphere. Each has also sent hundreds of (TTPs) and (AFGs) to the ground, with troops comprising a brigade which is totaling approximately two and a half thousand well-equipped and well-trained Grolz soldiers.

Eponan's ground forces, with their mechanized mobile weapons, were expecting the Grolz on their soils at any moment. They had their air defense weapons trained on the descending Grolz fighting crafts.

When (TTPs) and (AFGs) were near approach to the ground, Eponan forces suddenly opened fire through their canons and set the descending vessels in a blaze followed by fiery explosions before crushing to the Terra Firma.

Those TTPs, which have landed successfully on the ground, disembarked swiftly and took their positions. They began their ground assault operations by engaging Eponan and Darkan ground forces. Each side discharged their deadly ordinances. Plums of fire and smoke engulfed the buildings and caused its residents to flee their abodes into the streets in a frenzy.

There was immense confusion and uproar on the highways and on the thruways. Crowds were trampling over the strewed and chard dead bodies in the streets. Some were looking for their loved ones among the dead, hoping that they would not find their corpses and considering them to be still alive.

The mayhem left the cities and the nearby towns in flames and in ruins. Casualties mounted on both sides. The streets and the highways were littered with the bodies of Grols, Eponan and Darkan soldiers and destroyed war machines, but for now, Grolz seemed to have had the slight upper edge.

More Eponan space fighters from different sectors of the planet left the atmosphere to engage in a firefight with four enormous alien motherships that had just arrived above the planet's atmosphere. However, the very first Mother Ship was not immune from its impending peril. A few Eponan pilots under the command of Captain Sakreg have managed to concentrate their efforts on this huge starship.

Captain Sakreg and his team delivered their destructive and deadly ordinances at strategic locations on the starship. Suddenly at first, short bursts of fiery explosions jettisoned from its surfaces like a volcanic eruption that have. Soon after, flames engulfed the entire ship and its fiery parts scattered throughout the space by means of explosions.

Before the ship incurred its destruction, many small escapes began to leave the ship expeditiously through its various ports. Their purpose was to take a chance and hope against all odds to land unharmed on the planet despite the ensuing war on the ground.

Captain Sakreg is young. In his mid-twenties. He has been serving the Eponan's space force division for two Eranduh years, which is equivalent to three Earth years. His superiors considered him to be a soft-spoken, mild-mannered, and seasoned soldier. Despite the fear he faced in the battles, he was a true risk-taker.

Just when Sakreg and his colleagues had set the mothership ablaze, he broke away from the fighting coalition, because two Grolz fighting crafts began to pursue him diligently. His vessel meandered sinuously through the space to escape the chevying Grolz fighting crafts, but regardless, they managed to stay on his tail.

Sakreg acknowledged the red-hot ionized projectiles that were escaping Grolz gun barrels in a fast and successive burst. These projectiles were whizzing very close to his craft but were missing their intended target.

Sakreg was well skilled in handling his Starfighter to evade the destructive projectiles that were bursting from Grolz Starfighters. However, unlike him feeling the way he was feeling, now, for the first time, he felt consternation and trepidation creeping into his heart. Soon, the fear of death began to materialize and overwhelm his heart and mind. The thought of being a casualty of war was becoming more and more of a real thing with each passing second.

Suddenly, Sakreg's dashboard emergency pulsating light lit up bright red and moments after—a loud and cacophonous pulsating sound of an alarm ensued. It was obvious; the pursuers were right behind him and had his craft in their crosshairs. The Grolz fighter jets had a lock on his craft, tagged for a kill.

Sakreg's heart raced, and his eyes opened wide in fear by glaring at the red and pulsating emergency light on the button. This was the time when his craft could experience the oblivion and him in it. His Sweat exuded from every pore in his body, his hands began to tremble uncontrollably, and his breathing became heavy and audible.

Sakreg felt at any given moment now, his pursuers were able and were in the position to obliterate his craft. The challenge he faced to stay alive has become insurmountably hard and began to lose hope fast.

Sakreg didn't think for a moment that he was going to stay alive in the next minute or two. The thought of death overwhelmed him. He didn't desire to die. He had too much to live for—his wife, whom he loved very much, and so his kids.

Sakreg began to brainstorm, and then, in an instant, he conjured a brilliant evasive maneuver that may have ultimately saved his life. He learned an evasive maneuver in the flight school. Suddenly, Sakreg executed an immediate "High-G barrel roll, having the craft's nose upward in an ascending order." This action was his final defensive maneuver, and this action rendered success. This execution of his craft left much-needed space between him and his pursuers.

In the interim, at a certain distance, approximately at two o'clock position, Sakreg caught sight of a large, white in color and slowly whirling discoid having brightly lit extremities, but having an ink black center. Sakreg immediately realized that this phenomenon must be a "Wormhole."

Sakreg decided to enter this wormhole right through it. He didn't care where he might end up on the other side. His intention was to escape his pursuing foes and to stay alive. Otherwise, his life in the living world would have been a very questionable issue should he have remained in pursuit of his foes, he thought.

Sakreg realized the wormholes normally don't stay active long periods of time in space. He learned that in his science class. Therefore, he purposely engaged the after-burners and increased his speed to make sure he would go right through it before the wormhole collapsed on itself and disappeared.

Sakreg's craft shook and rattled from excessive speed but managed to make it through the wormhole. He looked at the bright side and hoped that he wouldn't have to entertain the company of his adversaries on the other side.

While Sakreg was moving through the wormhole, he passed out and became unconscious. He had no realization of time lapses. It could have been hours, days, perhaps months, or years.

Suddenly, Sakreg opened his eyes and realized everything around him was black; there were no stars, no planets, and he didn't know whether he was moving or he was stationary; there was no reference point anywhere. Some of his lit-up counsel gages had a distorted reading, and some were out of order.

Suddenly, Sakreg witnessed a small but brilliant white dot that kept on getting larger and larger until it came to resemble a hello-like phenomenon. Soon, Sakreg realized that he was getting closer and closer to the exit point from the wormhole. Sakreg's craft jettisoned from this wormhole a great speed with his fighting vessel still intact.

Suddenly, Sakreg described a huge planet looming fast before his orbs. The humans called it "Jupiter." (This planet is found in the 'Milky Way' Galaxy and is the fifth planet from the sun).

After a few minutes passed, Sakrag realized, none of his pursuers had come through this wormhole, and soon he expressed extreme illation. Sakrag exploded his emotions in the form of a guffaw. He felt having a new lease on life, decided to make the best of it by exploring new worlds, and desiderating one to make it his home. However, Sakreg had no idea where or what part of the universe this wormhole ejected him into. He hoped to locate a hospitable planet so that he could survive and move on with his life and thrive.

Sakreg turned on his craft's special sensors and found them to be functional. Sakrag suddenly brokered a wide smile, thinking if these sensitive devices on board were still functional, then the rest of the warcraft must be working as well.

These sensors were located on the ceiling of the craft's canopy; they were to determine his location on his own home planet, but they couldn't get the answer he was looking for. The sensors were also to take a statistical reading of the planet Jupiter, especially its atmosphere. His findings of the planet were not conducive to bear life that he knew of, because it was mostly comprised of hydrogen, helium, and methane. And furthermore, his sensors were to detect if there were signs of life on this brilliant and colorful globe down below. Sakreg became dismayed. He couldn't detect any life-form roaming on this planet.

The size and the swaths of this beautifully colored planet with its whirling atmospheric features in which it housed over nine hundred miles per hour wind speeds and along with its ever-prominent red spot, these features have literally enchanted Sakreg and vastly mesmerized him. Sakreg's instruments also depicted that this planet had no solid surface, and he concluded that this planet must be a gas giant; also, at the same time, his sensors were picking up emissions of radiation, which was totally not conducive to bear life.

Sakrek's craft sensors couldn't locate his whereabouts and the world where he came from, but managed to lock his exit coordinates lest he desired to get back home and be with his family once again. He aspired that they would still be alive and well when he returned.

CHAPTER 5

While Sakreg was in orbit around the planet Jupiter, attempting to extract data, he witnessed a large piece of rock that was hovering stationary above the planet's atmosphere. Sakreg's starfighter was at a safe distance from this large slab, but this chunk was looming larger and larger as he was getting closer and closer to it.

Sakreg realized he was on a collision course with this mammoth rock formation. Sakreg acknowledged his speed and decided to slow the craft or change its course, but on second thought, he decided to investigate this large, broken piece of a planet. But one thing disturbed Sakreg's thoughts; he questioned silently, *"Why is this slab of rock remaining stationary where it should be moving like an asteroid or a comet at a great speed, or it should be orbiting this giant planet like one of its moons otherwise, this rock should fall into the atmosphere by the planet's strong gravitational pull, or be hurled into the wide-open space with great speed. I wonder what magical forces are holding this thing stationery. I must find out."*

This rock was significantly large and flat in its appearance. It had uneven surfaces, just like a rock should look. It measured approximately five football fields long, three football fields wide, and one football field in height.

Sakreg also knew that this planet was a gaseous planet; therefore, certainly, this rock couldn't be part of it. Then he questioned in his head, *"Where did this rock come from"?* The unanswered questions that were in his head motivated him to further make his mind to investigate.

As Sakreg closed the distance between him and this very large solid article of unknown origin, he reduced his speed, circled around it, and decided to assay its composition. He also thought to make a touchdown on its surface and acquire a sample just to placate his curiosity.

As Sakreg was hovering slowly over this mammoth rock, he suddenly experienced a burst of instance beam of light that encompassed his craft in its entirety. The light engendered an overwhelming tug that slowed his craft to a standstill position. This light was originating from the surface of this huge boulder. He thought this phenomenon was strange. *"How could a rock emanate light and impede my movements to a degree of standstill?"* He thought silently, and fear was growing in his mind. Sakreg knew there was no mechanical apparatus attached to the surface of this rock to cause such an event to happen, so he thought, *"This conical beam must have originated from somewhere inside this rock."*

Suddenly, it dawned on Sakreg that the area of the beam where it commenced from—the beam must have been covered by a holographic image that portrayed a rocky feature to dupe the passer into thinking that the immediate surface is part of the rock's feature.

Sakreg decided to leave the immediate vicinity to get away from this blazing light, thinking this could be a life-threatening situation and didn't want any part of it, but the beam had a lock on the craft from the start, *"What—my engine just died. Oh damn—my console lights went out too"!* Said out loud in an anxious voice. The illumination of the cabin was only by the outside light source that surrounded his craft.

Sakreg had no power and no control of his onboard instruments to do anything, let alone attempt to fly away like a bat out of hell to save his life from this unknown danger. He realized His craft was slowly descending to the surface despite his effort to escape. *"Well, hell, it looks like I am descending. Damn it, there is not much that I can do now. I can't seem to get away even if my life depended on it. Whatever this thing is causing my ship to descend, I must face it whether I like it or not,"* thought Sakreg aloud to himself.

Soon, Sakreg's craft entered the belly of this rock and then rested inside a well-lit and commodious room. Sakreg felt dumbstruck. His eyes scanned the entire room frantically to locate any danger that he might have to encounter and come up against. But to his surprise, he found none and realized that the room was devoid of equipment, such as stationary and moving machines. *"Oh sh**, where the hell am I? And what the heck is this place? This rock must be a spaceship. It certainly filled me. All right. What am I going to do now? I suppose I must wait and find out.* It seems, *I have no choice in this matter. I am here, and I must face whatever that comes my way"!* Sakreg said outloud with angst.

Sakreg knew right then that an unknown situation or trouble was waiting to happen and soon it should ensue in his path. He felt hopeless to get away. And that he must wait here inside this thing, however, the length of time it takes.

Sakreg, in his mind, reaffirmed to himself that this large piece of rock was not just a huge piece of a broken part of a planet; it was a "spaceship for sure". It was life with technology, but so far, it was devoid of life. Sakreg wondered to whom, to what race, or to what civilization this enormous spaceship belonged to, and what is it doing out here above this inhospitable gaseous planet.

Sakreg began to introspect and protest the questions in his mind, *"I wonder—am I going to die here or come out alive? Why I am being pulled to this place? What do they want from me whoever or whatever they are? Am I going to be their Lab specimen?"* His body began to react to his unanswered questions. He felt the ongoing butterflies in his stomach and his heart kept on beating fast.

Suddenly, he heard a startling mechanical movement sound. At first, he thought something ominous was going on in this place and was about to burst right before his eyes. He immediately scanned the area for movements and found none, then elevated his head toward the ceiling and realized the ceiling gates were slowly shutting down and began to think; *"Damn it, I feel like I am being trapped here inside my craft against my own freaking will and with no room to react defensively."* Sakreg had very unease of mind, and at the same time, his eyesight was frantically roaming everywhere to detect movements that may endanger his life.

Sakreg heard more noises, but this time, it was coming from the walls. These sounds were the sounds of machines attempting to pressurize this enormous room with atmosphere.

Sakreg was still feeling very jittery. His hands were trembling and sweating from the fear he was feeling. His breathing was becoming heavier and audible. He didn't feel secure being alone inside this enormous alien star-cruiser, and at the same time, he didn't feel right being confined inside his own ship, and not having the ability to set himself free to disembark and to set his feet on the ground because he couldn't open his canopy. There was no power in the craft that he was sitting in.

Sakreg felt all alone. There was no one inside on his side to protect him from harm; he was expecting it to materialize at any moment. His eyes remained wide open, canvassing the room for anomalies. Suddenly Sakreg experienced strange and unusual sounds that were coming from the machines. The cacophonous and strident sounds were likened to ferocious monsters ready to devour their opponents.

Chemistry, like human Adrenaline, rushed through Sakre's veins. He was sure that at any given moment, now something was about to burst or evince itself right before his orbs. He had nowhere to run or hide. His heart still raced in its cage right from the start of his descent, and he felt his blood pressure was still elevated in anticipation of the unknown.

Suddenly, an autonomous flying drone released itself from the ceiling and silently and gracefully descended over Sakreg's starcraft. Sakreg's eyes glued on this drone. He followed its every move that it made. The sphere measured approximately two feet in diameter. It had a polished gunmetal color.

This orb hovered approximately ten feet above his craft and shined an intense pulsating red beam that panned out approximately forty-five degrees from its bottom surface and began to move slowly until it scanned the entire craft. After it conducted its full examination, it went back to the ceiling and attached itself to it.

Sakreg thought silently, *"This drone must have gathered data on my craft. And the data must have been transferred to the command post already. Now, the entities of this spaceship must have knowledge of my presence here. They will be sending their emissaries. They will either be friendly or inimical that are trigger happy and ready to kill on sight".* The machine noises that were involved in pressurizing the room suddenly stopped. Quietness prevailed at last—at least for now.

Lights and more lights were everywhere inside this huge cubicle. Sakreg again swiveled his head slowly to his left and to his right to locate any motion or a presence of some sort. At any given moment, he was expecting a life form, or a bunch of armed robots to merge through the huge gates on his left, but still, there was none to detect, and he wondered why.

Sakreg depressurized his headgear, pulled his helmet slowly out of his head, and placed it on his side. He was still breathing the air that was inside his cabin. He braved and opened a vent to let the outside air to flow into the cockpit. His intention was, to assay the air that belonged to this huge rock-like spaceship.

He inhaled deep through his nostrils and felt no discomfort of any sort. To his surprise, he acknowledged that he could breathe the air of this alien ship and felt a sense of relief.

Suddenly, his whole flight counsel lit up. The instruments and the gadgets came to life. Sakreg became elated and realized that now he had power in his starfighter, but he wished that the ceiling was open and that he would fly away quickly.

He turned on his silent beckon that was wrapped around his wrist to set his immediate location in this spaceship so that he could find his way back to his ship just in case he made it alive.

Since there was power in his craft, Sakreg could now open the canopy and jump to the ground on a gray and shiny slabbed. The floor appeared super clean, as if there was not even a particle of dust on it.

Sakreg opened his canopy and jumped to the floor. As he stood erect, he slowly turned his body around 360° and scanned everything in his sight to hear and detect anything that was out of the ordinary, and then he went around his craft to examine for any damages that he might have incurred during the time of exit from the wormhole and found none and was comforted.

Sakreg thought this place could be a reception area but was devoid of life. He silently questioned himself, *"Where are the greeters? They should have been here already."*

At a distance, to his earth south there was a huge gate that he had knowledge of all along and turned his attention to it occasionally. This gate was large enough that his starfighter could have easily passed through it. He appeared dwarf in comparison to the gate that was before his sight. Sakreg thought, *"Could the inhabitants of this spacecraft be so enormous in stature that would have prompted the gates to be built so tall?"*

Suddenly, he heard a clank and a squeak sound, and then, within a few moments, in a swift action, the gates parted half to the left and the other half to the right. Fourteen towering and mesomorphic beings surged through the gate expeditiously and in unison. They marched in cadence toward Sakreg, and when they came close, they formed a circle around him.

These beings wore black armor on their black uniform with helmets completely encapsulating their heads and their shoulders. They displayed no visible flash, no sound, and wielded formidable weapons in their hands.

Sakreg remained frozen in his position ever since he saw the arrival of these beings through the gate. He didn't run or hide nor twitch a muscle. He glared at them apprehensively and thought silently, *"O no, I am going to be a fodder for these beasts. At this moment, I have no fighting chance with these freaking creatures, whatever they are. For now, it would be better for me to stay calm and cooperate with them, and just maybe, I might have a chance to live and talk about it."*

Despite of this alarming situation, Sakreg found himself managing to keep his composure dispassionate. He didn't desire to alarm these creatures of the fear he felt in his veins. However, back in his mind, he thought he had seen these beings with their uniforms somewhere before, but where, to be exact, he couldn't remember.

Suddenly, the team's commander blurted a few words to his teammates, and as a result, they opened their helmet visors to get a better look at Sakreg. Besides, they thought he was not going to pose trouble, because he was surrounded, outgunned, and outnumbered.

Commander Narmoop approached Sakreg, frowningly glared at every inch of his body as he silently and slowly circled around him.

"No doubt, he is an Eponan! We, the Ongumas, should have exterminated every one of them while we had the chance, then we wouldn't have to meet the thing that you see in front of you today! Only God knows what he has purposed for us now that he is here! No doubt, he is dangerous. But have no worries, we'll extract every bit of information from him, then we'll kill him, lest he bring harm to any one of us!" blurted the commander vehemently to his team.

Commander Narmoop went back to his position and ordered his first officer, who was second in command by the name of Yinoot, to disarm Sakreg. The officer expeditiously responded to the commander's order, approached Sakreg within two feet of him, and glared down begrudgingly at his face. This officer stood head and shoulder above him. Their eyes meet in ire and Sakreg anticipated soon a life-threatening conflict to be ensued between them.

Yinoot soon realized, as his commander stated, Sakreg did surely belonged to the Eponan race. Yinoot was very young when his ancestors' the Ongumas, conquered the planet called Eegroag, where Sakreg grew up.

Yinoot became alone after his parent's death and wandered aimlessly in the streets of the town. An Eponan Soldier rescued him from harm's way and brought him to the family, then raised him like one of his own.

They instilled in him Eponan values and standard protocols. Yinoot was ever grateful and proud that an Eponan family raised him to become who he is now: a remarkable, sensitive, intelligent, and intrepid soldier.

Yinoot came within whispering distance of Sakreg to disarm him, then surreptitiously whispered in his ear the word *"Rooktok."* It meant "The crazy one" in the Eponan language. Sakreg remembered only one person used to call him that name, and it was Yinoot. When Sakreg was a kid, they used to play together and banter with each other, and as a result, they both became dear friends.

Sakreg felt at ease and thought, *"Excellent—there is someone here, who happened to be a dear friend of mine from the younger years. It must be Yinoot, no doubt, and now, either by fate or by accident, we meet again. He might just be my ticket out of here alive."*

Yinoot disarmed Sakreg and then handed the weapon to his commander. The commander assigned four of his soldiers, Sergeant Owaha, Private Tarwa, Private Evoto, and Corporal Norjra, to stay here and guard Sakreg's star craft and that they will have four other teammates to relieve them within two hours. The commander signaled the rest of the team to move forward along with Sakreg being in the center.

CHAPTER 6

Commander Narmoop and the rest of his team, along with Sakreg, exited the gate that they entered from. They marched briskly in unison and in cadence through a wide corridor where either side was filled with broken down crafts, machines, tools, hoses, engines, large electronic diagnostic devices, and a few technical repair crewmembers working on dismantled Starfighter engine parts. These technical team members froze in their positions and focused their eyes on the moving soldiers. They were in such a mental state as if they were watching a parade moving by and were somewhat entertained. Within moments, they realized that a strange being was walking in their midst. These technicians were pointing their fingers toward Sakreg and were chatting amongst themselves having a surprised and bewildered expression on their faces.

Suddenly, two spheroid-flying robots approached the marching group and hovered approximately ten feet above their heads. They moved as the marching group moved, then suddenly and swiftly, they parted to a different location in the starship.

After the commander and his troops, along with Sakreg, marched for a little while, they reached an area where they had to meander through the not-so-well-lit narrow corridors until they arrived at a much wider and open area accommodated with a higher ceiling. Commander Narmoop decided to pause here. He pulled his map to decide in what direction he must go to reach his destination, with the rest of his crew following him. His purpose was to take Sakreg to a holding place set for the prisoners. However, in the meanwhile, the autonomous flying weaponized robots were whizzing through the corridors and over their heads to guard the spaceship from intruders and dangers and alert the command post of any malfunction in any sector of the ship.

In this region there were many corridors that lead to different sectors of the ship, and there were gates with some sort of writings on them that described a specific section or department. However, all the writings were cryptic to Sakreg.

Suddenly a discordant loud sound emanated from inside of a closed gate. It felt as if a huge glass just shattered, and then, within moments, a strident and cacophonous scream ensued. The shriek belonged to a certain alien life form that was kept inside the gate for observation. The commander and his crew, including Sakreg, all heard the shatter and the shrill loud and clear. The earsplitting cry seemed to have originated from inside the Specimen lab that was located close to their vicinity.

In this Lab, the occupants of this ship kept previously captured alien species inside huge tubular glasses that were filled with life-sustaining liquids. The lab scientists subjugated these alien specimens in various experiments. Sakreg was going to be their next exhibit in the lab. The scientists were to place him in an enclosed glass like tube and hang him suspended from the ceiling until his turn came for the scientists to perform various tests on his body, possibly including dissections of his body parts. The commander signaled two of his crewmembers to investigate the sound that reverberated through the walls of the Specimen Lab.

The commander summoned an investigative team comprised of Second Lieutenant Omeh and Airman First Class Eegroj. They were to investigate the specimen incident. These two glared at each other at first in distress then they switched their sight toward the commander with discontent. Omeh said, "You know what you are getting us into, don't you, commander!"

"Yes, yes, as a matter of fact, I do, and I know you both are very capable of handling any situation that comes before you. Both of you are trained well for this purpose, and that is why I have chosen you two to take on this task—so, get going and don't come out till you take care of the matter at hand, is that clear?"

"Yes sir," replied both with slight discontentment. They knew they wouldn't dare to challenge the commander's order; otherwise, they would incur an immediate decision of execution by the commander, and the rest of the team would have to carry out his order.

"Are you ready, Eegroj?" asked Omeh.

"Yes, I am sir," Said Eegroj.

"Very well—I know we can do this, so let's get going," said Omeh.

"Yes sir," said Eegroj.

The two that were summoned left the team with an expression of dread on their faces, but despite, they proceeded toward the Specimen Lab. They knew they were in a great deal of unknown danger and that it may have to cost their lives. Who knows what kind of alien creature they will be encountering and confronting inside, and what are its capabilities? Possibly, a mayhem or a slaughter must be expected. The technicians that were inside perhaps had already encountered the full brunt of the alien's wrath and experienced their own bloodbath. Both crewmembers knew that they were going to be right in the middle of fighting off the loose alien. A huge, closed gate that belonged to the specimen lab loomed before their sight.

"Look Eegroj, as soon as the gate opens, we must run to get in and get in fast. We have two seconds before the doors get closed shut. We don't want to be in the middle. Otherwise, we will be crushed to death. Is that clear?" asked Omeh.

"Yes sir," said Eegroj.

Omeh stood facing the gadget on the wall. With a few punches by his beefy fingers on the buttons, the huge doors parted swiftly, one to the left and the other to the right. Eegroj and Omeh swiftly entered a thirty-foot by eight-foot wide not-so-not-so-well-lit corridor that led to the Specimen room.

The two drew their heavy Weapons out of their weapon's compartment situated on their backs. The doors instantly shut behind them, and the two remained inside and apart from their teammates.

Omeh and Eegroj glared at each other briefly in despair, and Omeh said, *"This is it. We are in. Now we have to face the thing that made a bad noise and whatever else may have to come our way."* Omeh signaled Eegroj let's get moving. Hearts began to pound fast. They had no idea as to what was waiting for them inside. They anticipated some unknown creature with some degree of danger that must be lurking surreptitiously inside this room, and eventually, it may have to cause their demise should they not be careful.

They both reached the end of the corridor, stopped in their tracks, and briefly scanned the area for anomalies; they realized things were not out of order, strangely quiet and no sight of the alien creature. However, they noticed the broken container that the alien was kept in. It was slightly swinging to the right and to the left. The blue fluid that was in the container now it was now all over the adjacent counters and the floor.

"I don't see any creature here sir," said Eegroj.

"And I don't see any Lab scientists here either," said Omeh.

"Yes sir, where are the Lab workers? Shouldn't there be at least a few of them monitoring these gadgets?" asked Eegroj.

"Yes, you are right; there should be a few at least. I wonder what happened to them and where did they all go? I hope they are not dead," said Omeh.

"We'll find out soon, won't we sir?" asked Eegroj.

"Yes, I suppose and no doubt we will," said Omeh.

"It's time for us to split. You take the right, and I will take the left. Be careful and holler if you find anything unusual," said Omeh.

"Yes, sir I will, and you do the same. Let's do it," said Eegroj.

The lab room appeared well-lit and commodious, with many rows of elaborate electronic counsels having many buttons, levers, rotating nobs, beakers, colorful and bubbling liquids, and many mechanical devices. There were also many long and tubular glasses that were still hanging from the ceiling in each passing row. Inside these tubular glasses were alien species that were large and small, having grotesque figures, and were on their life support systems. They all had a fixated stare and seemed to be in suspended animation.

Omeh and Eegroj both split and walked slowly in a stealthy manner. Eegroj turned right towards the south wall, and Omeh turned left towards the north wall, and both proceeded to move toward the back of the room. With the communicators tied on their wrists, Omeh blurted in a very low voice and said, *"Did you see anything yet."*

"No—not yet sir, but I heard a noise. It sounded like a heavy footstep, but I can't tell where it came from sir, did you hear it sir?" asked Eegroj.

"No, not really," said Omeh.

"Sir, come to think of it, I think it came from the back of the room sir," said Eegroj.

"All right then, just be careful, do you hear me?" said Omeh.

"Yes sir, I am careful sir, but I don't feel good about this sir! Whatever it is, it could be moving now, and this thing could be anywhere here, waiting to make a meal out of us. Just be careful," said Eegroj.

"Yes, yes, I am all eyes and ears," said Omeh. He was at the third row and Eegroj was just reaching the sixth row down. Eegroj suddenly grimaced his face in disgust. He witnessed two lab personnel on the floor and in the pull of blood.

"Sir, you better get here fast!" yelled Eegroj. There was terror in his eyes.

"Why—did you find something?" asked Omeh.

"Yes, something terrible sir! You had better get here fast sir! Three lab people are dismembered and dead and are drenched in blood sir!" said Eegroj.

"Where!" said Omeh.

"Right here, sir right where I am standing sir!" said Eegroj. Omeh ran toward Eegroj and discovered the three dead lab personal who were laying on a bloodstained floor with their

uniforms covered in blood, just as Eegroj had described. Omeh took a few steps back, grimaced his face in disgust, and acquired an aghast expression. His hands began to tremble as he knelt to get a pulse from one of the dead lab crewmembers. To his dismay, he couldn't find any pulse and claimed that they all must be dead, for the very fact that he detected no movements from the crewmembers that were laying on the floor, he then pulled their dog tag off their necks and placed them in his pent pocket and said, *"Damn, I don't know what we are dealing with here. That could have been us dead on the floor. This is getting scary. I don't like this. I hope we get out of here alive. Damn it, I don't understand one thing, why we haven't seen this freaking creature yet—that really disturbs me. The room was locked when we got here, so there should be no way that the creature should have had the means to escape. It must still be here among us in this room, and perhaps now it is watching and studying us. It could be at any moment that thing decides to attack us. Look, Eegroj open your eyes ten-fold and be very careful while I go back to the north wall. As I have said, please be very careful. Do you hear me? I don't want to lose you too."*

"Yes, sir," said Eegroj.

"Fine then," said Omeh as he scurried silently toward the north wall with his back arched toward the ground as if he was out hunting for something and having his finger glued to the trigger of his weapon, brandishing it every which way but straight. Suddenly, Omeh's communicator blurted.

"This is Commander Narmoop. Do you copy Lieutenant Omeh"?

"Yes sir, I copy," said Omch.

"*Great—then can you give me an update of the situation inside? It has been a while, and I haven't heard anything from you yet,*" said Commander Narmoop.

"*Well sir we have three dead lab-personal here. This seems to be something very recent sir. We'll inform you should we find anything further, sir,*" said Omeh.

"*Did you say three dead lab personals?*" asked Narmoop

"*Yes sir, that's what I said,*"

"*Can you tell me their names?*" asked Narmoop.

"*Yes sir,*" said Omeh and managed to pull the three dog tags out of his pent pocket and read their names.

"*Sir, their names are Renepon, Nikrep, and Ranure,*" said Omeh.

"*Oh damn, they are such a loss. They were the best we had in their field. All right, do you need a backup?*" asked Narmoop.

"*No sir, we could handle it ourselves,*" said Omeh.

"*In that case you both be careful. Do you hear me?*" said Narmoop.

"*Yes sir,*" said Omeh.

"*Very well then, don't let us hang around here for long; we have a prisoner to interrogate,*" said Narmoop, the commander.

"*Yes sir, we'll do our best to find and neutralize the situation at hand,*" said Omeh. Omeh proceeded to move toward the back of the room.

Despite the temperature-controlled environment that they both were in at the time, the milieu around Eegroj was becoming unusually calescent.

Eegroj flinched, thinking something was nearby and about to cause a detriment. He slowly took a few steps backward. His senses were on high alert. He was contemplating whether to stay or run for a cover. He felt solicitous. Fear harbored in his mind. His heart began to beat fast. Beads of sweat began to roll down his cheeks from feeling angst and heat. Eegroj briefly shifted his sight to the ceiling to see if there were vents that may have produced the temperature change around him, but there were none. There were no vents on the ceiling, but there was one vent on the west wall at the back of the room and it did not seem operational now.

"Hey Omeh, do you feel a temperature change around you?" asked Eegroj, using his wristband communicator.

"No—why should I have?" said Omeh.

"Then why is it noticeably hot here around me?" said Eegroj

"I don't know! I don't know what to tell you except be careful!" said Omeh.

"Ya, I am careful, but I feel something is wrong here. Let's get out of here now Omeh," said Eegroj

"Now—you know we can't do that. We can't get out of here until we neutralize the thing that we're after. This is the commander's orders. You were there when you heard it. You and I know that we can't violate the commander's orders otherwise; you know what's going to happen, right? I don't have to tell you that," said Omeh.

"I suppose we don't have any other choice here, do we, sir?" asked Eegroj.

"Now you're getting it. We're going to do our best to stay alive and kill whatever is loose here, and that will be the end of the story. Is that understood?" asked Omeh.

"Yes, I suppose!" said Eegroj with trepidation.

Eegroj took slow steps forward toward the back of the room where suddenly a creature fierce in continence began to materialize and loom before his orbs slowly. Eegroj froze his steps, and his eyes bulged in angst. His Heart continued to pound as if it was going to jump right out of his chest. He glared attentively and silently at the creature, knowing that death was staring at him right in the face.

Eegroj did not even move a muscle for approximately ten to fifteen seconds, then slowly raised his wrist to his mouth and with the breathy and quavering voice, he said, *"Omeh—are you seeing what I am seeing?"*

"See what? What am I supposed to see Eegroj? Everything is normal here."

"You mean you can't see this freaking monster staring me right at my face?"

"What monster. Are you hallucinating? We've got to talk about this when we get out of here," said Omeh.

"No sir, I am not hallucinating sir. I am afraid, very afraid now. This thing is real as it comes, sir, and I am in real danger now. Please—do something quick, or soon I will be history," said Eegroj.

Eegroj didn't wait for Omeh to act. He slowly heaved his large weapon with his trembling hands and bulging eyes, then aimed it right at the brute beast, and right before he pulled the trigger, the monster gapped its enormous mouth that could have easily swallowed his head in full. It displayed its razor-sharp and menacingly large teeth, and at the same time, the beast expeditiously closed the distance to approximately a foot between it and Eegroj.

Suddenly, two elephant-tusk-like features, two inches apart, having very pointed ends, jutted out two feet in distance lightning fast and impaled Eegroj in the chest. The tusks came out from beneath the lower jaw and were strong enough to heave Eegroj a few feet up into the air and draw him to its mouth.

The creature bit off most of his neck and part of his shoulder. Then it dropped him to the floor. His head dangled as if there was no support. It appeared almost severed from his body. Eegroj laid on the cold ground in the pull of green blood while his body twitched a few times, eyes wide open, stared through his helmet nowhere in particular and soon gave up the ghost.

Omeh's chin dropped in sheer amazement. Fear gripped his heart. He thought silently, *"Oh my Kruma,"* (Kruma is the god they worship) *what had just happened here? I should have believed him when he faced that damn invisible creature, and here I was, thinking he was hallucinating. Eegroj is gone now, damn it, how stupid I could have been not to believe him!"* Omeh immediately opened fire in Eegroj's direction; green balls of energy particles escaped from the barrel of his rifle to engage the creature who was at large now. There was no evidence of a hit. He had no clue of the creature's whereabouts in the room and began to ruminate silently.

"I know I am going to be next to bite the dust. This thing is going to come after me at any moment now, and if I can't see it,

how am I going to kill it?" He brought his wrist to his mouth and blurted through his communicator, *"Commander, do you copy?"* asked Omeh.

"Yes, I copy you Omeh. Go ahead. Do you have anything to report?" asked the commander.

"Yes sir, I do. Eegroj is dead. Most of his neck and part of his shoulder are gone, and ripped clear from his body, blood everywhere sir. Sir we have an invisible creature here in our midst in the room. I am all alone now, and I don't know where this damn beast is! I need help, and I need it now before I'll be the next victim here! Do you read me, commander?"

"Yes, I read you loud and clear Omeh—but you should know that I can't risk opening the doors for you, now that I know the beast is invisible and loose. *We must contain him inside the room, lest the thing you are talking about decides to escape and endanger the whole mothership. I can't allow that you should understand that. And you shouldn't try to open the doors yourself either. You do see my point, don't you?"* asked the Commander.

"Then—you are going to leave me here to die, aren't you, aren't you!" said Omeh.

"Well, you know—I wish there was something I and the rest of the crew could do to help you Omeh. Unfortunately, you must deal with it yourself. There is no way we can get in unless we open the door to the specimen lab, and then it may be too late. This thing could be out, and as I have said before, it would be endangering everyone on this ship. Hopefully—you will kill it, and you will come out as a hero and do us all good. I know you would have done the same for me if I was in your circumstance, wouldn't you?" There was sulk in Omeh's end.

CHAPTER 7

Omeh began to think silently. "I must create a strategy to survive. I am not planning to die here alone like my partner. The creature must be watching all the moves that I make, and if I attempt to hide anywhere, the creature must and will know my whereabouts. So, —for now, I must stay in the open ground, but how long must I be alone with this invisible creature and those things that are hanging from the ceiling; they are giving me the creeps, and why this thing hasn't attacked me yet. It has been more than a couple of minutes since the death of Eegroj. I simply can't spend the night here, and I can't have a shuteye if I must sleep, lest I don't wake up in the morning. I have to set a trap and then blast him with my rifle," thought Omeh while swinging his weapon everywhere.

"Omeh, this is the commander do you copy?"

"Yes sir, I do."

"Great, I am glad you are still alive. Were you able to utilize the environment?"

"No sir, not yet," said Omeh

"Well, that is not good news that I am hearing from you. I thought by now you would have already accomplished the mission. I tell you what. I am going to give you fifteen more minutes to take care of whatever is inside. After that, I am going to shut down the life support system and suck all the air and moisture from inside the room you're in. You are aware of what's going to happen then—right?"

"Commander, have you gone mad! This is insane! This means you are willing to kill one of your crew, aren't you!"

"Well, Omeh, I must do what I must do to save the ship from the creature that you are talking about, even if it has to cost one of my member's life, and sadly, it had to be you. You must understand my true intention here Omeh, and please don't take it personally. I wish you the best and hope that you come out of there as a victor, not as a victim. Well, with no further ado—the time will start-----now!"

"Commander Narmoop, this is Lieutenant Poyt from the prisoner interrogation department. Do you copy?"

"Yes—I do copy. Go ahead; I am listening. This is Commander Narmoop. State your inquiry, Lieutenant Poyt?"

"Yes, yes—I was wondering what became of the prisoner I was supposed to receive a half an hour ago. What's the holdup commander?"

"There is no hold-up, and there is nothing for you to be concerned about! You will receive your prisoner shortly! There is no more for me to say! The commander is over and out," Poyt acquired a dumbfounded look on his face, then turned around and began to converse with his assistant by the name of Emogra, "It's so unlike of the commander to be late in anything, let alone now. His statements were curt, as if, he was hiding something and didn't want to share.

"According to the map I see on my screen, the commander's last communication came from near the Specimen Lab, which is not so far from here. Emogra, you know where it is, don't you?"

"Yes sir, I do," replied Emogra.

"Exellent, then here is what I want you to do, Emogra. I want you to take a few deputies with you, then go and find out what's holding him and his crew for such a long time. Do it quickly and let me know if I should sound the alarm or not. I am concerned, very concerned. We don't want to start an alien hunt on this ship. God knows what this prisoner is capable of doing," said Poyt.

"Yes sir," said Emogra. He took a few fully armed deputies with him as Poyt commanded and moved on to reveal what Narmoop is up to now. Emogra and his deputies soon arrived at the scene.

"What brings you here, Emogra?" asked Narmoop with discontentment in his expression. "Did you think I might not be able to accomplish the mission that is set before me? That is why Lieutenant Poyt has sent you here to check my competency!" asked Narmoop vehemently.

"No, no sir, nothing in that nature, sir—take it easy now, take it easy, no one is accusing you of incompetency, and why are you so upset? Said Emogra.

"Because I know darn well that you are in violation of space trooper code "ARY258" that portrays you are lying to me, and you know the consequences of lying, and I am sure you have read the code yourself, you must!" said Narmoop.

"No sir, no, no, that's not true. I am not lying!" said Emogra with a concerned look on his face.

"No, I think you are lying to me," said the commander and signaled his crew to get ready to blast Emogra and the few members that he brought with him.

"All right, all right, you don't have to resort to violence, Commander Narmoop. We are all here to do our jobs. You have yours, and I have mine. Please tell your crew to set their weapons down. Let's all be in cooperative mode." The commander signaled the crew to set their weapons down.

"Fine then, let's hear the truth. The floor is all yours," said the commander.

"All right, since you put it that way, we are here because Poyt had sent us. He wants to know what's the holdup on your end sir, and he sent us to assist you in your mission should you have the need for us. Yes, to assist you, and nothing more than that sir!" said Emogra.

"Well, in that case, I thank you, and I thank Poyt, but no thanks! I don't need your help! Understand! I have all the help that I need here. You may go back to your quadrant!" said Narmoop with discontent and with a slight anger in his voice.

"Is he the prisoner we are going to interrogate sir?" asked Emogra, pointing his finger toward Sakreg.

"Yes, for your information, he is the prisoner!" said Narmoop. Emogra approached Sakreg, circled around him, and said, "He surely looks different from anything I have ever seen so far. Is he alone here, or are there more of him lurking around, and that, we have to find out later as to their whereabouts sir?"

"I see your concern, but don't worry, he is all alone here! We have secured his ship in the landing-bay. Anything else you need to know?" asked Narmoop.

"Yes. Then I would say, as long as we are here, we will take him with us and relieve you of further obligations sir," said Emogra.

"Really! You know darn well that is not going to happen. This is my responsibility from the get-go. I was entrusted with this operation by the first in command of this ship, and you know whom I am talking about," said Narmoop.

"Let me guess. It must be the Admiral Odnanra, isn't that right?" said Enog, one of the Emogra's crew members.

"Yes, you've guessed it right. It is Admiral Odnanra, and I am committed to accomplishing my mission set before me. Don't you forget that? Is that clear?"

"Yes sir, that is very clear sir," said Emogra.

"Then, I would suggest you go back to Lieutenant Poyt and tell him what I have said, and in a short while, I will see you with my prisoner at your compound—is that also clear?" asked Narmoop with slight irk in his expression.

"I suppose!" said Emogra with a discontented expression on his face.

"Very well then; our discussion here is over," said Narmoop.

"Not so fast commander. You still haven't answered my question, and that is—why are you hanging around here where you must be moving toward the compound?" asked Emogra.

"All right—I am going to explain it to you just so that you get out of my sight. We heard unusual noises coming from the Specimen Lab, and we stopped to investigate the source," said Narmoop.

"Specimen Lab, you said? Isn't it the place where we keep alien creatures in there for further study?" asked Emogra.

"Yes—that's what I said."

"And you said you heard unusual noises coming from inside the Specimen Lab. You know—that could spell trouble here sir! Who knows what could be lurking inside the Specimen Lab right now and wanting to become loose? Have you notified the command post?" asked Emogra.

"No—not yet. I don't need to alarm the command yet. It may just be nothing to talk about; I will inform the command should it become necessary, and I think you are going too far with this. Contain your imaginations at bay and Leave the emergencies for us to handle. We don't need you to get involved. Thank you! Everything is in control," said Narmoop.

"I don't believe that for a second, but I do see that our presence here is not appreciated. Come on, crew, let's head back to the compound where we are needed, and for your sake, sir, I hope you are right that everything is in control," said Emogra, and they all turned around and left.

"Lieutenant Neeyug, how much time is left to shut the life support system in the Specimen Lab?" asked Narmoop.

"Five minutes sir," said Lieutenant Neeyug.

"Very well," said Narmoop.

"Omeh, do you copy? This is Commander Narmoop."

"Yes sir, I copy you loud and clear," responded Omeh.

"Is there any progress in your location?" asked Narmoop.

"There are movements here and there, but the creature is not visible, as you know, and I don't understand why it hasn't attacked me yet," said Omeh.

"You must take care of the situation that is entrusted to you, and you need to do it fast. I mean very fast. You have five minutes of life support left before we turn it off. Do you hear me well?" asked Narmoop.

"I understand commander. I'm doing my best," said Omeh and began to search for the creature in the room. He pointed his weapon toward the sounds that the ship was making, thinking it was the beast that was the culprit, but there was no creature in the room.

The west wall had a vent that blew hot or cold air; also, it controlled the purity of the air inside the Specimen Lab. The presence of these large Specimen Tubes temporarily obscured Omeh's sight from noticing the vent on the west wall.

Soon after searching for the creature, Omeh acknowledged a vent without a screen. He thought that was odd, shouldn't there be one in its place, but there wasn't. He looked around and noticed a yanked screen strewed on the ground at some distance from the vent. He immediately came to realization that the beast was not present in the room and that it was somewhere in the air ducts of this ship.

"Commander—this is Omeh. Do you copy?"

"Yes Omeh, I copy you loud and clear. Do you have good news for me?"

"No Commander, but I have something to tell you, and it is more alarming now."

"What—is it now? All I hear is bad news from you," said the commander.

"Sorry for the bad news sir, but I have to tell you one thing that you must know. You probably won't believe this when I tell you. The creature is not in the room."

"What! What—did—you just say?"

"You've heard me right commander. The beast is not in the room!"

"It can't be. You must be wrong. Look harder!"

"Let me explain sir. I have witnessed the vent screen on the west wall; it has been compromised. He may have easily gone through it. I am very positive now the creature is somewhere in the air duct system sir! I suggest you abort the notion of cutting the life support system from the Specimen Lab sir."

"Affirmative will do as you have suggested," said the commander.

"And now unlock the door so I can get out sir," said Omeh.

"Not so fast. I still have slight doubts about what you have said, and for that reason, the doors will still have to remain shut. The commander is over and out."

CHAPTER 8

There is an inlet vent on the east wall of Specimen Lab right above the entrance doors. The vent operates through some sort of vacuum system where it sucks the air from outside the room and then channels it through the filtration system. After it does its filtration it disperses the pure air into the Specimen Lab.

Suddenly, the screen on the inlet vent, along with its filtration system, blew out violently with a loud noise. The vent with its filtration system fell to the ground and tumbled a few times, then stopped.

The commander and his crew became startled and confused. They all had perplexed expressions on their faces, and in response to their natural reflexes, they all pointed their weapons immediately toward the direction of the vent, but they witnessed nothing that came out of the vent and wondered what had just transpired here.

Few crewmembers opened fire instinctively but availed no result. There was nothing out there to shoot at. Fear gripped their hearts. Weapons didn't come down from their intended target.

Soon after the blowing of the vent screen, there came a brief thudding noise as if something had just landed on the floor. Only Sakreg, with his keen hearing, heard the thudding sound and said, *"Yinoot, something is wrong here. Prepare to run,"*

"Why, why should I run?" said Yinoot (Sakreg's friend)

"Let's be on the alert. I heard a thudding sound as if a creature of some sort had just come out of that vent moments ago and landed on the ground nearby. The creature must be around here, and this thing must be invisible," said Sakreg.

"You have determined all that just by a single thudding noise that only you heard, and no one else did?" said Yinoot.

"Yes Yinoot, trust me, I am not wrong here. Something worse is just about to happen. Everyone's life is in danger here. Please warn everyone, and let's all get the hell out of here, and let's do it as fast as we can to go to a safer place, and please alarm the command unit about this creature being out in the open before we acquire any casualty here," said Sakreg.

"Do you know where the creature you are talking about is now?" asked Yinoot.

"No, the creature is silent right now. Maybe it is deciphering who to attack first, but I believe it is close by, and we don't have much time to escape the danger if we terry any further," said Sakreg.

Suddenly, the creature shook its head up and down violently, then stopped a second or two, then gaped its mouth wide open. From its mouth burst out six more creatures, and within a few seconds, they became fully developed and invisible like its mother. Four have dispersed into the corridors of the ship with celerity, they were hungry and were seeking whom to devour. Two decided to accompany the mother creature to entertain the meal that was before their sight.

"Oh no, I feel there is more than one now!" said Sakrag.

"Commander, the prisoner is sensing the presence of many invisible life forms somewhere around here, and he thinks it is very dangerous right at this moment. He wants all of us to run fast for safety and inform the command post immediately," said Yinoot.

"You must be out of your mind, Yinoot. We will evaluate your mental stability when the time allows! How would you understand what he had said to you? You know that he is totally alien to us?" asked the Commander, Narmoop.

"There is one story you don't know about me commander," said Yinoot.

"Really! And what is that one story that I must know about you?" asked the commander.

"You see commander, we invaded their planet when I was a child sir. You should remember your history. My mother and my father fought the war of annihilation on the planet called Eegroag. This is where our prisoner comes from, and yes, I do understand his language very well, because their race raised me. My parents left me and abandoned me. I didn't know at the time whether they were dead or alive," said Yinoot.

"This piece of information about you I wasn't aware of. Considering what I know about you now, you may interpret for us what we need to know from this alien. However, on the first note, we are not running anywhere. This is what we're trained for. We will face this challenge and eliminate this menacing creature here and now. Is that clear to everyone?" asked the commander.

"Yes sir!" replied all with a concerned look on their faces.

"Very well then; that's what I want to hear! Now, keep your eyes and ears open. As you know, we are not dealing with an ordinary creature here. This one is fierce and possibly very deadly. It is invisible. Even the drones aren't able to detect them, as you have all seen. Four drones just buzzed right through here, and we had absolutely no response from them, and it has

already..." Just before the commander ended his statement, a projectile flew a bullet fast out of nowhere and struck the commander right in the neck. The impact was so powerful that it penetrated through the thick neck armor, pulled him up a couple of feet into the air and cut off his air supply instantly. The projectile was approximately three inches in length, half an inch in diameter, and had a very pointed end.

The commander struggled for air. Blood began to pulse out of his neck and contaminated his clothes, his hands, and the floor. He must have compromised an artery; a second later, he fell to the ground holding his neck with both arms and within moments, his body began to twitch and soon became motionless and died.

The crew immediately opened fire in the direction of the projectile that struck the commander, but their efforts resulted in no avail. There was no kill in sight. Soon, there was another victim of the same sort, another from a different direction and another... They all fell to the ground, immersed in their own blood, and all died instantly.

"Yinoot, as I have said, there is more than one creature here. Let's get out of here fast before we become their next victim. Let's go now, go, go, go!" said Sakreg. They left the crew, and both ran as if their lives depended on it, but two crewmembers followed them to find a hiding place quickly.

Two spheroid robot drones flew side by side through the hallway, where the commander and most of his crew became victims of the invisible creatures. The drones quickly halted in midair and hovered right above the dead bodies. They shined a beam of light upon them to identify their corpses.

Suddenly, the drones fell from the air to the hard floor in a freefall and rolled a few times, then stopped. The dotted Lights on their surfaces flickered a few times then that too gone dead. This incident occurred all over the spaceship. There were no more drones flying in the air anywhere in this huge starship, and the floors became littered by their presence.

"Commander, this is Lieutenant Omeh, do you copy"? There was no answer. *"Commander, please respond,"* still there was no rejoinder. Omeh's ears registered the discharge of weapons and desired to know the upshot, whether the beast was dead or still alive, or it was still in the air ducts.

Omeh felt he couldn't stay in the Specimen Lab any further and decided to take a chance and climb the west wall to get into the air duct. With some effort on his part, he managed to do so. Inside, the air duct was dark, dusty, crampy, and muggy. Hands and knees embraced the base of the meandering air duct and Omeh moved agonizingly slow.

Omeh slowly slid his large hand-held weapon on the base of the air duck as he slowly propelled his body forward thinking the alien beast could be near his proximity. He was careful not to make noise, lest he draw attention from the creature.

Omeh's attempt was to understand what was on the other end of the air duct and that he hoped to free himself from ever hauntingly and creepy Specimen Lab that was full of alien life forms in translucent tubes hanging from the ceiling, also to free himself from four dead and mutilated bodies inside the specimen lab.

He approached the near vicinity of the inlet air duct that was situated right above the entrance door of the specimen lab and was approximately twenty feet shy from it. He immediately noticed the mash and the filtration system that covered the entrance of the air duct was no longer there. He swiftly decided that the creature must have been out already. *"Why should the creature hang out in the air ducts? There are plenty of flash out there to feast upon,"* he thought.

Omeh silently approached the edge of the destroyed inlet vent and surreptitiously stuck his head slightly out of the compromised vent to have a glance at the environment down below at the ground level. He witnessed there were three creatures, bright red in color, having long spiky and segmented tails like scorpions, extending approximately two feet from their bodies, and a pair of muscular legs that contained three toes on each claw-like feet accompanied with very sharp curved nails at their ends.

The creatures had stout shoulders accompanied by two buffed forearms, and at their ends, it contained two claws, possessing three digits on each claw and at the end of their claws, there were large and very sharply curved nails.

Their craniums were large. Their temporal lobes were multi-faceted but flat at the apex. They had an extended bony occipital region that narrowed at the end and curved upward, housing a sharp hook that was like that of a scorpion's tail sting.

At each side of their noggins, two large purple orbs were having solid pupils used for sight. They had an enormous gaping mouth. In the center of their upper jaws was a single, protruding, and profoundly large tooth. This tooth was menacingly wide, curved and pointed at the lower end, which was followed by sharp and jagged, but smaller teeth in the background. On the lower jaws, two large and protruding pointed teeth were accompanied by smaller, sharply notched teeth along its perimeter.

For now, these monsters were amazingly visible. Apparently, when they had to feed on something, they would have to lose their invisibility and become detectable. These creatures were hunched over their prays and were very busy tearing into their meat, cutting large portions of muscles, blood vessels, and nerves with their huge K-nine-like teeth and were voraciously munching on their prey that were eviscerated, bloodied, dismembered, and were already a carrion. These were the bodies of the crewmembers, including the commander.

Omeh was silently observing all that which was unfolding before his sight. The scene was too lurid for his senses. He grimaced his face in full disgust, anger, and trepidation. His body convulsed from the horrid sight that he was witnessing before his eyes. These were his crewmembers, whom he dined and drank with, joked and laughed with, but now, they have become nothing else but a lunch for these unknown creatures.

He briefly shut his eyes, thanked his maker, and thought, "How lucky I must have been by not being outside with the commander and the rest of the crew, when I desired to be out of the Specimen Lab."

He thought to use his weapon to eliminate the creatures but noticed there was not sufficient room in the air-duct to freely heave the rifle and take a decent aim at them and shoot. He decided to wait until they were out of the way, then jump to the floor and inform the command post, then hide until he decided how to deal with these invisible beasts.

These brutes seemed to have devoured almost all soft tissue and some part of their skeletal bones. They stood erect on their two strong legs and appeared towering. They were approximately eight feet in height and ambled like the rest of the crew on the ship, one leg at a time.

The creatures began to banter physically with each other, making strange, rapid and repetitive sounds like the woodpeckers do when they are picking on the wood but in a flatter tone. Omeh felt that they were happy and gloating in their kills.

Omeh stepped back a little so that he wouldn't become an obvious target of observation, but in the process, he managed to create the sound of sliding metal. His weapon was sliding on the base of the air duct. The creatures suddenly stopped in their activities and concentrated their sight on the inlet air duck.

Omeh realized they stopped playing with each other. They must have sensed a life-sustaining presence, and now there was a distinct possibility that the creatures had already discovered him.

Omeh strenuously moved his body in confined and limited space to be ready to shoot should they come in through the inlet air duct. He didn't care about making noise anymore, because he was sure that they had already pinned his whereabouts and that he was going to be their next target of the meal. His heart rate, blood pressure elevated, and trepidation set in, he thought— *"Will I be the next on their menu?"* Omeh mustered sufficient gallantry and pulled his body to the edge of the air duct one more time to witness the situation at the ground level. He noticed the creatures were just beginning to transform right before his eyes to the point where they had now become invisible again. Omeh thought they would be charging through the vent at any moment, but at least they would have to do it one at a time.

Omeh managed to slide back about ten feet in haste to give himself ample space from being in harm's way. With much afford, he readied his weapon and pointed it forward right at the opening of the air duct, thinking that the creatures may charge through at any given moment. He thought, *"At first, they must make an impact noise on the wall, and when they attempt to enter through, I will see their heads first, and then I will have the chance to blast them one at a time until they are none."*

Just as Omeh predicted, there was an audible struggle at the mouth of the inlet air duct. It was an attempt by the creature to get a foothold on the wall so that it could stick its entire body in. This was an easy decision for Omeh to make. He pulled the trigger once when the creature extended its head into the air duct. A bright green ball of ionized projectile left the nozzle of Omeh's weapon and struck the creature right at the upper head.

Suddenly, Omeh heard a loud and strident scream like that of a banshee, followed by a thudding sound. *"Yap!"* Omeh yelled, *"One down and two to go."* He suddenly felt elated and expected the other two creatures to execute the same act as the first one did, and that he may also have to blow them away.

Omeh waited a minute or two; no creature evinced itself at the inlet air duct, and he wondered why. *"They are smart. They know that they will be blown away. Now, they must be up to something and are planning my demise somehow. I wonder if they are already inside the Specimen Lab by using some type of means to get in? Their intention must be to get at me from behind through the specimen lab's west wall air duct. That is the only way to get at me,"* thought Omeh silently.

"Damn! I wonder if I should blow the air-duct that is behind me to leave as much distance between them and me. Heck, if I do that, it might weaken the structure of the air duct, and maybe it wouldn't be able to carry my weight, and then it will collapse;

it will be certain that I will fall to the ground along with the air duct and then I will be confined in the Specimen Lab with no chance to exit or escape." Omeh decided to abandon the plan.

Omeh slowly crept forward toward the entrance of the inlet air duct to have a better understanding of the situation down below. It was his only chance to free himself from the Specimen Lab, but the environment may have been fraught with the danger of invisible creatures, and they may just be waiting for him to make the dammning move.

CHAPTER 9

"First-officer Yinoot to the main bridge come in, please."

"This is the main bridge, Admiral Odnanra on the comm. Go ahead Yinoot."

"Admiral, we have a code red situation in the Specimen Lab. There are many casualties here including commander Narmoop. I am requesting assistance sir. A deadly creature from the Specimen Lab is on the loose. The creature is multiplying by droves as we speak. I don't know how many are there right now. But now, I would say they may be everywhere in this ship. I am in a hiding place along with my two teammates, but the rest of my crew is dead."

"What about the prisoner?" asked the Admiral Odnanra?

"The prisoner is fine and is under my custody sir," said Yinoot.

"Very Well, Lieutenant, keep an eye on the prisoner, don't let him get away. Keep calm. The help will be on its way soon. By the way, do you have any information about the drone malfunction?" asked the admiral.

"What drone malfunction sir?" asked Yinoot.

"Never mind, apparently, you have no idea about the drone situation. We'll be in touch. The admiral is over and out."

"Admiral Odnanra to Captain Yilow; come in, Captain Yilow."

"Yes Admiral, this is Captain Yilow. I hear you loud and clear sir."

"We have two security issues that needs to be addressed as soon as possible. Your first assignment is to investigate the drone's malfunction. Find out its cause and see if you can get them back into the air.

The drone room is not in communication mode. I can't get through to them. Something is wrong over there. Find out and report as soon as possible. Your second assignment is that you need to attend to the Specimen room and address the emergency there. Apparently, a Lab creature is loose, and we have casualties there. Be careful, Captain. According to Yinoot, these creatures are multiplying fast. They may be everywhere by now. Just be careful, do you hear me?"

"Yes, admiral," said Captain Yilow.

"Fine then, the admiral is over and out."

"Lieutenant Sesmo, this is captain Yilow speaking. Can you hear me?"

"Yes sir, I hear you loud and clear, sir," said the lieutenant.

"Fine then, get the special Ops unit to the briefing room within five minutes. I have important news I want to share with everyone."

"Yes sir. It must be urgent," said the lieutenant.

"Yes, it is very urgent," said the captain. The lieutenant dispatched a twenty-five-member team to the briefing room, and within four minutes, they were all in the briefing room waiting for Captain Yilow to arrive.

"Hey lieutenant, what's this all about?" asked one of the teammates.

"I don't know the details, but all I know is that it is very urgent. We'll all find out soon, as soon as the captain arrives, which will be at any minute now," said the lieutenant. Moments later, Captain Yilow walked hastily into the room.

"The captain is in the room," yelled the lieutenant and everyone stood up at attention.

"Be at ease team, and take your seat," said the captain.

"Lieutenant—are all members accounted for?" asked the captain.

"Yes sir," said the lieutenant.

"Very well then, take your seat, lieutenant," said the captain. The room was devoid of palaver. All orbs were fixated upon the captain, and everyone with a concerned look on their faces was patiently waiting for the captain to hear what he had to say.

"Team, I have come across two disturbing pieces of information from Admiral Odnanra, and we need to address them now. I really mean now. First, you all might have realized that the drones on this ship are out of commission. As soon as Admiral Onanra realized that the drones were down, he contacted the drone-room, and their response was, 'we are working on it.'

"After a little while, Admiral Odnanra attempted to contact them again, and there was no response. I think there must be a sabotage of the drones conducted by rogue personal. We need to investigate and find the source, who and why. The second point I want to make is that we need to address the emergency that popped up in the Specimen room. I hate to say this—but we have casualties. I don't know how many, but we'll find out soon.

"The admiral informed me that a creature is loose in this spaceship, and it is multiplying fast as I speak. We have no idea what that creature looks like, what its capabilities are, and how many are there right now. For all I know, it could be in the hundreds by now. Who knows. We all must be on our toes and deal with this problem head-on. It might take a while to contain them, or they will contain us if we are not carful.

"They're considered extremely, I mean, extremely dangerous. I will tell you, team that we will have our hands full in dealing with the unknown creatures that are lurking now in this ship. We must attend every corner of this ship to find them and destroy them. We can't afford to leave one alive lest they multiply again.

"Right now, they may be hiding and waiting for us to show up, and who knows, they may already have claimed more lives than the specimen room incident. As I have said, we must be on our toes at all times.

"We have no choice in this matter. We can't lose. We must win; otherwise, our lives and the lives of everyone on this ship will be questionable. This is the time when we as a team must put all our training, resources, and expertise into use. Any questions?" asked the captain. There was no response from anyone.

"All right then, if there is no question—Lieutenant Sesmo, I want you to take fifteen ungs from this crew and head immediately to the Specimen lab to rescue the first officer Yinoot, two of his team-mates and make sure the prisoner does not escape, then we will have another headache to deal with. Report when you have accomplished your mission.

"I will take the rest of the crew to the drone control room to fix the problem there. If you need further assistance at the Specimen lab, then we'll meet you there. Otherwise, we'll go back to the head-quarter; is that clear?" asked Captain Yilow.

"Yes sir," replied the First Lieutenant Sesmo.

"All right, Lieutenant, choose your team?" asked Captain Yilow.

"You heard the captain—I need fifteen of you in my team. Please step forward those who want to join me?" asked Lieutenant Sesmo. Within moments, he had fifteen members for his team.

"All right, lieutenant it looks like you have all your team ready. Now, take your ungs (men) and move on," said the captain.

"All right, team, step outside the briefing room and get into formation," said the lieutenant and everyone in the team followed the command.

"All right ungs, you heard the captain. There is a real danger out there. We have no idea what kind of creatures we are dealing with. The onus is on us to take care of this issue. We must work as a team and always lookout for each other's back. Our mission is cutout for us. This is what we're trained for. There is no turning back. We must destroy all the creatures that are loose on board where-ever we find them. This could be a long-time battle until we destroy them all. Is that clear?" said the lieutenant.

"Yes sir"! They all replied in unison.

"All right ungs, let's move it!" said the lieutenant.

The fifteen tall and burly ungs, well-armed, well trained in Special-Op's, expressing fierce continence, dressed in black, wielding heavy weapons and sophisticated electronic gadgets have begun to move rapidly, but at the same time cautiously and silently, also in unison through the not so well lit, steely, and pipe-laden corridors of the ship.   Their destination: The Specimen Lab sector to rescue the ungs who have found themselves in a life-threatening situation, including the alien prisoner "Sakreg".

These Special-Ops team members have their eyes wide open. However, they were displaying concerned experessions on their faces. They were randomly swinging their plasma rifles up and down, left and right, and were occasionally turning around to witness if there was anything unusual lurking behind them. Despite their training and expertise, they still had a considerable amount of fear and trepidation lurking in their hearts and minds in dealing with this unknown situation, because they had absolutely no knowledge of the creature's attributes and its capabilities.

Suddenly—Lieutenant Sesmo made a motion with his hand for the team to stop, and he blurted, "My sensor is picking up movements two hundred feet up ahead. This is strange. We should be able to witness whatever is out there, but I can't see anyone or any life form and is registering more than one. I count five, to be exact. Can anyone confirm that?"

"Affirmative sir!" said all in a few seconds interval.

"Prepare to engage. Fire at will!" said the lieutenant. Right before they opened fire, the signal suddenly disappeared.

"Lieutenant, what just happened here? I've lost the signal," said one of the soldiers.

"I don't know! Mine has gone too!" said the lieutenant, as the rest of the crew said the same thing.

"Lieutenant, do you think it was a false alarm?" asked one of the crewmembers that stood next to the lieutenant.

"I don't think so. Not all of us will have a false signal. There was something out there, but not anymore. However, whatever they are, they must still be here, and in the corridor, they can't be anywhere else," said the Lieutenant.

"What the heck is going on here lieutenant? I don't like this!" said one of the crewmembers.

"I don't know. I don't like it either, but let's not panic. Let's all keep our cools now, and let's use everything that we have learned and trained for. Like it or not, we are here and we must deal with this unknown that faces us.

"So, keep your eyes and ears open and be alert at all time. None of us have any idea as to what we're dealing with here! Our sensors did pick up their presence, but the creatures were not visible anywhere. I would say we are definitely dealing with creatures that are small, and they can hide anywhere in the corridor, or we are dealing with large ones who happen to be, as I have said before, invisible; that is why we can't see them, but that doesn't mean they are not here. They must be here now in this corridor, nowhere else," said Lieutenant Sesmo.

"Sir, how are we going to shoot them if we can't see them," asked one of the crewmembers.

"Well, if they are invisible, then we have no other choice but to shoot indiscriminately weather we see them or not," said the lieutenant.

The lieutenant thought it through again about the creatures' whereabouts, and he came to a solid conclusion that the sensors could not have lied and that the creatures were in the corridor, and they were invisible. He yelled, "Open fire!" Forthwith, he opened fire, and soon all opened fire.

Suddenly, a few bright, thick, and gray bellowing clouds laced with occasional burst of fire ensued from the creatures. They were approximately thirty feet away from where the lieutenant and his team were. Within few moments, very loud and strident agonizing sounds filled the corridor as if many souls were in a great pain.

The bellowing clouds changed form and became like a tornado, five individual ones to be exact, and quickly descended to the ground, then shrunk to nothingness and created five piles of ash-like material on the floor close distance from each other.

"Wow! That was strange, and they were very close. What was that lieutenant? What the hack are we dealing with here?" said one of the crewmembers who stood near the lieutenant.

"I don't know. But one thing I know now—they are invisible for sure. I hope this is it, but of course, that is not going to be the case. As I have said, there may be hundreds of them by now. However, we still must attend the emergency at the Specimen Lab. I have a feeling that we may have to deal with more of them creatures when we get there. So, let's all be ready like always," said Lieutenant Sesmo and at the same time, he let the pile of ash that he picked up from the floor allow to flow down from between his fingers.

The lieutenant and his team moved cautiously through the rest of the corridor, and when they reached the end, they turned left and there it was—the specimen lab at approximately three-hundred feet away from where they stood. The crew descried the mutilated flash and skeletal remains of the Ship's crewmembers. They appeared as if vicious creatures had consumed their body parts. There was blood everywhere, some parts of their guts and body organs strewed here and there. They all grimaced their faces in sheer disgust, and the smell of their remains was overwhelming.

Suddenly, the sensors on their weapons alarmed them again.

"Just as I thought—they are here," said the lieutenant.

"Lieutenant, my sensor is indicating there are two somewhere near us," said one of the crewmembers, and everyone confirmed the amount, including the lieutenant.

"All right ungs, you all know the drill. Let's be careful. I don't want to lose any of you. Do you hear me?" asked the lieutenant.

"Yes sir!" responded the crew almost in unison.

"All right then, let's kick ass," said the lieutenant.

"Lieutenant, they are moving fast and are heading toward us," said one of the crewmembers, moments later a silent projectile came out of nowhere a lightning-fast speed and struck one of the crewmembers right in the neck, and the crewmember couldn't take another breath, fell fast to the hard ground, and died. A few teammates that were in a close approximate to the one who just died opened fire toward the direction of the projectile, but the result was abortive. Soon, few more became victims of such death. All crewmembers began to fire 180° indiscriminately, hopping to engage those unseen creatures.

The Second Lieutenant Omeh was observing the ground-level situation from the life-support air duct. He concluded that the creatures were no longer in near proximity to cause any harm. He jumped to the ground and rolled a few times to absorb the strength of the impact, then he got right back to his feet and ran eastbound toward the rescue team to assist them in their fight against the creatures.

Four crewmembers including the lieutenant remained alive to battle the brutes. They fired randomly but in the wrong direction. However, from the angle of Omeh's observation, he witnessed a slight, phantom-like disturbance in the air. He immediately came to realize that the fiends must have been causing these anomalous distortions in the air. Omeh immediately opened fire and struck the two creatures.

Suddenly, a high-pitched jarring sound ensued. Thick black smoke embodied the creatures, then the smoke bellowed like cumulus clouds and hovered approximately ten feet above the ground for a few seconds. Then the clouds churned fast and became tornados like whirlwinds, two to be exact, and shrunk to the ground, then became a pile of ash-like material.

The lieutenant and the rest of the remaining crew ran toward Omeh. Upon their meeting, Omeh rendered a salute by extending both arms straightforwardly, hands in a horizontal position, fingers extending forward and touching each other and accompanied with a slight bow of the head. The lieutenant rendered the same salute.

"Good job, lieutenant. I am Lieutenant Sesmo, and you must be?"

"I am Second Lieutenant Omeh. Thank you for responding to my emergency, Lieutenant Sesmo," said Omeh.

"No, no, no, I must be thankful to you, Lieutenant Omeh. You have saved our lives. However, you were not the one who dispatched our unit to the Specimen Lab. It was First Lieutenant Yinoot."

"It must have been. He was one of our senior crewmembers in charge of handling the prisoner, and we were all supposed to be in support of Lieutenant Yinoot in escorting the prisoner to the prison ward."

"Where is the prisoner now?" asked Lieutenant Sesmo.

"I, I----don't know. Lieutenant Yinoot will have to answer your question when you find him sir."

"And where is Lieutenant Yinoot now?" asked lieutenant Sesmo.

"Then again, I don't really know sir. Please let me explain."

"Go ahead, I am listening," said Lieutenant Sesmo.

"You see—Commander Narmoop ordered my partner and me. By the way, my partner is dead at this moment. As I have said, the commander ordered us to enter the Specimen Lab to ascertain the source of the shattering sound that originated from within, and when I attempted to exit that inlet air duct, all I witnessed was this carnage, the death of my crewmembers including the commander Narmoop," said Omeh.

"Who was your partner?" asked Sesmo.

"He was the Airman Eegroj sir," said Omeh.

"How did he die?" asked Sesmo.

"He was attacked by the same creatures that I shot a few minutes ago sir. His body is still on the floor inside the specimen room over a pool of blood sir," said Omeh.

"And how did you stay alive?" asked the lieutenant.

"I don't really know sir. For some odd reason, it stayed away from me. Maybe he didn't like me somehow and wanted to get away from me. The thing jumped into the air duct and escaped the Specimen Lab through the air-ducts and attacked my crewmembers, including the commander," said Omeh.

"Who was your commander?" asked the lieutenant.

"Well, as I have said before—he was Commander Narmoop, you are looking at him," he was pointing at one of the eviscerated bodies that were lying on the ground along with the rest of the crew in a pool of blood."

"Is that him?"

"Well—I believe so. As you see, there is nothing left of him except some of his bones, a few pieces of his flash and some parts of his uniform. However, that's his nametag next to his remains on the ground. He wore a special red nametag different from the rest. That is how I knew it was him."

"Narmoop ha, the famous Senior Grade Commander; I knew him well. He was one of the finest officers and a total perfectionist. He also was a hard act to follow. He was headstrong; everything must be his way, or you were in trouble. I worked with him briefly before we embarked on this space mission. He was also my commander in senior grade.

I am very sad about the loss of your commander and your crewmembers, Omeh. He was a fine commander, after all, but since he is no longer extant, you will be working with us from now on. I would like to welcome Second Lieutenant Omeh to our unit. I am sure the captain will have the final say so about you becoming part of our unit, but I do not anticipate any problem here.

We need a few good ungs like you on our team. However, coming back to what happened here, you will tell us all that we need to know, but in more detail, of course," said the lieutenant.

"Very well then, let's pick up the belongings of the deceased, including their weapons, oh yes—also that shiny weapon on the floor. I have never seen such a weapon. Is this something new?" asked Lieutenant Sesmo.

"No sir. I believe that belonged to the prisoner sir," said Omeh.

"Did you say it belonged to the prisoner?" asked Sesmo.

"Yes sir," said Omeh. Lieutenant Sesmo picked the weapon from the floor and examined its unique features.

"Do you know how to use this weapon, Lieutenant Omeh?" asked Sesmo.

"No sir, but I would suggest you exercise extreme caution sir. You would never know the destructive powers it may contain until you discharge it," said Omeh.

"Yes, yes, I know. We will handle it carefully," said Sesmo, inserted between his belt and his uniform.

CHAPTER 10

A few minutes after Lieutenant Sesmo's departure toward the Specimen room, Captain Yilow and the rest of his squad began to move toward the drone room to investigate the anomaly in question. Two minutes passed their initial start. Captain Yilow suddenly beckoned his crew to stop.

The captain and his crew glued their eyes toward the ground. They described many two feet in dimeter sand piles on the floor. They have never witnessed such sand piles in this ship. They were all wondering where these piles of sand came from and what could portray the nature of this unique and outlandish scene.

The crew counted thirteen Piles of sand on the floor. The captain knelt next to one and sampled the sand-like material with his fingers. It felt like real sand to the touch, and I still couldn't figure out how these piles of sand got here in the first place.

Captain Yilow didn't think of any harm that could come from these piles. He pulled his camera out and acquired photos, then scooped some and placed them into two small vials for examination. It was a standard operating procedure to have tools like vials in their position just in case they arrived at the unknown situations they just encountered. The captain summoned a cleanup crew to clean these piles of sand, and then they continued their mission toward the drone room.

"Captain, my sensor is going wild. There is something going on approximately ninety-four feet away. It is not one of us, and it is moving toward us," said one of the crewmembers. Shortly, everyone confirmed, including the captain, but there was nothing

out there physically to witness and confirm their readings to be correct.

"Captain, what do you suggest?" asked Seargent Emoh, who was standing next to the captain.

"All right ungs whatever it is, whether you see it or not, if your signal reads thirty feet, then open fire, is that clear?" asked the captain.

"Yes sir," said all.

Suddenly, the creatures materialized. They gaped their mouths and flaunted their teeth to instill fear into the spectator's minds. Captain's crew was ready to open fire, but just before their attempt to do so, they realized the creatures were in great pain and agony. They slightly lowered their weapons and fixated their sight on the creatures as they fell one by one and dematerialized into a pile of sand by their death routine.

"What----just----happened here captain?" asked Sergeant Emoh.

"Something killed them, I don't know what, but whatever it was, I am very grateful for it," said the captain.

"I think it was your face or your stench, but I think both your face and your stench that they couldn't stand, Sarg," yelled one of the teammates. The rest chuckled, but some broke out into full laughter.

"All right that's enough. We have a mission to accomplish here. Let's get serious for a change and move on," said the captain.

"You have to admit, sergeant, the comment was funny," said the captain and broke out into a chuckle.

"You too captain! One thing you should know—that's all a pile of shit. For your information, the women go crazy on me, and they love the way I smell—ok!" said Sergeant Emoh.

"Woe, woe woe—Hold your jet Sarg. No need to get testy here; I am just messing with you. Don't take it personally. You're too sensitive—relax. We have a mission to accomplish. We must be levelheaded to think straight, got it?" asked the captain.

"Yesssss sirrrrr. No need to worry; I am cool," said the sergeant. As they closed the distance between themselves and the drone room, they witnessed one of the ship's crewmembers shut the entrance door of the drone room quietly. It appeared as if his plan was to abscond, but he paused for a short time and glared at the arriving security crew rather apprehensively. There were approximately six school buses in the distance between them.

Suddenly, the ship crewmember absquatulated from the drone room. The captain and his team dashed to capture this anomalous lily-livered decamping ship resident to ascertain the reasoning behind his evasion.

The investigative team arrived at the entrance door of the drone room; the captain summoned four of his members, including Sergeant Emoh, to pursue the fleeing subject then the captain and his remaining crew entered the room. What they have witnessed was appalling. They have witnessed four controllers dead, two sprawled on their chairs with their necks slashed and soaked in their own blood, and two were on the floor, having their guts out and full of blood on the hard ground.

The captain registered the names of the deceased in his handheld miniature electronic device, acquired many photographs, collected evidence, and called for the proper authorities to clean the bloodstains and to transfer the lifeless bodies to a proper department to further collect evidence. The captain and the crew realized the computer monitors were pulsating a text message, "THE DRONES ARE DEACTIVATED. ENTER THE NEW CODE TO REACTIVATE."

"Captain, it appears that the drones were hacked. Whoever it was, he or she must have been very knowledgeable about the drone operations and decided to rewrite their program and issue a new passcode for them to reactivate. I don't know how long it will take the computer team to restart the drones, sir. They must find the virus and erase it, then reprogram the drones and re-issue a new code," said Sergeant Nibuo.

"Whoever it was—must have had a sinister plot to harm everyone in this ship. I would say this ship is in danger of mutiny. We must do everything in our power to find and prosecute the perpetrators of this heinous crime and stop them dead in their tracks before they stop us," said the captain.

Suddenly , the captain and the rest of the crew heard a noise and many metallic tools just fell to the ground. The noise originated inside a room that was not too far from the main control room. Everyone froze in their positions and glared at each other in obfuscation; it was as if something very odd had just transpired.

The captain and his team drew their weapons and glared at each other in silence. They attempted to ascertain the source and the direction of the noise. The captain immediately beckoned the team with his fingers and soon with his hand to follow him.

Captain Yilow deciphered that the noise came from the north of the main control- room. They all quietly followed him and ambled slowly toward the room in question; they soon arrived at the door and gathered right about it, pointing their weapons at the door.

The captain slowly and silently twisted the doorknob, but it only turned a little and then stopped. It is a locked door, he concluded.

The captain knocked at the door three times with his fist and said, *"Open the door now, this is the security. We know you're inside. Give yourselves up peacefully or face the consequences. Do it now!"* said the captain in a loud voice. The captain waited for a few seconds to hear a response, but there was none.

"Did you hear me? Come out peacefully, or we're coming in even if we must break this door," said the captain.

"How should I know you are the security? For all that matter, you could be lying, and you want to kill me like you have killed the rest of my team!" she blared from inside.

"What is your name?" asked the captain.

"You don't need to know my name. You need to leave me alone! I despatched the security, and they will be here in any minute, and if I were you, I would leave now. Otherwise, you will be in deep trouble I assure you of that!" said Noyt.

"Look—I am the Captain, and my name is Yilow. I am the head of the security. You should have nothing to worry about; please open the door now so we can help you. I want to find out

what happened here. I am sure you have seen everything that went on here, and I think you can identify the culprits who committed this heinous crime, so please open the door now and let me help you?" asked the captain.

"Oh—you're good; you're really good at pretending you are the captain of the security. You almost had me convinced, but I still have my doubts. How should I really know that you're telling me the truth, ha? I tell you what—I am going to ask you a question only the real security captain would know the answer. Otherwise, I am not opening the door. Besides, I am armed. If you break-in, I will kill you. Is that clear?" Noyt asked.

"Yes, yes, I would say that's fair—go ahead. If that's what it will take to make you believe what I am saying is the truth, then just make it fast. Time is of the essence hurry up," said the captain.

"Yes, that's what it will take! Are you ready?" Noyt asked.

"I said yes, I am ready. You know, you are getting on my nerves now, but go right ahead, ask the question and make it fast. I don't have time to play with you," said the captain.

"All right, here it goes. Tell me the security passcode if you are Captain Yilow, the security code that was assigned to us three days ago by the security department. What was it?" asked Noyt.

"As a matter of fact I did assign that security code. How could I forget it? It was "THE BIRDS ARE GOING HOME," said the captain.

"Excellent—then you are telling me the truth." She came to the door in a hurry and opened it.

"It is about time you have opened the damn door. We have lost lots of precious time because of you. However, you have lots of explaining to do Private Noyt. That is the name I read on your shirt is that correct?" asked the captain.

"Yes, that is the correct captain. Noyt is my name, and I will explain everything that I have seen, but it is better to be safe than sorry, don't you think so, captain?" she said.

"Yes—I suppose!" said the captain begrudgingly.

"All right ungs search the room to see if anyone else is hiding here," said the captain.

"Why! You think that I might be harboring a fugitive here and that I am pretending all this?" said Noyt.

"Yes. How should I know that you are not one of them? For all that matter, you could have killed your team, and you are making yourself look innocent of all this mayhem," said the captain. The crew went ahead and looked everywhere inside the room to locate the malefactors but found no one in the room.

"It is all clear sir," said Sergeant Nibuo.

"Very well sergeant—private Noyt, I suppose—so far, you are in a good standing. However, you will be coming with us to the headquarters, and you are going to tell us all about what had transpired here, but while we are here, can you at least tell us if you can identify the killer or killers?" asked the captain.

"Well—no sir, not really," said Noyt.

"What do you mean not really!" asked the captain.

"I mean, I saw what happened here, but I couldn't identify the killers, because they were wearing space helmets and their visors. As you know captain, the visors are mirrored as usual. It

would be obvious that I wouldn't be able to see their faces. However, I noticed one of them had a bad gash on the surface of his right hand, and it was bleeding," said Noyt.

"Great, at least we have something to go on with, but where were you when all this was happening with that? I mean, how did you stay alive when everyone else is dead?" asked the captain

"Good question. You see captain, I was in that room." She pointed to the room with her finger. *That is where we keep our drone maintenance records. I was attempting to find a certain drone maintenance record in there and that is when all the mayhem happened.*

I heard a commotion at the operation area where my teammates sat and monitored the drones and immediately realized something was going wrong. I stuck my head slightly out the door to see what was going on in the control room, and I saw two ungs using something sharp and stabbing the operators. I got scared, very scared. I knew I couldn't fight them. I decided to tiptoe to the room that I was in now. I was careful not to make noise, and then I shut the door behind me and locked myself in for my safety.

Soon, I heard footsteps in this corridor that you are standing on, and I knew instantly that they were coming for me. I was going to be their next victim, and sure enough, they came right here and attempted to open this door, but they couldn't, and after a few minutes, they left in a hurry. That is all I know," said Noyt.

"Thanks for all your information," said the captain, then he grabbed his communicator and began to blurt,

"Sergeant Emoh, have you been able to apprehend the fleeing suspect yet?"

"No sir, not yet we're still running after him to catch that bastard sir. He is giving us the runaround. I don't know from where he gets all his energy. We're having a difficult time catching up with him. He must be on drugs, we'll investigate once we catch up with him, but don't worry, sir we'll get him soon, I promise you that," said the sergeant Emoh.

"I hope so for everyone's sake, sergeant!" said the captain.

"Captain, your tone of voice sounds serious to me. What do you mean by that?" asked the sergeant.

"For your information sergeant, we have four dead ungs in the drone room. It is imperative that you catch whoever he is, so that we can question him for all the murders.

We might have a serial killer in our hands, or a mutiny in progress. Oh, one more thing: ask him if he knows the new code to reactivate the drones again. My guess is that he knows it. However, do you need our assistance now?" asked the captain.

"No sir we don't need any help. We're just about to wrap this pursuit, but I am greatly saddened about the murders. Captain if you don't mind, must end this conversation because my team and I are all out to catch this suspect while I am talking to you," said the sergeant.

"Fine then—get him, and get him to talk, but don't kill him. As I have said, we need to question him. We need answers quickly. He may not be working alone. Is he armed?" asked the captain.

"No sir, it doesn't look like he is armed. He is wearing a tight uniform and there is nowhere he can hide any weapon sir," said the sergeant, Emoh.

All right then, just be careful. The captain is over and out."

The suspect, while he was running, twisted his upper body to look behind him so that he could take a gander at his pursuers. Just then, he suddenly tripped over a strewed small drone, it was one of the many that were on the floor. He lost his balance and fell hard on the ground, rolled a few times, then laid on his back, holding his bent right leg at the knee and tucking it close to his chest, attempting to restrain his knee movement to minimize the pain he was experiencing. But while he held his knee in a bent position, he wallowed to his right and to his left and bawled, for he was in great pain.

Sergeant Emoh and his crew caught up to him. They all panted from being breathless and exhausted. The crew surrounded the suspect with weapons pointed right at his head while attempting to catch their breaths.

Sergeant Emoh made a motion with his hand and said, *"Point your weapons down. He is not going anywhere. Besides, he is not armed."* They all complied.

Sergeant Emoh had his upper body bent forward from sheer exhaustion and his hands were resting on his thighs for support. His chest rose and fell from rapid breathing. The sergeant was older than the rest of his crew by many years but was still spry.

After gathering his breath, he stood erect and blurted, *"Damn it, you gave us quite a run, Mr. I would say you almost got away at least for now. Where did you get all that energy for running?"* asked Sergeant Emoh.

The fleeing suspect was unable to heave his body off the floor, for the pain in his right leg was great, but despite his pain, he glared at the sergeant and managed to deliver a slight smirk on his face, then suddenly blurted and said, *"I eat a box of crackers in your mother's bed sergeant."* The crew burst into a big giggle.

"You know, that wasn't nice. I should just shoot you for saying that," said the sergeant.

"Who said anything about being nice here sergeant, especially when you and your cronies have surrounded me with their weapons pointed right at my head, ha! —That will do well with you shooting an unarmed and off-duty ung. That's going to make you look sooooo good. Heck, you might even get a promotion from scumbags like you," said the miscreant.

"Well, isn't that a sham for you to even get caught by a scumbag like me? *And now you have nowhere to run. What a bummer. I guess you have sealed your fate now,"* said the sergeant.

"I guess I did," said the suspect.

"Hey, sergeant, are you going to let him talk trash to you?" said one of his crew.

"I think we should shoot his ass right now!" said another crewmember and pointed his weapon right at the suspect's head.

"Put your weapon down!" said the sergeant. The crewmember hesitated. *"I said put your weapon down right now. That's an order!"* said the sergeant. The crewmember scowled at the sergeant, hesitated for a few seconds, then complied.

"Now that's better. I thought for a moment that you were going to pull that trigger," said the suspect, and he turned his head and faced the sergeant and said, *"And for you sergeant, bravo, many kudos to you. I suppose I am your catch of the day,*

aren't I. Now, let's see who is going to shoot me first you or your hysterical sidekicks?" asked the suspect.

"You know—for a little fart that you are, you sure have a big freaking mouth. You see—your shit can't come out of your bottom end because you are anally retentive, and that is why your shit must come out of your mouth. And your big stinking mouth is going to get you in biiiiiig trouble one of these days if you survive this day with us. I'll shoot your ass if you misbehave from now on and don't cooperate.

"Now, let's get back to the business of providing us with the *information that we are looking for. You had better cooperate, or else you are going to make me so mad, very mad indeed; I wouldn't be responsible for what I will do to you next. Have I made myself clear?"*

"Wow sergeant, you are scaring me really bad. My heart just jumped out of my ribcage from sheer shock and fear, and now it is on the floor. Please don't step on it, and you know what else— I am shaking in my boots and shitting in my pants. Sergeant, please don't tease me like that. I am getting a hard-on," said the unscrupulous, and the sergeant's team broke out in a cackle.

"Hey sergeant, you have to admit, he is amusing," said one of the teammates.

"You find this to be amusing - ha! He is being stupid and a numbskull. He doesn't seem to understand or realize how much trouble he is in right now!" The sergeant turned around and faced the suspect and said, *"All right, enough of your craps that you are putting out; didn't your mom teach you how to brush your freaking teeth to get rid of all the filth that's coming out of your mouth? Just answer my damn questions that I am about to ask*

*you, you piece of s**t that you are!"* said the sergeant and pulled a small device from one of his side pockets and pointed it right at the suspect. The device printed out his face on the screen and then read the contents of the device. *"I see your name is Tekope, Sergeant Tekope that is, and your position is a software engineer and a computer programmer,"* said Sergeant Emoh.

"Wow sergeant, you can read. I am impressed. You are doing well for a dumb schmuck like you sergeant. But I'll bet you haven't read a book in your freaking life, have you?" said Tekope with a little smirk on his face while occasionally grimacing his face from pain.

*"Look, you piece of s**t, stop lollygagging around with your smartass rejoinders. We don't have all day to hear your craps!"* said one of the sergeant's teammates by the name of Zopaque while charging toward Tekope with fierce continence and wielding a weapon in his hand, pointing it right at Tekop's head, and coming so close as to touching Tekop's head with the business end of the barrel.

Tekope swiftly swung his arm and pushed the weapon away from his head, then with posthaste, grabbed the barrel end of the weapon and pulled it toward himself. Zopaque didn't let go of his weapon, in a result, his body moved toward Tekope. Tekope then executed a quick kick with his good leg, and his boot struck Zopaque right in his groin.

Zopaque let go of his weapon, grabbed his balls with both hands, went down rather hastily, wallowed on the floor to his left and to his right repetitively, and screamed aloud in agonizing pain while still covering his balls with his hands. Sergeant Emoh quickly kicked the weapon that was in Tekop's hands with his foot; the weapon flew away and landed approximately ten feet away. One of the teammates ran and grabbed the weapon off the floor so that Tekope wouldn't have an excess to it.

"Look what you've done to my teammate," said Sergeant Emoh.

"Oh yes, it looks like I busted his nuts—he deserved it! Now he doesn't have any balls to get back at me," Tekope, despite the pain in his right leg, managed to let out a mean and sarcastic guffaw.

"You know, you are one sick bastard, I am going to charge you with assault and battery, you nincompoop," said the sergeant.

*"What! What is the reason you're going to charge me with assault and battery for defending my life from one of your freaking beasts! You should have better control over your crew, or someone else will deliver it for you like what I have done to one of your henchmen. You lack leadership. You need to resign from your freaking post. You, incompetent worthless s**t,"* said Tekope.

"Sergeant, he's got a damn big mouth by attempting to challenge your leadership. You need to stop him now, or I will," said his closest hobnobbing friend by the name of Hevorek.

"Don't worry, Hevorek. I wanted to see how far he was going with this attitude. However, it is time that I am going put him in his place," said the sergeant and turned around and faced Tekope, then said, *"I don't want to hear any more wisecracks from you and you better cooperate with me or else. Now I am going to ask you a question, and you better answer me just what I want to here as I have said, no more wisecracks from you, and if you do, then you will be facing severe consequences. Is that*

clear to you?" asked the sergeant. Tekope glared at the sergeant's face, realized his seriousness, and remained silent.

"Now that's better. All right then, when you caught the sight of us coming toward the drone room, why did you have to run, and what were you doing in the drone room alone?" asked Sergeant Emoh.

"Damn, sergeant, here you go, you ask too many questions. It's making me dizzy!" said Tekope. The sergeant and the team broke out in a chuckle. The sergeant turned around and faced the team and said, *"Hey guys, we have a comedian here besides his wisecracks."*

The sergeant turned around, then faced the suspect with a stern expression and said, *"Look here, you jerk. I told you no more wisecracks from you. Let's get one thing straight here. It is my job to ask questions, and it is your job to answer them. Do you hear me?"* They locked their glowering eyes at each other, followed by a brief silence between them.

"If you insist," blurted Tekope with hesitation.

"Well then, don't make me wait! Answer my damn question!" said the sergeant.

"You all suck, you know! I am not answering any of your damn questions, so don't even try," said Tekope.

"Oh really!" said the sergeant, *"how about now,"* he kicked Tekope's right leg, and Tekope screamed aloud and wallowed in pain.

"Hey, hey, what do you know, from the sound of your scream, I might have fractured your freaking bones, which I did with no charge, aren't I nice. Next time, it's gonna be your left one, and

I am going to make sure that you will not walk again, will that be ok with you?

"Not so!" said Tekope.

"All right then, it behooves you to talk. So, was it worth what you did in the drone room? Didn't you know running wasn't going to pay off for you, and it wasn't going to lead you to your freedom? Eventually, you were going to be caught, or possibly be killed in the process?" There was silence with Tekope, but he was still agonizing in his pain.

"Now that you can't run anymore, you are going to tell us everything we need to know as to what had happened in the drone room and why the drones are down, and if you don't tell us what we need to know, you know very well what's going happen to you—right?" said Sergeant Emoh.

*"Oh—you're scaring me, sergeant! Again, please don't tease me like that! And by the way, don't you see me sweating like mad? Look sergeant, I aint telling you jack s**t do you hear me?"* said Tekope, the insurgent.

"Ya, I hear you! You must be a hard shell to crack. You know, as I am looking impatiently at your left leg to break, just tell me where your pain threshold is from zero to ten?" asked Sergeant Emoh.

"Why—I don't know, and I don't care to know," said Tekope. The sergeant kicked his right leg again with his boots this time much harder. Tekope screamed and wallowed in pain.

"Now tell me where your pain threshold is?" asked the sergeant.

"Damn it, if you must know, you hurt me so damn bad!" said Tekope.

"Well—is that right? I haven't gotten your left leg yet. But I am running out of patience fast, and I am about to break it for you, as I have said, with no charge, and from the looks on your face, I suppose you have a very low threshold for pain. In that case, I hope I have your attention now. And if you don't want any more pain, then you need to answer my questions without hesitation. Is that clear to you?" asked Sergeant

"And if I don't, then you're going to hurt me more, aren't you?" asked Tekope.

"Well, duhhhhh. What a stupid question. I thought you were smarter than that. You really disappoint me, sergeant Tekope. I suppose it only comes from stupid ungs like you. What do you think I was going to do? Kiss your freaking ass and tell you have a nice day? Ha, well, of course, I was going to hurt you more, even to the point of killing you, if it had to come to that! Do you leave me with any other choice? I am going to hurt you so damn bad that you're going to hate your mother who brought you to life, and I am going to be the worst freaking nightmare you have ever had. Do you hear me? Now, where were we—Oh yah, you were going to cooperate and tell me all that I needed to know— right! Riiiiiight?" asked Sergeant Emoh, and his hand was going towards Tekope's injured leg.

"All right, all right look, I didn't kill the ungs in the drone room!" said Tekope.

"Reeeeally! —who said anything about the killings in the drone room?" asked the sergeant Emoh.

"Well, from the tone of your voice, which is a pain in my ears, I anticipated that you would have known a thing or two about the drone room incident, and I wanted to tell you that I didn't kill them—okkkkk!" said Tekope.

"Really—if you didn't kill, then who did? Besides —you were the only one we saw leaving the drone room and nobody else." said the sergeant.

"Yah, yah—as I have said before—I didn't kill them, ok!" said Tekope.

There was a pause for a few seconds between them with intense stares at each other's faces.

"Come ooooon you could tell us", said the sergeant.

"If I tell you, then I am a dead ung for sure," said Tekope.

"Reeeeally! —in that case, from whom are you afraid? You must be working for someone or some group here on this ship; there must be more of you around, or maybe you are collaborating with the alien that we have caught," said Sergeant Emoh.

"What alien you're talking about? Do we have an alien on board?" asked Tekope.

"You're acting naiveté as if you have no idea what's going on in this ship."

"No, I don't," said Tekope.

"Stop pretending. We have the alien in custody, and he will be telling us everything we need to know. But you know? — I am sensing a plot to overthrow the ship's command. Is that why the security drones were down so that you and your group, whoever they are, or possibly the alien we've caught—you're

going to tell us anyway—could do your heart's desire without detection? Answer me, isn't that right?" asked the sergeant.

*"Private Rigog, I want you to cuff this piece of s**t now."* Private Rigog followed the command.

"Now that you're in our custody, did you know that we have the authority to do what we want with you? We can even terminate you now—here on this spot; so it behooves you to cooperate with me. You see, I don't really need you. Why you might ask, because, we have someone who saw everything that went on in the drone room. We don't need you. What we wanted was corroboration, your statement versus the witness who saw everything—you have ten seconds to start blurting what we need to know. Otherwise, you are going to meet your maker, and I mean it. We'll start now," the sergeant began to count from ten down to zero.

"Ten, nine, eight, seven, six, and five."

"All right, all right, you win. Stop the count," said the suspect.

"Does this mean you're going to cooperate?" asked the sergeant.

"Yeeees!" said the suspect in reluctance.

"All right then, you must answer all my questions. Otherwise, I will continue to count down to zero, and you cut me off at five," said the sergeant.

"All right, all right, what is your question, sergeant? I will tell you everything you need to know, but first, you must promise me two things," said Tekope.

"Oh really?" said the sergeant.

"Yes, really," said Tekope.

"Otherwise?" asked the sergeant.

"Otherwise, no deal!" said Tekope.

"Look, you scumbag, you are in no position to make deals here. Do you understand me?" said the sergeant.

"Don't you want to catch everyone who is involved in the Drone-room incident? Look here, sergeant, if you don't cooperate with me, you will never find out anything that you want to know, and who knows, by then, it could be too late, and it will get very ugly indeed," said Tekope.

"All right then, you have made your point. What is it that you want now? Oh yes, I know what you want: a red lipstick, a lollypop and a pink dress that will fit you, right?" asked Sergeant.

"Sorry Sergeant, I hate to disappoint you, but you're not my type. Look, if you are into these kinds of things, then don't force your desires on others," said Tekope.

"Nice comeback. It looks like you are smarter than you look.

All right, all right, what is it that you want?" asked Sergeant Emoh.

"I am glad you came to your senses Sergeant Emoh. I was beginning to worry about your intelligence and your convictions. Ok, first, I want immunity; second, I want protection. That's all I want. Can you deliver that?" asked Tekope.

"That's a tall order. I don't know if I can deliver that for you," said Emoh.

"Well, you better deliver it if you want to wrap this whole thing fast," said Tekope.

"Well, I can't make that decision about your request. The commander must make that decision. But all I can say to you is that I'll fight for you in court, and I will do my best to get your wishes, and that's not a lie—how about that?" asked Emoh.

"All right, I think that's a fair answer," said Tekope.

"I am glad you came to my terms. Now, can you tell me about the murders in the drone room? Did you kill the drone room associates; answer me truthfully this time?" asked the sergeant.

"Look as I told you---no! I didn't! Didn't you hear me say I had nothing to do with the killings? What's the matter with you? Are you deaf or something, or maybe I think you are losing your marbles," said Tekope.

"Stop being a smartass again. Just answer my damn question!" replied Sergeant Emoh.

"Ok, what was your question now?" asked Tekope.

"Ok—if you didn't kill the occupants of the drone room, then what were you doing in there?" asked the sergeant.

"My job was to reprogram the drones, and that was it. However, when I got there, they were already dead," said Tekope.

"You know, you have to realize that you did a lot of damage to our drones and our security system. Now, all drones must be reconfigured and rebooted. This is going to take a long time to do all that. Who knows, perhaps we have lost many drones already as a result of your action, and they could be beyond repair.

"Tell me now, who killed the drone room associates if you didn't kill them?" asked Sergeant Emoh.

"Ursha, with the rank of captain in Alpha squadron, and Mewa in the rank of lieutenant, both murdered the people in the drone room. Captain Ursha happened to be the leader of the group. Captain Ursha's group consisted of ten ungs, and I was one of them. I didn't want to participate, but they got me at gunpoint and compelled me to cooperate with them because I had the skills they needed," said Tekope.

"Does Ursha have any distinguishing marks or tattoos?" asked the sergeant.

"Yes, he has a scar close to his right eye," said Tekope.

"All right then, what was the group's intention to accomplish?" asked the sergeant.

"Their intention was to take over the ship," said Tekope, the suspect.

"Why!" asked the sergeant.

"Ursha wanted to take the ship to a certain destination only he knew how to get there. For that, you must ask him for the answers. I don't know. He promised every one of us a handsome payment where we would be well off for the rest of our lives and provide us with high positions in the government where he would be the ruling party," said Tekope.

"Is that so?" said the sergeant.

"Yes, that is so," said Tekope.

"All right, what are the names of those who were involved," asked the sergeant.

"*As I have said, the people are Ursha, Lamsel, Pehot, Rantak, Mewa, Nakra, Thosad, Tinsap, Foho, and I Tekope. All these ungs are under Ursha's command,*" said Tekope.

"*Good, I am glad you have pulled through. Otherwise, seriously, you wouldn't be alive right now. Oh, by the way, there was no corroboration. I just made that up so it would be easier for you to spill the information we needed,*" said the sergeant.

"*All right, you've got me on that. I admit, I'm duped. Good job, sergeant—but now what?*" asked Tekope.

"*What do you mean now what? Now we're gonna take you to the station for further questioning,*" said the sergeant.

"*And then?*" asked Tekope.

"*And then we'll take you before the judicial committee and they will decide your fate, which doesn't look so promising—and you know what I mean by that, don't you?*" asked the sergeant.

"*Ya, ya, it means a death sentence. Look Sergeant, I gave you everything you've asked for, doesn't that mean anything to you and to the committee? Besides, I didn't do it by my free will. I was forced to do it, and if I wouldn't cooperate, they were going to kill me right then on the spot,*" said Tekope.

"*That might play a role in their decision. It might mitigate your sentence, but I can't promise you that. They might take you to a distant planet and leave you there, and then it will be up to you how to survive, and who knows, you might just like it and make friends there,*" said Sergeant.

"*Look sergeant…*"

"Shut up. I'm going to talk to the captain now. Don't interrupt me," said the sergeant.

"Captain, this is Sergeant Emoh. Do you read me?"

"This is Captain Yilow. I read you loud and clear, sergeant."

"We got him. The suspect is in our custody. He confessed to the crime he committed, which was to override the drone instructions to render them inoperable by setting a new code. I am sure he is going to help us to reset the drones with the new code.

"However, according to his input, he is saying he didn't kill the drone room operators. Two ungs on their team of ten did commit the murders. His name is Ursha and Mewa. Ursha and Mewa are ruthless and very destructive entities. These two have no regard for life."

"Ursha is the leader of the team. Please be aware of their presence. They are armed and are very dangerous. They will stop at nothing. Their mission is to commandeer the ship and direct it to a certain destination, which is unknown to the suspect in our country and to us at this point in time," said Sergeant Emoh.

"I think there could be more of them, not just ten," said Sergeant Emoh.

"Does the killer have any distinguishing mark, or some kind of physical factor such as a tattoo, scar, or something else that will set him apart from the rest?" asked the captain.

"Yes, he has a half an inch scar next to his right eye," said Sergeant Emoh.

"Very well sergeant. That's good information. Should we run into him, we'll apprehend him on the spot. Is there anything else you want to add, sergeant?" asked the captain.

"No, not right now, but we are heading to headquarters for further questioning of the suspect," said the sergeant.

"Very well, then we'll meet you there as well—Captain Yilow is over and out."

"All right ungs, you've heard, I just had a conversation with Captain Yilow about the ten criminally minded ungs, but he thinks there could be more of them, possibly sleeper cells ready to inflict harm on every resident of this ship in a moment notice. They have already killed a few. They wouldn't hesitate to kill more. These ungs are armed and are very dangerous. So, we need to be on the lookout we may have to confront them any time soon; any questions?" asked the sergeant.

"If we see them face to face, sergeant, are you going to exercise the shoot-to-kill on-the-spot option?" asked Private Obnitra.

"If we have to, it depends on how they behave. However, if the court finds them guilty, then you should all know the verdict —which is a 'death penalty' including all their accomplices. Our job will be to apprehend them and deliver them to justice," said Sergeant Emoh.

CHAPTER 11

"Sakreg, it is truly amazing to see you again, especially in this part of the universe, and strangely finding you here on this ship, mind you. I thought I would never see you again, but here you are. How did you ever find this ship in the first place? You know that you are a galaxy away from home, did you know that?" said Yinoot.

"No—no I didn't know that. Really, are you serious? I am in a different galaxy?"

"Yes you are Sakreg," said Yinoot.

"I knew I was Damn far away from home, but I didn't know that I was in a different galaxy. No wonder my readings in my craft were inconclusive.   Now that I am in a different galaxy, I don't know if I will ever be able to get back home to see my folks, my friends, my wife, and my kids. I have already missed them a lot. However, I want to go back so bad. It hurts me to think that it is almost impossible.

You know—I was being pursued by two freaking Grolz fighter crafts. After I destroyed their mothership. The damn thing was huge. And the fighters got on my tail; they almost got me killed," said Sakreg.

"You're telling me, you have destroyed their mothership?" asked Yinoot.

"Yes, I did. There were many casualties on both sides, along with three of my pilots. There were four of us on our way to destroy the Grolz mother ship; three of my pilots didn't make it; their vessels were blown up by Grolz's fiery projectiles, and they died instantly. But thank be to god, after I had destroyed their mother ship, I managed to escape unscathed despite the two that were on my tail for a while. I couldn't break loose from them. If it weren't for a wormhole that I went thru, I wouldn't be talking to you right now.

"After I went through it, I was so happy that they didn't make it to the other side with me and I have no idea what happened to them. I didn't have the desire to fight my pursuers in this part of the universe.

"I soon decided to find a suitable planet to live on for the rest of my unfortunate life, and perhaps alone. I wouldn't want to stay in space forever.

"However, the ship that we are in now, I thought it was a huge freeking rock at first. I thought this was a broken piece of a planet. I haven't seen such a huge piece of stone floating in space and thought to explore it and maybe I would learn a thing or two. I had no idea, and it never crossed my mind that this huge slab could be a spaceship. You guys did a very good job disguising it.

"As I was moving across its surface, suddenly, a tractor beam locked on my Starfighter. I was fully surprised. I said to myself, what? What the hack is going on here? I got scared, very scared indeed. I said to myself, am I going to be stuck here on this rock forever?

"At first, it didn't cross my mind that the intense light could be a 'tractor beam.' I thought I was experiencing some sort of anomaly, a universal anomaly unknown to me. I said to myself, first the Wormhole and now this thing, whatever it is. I did everything to get away from the light, but the beam was too powerful; I couldn't free my ship from it, I was slowly drawn inside this god-forsaking rock, and the rest is history," said Sakreg.

"I'm so sorry for what happened to you. I'll make sure that you will get out of here in one piece. By the way, you said the ship that you destroyed was a Grolz ship; I never heard of them. What did they look like? Can you describe it to me?" asked Yinoot.

"Oh, it is hard to explain. One thing I know is they were the ugliest freaking creatures I have ever seen in my life. Their ship was huge and spiky,"

"Did you say spiky ship?"

"Yes, that's what I said, spiky."

"Oh my —I think I know them," said Yinoot.

"Do you really!" asked Sakreg.

"Yes! We had some run-ins with them too. They fight like beasts. They have no feelings. They are good at one thing: to kill, destroy, and pillage. We called them Odraks. So, —it wasn't only us who decided to destroy your race, it was also the Odraks.

Sakreg—I am so sorry for what my people have done to your planet and to your species. We have learned to go to the stars, but we still haven't learned to respect life.

I was a child when our race invaded your planet. I see all the brutality and the mayhem that took place on your planet, and I would say, to this day, it is still fresh in my mind. It is one of my life's mental insults. I occasionally experience flashbacks of all the mayhem I have witnessed, and as result, I feel dysphoric for some time. I suppose I will have to take it with me to the grave.

I can't seem to shake it out of my system. I remember it well as if it happened yesterday."

"It's not your fault, Yinoot. You were a kid at the time. Don't take it hard on yourself. You must get over it. Otherwise, it will slowly kill you," said Sakreg.

"I haven't shared my inner thoughts about how bad I felt growing up in a battle zone. I want to go on talking about it. Maybe this way, I will get it off my chest," said Yinoot.

"Fine, I am all ears. By the way, are we safe being here right now?" asked Sakreg.

"Yes, yes—we're safe, so as two of my teammates here," said Yinoot.

"Excellent, then go ahead and talk about your past Yinoot. I want to hear it," said Sakreg.

"All right, where was I?" asked Yinoot.

"I think you were going to start telling me what things happened to you during the war when you were a kid," said Sakreg.

"Oh yes, I remember, during the war—I got lost in the city. I was roaming the streets like a renegade, barefooted, hungry, and crying about losing my parent.

"I remember Plasma projectiles were flying in every direction, including "Electro-bombs," having them dropped by fast-moving, huge flying spherical drones, destroying buildings, turning them into heaps of rubble, killing and maiming innocent people, your people at that, and witnessing their body parts flying everywhere. I still don't know how I managed to stay alive and maintain my sanity while all that was going on around me.

"You know—I was six at the time. However, coming back to my parents—to this day, I don't remember what really happened to them. Soon, I came to the conclusion that they must be dead. Perhaps their lifeless bodies were lying somewhere on your city streets. Maybe it was good that I didn't witness their corpses. Otherwise, I would have lost my mind.

"You see, my mom and dad were in the military. Their unit was to support the front-line operations. One early morning, my parents received a call from their unit commander to report for duty as soon as possible; their command post was under fire from your people. They kissed me goodbye and said, 'Don't you worry son, we'll be back soon. Don't go anywhere. Don't go outside and play with your friends. You should know better that it is dangerous out there.'

"My folks went out to report for duty, as I've said, but never came back. I don't think their intention was to abandon me; they loved me a great deal. Anyway, when they left me, I didn't have anyone to carry on a conversation with. I felt very lonely and scared by every little noise the house-made, especially at night. Besides, after staying home for two long weeks, I occasionally looked out the windows. I gazed at the troops passing by. I hoped and wished that my parents would be walking along with them, and then to see my mom and my dad walk through the front door so I could give them a big welcome home hug, but that resulted in disappointment. There was no mom, and there was no dad.

"There was nothing left to eat or drink in the house. I knew then I couldn't take care of myself any longer by staying home, and for that reason, I went out to the streets to find food and take care of my needs. I didn't care about the dangers anymore. I had to have sustenance or die.

"When I was out there in the streets searching for food, I was also hoping that I could run into my parents or someone who knew where they were. With tears in my eyes, I went around asking people—have you seen my parents? All they did was shake their heads, disavowing their knowledge of my parent's whereabouts.

"However, after a while, I lost hope of finding them alive. Thinking that they might be dead anyway, but that thought was a big blow in my life in many ways. They were all I had. They were my beloved parents, whom I needed very much.

"After a while, I became convinced that my mom and dad must have become casualties of war. Otherwise, they would have returned home to take care of me. As I've said before, my parents wouldn't abandon me for any reason, and I knew that. I knew they loved me dearly; they wanted the best for me, and I loved them too.

"They were concerned about my welfare, because of the kind of work they chose for their lives. Being in the military at the time was a very dangerous occupation. They often talked amongst themselves as to what was going to happen to me and who was going to take care of me should they both bite the dust.

"I used to hear their conversations from my room while they were in the living room talking and planning my future among themselves. Frankly, I was worried about them every day. They thought I wouldn't hear any of their conversation, but I did, and I was concerned about them constantly. I spend many sleepless nights thinking and praying about their safety.

"However, I am so grateful to your species, because after the alleged death of my real parents, your people came to my rescue. I learned your language and your protocols. Despite my physical and racial differences, my new parents welcomed me into their house and took very well care of me. I would say they did as good of a job raising me as my real parents did. They adopted me and treated me like one of their own and I am very grateful for them.

"Now that I met you here, I recognize that it was you, the Rooktok (the crazy one). You always liked to jump from high places and occasionally hurt yourself. I am so glad you didn't break any bones. Anyway, that's why I used to call you Rooktok. However, now that you are here by fate or by destiny, I am freaked out seeing you here in this part of the universe.

"I would have never imagined in a million years to be able to see you again, let alone in this part of the universe and, as I have said, on this ship. But it must be fate. Yes, it must be a fate.

"I remember when I lived two blocks away from your house; I used to come to your abode, and we used to play together using each other's toys and tell scary stories. Do you remember one day when I was playing with firecrackers, my clothes caught on fire, and you saved my life that day? I was terrified, but thanks to you for saving my life. If it weren't for you being there, I wouldn't be here today. You are my hero," said Yinoot.

Sakreg cracked a slight smile and said, "How can I forget that event. I was scared as you were. I didn't want to lose my best friend, especially in a fire. I remember that terrifying moment clear as a day," said Sakreg.

"I knew you wouldn't be able to forget that event. Anyway, as I grew older, my new parents became ill, and they too passed away, and again, I became alone, but by then, I felt lucky to be old enough to take care of myself. I remember you were thinking of joining the military and I knew then I was going to lose you as a friend.

At that time, most of my people have already left your planet. There were only a few remnants left. The time came that what's left of us was also going to have to leave your planet, so I decided to leave with them and here I am talking with my best friend about our past.

I knew if I had decided to stay on your turf, I was going to be a spectacle, perhaps I would have been the only alien on your planet, and I wouldn't think your people would have treated me as well as you or my new parents did.

Now that you are here, I said to myself, I am going to do everything possible to help you get out of here in one piece, especially right now when you are in trouble with my people. I owe you one Sakreg," said Yinoot.

"By the way, what brought you folks to this part of the universe, and do you know where we are because I don't?" asked Sakreg.

"We are in the galaxy called Zeltra (Milky Way). We are far, far away from our galaxy, 'Ronepar' (Andromeda). What happened was that—the supreme commander summoned us to go and help our fellow soldiers who were fighting the occupants of the planet called Pukrav. This planet was number four of the twelve planets in our solar system.

"As I was saying, we were on our way to help them, but in the middle of the course, we encountered something very strange. "To this day, we can't tell what it was. It was like a vapor but a sparkling vapor at that. It was blue in color. It was beautiful and mesmerizing, almost hypnotic. This thing was vanishing and reappearing every fifteen seconds. We have never seen such a phenomenon.

"This thing was large enough that we couldn't escape it, and we felt it was drawing us to it. In result, we had to go right through it. It felt like we were inside of a portal of some sort. Things were very ambiguous and dark. We were witnessing bright Light particles whizzing by extremely fast and we had no idea where we were or what this thing was.

"Suddenly, everything became black. We had no inclination of time or space. It felt as if we were in a twilight zone, and when we saw stars, we knew then we were out of this thing, whatever it was. Then, we also knew that we went through a portal. It wasn't a wormhole-like phenomenon that you went through, I assure you of that.

"At first, when we decided that we were out of this anomaly, we had no idea where we were, or what part of the universe we were in, but soon our computers figured out the galaxy that we are in now, and as I said before, it is the galaxy called Zeltra (Milky Way). In this galaxy, we encountered this unknown planet. There is something about this giant gaseous planet—we are yet to name it. We found out that this planet was energizing or batteries, and that is why we are here, but it won't be long before we leave this planet's atmosphere and move on. We don't know yet where we will go, but we will attempt to go back if we can," said Yinoot.

"How did you get this freaking creature, this thing we are fighting inside your spaceship?" asked Sakreg.

"That is a good question. It is going to take some time to explain," said Yinoot.

"Wait a minute, I hate to break our conversation, but are you hearing something?" asked Sakreg.

"No, why?" asked Yinoot.

"I am hearing footsteps, as a matter of fact, many of them," said Sakreg.

"Really?" asked Yinoot.

"Do you think it is the creatures?" asked Yinoot.

"It sounds like them. Yes, I think it is the creatures," said Sakreg.

Suddenly, Yinoot and two of his crewmembers heard a fast-moving heavy footstep coming from nearby whole-way and were heading westward. It seemed the footsteps represented more than one entity, perhaps seven, ten, or possibly more. They were moving together with a purpose and a plan.

"You are right Sakreg, now my two crew members and I can hear them tracking down our way. You sure have good ears Sakreg," said Yinoot.

The corridor had plenty of lights. There was no dark or shadowy place. Everywhere was visible. Yinoot, his two crewmembers, and Sakreg were hiding in an elevated place, which had a nook somewhere between the ceiling and the floor, but despite the sound of the footsteps that they heard, they couldn't detect any physical beings. They quickly concluded the invisible creatures must have been passing through the pathway.

"These creatures must be multiplying fast. Who knows how many there are now on the ship? I hate to frighten you Yinoot, but by now, they could very well be in hundreds, may even be in thousands, and they might even take over this ship soon.

"How can we fight something that we can't see? They would take us out one at a time if they had to until there is none of us left to defend this god-forsaken ship.

"I came to a firm conclusion that it is not safe to be in this spaceship. We need to get you out of here fast. You don't belong here," said Yinoot.

"Your point is well taken, Yinoot. Well then, in that case, if I am getting out of here, you are coming with me. I got an extra seat in my star-fighter; besides, I could use company," said Sakreg.

"It's not all that simple Sakreg. We still must fight the guards that are hanging around your ship and the invisible creatures along the way. They could be everywhere by now, and who knows what else we have to encounter or contend with," said Yinoot.

Yinoot and two of his crew members, including Sakreg waited until the sounds of the footsteps disappeared, then they came out of their cubby hole and jumped twenty feet to a hard metal ground. They drew their weapons immediately and situated themselves two on each side of the fifteen feet wide corridor then proceeded cautiously by heading eastward. They were fully aware of their exposure to the elements of danger. They had no choice but to brave the circumstances as it would unfold right before their eyes.

The corridor angled to the left at about three bus sizes away.

They heard the sounds of footsteps, but this time, they sounded different from the previous pace of the invisible creatures, and it was coming from beyond the curve of the corridor. It sounded as if many soldiers were heading their way, and Yinoot was concerned about Sakreg's safety. The sounds of the footsteps became louder with each passing second.

Suddenly, the soldiers loomed before their sight. They all drew their weapons and were ready to shoot at each other. Yinoot screamed loudly, "Don't shoot, it is I, Yinoot. He is my long-time friend, pointing at Sakreg. He doesn't pose any danger. Let's all put our weapons away." They all pointed the business end of their weapon down toward the ground and glared silently at Yinoot and his strange-looking friend Sakreg for a few seconds to absorb the reality at hand.

"I am Lieutenant Sesmo, part of the security Special Ops team, and on my right, these are my crew, what is left of my team."

"I am the First Officer, Lieutenant Yinoot, sir; second in command of my unit, but this is what's left of it. On my right, these are my two crewmembers, Private Norg and Private First Class Kunra, also here with me on my left. His name is Sakreg; he is my long-time friend," said Yinoot.

"You have said he is your friend? He sure looks different in fact very different indeed—to the point where he could be considered an alien, care to explain?" asked Lieutenant Sesmo.

"Yes, he is an alien to every one of us here…" Right before Yinoot finished his conversation, the lieutenant blurted.

"Wait a minute! Isn't he the prisoner that was supposed to be transferred to the interrogation room?" asked the lieutenant.

"Yes, as a matter of fact, he is," said Yinoot.

"Then, how is it that you claim he is your friend?" asked the lieutenant.

"I will explain sir. Lieutenant, do you remember your history? Does planet Eegroag mean anything to you?

"Not really, that must have been before my time."

"Yes indeed, that must have been before your time. You see, Eegroag happens to be the planet he came from, the planet that we invaded a long time ago. At that time, I was a child. I lost both of my real parents in the war, and then a nice couple from his race came to my rescue and raised me to be who I am today; besides, we used to play together when we were kids, and yes, I also speak his language.

"We grew up together. One time he saved my life from a certain death, and today, I owe it to him to save his. You all understand that, don't you? There is one more thing I want to add—he doesn't pose any threat to any one of us. As a matter of fact, I want to count him as one of us, and he just might save your lives today, as he did mine. I guarantee you that he will be an asset rather than a liability. As I have said, he doesn't pose any danger to any of us," said Yinoot.

"I hear what you are saying, lieutenant. It is good to know that you trust him entirely and that he is not going to create any danger to our people. I want to tell you that we will be watching every move he makes. Should we detect any aberrant behavior on his end, then he will be dealt with swiftly, even if it means killing him. Is that understood, lieutenant?" asked Lieutenant Sesmo.

"I believe your statement is fair. As I have said before, He will not pose any danger to any of us," said Yinoot.

"By the way, how did he ever get here and what is he doing in our ship anyway," asked the lieutenant.

"You see sir, he came out of a wormhole and landed in this part of the universe, and when he saw this ship, I kid you not, he thought it was a large piece of rock," suddenly, everyone began to chuckle at the statement, including Lieutenant Sesmo.

"I could see why he thought that way," said Sesmo.

"He thought perhaps this rock was a broken piece of a planet in this solar system, or possibly it came from beyond and now hovering aimlessly in space, so he decided to explore this piece of rock. Then suddenly, a tractor beam pulled him inside.

We were aware of his presence around the ship. The security informed Admiral Odnanra of this impingement. He dispatched our squad to handle this incoming intrusion. Captain Narmoop was the commanding officer in charge of this operation. He decided to take the prisoner to the interrogation room to glean information and ascertain everything about him, but as you see, there is no need for that sir," said Yinoot.

Suddenly, Lieutenant Sesmo swung his arm behind his own back, grabbed and heaved the hand-held weapon that was tucked halfway inside his pants and brandished it in the air.

"Yinoot, please tell him to be very careful with that weapon in his hand," said Sakreg.

"Lieutenant, the weapon in your hand belongs to my friend Sakreg. He asked me to tell you to be very careful with it," said Yinoot.

"I suppose he wants it back—right?" said Sesmo.

"As a matter of fact, yes, he does. That would be nice sir. I told you he doesn't pose any danger sir. You have no reason to feel apprehensive," said Yinoot. Just then, Sakreg heard many hard footsteps way at a distance inside the corridor and were heading east. Whatever it is, it must pass through them. No one else heard it except Sakreg.

"Yinoot, I hear heavy footsteps and the same smell that I smelled when your team was attacked by them invisible creatures. I believe we need to be ready now to confront them. They will be here any minute now. Please inform him," said Sakreg.

"Lieutenant—Sakreg just told me that we will be confronting fast-approaching invisible creatures. They will be here at any minute now. He heard their fast-moving footsteps and their unique smell sir," said Yinoot.

"All right, team, get ready to shoot. You heard Lieutenant Yinoot; the creatures will be here at any moment, and we're in their path," said Lieutenant Sesmo and hurled the shiny weapon toward Sakreg, he caught it in mid-air and than executed certain operations to activate it.

"Lieutenant, I don't have a signal on my sensor. I am not picking anything," said one of the teammates who was close distance to Sesmo.

"Does anyone have any signal," asked the Lieutenant Sesmo. There was a response "No" from everyone.

"These creatures must be evolving fast. We are going to need better tools to reveal their where about, but for now, our sensors are useless to detect the incoming creatures. I suppose we must rely on your friend from now on Yinoot," said Sesmo.

"Sakreg, their sensors are not picking any movements ahead. You need to tell us if they are close enough so they can shoot them bastards to oblivion. You will have to give us the signal to shoot," said Yinoot.

"All right, I will," said Sakreg.

"Lieutenant, he agrees to help," said Yinoot.

"Very well, troop, be ready to engage at Sakreg's signal."

"I hear more of these creatures on their way here; they are at some distance and are coming from behind us this time," said Sakreg.

"Oh great, we have them coming from front and back. Now, we should feel sandwiched between the oncoming creatures. All right upon Sakreg's signal, you, you, and you cover the back and the rest of us will cover the front," said Sesmo.

"Yes sir, responded the teammates." They all waited quietly for Sakreg's signal. Suddenly Sakreg pointed at the rear flank to engage the oncoming creatures, and the team opened incessant fire, in result, all fifteen creatures died the same way as they did their predecessors before them, and while the rear flank was firing, the front flank had the signal from Sakreg to fire the creatures that were coming from the front. There were twenty-five of them, and all died the same way as their ascendants did in the ship. After all the black clouds and the tornados had settled, Lieutenant Sesmo approached Yinoot and thanked him for his assistance and blurted by saying,

"Yinoot, knowing that you have lost most of your team members, I would like to extend my invitation to you to become part of our team from now on, provided that captain Yilow will agree with my decision. Do you accept the position?" asked Lieutenant Sesmo.

"Well yes, sir, why not," said Yinoot.

"Excellent; I will be informing Captain Yilow of your decision. I don't foresee any problem arising ahead. I would like to welcome you in advance to our security special op unit, just as I did with Second Lieutenant Omeh. Should you become part of our unit permanently, you will be receiving extra training. I am very sure that you will do fine.

"Team—for the time being, you will also be receiving orders from Lieutenant Yinoot. However, we will officially ratify him to be part of our unit upon Captain Yilow's approval. Is that clear?" said Lieutenant Sesmo.

"Yes sir," responded the rest of the team. Lieutenant Sesmo turned his face toward Sakreg, walked toward him, and glared at his face. Their eyes locked on each other, and they were silent for a moment or two, then Lieutenant Sesmo blurted,

"Yinoot, how would you say thank you in his language."

Yinoot responded by saying, "Do mash ta da hey."

Lieutenant Sesmo blurted, "Do mash ta da hey."

"Yee kro ma hayo," said Sakreg; its interpretation is, (you're welcome)

"Very well then, Yinoot. When it comes to your friend Sakreg, we will see that he will get out of this ship safely; he earned it."

"Thank you, sir," said Yinoot.

CHAPTER 12

"A loud digital ringtone pervaded the corridor through the wrist communicator of Lieutenant Sesmo. Lieutenant Sesmo pushed a button on his communicator and brought it to his mouth, then answered, *"This is Lieutenant Sesmo. Go ahead."*

"This is Captain Yilow, what is your position?"

"My position is ten, five, niner sir," said the lieutenant.

"Oh, I know where that is. That is a little farther west of the Specimen Lab. Were you able to find Lieutenant Yinoot," asked the Captain Yilow.

"Yes sir, he is right here with me, along with his two teammates and the alien sir," said Lieutenant Sesmo.

"The alien!" asked the captain.

"Yes sir, the alien sir," said the lieutenant.

"Wasn't he supposed to be in custody for interrogation?" asked the captain.

"Yes sir, it sounds unbelievable, but the alien turned out to be a childhood friend of Lieutenant Yinoot sir."

"What!" Replied the captain.

"Yes sir, you heard me right. They grew up together, and the alien was here by mistake."

"What do you mean by mistake," asked the captain.

"Well, it is somewhat a long story, sir. Lieutenant Yinoot and I will explain everything when we get back to the headquarters sir.

One more thing, captain; this alien saved every one of our lives just a little while ago from the creatures that were lurking in the ship. If it wasn't for him sir, we wouldn't be here talking to you right now sir."

"Is that right," said the captain.

"Yes sir, I really appreciate his help. He is very benign sir, and I wouldn't mind having him in my team sir. We are very grateful for his help sir. However, we are going to see him leave this ship in peace sir. There is no need for interrogation of the alien sir. As I have said before, Lieutenant Yinoot and I will explain everything when we get to the headquarters sir," said the lieutenant.

"Fine then, lieutenant, I trust your judgment on this. However, the reason for my call is that—Sergeant Emoh apprehended a suspect who was involved in the drone room incident. He got him to confess to his crime, which was the downing of the drones, but there were also killings in the drone room beside the drones that were down, and he confessed to the names that were involved in the killings, and the names he gave us was "Captain Ursha, and the other, the captain paused a few seconds then blurted. *It doesn't come to mind for now. Anyway, there was another one involved with Captain Ursha. You will find out soon. These two were from Alpha Squadron. One more thing lieutenant—captain Ursha has a recent scar on his right hand and also a scar on the right part of his face close to his right eye. If you run into him, arrest him immediately. Is that clear, lieutenant?"* asked Captain Yilow.

"Yes sir," replied Lieutenant Sesmo.

"Fine then, there is no further discussion. The captain is over and out." Lieutenant Sesmo pushed a button on the communicator and rested his elbow from being at a bent position, then he turned around, faced Lieutenant Yinoot, and said, *"Lieutenant— which sector is the alien spacecraft located?"*

"Sir, it is in the craft landing bay Alpha One Bravo Nine sector, on the western quadrant. It is a good walking distance from here we must pass the armory. Four of my crew members are securing his craft as we speak. I hope they are still alive, and those creatures didn't get to them yet," said Yinoot.

"Well then, that shouldn't be a problem convincing your teammates to cooperate with us, and there is no way the creatures could get inside the landing bay without opening the gates. I would say your friend would be out of here in no time.

However, now that we realize his special capabilities, we really need his presence here even more. He could be very useful to us. We need him for our survival. He literally saved our lives last time. We are very grateful to him, but we must do what we must do and have him leave this ship and fulfill his desire. We can't keep him here against his will," said Lieutenant Sesmo.

"Yes sir, I agree with you. That will be a sensible thing to do. However, it will be sad for us to see him leave. I'll probably never see him again, but when it comes to dealing with my teammates in the landing bay, we shouldn't have any problem convincing them to cooperate with us," said Lieutenant Yinoot.

Lieutenant Yinoot's team and Lieutenant Sesmo's team began to move toward the landing bay sector A1B9. Their eyes were wide open in anticipation of the unknown. Muscles were tight, and expressions were tense; they were ready for any conflict that would come in their way.

Suddenly, at a distance, they witnessed three distinct disturbances in the air, spasmodically pulsating and unevenly flickering faint blue lights. They all stood still, weapons pointed right at the quivering lights and silently glaring at the event, not knowing what the outcome was going to be. Suddenly, the faint blue lights changed their color to a bright tawny color, and from it came out the creatures.

The creatures appeared as if they had lost their fervor, and when they began to move. They huffed and puffed and staggered like a drunkard person. One of the creatures began to tread toward the team with malice in its mind, and the other two creatures stopped in their tracks. They raised their heads to a horizontal position, eyeballed the team for a few seconds, and then, their knees buckled. They screamed loud like a banshees as they fell face down to the ground.

Suddenly, their bodies pulverized as if millions of ants were busy eating their flash to nothingness. All that remained was a pile of sand-like particles on the ground. The one that was still alive, and was still charging toward the team, too, experienced the same fate as others did.

"Yinoot, these creatures were ill, very ill indeed. I think I know why and how they got ill. You're going to see more of them die the same death as these creatures did. I believe your ship is saved from these things, whatever they are," said Sakreg.

"How did you come up to such conclusion Sakreg?" asked Yinoot. The Lieutenant Sesmo turned around and faced Yinoot and Sakreg then asked

"What are you two talking about?"

"Sir, it's about them, the creatures'," said Yinoot.

"What about the creatures? I am glad they are dead." said the lieutenant.

"Sakreg thinks these creatures were very ill, and he says he knows how these creatures became ill and died before our eyes, and he also thinks that all of them will die the same way as these creatures died," said Yinoot.

"Really, I would like to hear that," said the lieutenant.

"Sakreg—Lieutenant Sesmo wants to hear what you've got to say about them creatures, why they died the way they did," said Yinoot.

"It is simple. You see Yinoot, when these creatures killed your teammates and consumed their bodies, they became infected by a bug that is innate within your race, or there was a certain chemistry in your bodies that made them ill to the point of death. Since they multiplied from within themselves, the bugs or the deadly chemistry multiplied along within their new bodies. Hence, they all now have the same killer agent within themselves, and it will be a matter of time before they all get sick and all are going to die the same way as these creatures did," said Sakreg, and Yinoot translated to lieutenant what Sakreg had said.

"I believe it makes sense, a perfect sense, what your friend has said Yinoot, and that is very encouraging news to my ears. Now, let's keep on moving toward sector A1B9 to witness your friend's departure. At the same time, we can't let our guards down," said Lieutenant Sesmo.

As they began to head toward the sector, halfway to their intended destination, they came across many piles of sand on the floor depicting the death of the creatures. However, everyone grimaced in horror and wroth when they witnessed the appalling scene of the mutilated bodies of their comrades.

There were pools of blood here and there, bloodstained floors, walls, and hallways nearby. In addition, there were many body parts: arms, halfway-eaten legs, and lacerated abdomens with guts pulled out of their place. These dead bodies belonged to their dead comrades, with their body parts strewed here and there and everywhere. Despite the fact that these creatures were dying, the crew was still not free of the fear that had gripped their hearts ever since they challenged the creatures.

Lieutenant Sesmo and the rest of the team attempted to identify the deceased bodies one by one, but some were unidentifiable because nothing was left of them except the skeletal remains. The lieutenant dispatched a cleaning crew to pick up the carcasses of their crewmembers.

Lieutenant Sesmo and his band, along with Sakreg, moved on lumbering evermore cautiously toward their intended destination, thinking that this area must have been a hotbed of activity for the voracious and mortiferous creatures.

Lieutenant Sesmo and the rest of the team drew their weapons in anticipation of more carnage; eyes filled with fright and distress, they scanned their immediate and distant environments for any anomalies. The lieutenant and the crew were ready to encounter and embrace the danger that they may have had to brush within their path.

As Lieutenant Sesmo and Lieutenant Yinoot's team were on their way to the A1B9 sector, they had to pass the armory department first. Suddenly, nine ungs dressed in black wearing eye masks were just about to exit the armory room with weapons in their hands when Captain Ursha witnessed Lieutenant Sesmo and his crowd heading his way. He instructed three of his crew to stay inside the armory and observe what was about to happen.

"In case of trouble, I want you three to wait for my signal. The signal is going to be a "loud cry of distress" coming from me, and then, I want you to launch a quick attack to subdue the situation and turn it in our favor. Is that clear to three of you?" asked Ursha.

"Yes sir," replied the three.

"What's now Ursha? Heck, them being here wasn't in the plan. What are you going to do now?" asked Lieutenant Murmo. Ursha was thinking silently as to how to answer Murmo when Sergeant Tilkud began to blurt,

"I think someone gave out our position away and that is why they are here, and they are here to arrest us. That means the death penalty to all of us."

"I agree with Tilkud. They must be here to arrest us. Someone snitched on us, but despite that, we're not going to let these bastards arrest us or do away with us! By the way, where is Tekope? We haven't heard from him yet. He was supposed to report half an hour ago," said Ursha.

"Sir, I attempted to contact him a few times, but there was no respond from him," said Lieutenant Murmo.

"He is not answering. That is a dead giveaway; it could only mean special ops security caught him no doubt. In that case, he

had already spilled the Grums (bean-like food), and that is how the security knew where to find us.

He is the snitch. Now we're in deep trouble, but relax, all of you. I'll handle this, and if Tekope did talk with security, then he is a dead ung for sure, either by the justice or by us. It would be better if we get him first," said Ursha.

"Captain, don't you think we should run now while we have a good amount of space between us and them? After all, they are getting closer every passing second," said Lieutenant Murmo.

"No, we shouldn't run! They may think that we are the criminals that they are looking for, but if we don't run, this way, we might have a better chance to let them know that we're not the ones that they are looking for," said Captain Ursha.

"Sir you're taking an awful big chance by sticking around to entertain their questions. I would say let's get out of here fast captain!" said Lieutenant Murmo.

"Are you questioning my decision, Lieutenant!" asked the captain.

"No sir, I am just basically making a statement, nothing more than that sir," said the lieutenant.

"I hope so; otherwise, you're in trouble with me! Address your statements when you are told to do so. Otherwise, shoot your mouth. Is that clear!" asked Captain Ursha.

"Yes sir!" responded Lieutenant Murmo. Lieutenant Sesmo and his team came within fifteen feet of Ursha, and his henchmen then stopped.

"Lieutenant Sesmo—that's what your name tag says, is that right?" asked Ursha.

"Yes, that's correct," said the lieutenant.

"So, lieutenant what brings you out here? You are far away from your post. Are there any urgencies that I must be aware of?" asked Ursha.

"I am looking for two ungs who have murdered the drone room occupants for some personal endeavor or gain. However, I didn't get your name and rank. You should have a nametag and a rank attached to your uniform like everone else in this ship, but there isn't. You are out of uniform, and what's up with these masks? These masks are not in the ship's uniform codes either and why are you and your team wearing them unless you all have something to hide from rest of us," said Lieutenant Sesmo.

"Well, first of all, I am very saddened by the murders of the drone room occupants. I hope you will find the perpetrators of this heinous crime. However, don't get ahead of yourself about us not being in uniform and the masks we are wearing, it is not important for you to know the reason, but you may know my rank. My rank is captain, and I outrank you lieutenant," said Ursha.

"You have mentioned your rank but not your name; was that deliberate?" asked Lieutenant Sesmo.

"Yes, it was a deliberate attempt, because you don't need to know my name lieutenant," replied the captain in the mask.

"Wait a minute, I need to know your rank but not your name, isn't that right?" asked Lieutenant Sesmo.

"Yes, that is right!" said the captain in the mask.

"You should also be aware when it comes to security matters; any rank will have to outrank you, and you must follow the security instructions no matter what rank delivers it. So, you say

you are a captain, which I am not so sure of at this moment, then I demand to see some sort of identification from you. Until then, I want you and your crew to remove your masks now, and That's an order!" said Lieutenant Sesmo.

"You have made your point, lieutenant, I grant you. However, you have no need to see my identification. You are best to move on now. You are beginning to vax me with anger! You have better things to do than aggravate my nerves and annoy me and my crew with your nonsensical inquiries and demands!" said the masked captain. Lieutenant Sesmo immediately pulled his hand-held weapon, and so did the rest of his crew, including Sakreg.

"Sir you and your crew are now under arrest for violating the ship's ordinances and my orders. Make no sudden moves unless you want to meet your maker. Put your hands up in the air where I can see them and drop slowly on the floor. Lay a prone position and spread your arms wide open. Do it now!" the lieutenant expressed vehemently.

One of Ursha's teammates pulled his weapon, and just before he took aim at Lieutenant Sesmo, a burst of red plasma projectile ejected from the nuzzle of Sesmo's handheld gun and struck the instigator right on his chest. The impact of the projectile pulled him up two feet off the ground and then landed him on the ground with his back, embracing the cold steely floor, and contaminating his attire with the blood that was gushing out of a huge hole on his chest. With insufferable pain, soon after, Private Gulkal gave up the ghost.

"Lieutenant—you've just shot one of my crewmembers! That wasn't necessary! You will have to answer for that!" said the masked captain.

"What's now boss—Gulkal is dead?" said Sergeant Tilkud.

"Shut up Tilkud, I will have this under control soon," said the captain in the mask, then turned around and faced his crew and said, *"Let's all do what he says for now!"* Five of Ursha's henchmen and the masked captain himself slowly and quietly went down to the floor and assumed the position as Lieutenant Sesmo ordered and were silently waiting for his next instructions.

"Sargent Grelgon and you, Private Enobue, I want you both to disarm them and tie their hands behind their back and then remove their masks one at a time. If they give you any trouble, I want you both to exercise the shoot-to-kill option. There should be no hesitation is that understood," said Lieutenant Sesmo.

"Yes sir!" responded both and they moved with a quick pace toward the masked ungs with their weapons pointing at their heads. Private Enobue approached Ursha, disarmed him at first and then tied both his hands and pulled his mask off. Lieutenant Sesmo noticed the big scar above Ursha's right eye. He quickly approached Ursha and knelt, then he examined his hands, it was sure enough, there was a freshly made gash on his right hand.

"Well, well, well, who do we have here? If it isn't the infamous Captain Ursha, the most wanted ung in this ship. You must be the murderer of the drone room occupants, Captain Ursha. That is your name, isn't it? And don't lie to me," said Lieutenant Sesmo.

"What makes you think I am the Captain Ursha?"

"Because we caught one of your henchmen, his name is Tekope. You are familiar with that name, aren't you, and don't say no," asked Sesmo.

"Yaaaaah------unfortunately I am familiar with that name. He is a dead ung for sure," said Ursha.

"Not so fast, you scumbag. The justice will most likely get you first. You see, he told us everything we needed to know about you and your pathetic plan," said Sesmo.

"I thought he would do that. He is a dead ung, for sure. If I don't get him, someone else from my team is going to get him soon, very soon," said Ursha and attentively eyed Private Obnitra, who was part of Lieutenant Sesmo's team, in anticipation of help. Ursha previously had brief synoptic interludes with Obnitra in regards to recruitment and him becoming a part of Ursha's team member. Lieutenant Sesmo quietly acknowledged the essence of Ursha's gaze at Obnitra and thought to handle the situation when he got back to the headquarters.

"Who is that someone else? That was your accomplice who joined you in your killing spree?" asked Sesmo.

"Don't ever think that I am going to tell you anything. You see, I have my people that you have no idea of; if I were you, I will watch my back at all times, lest you encounter a lethal accident by one of my ungs," said Ursha.

"Is that a threat?" asked Sesmo.

"Weeeell, you could take it that way if you want to," said Ursha.

"I should shoot you and your henchman right here and right now and be done with," said the lieutenant.

"Yah, you really should. Did you know that now, as we speak, you and your crew are being watched, and if anything happens

to me or if I signal them, they are going to charge on you and kill every one of you!" said Ursha.

"Where are they?" asked Sesmo.

"They are here, but you can't see them. That is all I am going to say," said Ursha.

"What! Are they ghosts?" asked Sesmo.

"No, they are real ungs like you and I, but soon they are going to make you become a ghost," said Ursha.

"Is this one of your tricks that I must believe?" asked Sesmo.

"It is up to you to believe me or not. What I am telling you is a fact," said Ursha.

Suddenly, Captain Ursha delivered a profound bawl as if he had a paroxysm of heightened pain. This was the signal intended for his hiding crew to come forth for their assistance.

Three ungs bolted out of the armory, having their weapons drawn. They moved hastily, and at the same time, they blustered, commanding everyone to drop their weapons or be shot. Lieutenant Sesmo extended his hand-held weapon to fire, but a red plasma projectile struck his right shoulder, and with the force of its impact, the lieutenant lost his balance and fell to the floor on his back. Blood began to spew and contaminate his clothes and the floor.

The lieutenant appeared bewildered by the impact of the round he received and demonstrated his agony and pain on his fuming face. Within a split second, the whole Sesmo's team opened fire without hesitation. The plasma shots littered the air. Ursha's team didn't have a chance to fire another round, and soon everyone in Ursha's team died, including Captain Ursha.

Sergeant Krama immediately knelt beside Lieutenant Sesmo and slowly moved the scorched part of the uniform away from the affected area to witness the extent of the flesh wound. Sergeant Krama witnessed Lieutenant Sesmo slipping in and out of conciseness for the very fact that he had lost a great deal of blood.

"Are you all right, lieutenant?" asked the sergeant.

"I suppose-------- I can't sssstay like this laying on the floor," said Lieutenant Sesmo, grimacing his face in pain.

"Don't attempt to get on your feet and please don't move. I will dispatch the medics right now and they will be here in no time, I promise you," said Sergeant Krama.

"Very well sergeant, inssssssstruct the medics to---------arrrrrive soon," said the lieutenant.

"Yes sir!" replied the sergeant and called in for the medics as the lieutenant instructed him.

"Sergeant------ you see that ung," the lieutenant slowly raised his hand, and with his finger, he pointed at Ursha, "I want-----you------to pull his--------iden---tification and bring it to me," said the lieutenant.

"Yes sir," replied the sergeant and stood on his feet at once, walked briskly towards the laying corpus of Captain Ursha, pulled his idea from back pocket, and brought it over to lieutenant Sesmo.

"Now please-----read the name on the iden---tification," asked the lieutenant.

"Yes sir," said the sergeant.

"*Commanding Officer, Captain Ursha, Special cyber-Unit, Alpha Squadron,*" said the sergeant.

"*Thanks, that's------what I thought. He was the------- murderer of the--------drone room personal. We had the right ung all along. I must, -------I must report---this to Captain Yilow as soon as possible.*" The lieutenant then took a deep breath and sighed. "*He will be delighted with the news,*" said the lieutenant. The lieutenant attempted to elevate his wrist toward his mouth so that he would communicate with the captain but couldn't for the pain was alarming.

"*Sergeant Krama------ I-----I want you to----- use your communicator to address Captain Yilow-----of the events---- that took place here,*" said Lieutenant Sesmo.

"*Yes sir,*" replied Sergeant Krama. He pushed a few buttons on his communicator and then said. "Captain, this is Sergeant Krama do you copy?"

"*Yes, I copy Sergeant. Go ahead,*" said Captain Yilow.

"*Well, we have your murder suspect and his team on the floor. They are all dead. His description and the name matched the one you have provided. One thing I am going to tell you sir, but please don't be alarmed; Lieutenant Sesmo took a round from their blaster on his upper chest, but I believe he is going to make it through. The medics are on their way,*" said Sergeant Krama.

"*Where are you now,*" asked the captain.

"*I'm at the location very near the Armory,*" said the lieutenant.

"*Near the Armory, what the heck are you doing that far off?*" asked the captain.

"Well sir, we were on our way to the Landing Bay, alpha one bravo niner sector, to see the prisoner leave the ship; in doing so, we had to pass the armory to get where we are sir," said the sergeant.

"Very well then, tell the lieutenant that he will be debriefed when he gets well. I will be sending the forensic personnel for a full investigation of the incident. You tell the lieutenant I'll see him in the sickbay. The captain is over and out."

CHAPTER 13

Huge, motorized double doors, gray in color, swung fast and forward from the infirmary bay 9A2C sector. Instantly, the light inside the infirmary overwhelmed the exit path, and within moments, out came two tall medical personnel outfitted in a green uniform, riding on a small and fast-moving hovercraft that hummed as it hovered three feet above the hard-steely ground. They maneuvered through many narrow and wide semi-lit corridors and instinctively avoided the piles of ashes that were on the floor where the creatures had died and left their pulverized remains.

The medics reached the Armory in less than two minutes, made a sudden stop in midair then slowly descended to the floor. The medical personnel quickly disembarked from their machines and trotted toward the lieutenant, who *was laying on the ground.*

"Are you the Lieutenant Sesmo?" asked Sergeant Elav, the lead medic.

"Yes----- I am," said Sesmo.

"Very well sir. I see you have lost lots of blood. I am surprised that you're still alive," said Sergeant Elav.

"As you see, -------I am hit in my --------right shoulder with one of their -------- blasters," the lieutenant pointed at the corpse.

"Yes, yes I could see that. However, the bleeding has stopped. That is a good sign. At this moment, your condition is not life-threatening. However, I am concerned about the danger of infection sir, which is common in such situations, and it could get ugly. Sir I am going to unbutton the shirt so we can get to the

affected area. We need to sanitize the wound as soon as possible," said Sergeant Elav.

One of the two medics prepared the sanitizing solution by tearing a few sealed packages and mixing them together, forming a compound and inserting the freshly made compound in a translucent tubular container.

"Sir this is going to sting a little, but I am sure you could handle it," said one of the medics, and sprayed the content on the wound.

The lieutenant expressed a slight contortion of his face. He didn't desire to evince the paroxysm of pain he was experiencing.

"We'll have you in the emergency room in no time sir." Elav blurted. From a distance, he took a quick gander at the deceased bodies, and ruminated in his head; what could have caused the security to end the lives of these ungs? What dastardly or nefarious deeds they must have committed to cause their demise?"

"They are not the ones------you should-----be concerned about. They------truly deserve------the death they embraced," said the lieutenant.

"Really, there must have been a lot that went on here! We don't see this kind of thing every day, and I hope we don't have to ever," said one of the medics, and as he spoke, he pulled a little box from the transport machine and laid it on the floor, then pushed a thumb-size black button. Suddenly, the box began to unravel quickly, and it became a hovering gurney. It hovered approximately two feet above the ground and danced in the air with restricted movements.

"Sir we're ready whenever you are," blurted one of the medics.

"Fine, I feel much better. The pain has subsided a great deal, thank you."

"It was the medicine we gave you on the wound sir," said Private Advak, one of the medics.

"Excellent now I want to part with a few instructions to my team before I embark on this black stretcher," said the lieutenant.

"Fine sir, go right ahead, but just that you should know, we have few minutes to invest here. That's all the time we have sir?" said one of the medics.

"Fine, then I'll make it short." He turned around, faced Lieutenant Yinoot, and said, "Lieutenant, I want you to continue in your mission to see your friend Sakreg leave this ship safely. Take all the ungs with you. You are in good hands, lieutenant, with my team. Any question?"

"No sir, I don't have any question, but just get well sir," said Yinoot, and a few blurted, *"Good health, lieutenant."*

"Thank you all, and Godspeed." He turned around and faced the medics, then said, *"I am ready."*

"Fine sir, now we're gonna carry you and put you on the gurney—easy does it," said one of the medics. They carried his motionless body onto the stretcher, and with the push of a few buttons on one of the medic's wrists; he became secured on the bunk.

"Sir, we will be moving fast, but it should not concern you. Everything will be under control. You just close your eyes and enjoy the ride. We'll be there in no time," said one of the medics.

They got on their hover machines, pushed a few buttons and with a slight hum, they sped away along with the lieutenant on the flatbed.

"All right ungs, Lieutenant Sesmo is gone, as you all know— I am now in charge. Listen up crew; as per Lieutenant Sesmo's instructions, we will see my friend Sakreg take in his starship safe and sound.

I believe we're not going to have any more problems with the creatures, for they must all be dead by now, so I believe we have a clear path to the A1B9 landing bay. As you all know, that's where we're heading for his spaceship, and we are almost there. After approximately one hundred yards, we will turn left and head straight to the gates. However, we still must be on the lookout just in case there are a few remnants of the creatures that are still alive," said Lieutenant Yinoot.

Lieutenant Yinoot's new conglomerate crew moved ahead eastbound quietly in unison. They attempted to avoid the piles of sand on the floor. Their eyes and ears were attentive to their immediate surroundings, lest they witnessed the creatures materializing before their eyes. They reached one hundred yards without an incident, and now they had to turn left for the gates.

Lieutenant Yinoot's crew reached an area where on either side of their path were some dismantled spaceship engine parts, diagnostic equipment, and hand tools large and small. Some grease-covered tools were on the benches, and some were on the floor, but no one was around to run or maintain the machines and the diagnostic equipment.

There were also grotesquely dismembered bodies strewed here and there. The team stopped to identify the corpses that some were slouched on their workbenches, bathed in their own blood. Some of the dead bodies were pinned on the engine shafts and were dangling in the air lifelessly. Some were laying dismembered on the floor and imbued in their own blood. The stench of their dead bodies was overwhelming to the nostrils of the arriving team, and the sight of the mayhem was indelibly disturbing to their psyche.

"These ungs didn't have a chance to survive this onslaught. They didn't even have weapons to fight the creatures with sir," said one of the members that were in proximity to the lieutenant.

"Yes, I agree. Things really got out of hand here. Some rules must change! How many did you count?" asked the lieutenant.

"I counted three on my end sir."

"And you, over there!" asked the lieutenant.

"Sir, I counted four," said the one who was a little distance from the lieutenant. Soon, everyone announced their tallies. The total was fifteen. The lieutenant called in for the cleanup crew.

"All right, I believe we're done here. Now, we must move on," said the lieutenant. As they went further, they confronted the huge gates having double doors, and on its right side, there was a large inscription stating "AIB9 Landing Bay."

"This is its team. We're here—on the other side of this gate, lay Sakreg's starship and as I have said before, per Lieutenant Sesmo's instructions, we are here to see him depart safely, and that is what we're gonna do," said the lieutenant. He pulled his communicator and began to utter,

"Sergeant Owaha—this is Lieutenant Yinoot, do you copy?"

"Yes lieutenant, this is Sergeant Owaha, I copy you sir. Are you here to relieve us sir. We were supposed to have been relieved two hours ago, but no one showed up yet?"

"Not exactly sergeant, we are here to see the prisoner depart this ship safely. Is it safe where you are, sergeant?" asked the lieutenant.

"Yes sir, it is safe back here. However, should we be concerned of something sir, now that you have addressed a safety matter?" asked the sergeant.

"No—not at this time; however, you have no idea what most of us had gone through outside this gate," said the lieutenant.

"Like what sir. Can you elaborate on that thought sir?" asked the sergeant.

"You will be informed in due time, sergeant, and now I will be opening this gate to see the prisoner leave in his vessel. Any questions sergeant?"

"No sir, come on in."

"Fine then, the Lieutenant Yinoot is over and out." He placed the communicator back in its holster, took a few steps toward the metallic wall where the gate control counsel was located and pushed a few of its buttons.

Suddenly, the gate-panels made cacophonous noise as they swiftly parted one to the left and the other to the right, and Sakreg's star fighter loomed before everyone's eyes. They all admired its design and its construction and thought it appeared formidable. However, when Sakreg caught sight of his ship, his expression took an elated form, thinking his captivity here would soon be over and he would be out exploring new worlds, but on second thought, he was going to miss his longtime friend Yinoot and wasn't sure that he will ever see him again.

As they all stepped inside the landing bay, they ambled toward the starfighter and congregated around it. Suddenly, Lieutenant Yinoot blurted.

"To all of you, I address—here is my longtime friend who is about to depart from among us. It is a sad moment for me to watch him leave, because we have been friends since childhood.

He deserves many accolades because, as you know and experienced, he saved our lives from imminent death. If it weren't for him being here with us, we probably wouldn't be standing here right now. We owe him the Olomak salute.

He doesn't understand our language, but I speak his language. As I have said, I grew up together on his own planet that we have invaded long time ago. I am going to express our intentions and our appreciation to him in his own language so he will be aware of our intentions. Any question?" asked the lieutenant. There was a brief silence. Yinoot turned around and faced Sakreg, and before he opened his mouth to speak, Sakreg blurted by saying,

"Yinoot, you're coming with me, right?" asked Sakreg with a certain degree of excitement. Yinoot rendered a brief simile than said.

"I wished that I could, but my people need me here. I can't let them down Sakreg. I wish you safe journey home. Maybe we'll meet again some other time in a more auspicious way. But for now, I wish you 'god's spee'."

"All right------I respect your decision. But I want to thank you for saving my life from your own people. I owe it to you Yinoot," said Sakreg.

"No, no! We all owe you. If it weren't for your presence here, we would have been dead by now. I thank you for saving our lives from the creatures on board and all that you have done for us here. I will remember these events for rest of my life. I receive you as my hero," said Yinoot. Now depart in peace, my friend, and be safe. There were tears in their eyes as they glared at each other for a few moments.

Sakreg and Yinoot gave each other a worm hug that lasted more than a few seconds; then, they let go of each other. Yinoot took a few steps back, rendered a salute by raising both forearms to the chest level, and leaving a space between the hands and the rib cage, then hands pointing upward at a sixty-degree angle, and the digits in both hands touching each other, he then rendered a brief bow of his head. All team members responded with the same salute.

Sakreg felt honored and respected. He returned the same salute to Yinoot at first and then slightly swiveled his body and delivered the same salute to Yinoot's crew, then he made an about-face and ambled toward his craft. Sakreg climbed into the canopy and began to perform basic tests to ascertain the condition of his spacecraft while Yinoot and his team stood silently observing Sakreg testing his craft.

Yinoot had confirmation from Sakreg that the craft was every bit functional without even firing the engines, then Yinoot and his teammates made an about-face, and they all marched out of the "landing bay" in unison. The large gates closed shut behind them.

Immediately after the shutting of the gates, a spherical drone loosened itself from the sealing, descended toward Sakreg's craft, and hovered approximately twenty feet above it. A bright and coherent light beam ensued from the bottom of the drone and shined the surface of the craft. Sakreg realized that the beam was a tracker beam.

Within moments, the roof of the flight deck traversed to one side, exposing the blackness of the starry space above. Sakreg realized that the purpose of the drone was to lead him outside the bay into the space; therefore, he didn't fire his engines.

Now, there was nothing stopping Sakreg from leaving this huge ship. The drone pulled Sakreg's craft out into space, then suddenly, the beam stopped, and the drone descended swiftly into the landing bay. Sakreg started the engines after the tractor beams were off and jetted forward out into space like a bullet out of the barrel.

Sakreg decided to leave the uninhabitable, enormous gaseous orb along with its sixty-plus moons and its faint rings. Humans call this planet "Jupiter," but at the same time, he used the planet's enormous gravitational force to catapult his vessel towards the planet where the humans call it "Mars."

With great haste, Sakreg arrived at the outer edge of the red planet's atmosphere. He acknowledged that this planet was much smaller than the one he left, and it had a solid surface for a change. Also, the readings of his sensors were much different from the previous planet. His analysis of its atmosphere was mostly comprised of carbon dioxide and that its surface was red because of the presence of iron oxide.

Sakreg observed the hills and the valleys, the great fissures, the deep canyons, the sand dunes, the craters, and the large dust storms that were all over this planet, but didn't find any observable water, nor vegetation for a life source and was dismayed. He concluded that this planet was barren and hostile to life, especially the temperature—the coldest being at -226 °F. He again ended his orbit around this planet and used the planet's gravity to propel his Starfighter toward Earth.

He soon arrived at the outer realms of the Earth's atmosphere, and his sensors depicted 78.09% Nitrogen and 20.95% Oxygen. These were near the right number of gasses he needed for his air to breathe. From the space, Earth appeared beautiful for Sakreg.

He observed the brilliant blue welkin that extended approximately five hundred miles into the space. He then acknowledged the blue waters that encompassed most of the planet. Sakreg witnessed white and ubiquitous patchy clouds floating inside the planet's atmosphere, for him that meant rain, seasons, and the most important thing he noticed was the colorful land, the terra-firma.

He immediately took vital readings of the planet and found abundant life forms, a celestial sphere that is suitable for breathing, a temperature that could be endured, and water that could sustain his life. He broke out in total elation as if all his worries had disappeared all at once and thought in his mind, "This is it. I am going down to investigate, but first, I am going to circle around this planet before I land.

I must have found favors among the gods that I am still alive and am here. There is a lot to see, a lot to learn, and maybe a lot to love. I will make this planet my habitation, at least for now, unless otherwise specified by nature, and I'll call this planet Abakwa, it means 'the beautiful world' in his language."

CHAPTER 14

Drake Grenhr, he is a man in his early forties, six feet in height, burly built, blue-eyed, having midnight black hair, a slightly grayed Vandyke beard, and a tanned integument. He is employed by a prominent aerospace company located in Salem, Oregon. His position is a senior engineer in charge of top-secret government projects involving antigravity machines.

Drake's demanding long work hours was fomenting a marital conundrum at home, and his situation was irking his family also his psyche. For a change, he decided to take a long overdue, one-week vacation to spend his time camping alone in the wilderness to have a clear mind to decide the fate of his marriage and to get away from everyone, his work, meetings, schedules, projects, scientific experiments, and clients, including steel and concrete edifices, highways, and traffic jams.

A week prior to Drake's planned adventure, his son Jake received a call from his sister Vraya, a resident of Scottsdale, Arizona. Vraya requested Jake's assistance in installing new floors and kitchen cabinets. He was to stay at her abode for a duration of one month starting Monday.

As for Drake—it has been three months since his separation from his beautiful wife, Rebecca. Eight years of rocky marriage was hanging from a thread. He was not aspiring or desirous of losing her permanently. In fact, despite the volatile relationship he had with his wife Rebeca, his amorous propensities were still at their zenith, but despite the ardent amative feelings he projected towards his wife, at this moment, his ambivalence toward his marriage was the predominant factor in his relationship with his wife.

Rebeca dealt treacherously toward Drake. She was having various one-nightstands and numerous affairs with men in town, especially the one with a marketing executive of a prominent company; the affairs were ongoing.

Drake felt his hubris had been challenged. His constant mindfulness of her treachery and her wild affairs with other men fomented painful thoughts of leaving her and consequently clouded his mind by engendering dread and disgust about her duplicitous lifestyle, but at the same time, he despised the thought of being labeled as "cuckold" by his peers.

He needed this solitude to clear his gray matter from everything that could make him feel saturnine, woebegone, disconsolate, and befuddled about his marriage. Whether his determination to embark on such a camping adventure was to be commended or to be characterized as an insane notion, the determination was solely his own in the making.

It is late Thursday, July evening. The ornate Grandfather clock was a few minutes short of striking six o'clock. However, there was still plenty of sunlight before the event.

A recent model of black Chevy Camaro just pulled into Drake's driveway. On his left, the front porch was full of decorated and well-taken care of colorful floral arrangements in various beds and a well-manicured lawn with four feet high topiary-hedged fence.

Drake was in a much preparation for his adventurous trip. He was placing his personal camping supplies inside the haversack to be ready for tomorrow's trip. Suddenly he paused for a second or two to listen for the sound of the revving engine that just pulled into his driveway and the distant faint sound of the music that was playing in the car. Drake soon came to the conclusion; that it must be Jake visiting him this late in the evening and wondered why.

The music was loud in the car; Led Zeppelin was singing "Stairway to Heaven," which is Jake's favorite song. Suddenly, the revving of the engine stopped, and the music died. Jake stepped out of the car and slammed the door shut. He climbed a few concrete stairs, entered the front porch, and ambled toward the front door. He knocked with three gentle but distinct knocks at a specific frequency. It was Jack's signature knock.

Drake opened the door and noticed his tall and burly son standing with a smile on his face, wearing khaki shorts with a fancy untucked Hawaiian shirt and flip-flops on his bare feet, waiting to come inside.

"Oh—hi, Dad, can I come in?" asked Jake with a slight smile.

"Ya—ya sure come on in son!" said Drake with a surprised and addled look on his face.

"Were you expecting anyone this evening, Dad?" asked Jake.

"No—not really, son—I really wasn't. What brings out here anyway? Oh—by the way, didn't you have some sort of business meeting on the phone tonight?" asked Drake.

"Yaaaaaa, but I canceled it. I decided not to invest in the coffee business," said Jake.

"Why did you decide not to?" asked Drake.

"Dad, there were too many loopholes and unanswered questions, and the people that I had to meet with were out of state. I just didn't feel too comfortable investing with them," said Jake.

"All right son—I understand. From what you have told me, I would have done the same. You have made the right choice. You must go with your gut feeling, you know. I am proud of you son. You are making good choices. Logical ones at that, but then what really brings you out here? Do you need money?" asked Drake.

"No Dad, I am doing fine. I don't need money now. Thanks for the asking."

"Ya, sure," said Drake and continued stuffing his needs in the sack.

"Well, the reason I am here Dad, is that—I heard you were leaving for camping early in the morning, and I came by to say goodbye, and God's speed. You know I care about you Dad. You have taught me a lot, and I am grateful to you for that," said Jake.

"Well—well thank you, son, but told you that I was leaving. I don't remember telling anyone that I was leaving for a camping trip, not even you," said Drake.

"It was Grandpa Willy," said Jake as he observed Drake packing .45 caliber clips full of ammo inside his camping gear.

"Grandpa Willy ha?--------- Yaaaaaa—I remember telling him about my tomorrow's camping trip. It was about two months ago. He must have marked the date on the calendar. That is how he remembered."

"Dad, should I be worried? What the hack are you doing with the ammo, especially the kind of rounds that you are tucking in that clip? They are special kinds of rounds Dad, and are a lot deadlier than the normal bullets. You are not going to be out there killing someone and making sure that he doesn't get back up again, are you," asked Jake. Drake suddenly ceased his activity for a moment and fixated his glare on the floor as if being

in a great muse, then suddenly turned his head toward Jake and blurted by saying, *"Like who,"* asked Drake.

"Dad, you know darn well whom I am talking about. Like Mom's, you know who?" asked Jake.

"Oh, no—no need to worry son. Although that may not have been a bad idea, it is not worth it. It seems your mom has already made her mind up to be with that Jackass, the home wrecker. It is not worth going to jail for it.

"Listen son, no matter what I did to please her. I even worshiped the ground she walked on; I couldn't win her love, even if my life was depended on it. I know I am not gonna ever gain your mother's love no matter what I do. So, it is not worth going to jail for it. Do you understand me?"

"Yes, I do Dad, but it is sad and tuff to see you apart from each other. By the way, do you still love her dad?"

"Yes---and no, I don't really know right now. That is why I am going away to clear my thoughts and hopefully figure out my next move, and you know son, if things don't work out between us, then I am going to have to chuck it up to my experience and move on. Life throws so many punches and curve balls, and some of them hurt a lot, but you must learn to roll with it. Otherwise, you will pay a big price even with your life. Do you understand me, son?" asked Drake with a sullen expression.

"Yes Dad, I hear you. That would be the best thing you would want to do—just chuck it up to the experience and move on. I wished that it would have been as easy as it sounded—However, I just wished things were different between you two—Dad," said Jake.

"Ya, I wished the same son. And if you want to know why I am taking these special ammos with me, they are for my protection. I will never know what I will face in the wilderness."

"But then, why are you putting yourself in such danger where you might have to fight for your life? Isn't that counterintuitive? You don't need to do this, Dad. I don't want you to go. Just sort things out where you are—here!" said Jake emphatically.

"Yes son, I suppose I could stay here and think things out, but here—there is much noise and interruptions and memories in this city that would clutter my mind. I need to get away from everything, I mean everything and everyone, at least for a little while, son, and decide in a clear mind as to what I must do with my marriage and with your mom; besides, I like an adventure anyway. I haven't had that for a long time. You know I have been bogged down with work, and I thought getting away from everything was not such a bad idea after all, but don't worry son, I'll come out alive, trust me. I promise you that," said Drake.

"Ok-----I suppose there is nothing I can say or do to change your mind; could I? It seems you have made up your mind, Dad," said Jake.

"Yes, I have son," said Drake.

"All right, Dad, to change the subject, I have two things I want to share with you," said Jake.

"I hope you are not in trouble son," said Drake in a surprised posture.

"No, no, Dad—it's nothing like that. I want to tell you that I am leaving next week for Arizona to see my sister Vraya. She called me to do some work around the house. I am going to stay

there for about a month to finish everything and then come back."

"Well, that's excellent son. You get to help your sister, and at the same time, you may enjoy the country. There is a lot to see there. Ok—what time are you planning to leave son?"

"Well Dad, we are thinking of leaving sometime in the morning around 7.00ish," said Jake.

"You've mentioned us. Is there anyone else coming with you?" asked Drake.

"Yes Dad, it is my friend Marvin. He will be driving, and I will be flying back," said Jake.

"Excellent, you both could keep each other's company. It is a long drive. You know that son," said Drake.

"I know that Dad. Dad there is something else I am going to tell you," said Jake.

"And what's that now? I know it's not money, I asked you that already. I also know that you are not in trouble," said Drake.

"You're right Dad, it is not money, and I am not in trouble. Are you ready to hear this Dad?"

"All right, son----shoot," said Drake.

"Ok, here it goes------I have decided to join the Army," said Jake.

"Army! How did you ever come up with that decision, son?"

"I haven't told you this Dad, but I always wanted to serve my country," said Jake.

"Ya son, I am proud of you that you have such a love and commitment for your country. How about your wife Esmeralda? What does she think about your Army decision?" asked Drake.

"She is not too happy about my decision," said Jake.

"I see—maybe you should reconsider your thoughts despite of your love for your country. I think besides God, your family should come first above anything else son. There are too many divorces in this country. That is what's tearing this country apart. Don't be a statistic," said Jake.

"I get your point Dad! But it is too late now! I have already signed up Dad!" said Drake.

"Ohhhhh, I wished we had this conversation earlier. I suppose there is not much you can do now, is there? I am so sorry to hear about her disagreement with your military endeavors. This will affect your relations with your wife—son. Is there anything I could do to help?" asked Drake.

"No, I will work things out, Dad. You'll see," said Jake.

"Very well son, I hope you do for both of your sakes. Divorce is a nasty thing. Don't even entertain the thought if you can. That is why I am going away to think things over.

So, coming back to the Army issue, when are you supposed to leave?" asked Drake.

"October the 18th, Dad," said Jake.

"That is not too far from now, and I suppose you have signed up for three years. Is that correct?" asked Drake.

"Yes Dad, for three years, and if I like it, I will make it a career and be the best shooter in the country like you are Dad," said Jake.

"I like that in you. That is a positive thinking son. One thing I would like to part with you—be the best at what you do, and success will follow. Remember that, son----don't you ever forget it," said Drake as he finished his packing.

"All right, Dad I won't, I won't forget it. I promise. Oh, by the way, what time are you leaving Dad?" asked Jake.

"Well son, I will be leaving somewhere around 4.00 AM," said Drake.

"Why that early, Dad?" asked Jake.

"I am going up north to Washington State. It is about 4 hours drive, I think, maybe less, or maybe more. I don't really know. I had better start early so I can be there at least by 8.00 or sooner and start my day early," said Drake

"In that case, Dad, you need to retire early today so you can get all the rest you need and be ready for tomorrow. I won't be holding you up anymore Dad. I had better leave for now; it is getting late anyway. Be safe, you hear me Dad?" asked Jake. They hugged each other, and then Jake left.

CHAPTER 15

Suddenly, the strident and reverberating sound of the alarm pervaded through Drake's dark and unadorned bedroom. He grabbed his flashlight that was next to his pillow, shined the light at the clock that was on the lamp stand, and noticed that it registered three AM. Drake rubbed his sleepy eyelids with his buckled hands while he laid in a supine position on his bed, having no blanket on, wearing just shorts and a T-shirt. After a few moments, he sprang up out of his king-size bed and stood erect on a matted floor, then decided to starch.

Drake took a few steps, staggered at first, wore his flip-flops then began to walk toward the kitchen to prepare his morning Joe. Along the way, he began to rub his sleepy eyes again so that he would truly wake up from his oscitancy state.

When he was halfway through the corridor, he paused for a moment and turned on the corridor lights. And when he reached the kitchen, he turned on the kitchen light and prepared his robust Colombian coffee, and then he went to the bathroom to take a cold, quick, and exhilarating shower.

After feeling refreshed and fully awake, he wore his hiking gear, grabbed his brown tactical shoulder harness holster that hung on a tall coat hanger pole, wore it over his checkered long-sleeved earth-hued shirt, and covered it with his camouflaged hunting jacket. The holster housed a Smith & Wesson .45 Caliber semiautomatic pistol. He took a few extra clips full of .45 caliber rounds and hid them in his hunting pant pockets.

Drake is natural with handguns and rifles. He is well known and well respected in shooting communities all over the states.

His precision in engaging targets is nonpareil. (Marine Corps Distinguished Shooters Association considered Drake an expert shooter in small arms, one of the best in the country).

It is Thursday early in the morning. Drake grabbed his tall metallic coffee mug full of freshly made strong coffee, heaved his camping gears, locked all doors, and embarked into his brand new 4-wheel drive Cadillac SUV parked in his driveway and began to drive. He took a brief glance at his Chrono watch, and it displayed 4.00 AM, right in time to leave as he had planned.

The incandescent city streetlights hung on the long and arched poles. These poles were spread a few hundred feet apart and were lighting the dark streets, sidewalks, and front porches of the pristine residential homes. There were few houses with indoor lights on; however, most of the community appeared sound asleep, resting from their daily chores.

Drake made a right turn on an empty but well-lit street. He did not witness any sole that roamed the pavements. Drake briefly glanced to his left, the large city park that was enveloped with the blackness of the night. He moved his orbs up and took a brief glance at the full moon that was casting its light on the earth, pushing the darkness away to some extent and rendering its constant smiling face in his direction.

Drake felt the moon was bidding him a safe journey. He switched his orbs toward the direction of his drive, grabbed sight of the sky, and realized bright dots of the Milky Way Galaxy intensely peppered it.

After Drake had crossed a few streetlights, he embarked on Highway 5, his direction, northbound from his residence in

Salem, Oregon. The destination in mind is Washington State, near Adam's Mountain.

The Highway arching lights that lit the empty paved path stretched beyond Drake's line of sight. It was casting its brilliance on occasional and far-in-between steely motors that were racing toward their unknown destinations with impunity as if there were no constables on the road.

Suddenly, a sense of freedom merged in Drake's heart and mind. It made him feel nothing was going to stop him from achieving his endeavors. He took a few sips of his freshly made coffee and felt wide-eyed and alert, ready to conquer the day's events.

After being on the road for a while, Drake entered the state of Washington. He had his radio on and was playing his favorite song, "My Heart Will Go On," by his favorite artist, Kenny G, sounding on his sultry saxophone.

Suddenly, the music stopped in its mid-course, and the announcer on the radio came on to announce the breaking news, *"We interrupt this program to bring you the following news. Another bank was robbed late yesterday afternoon. This time, it was Ralph Farnham Bank. There were five casualties, three dead and two wounded, and the president of the bank is missing, kidnapping feared.*

The robbers got away with two million dollars in cash, and they are still at large. The authorities think there were three masked men who perpetrated the bank robbery. Tune in at 9:00 A.M. for the full story. Now, let's get back to our music."

"Damn it, when will the police get a handle on crime in the cities," thought Drake with a sullen expression.

After further driving, Drake got onto Highway 84, headed eastbound by crossing the Hood River Bridge. He then got onto Highway 14, which led to Highway 141, north to Mt Adams Rd heading north. He finally took the National Forest (NF 5603) road and drove for a little while, then took a nondescript path that snaked to a small open ground and parked his SUV.

Drake parked his car on the gravel and didn't witness anyone around, and that appeased him the most. He glanced at his wristwatch, it registered 8:25 in the morning. His arrival at this destination was at the right time, just as he had planned it.

Drake stood on the gravel and elevated his head slowly to the sky, then thanked God for his safe trip. He took a few deep breaths of unadulterated air, then exhaled slowly, smelled the forest aroma nearby, and felt refreshed for a change.

The temperature of the air felt balmy on Drake's skin, it felt as if it was in the lower seventies. There were a few white patchy clouds that hovered in the sky. However, there was this low, lingering, ubiquitous and obscuring brume in between the tall Grand firs, Douglas firs, Western hemlocks, Western red cedar trees and more. *"The sun will burn this haze, and it will clear soon. Then the day will be beautiful,"* he thought.

Drake hauled his haversack off the ground, secured it on his back, then gingerly slid down the not-too-steep slope to the valley down below, then began to tread towards the tall and not-too-distant Grand Firs. As he began to close the distance between him and the forest up ahead, he peered through the trees and noticed the sun's rays were bolting through as shafts of light, eliminating the leaves, the thick branches, and the thickets on the ground. The huge forest trees loomed bigger and taller with every step that he took.

Drake entered the timberland; he immediately wondered, *"What could be lurking here that might make me feel vulnerable."* He felt a little intimidated by the enormity of the trees and the dense foliage that encompassed him. Drake thought that he might have to encounter voracious carnivore animals like black bears, wolves, big cats, and perhaps snakes and possibly large poisonous insects and arachnoids. (However, wolves were scarce around this region).

He chose a no ordinary path that was created by humans. The path was nature's own making. He didn't witness any human footsteps anywhere and thought, *"No one must have set foot here yet,"* and felt content. As he ventured deeper into the forest, the sunlight dimmed a great deal all around him. It felt as if the daylight surrendered its power to the night. Inside the forest, the bright shafts of sunlight continued to break through the trees, shrubs, and foliage here and there to fight the darkness that was prevalent in the woodland. Drake sensed the pervasive and haunting aroma of the timber and stopped for a moment to take a deep breath. The scent of the flora that surrounded him pervaded his nostrils and overwhelmed his sense of smell in a very positive way.

Drake pulled a military compass from the top of his shirt pocket to ascertain his direction, and the needle indicated his heading was at 50° Northeast bound. And placed the compass right back in his pocket and thought he was heading in the right direction. The compass was passed from his grandpa Joe to his father, Tim, and then to him.

This trip was Drake's first in this part of the country. He was not an experienced camper and was not on his familiar grounds. In fact, he lived in the city most of his life, but had a strong foresight and an instinct as to how he should survive in this untamed wilderness and trusted his instincts to be right.

Drake pulled up his cell phone to see if there was any reception, but to his dismay, the reception was very poor, almost nonexistent. There were no cell phone towers here; therefore, he turned it off and placed it back in his camouflaged pant pocket to save energy. As Drake proceeded to move forward, little twigs and dead leaves crackled and broke under the weight of his body, and at the same time, branches of little trees and shrubs were beating his face, his chest and just about everywhere on his body and was impeding his path.

Drake pulled his long machete and began to swing left and right to lop the tall bushes and the thin tree branches from roundabout him. The direction that he was heading did not have the usual path that nature had created. Now he was creating his own path as he was moving deeper and deeper into the forest. Maybe at heart, he felt he was born to be a rebel and uninhibited person.

Drake felt empowered by experiencing a sense of freedom that embraced his heart and his mind. He seemed totally in charge of his life and of his decisions. No one was to tell him anything, or to dictate his time as to how he should spend it.

Drake noticed the beautiful and colorfully blossomed flowers and the large winged hovering kaleidoscopic patterned flying butterflies that surrounded the flowers; it enthralled him with delight. *"This is truly a magnificent and very tranquil sight, and it is something that I can get used to rather quickly,"* but suddenly his thoughts betrayed him, thinking, *"What the heck did I decide to do? Did I have to go this far to think thing over?"* this thought was slowly creping in Drake's mind as he continued in his path.

Suddenly, Drake lost the euphoria he once held a few moments earlier. He acquired an eerie and unsettled feeling of being totally alone here in this vast wilderness, a sense of *"what the hell I am doing here with no one around, no one to talk to, or share thoughts or feelings with, and being somewhere that I am very unfamiliar with, or being lost altogether, away from humanity, society and comfort. I am acting like a vagrant and an antisocial person,"* this thought has also encompassed his mind, and it disturbed him for a while.

Despite Drake's unsettled feelings, he continued treading the forest for one and a half hours incessantly. He carefully meandered through the hills, valleys, and slightly open and natural pathways that were devoid of foliage. His attempt was to find a resting place for his weary bones. However, despite the power bars he consumed along the way to maintain his energy level, his body still felt jaded and enervated. His breathing became a little more intense than the norm, maybe because of a certain elevation he found himself to be in. However, the tall and short trees with their dense and thick branches, shrubs, beautiful and colorful flowers, and chirping birds were totally overwhelming his mind and his senses in a positive way. But he couldn't help to think that he was truly lost here and wasn't so sure that he would be able to find his way back or come out of this dithery jungle alive. Drake truly felt alone and lost. There was just the blue empyrean above and the boscage down below that was all around him.

"Well, as long as I am on this path, there must be somewhere I could find a resting place where I could rest my bushed bones. I am getting tired," Drake thought to himself.

CHAPTER 16

As Drake continued being afoot, he saw a clear swath of damp ground that was laced with many freshly set large and small shoeprints and thought that should odd, in fact, very odd in this part of the territory. *"Who is in the right mind that would venture here in the middle of nowhere beside me? I suppose, now, I am not alone here,"* thought Drake and the notion disturbed him.

The shoeprints indicated there was more than one person here. Drake began to ruminate. *"If it is a case of people living here, then what kind of people am I going to encounter in this part of the wilderness? Is it going to be friendly and cheerful or toothless illiterate provincial mountain dwellers who are fractious and living off the land, wielding shotguns and shooting at every passerby? But what could be worst is that, maybe I will be meeting nefarious killers, crooks, thugs, or escapees from the authorities who may have to conspire my demise once they find me here,"* Despite the notion of whom he may find in his path, he decided to follow the footprints and expect the worst but hope for the best of what may come in his way.

After Drake traded an approximate distance of four buses in length, having his eyes always glued on the footprints, he came to a place where he had to veer left and face north to maintain the sight of these mysterious shoeprints on the ground. At this time, the shoe prints weren't the only items that caught his sight; he also described a large, rickety shack approximately half a football field away. The shack was constructed from the boles of trees, branches, and twigs. It had a pitched roof but no front porch. It had an entrance door that faced southward direction.

Drake was dumbstruck and thought, "*A shack in the middle of nowhere.*" There was no frippery here? He couldn't believe his eyes as to what this ramshackle hut was doing here. "*Who would be in the right mind, not counting the criminals, to live in this godforsaken wooded place and away from everything and everyone? Someone must be irascible or invidious, totally antisocial, austere and possibly a misanthropist to come up here and make this place happen,*" he thought.

This makeshift shelter had just two small windows, one on each side of the door, and they each measured about two feet square. These windows were covered with a thick cloth, maybe to keep the wind, the insects, and the big animals from entering the premises. These windows were approximately five feet above the ground.

For now, all is quiet here around the shack, as if no one has been living in this dwelling for some time, but the freshly made shoeprints led straight to the front door; it appeared as if it must have been a recent event. At this moment, Drake was not so certain if this shanty was occupied or deserted.

Drake pulled his .45 Caliber semiautomatic pistol, supported it with both hands, and pointed its barrel vertically. He moved quietly and surreptitiously. He went and hid himself behind a large tree trunk and waited for a couple of minutes to ascertain if there was going to be any activity around this cottage.

It has been a little while now. No one has yet entered or exited the cabin. Drake concluded that whoever they are, or whoever lives here—at this moment, they are not in this vicinity; but, still back in his mind, he was not so positive about his conclusion.

Drake thought again as he did before, *"To whomever these fresh footprints belonged, they could possibly be murderers. They could have already taken notice of my presence here, and now perhaps they might have set a trap for me, and they must be patiently waiting inside for me to show up in front of their door. If I should enter their premises, they will surely blow me away, or do with me as they please."*

Drake preceded toward the shed in a careful and stealthy manner by executing quick steps and occasionally hiding behind tall bushels and shrubs for a few seconds at a time and still not losing sight of the shack. At about three bus distances away from the front door of the shack, Drake slowed his steps to a snail's pace and maintained his .45 caliber semiautomatic handgun straight forward toward the front door. He held the gun with both hands, arms extended forward, finger on the trigger, and occasionally panned the gun left and right, and executed 360° turn to see if anyone was following him.

Drake was ever more concerned as to who was going to suddenly jump out of the door and surprise the wits out of him. His heart was beating fast, his hands were shaking slightly, and in result, he was inducing more pressure on the gun with both hands.

Fear gripped Drake's spirit, and he felt his blood pressure rose when he experienced the dull headache. This situation was not in his plan. Despite all the trepidation he felt, Drake couldn't forgive himself if he had eschewed or run away from this situation. His curiosity and his intrepidity got the best of him, and he continued forward toward the front door.

Drake approached the shanty quietly from the left side (west) and allowed a foot and a half distance between him and the wall.

As he approached the front door, he noticed the door was slightly ajar. He immediately swiveled his body 90°, and traversed across the door rather rapidly, then leaned his body up against the wooden wall of the shack east side of the door facing south into the wilderness. He didn't feel like tasting the shotgun or rifle leads from inside this abode. Drake still held the gun with both hands, but this time close to his upper chest, facing the barrel upward toward the sky.

"Oh God, let my wayward thoughts be wrong and that there be no one here, and I'll be happy to go on to my merry way," he prayed in a muffled voice. Drake let loose his right hand from the grip of the handgun but maintained his position; he then pushed the door slowly with his right arm while his back was still pinned against the wall. The door squeaked as he pushed, but he did not encounter a life-threatening situation yet. There were no rounds were fired from a weapon of any sort. He felt that was somewhat odd, but a pleasant surprise.

Drake waited a couple or three seconds, then immediately charged through the door, eyes wide open, arms forward, holding the gun with both hands, finger on the trigger. He swung the gun to his left and to his right in a rapid fashion. Drake immediately grimaced his face as a result of the stanch that was prevalent here along with a fusty atmosphere. His breathing became challenging, and he felt disgusted by the smell of animal ordure.

Inside the shanty was dark, devoid of furniture and amicable amenities. However, there were three blankets on the floor accompanied by "Augean stable." There were plenty of empty beer and whisky bottles strewed here and there, three wooden unadorned makeshift chairs, leftover food, and a large box covered with cloth and twigs that was shoved against the eastern wall of the living room; also, there were four battery-operated lanterns on the floor. Drake immediately thought, at least there are three filthy, mucky, and scuzzy people living here, possibly with a dog or two.

Suddenly, Drake heard a faint moaning and grumbling sound as if a man was in pain. It was barely audible. The sound was coming from another room that led from the living room.

As Drake approached gingerly to the second entry door, the whining sound became slightly louder, and he immediately determined that it was a male sound.

Whoever this ill person was must have been experiencing lots of pain prior to Drake's arrival, but perhaps became winded from screaming aloud for such a long time. In result, he had lost the vigor and the strength to scream loudly.

Drake thought if anyone was in great physical distress, or pain, the person might not be posing much trouble, because they would be preoccupied on how to alleviate or assuage the experience of pain or discomfort. As Drake approached the entry door, the whining became a little louder. Drake slowly pushed the door ajar, just enough so that he could stick his noggin through and have a clear visual of its surrounding to render a judicious decision. His finger was still on the trigger, and his pistol barrel was still pointing up in the air. He immediately took notice of a man lying on the floor, and where he was laid, he contaminated his clothes and the floor with his blood. However, there was no weapon in sight anywhere around the victim. He had his hands tied behind his back, and his eyes were barely open.

Drake relaxed his muscles, placed his gun back in its holster, pushed the door aside, and quickly went in and knelt down next to the victim who was in pain so that he could scrutinize the condition of this slain man and decipher the location of his life-threatening wound. Just as he was doffing his jacket to cover the wounded man on the ground, the wounded man blurted,

*"Are you----are you going to----finish me up? You, filthy bastard—you murderer. Why-----don't---you just go ahead and------do it. This time------do it right and get it-----get it over------with it! And get me out of my-----f***ing misery. You Son of a bitch!"* said the wounded man with barely audible voice and eyes flickering and attempting to stay open.

"Relax, I am not going to hurt you," said Drake.

"Why! ----Why not; aren't you one of them?"

"One of who, sir?"

*"I see---well---I recon------- if you are not one of them --------- then------- you must be a stranger here. How did you f***ing find ------- this no man's land? I thought no one could find me here. Are you here to------ rescue me?"* The victim responded in a hesitant and faint manner.

"Well sir—as much as I want to, but the phones don't work here to call anyone for help."

*"Oooooh S**t, I am really done for now ----- then------- I am really gonna die here."* He shut his eyes in despair. *My wife---- my wife, my kids----they don't even know------what in the hell is going on with me, or----- where in the hell I am at-----right now. All I know----they are very much worried about me. My wife--- my kids-----I am really going----to miss them. Oh s**t----why did this------had to happen to me?"*

Drake knew there was not much time left for him to live, even if he was in the hospital and on an operating table with the best doctors around him attempting to extract the bullet from his body.

"Please tell me how I can help alleviate your pain. You don't look well. It looks like you have lost lots of blood," said Drake.

"What happened here?" Drake was attempting to ascertain the severity of the man's wound that appeared on the victim's chest but was afraid to move him.

"Look, I am not a doctor, but I think I can pull the bullet out of your body. My dad is a doctor, and when I was a kid, he taught me a lot about surgery. Do you want me to help you in that respect?" said Drake.

"Well, if you are not a doctor or a nurse -------- I suppose --- ----there is really not much you can do -------- to help -------- me now, -------- besides, I know --------that nothing is going ------to help me now anyway-------even if you pull the bullet out of my--- ----body. I know, I perhaps------ I have an hour or less to live. I feel it. I sense it, so don't bother trying-------to operate on me. Thanks anyway------for the offer. You seem to be-------a good man. And as far as what had happened here, ---------- It's a long story. I don't think I have much time nor the energy to explain-- ---as I said -------- don't have the energy to tell you --------- about it." He let a few gasps and panted; then he shut his eyes again.

"My name is Drake. I would have shaken your hand, but it looks like you are not able to do so. What is yours?"

He opened his blue eyes and glared at Drake for a few seconds then blurted, "I am ------John Henklin." Just then, a severe paroxysm of pain shot through his chest and he screamed as loud as his condition allowed him, which was not much. A few drops of tears began to roll down from his grimaced and contorted face, and his body began to convulse uncontrollably. It appeared as if he was going into a shock. Mr. Henklin wasn't going to make it through another hour, as he said.

"Look here ------ Mr. -------- You need to --------get out of ------- here fast------because they-------may be returning soon-------and you will be-----their-------next victim. Go ------ go on, and get out of ----- here now while you can and let me die-------here. I know ------- I don't have—much time left anyway. There is nothing -------------- you can do here. Go on, get out of here----- hurry, hurry now -------- before they get here."

"All right, I am leaving," said Drake. He got on his feet, went to the living room, picked up one of the reeking blankets, and brought it to the victim's room, then picked his jacket up from the wounded man and replaced it with one of the counterpanes.

"I am leaving now," said Drake. Mr. Henklin did not respond. He did not move. There were no more convulsions, eyes were open, and there was an empty glare in no specific direction. *"It must be apparent that he passed away,"* thought Drake.

Drake paused for a few seconds and stared at the dead man on the floor, shook his head in dismay, then proceeded to exit the place. But, before exiting the vicinity, his curiosity got the best of him and he decided to find out what was in the big and makeshift box made from cut pieces of small logs covered with withe and black baize.

Drake swung his arm and shoved the twigs and the rest of the contents that were on top of the container aside on the floor and slowly opened the lid. There it was, oodles of money. His eyes opened wide in an utter surprise. He hasn't seen so much money in one place in all his life. The money was fresh and untouched, bundled up in one hundred dollar bills along with a company badge having a picture of a person on it, and it was Mr. Henklin's photo with a description stating "President" and the company was *"The Bank of Ralph Farnhan."* Drake immediately remembered the newsbreak while he was driving to his destination and thought that the three bank robbers were there, and the missing president of the bank was Mr. Henklin.

The sight of the money mesmerized Drake, for it was plenty. He imagined, *"What could I have done with all that cash."* Suddenly, he came to his senses and thought that he is not alone here. The occupants of this place may have to return at any moment, especially when Mr. Henklin warned him of their eminent return. He realized he had spent much time here, and now he should no longer linger here; his life could be in danger. He immediately closed the lid, replaced the top cover of the box with its original contents the same way as it was before, got on his feet, and went for the door.

CHAPTER 17

"Our plan worked very well. The robbery was a success. We had a very good disguise, didn't we? Nobody knew who we were, especially when we killed all the cameras, including the one in the parking lot. Now, for sure, the Cops can't track us, and to top that, we didn't leave any evidence that the Cops can trace us here.

"I learned well from my next-door cell inmate, Murdock. You guys know that he is a seasoned f***ing bank robber. He was a wanted man by many states. He did work alone. Bud damn! He was caught because there were two f***ing off-duty police officers in the bank while he was attempting to rob, and these A**holes arrested him right on the f***ing spot. They pulled the gun on him, and he didn't have the chance to respond. He also told me all the f***ing mistakes the bank robbers make to get them caught.

"I would say the only thing that went wrong with our plan was that Jackass, so-called president of the f***ing bank. He managed to pull my f***ing mask off my face. I hated it. I got so f***ing mad, I was going to kill him right on the spot, but I got distracted by you idiots, and I had no f***ing choice but to bring him here with us.

"I didn't want him to reveal our identity to the f***ing police. Well, here he is now, dead as a door and a nail, and no one will be able to find his f***ing dead body here, not in a million years. Now, there is nooooo one that could pin us down for this robbery. However, we must bury his ass in the ground when we get back to the house, otherwise, we are going to smell his decaying body, and that's going to be awful. It will be worse than the dog s**ts we are smelling all the time," said Roger Brauner.

Roger was Jeremy's brother (one of the three bandits) and was much more confident than Jeremy. Roger was Twenty-eight years of age. He was a prison escapee and wanted by the Minnesota state authorities. He stood just about six feet in height, watched his diet, and worked out every chance he could get, and consequently, he created a six-pack abdomen and became a muscular build in his upper chest. He intimidated the guards and occasionally got in trouble with them. Roger had black eyes, black crew-cut hair, with a thick mustache and made use of the rifle.

"I think we should do it again. It is fun. It gets my blood going," said Jeremy Brauner.

"You mean it gets your adrenalin going. You are stupid. It is not your f***ing blood, you dumb f***!" said Roger.

"All right, my adrenalin, whatever that is Einstein," said Jeremy.

Jeremy stood approximately 5.8 feet in height and was a bit stocky in the middle (possibly too many beers and sodas in his diet). He just had his twenty-fifth birthday.

"It looks like you're getting the taste of the money very well. I can see why it is fun for you. You know—I like that in you, Jeremy. You are finally gaining the f***ing confidence that you need in this f***ing business. It's about time b**ch. Keep it up otherwise, I will kill you myself—do you hear me?" said Roger.

"Ya—right! I hear you! You must think you are a hot shot don't you? But you're aint," said Jeremy.

"All right, all right, you are not only gaining your f***ing confidence, damn it, but you're also getting cocky! —I have heard enough of you. Just shut your f***ing trap, or else I'll do it for you! If you were not my brother, I would have kicked your mother f***ing ass—you bitch. Now that I have that off my chest, I feel better. Ok, enough of that. Now, when it comes to our next operation, let's plan it for this coming Monday.

"I'll go to town today and talk to our friend Tim Rolner, and I am going to tell him we need your helicopter expertise one more time to do our next f***ing job. We paid him handsomely last time, and I don't think he is going to refuse us this time. So, are we in?" said Roger.

"Ya, I am in," said Jeremy.

"How about you Ray, are you in?" asked Roger.

"Weeeeeell," said Ray. Roger stopped in the middle of his path, and so did the rest. Then Roger turned toward Ray and accosted him by coming really close to his face and then blurted, "What the f***! What does it mean weeeeeell? Don't tell me you are backing off or scared, you b**ch. I'll kill you myself if you back off. Did you hear me? There is no weeeeeell here— you're in and no questions asked—is that clear!" said Roger. Ray, realizing Roger's temper and his determination, succumbed to Roger's will and said, "Well —I suppose it is all right, I'm in, I am in! Now that you have twisted my f***ing arm, I don't have much choice here, do I?" said Ray.

"No, you don't! And if I sense you are thinking to stop partnering, you know what I am going to do to you don't you!" said Roger.

"Yes, I do," said Ray.

"Excellent, that is more like it! So now—we're all in the agreement. Then, I'll consider it's done," said Roger.

Drake heard these faint noises, as if they were coming from a certain distance. He held the cloth that covered the front windowpane and swung it slightly to his left so that he could have a peek at the sound source. Lo and behold, it was his worst nightmare just now materializing right before his eyes.

The bank robbers were approximately a little bit over half a football field away in the distance due west of the shanty. Drake espied three male adults afoot, trading cheek by jowl, wearing camouflaged attires, and wielding rifles and a shotgun. They were advancing to the shack where Mr. Henklin succumbed to his life-sucking wound. Also, there were two loose bloodhound Beagles, they were leading the path to the shack.

"If the bank robbers are the occupants of this crappy place, then I should consider them 'very dangerous' because they have robbed banks, murdered this bank president, possibly raped many women during their courses of the criminal carrier, and who knows what other scandalous and egregious deeds they may have all occupied their lives with and are culpable of. However, now that they are hiding in such boondocks where no one could suspect or find them out here—that is smart, very smart indeed," thought Drake.

Drake's heart began to pound fast in his chest. His blood pressure became elevated; Fear gripped every fiber of his being. He thought to himself, "What now; what the heck am I going to do? How am I going to get the hell out of here alive? I didn't come here for this crap, and I didn't come here to die. I don't want trouble, nor do I want to become like Mr. Henklin. I have to think, and I have to think fast and get the hell out of here, hopefully alive and in one piece before they get here."

Suddenly, the two leading Beagles began to canter towards the shack. Drake thought, "This should be indicative of the obvious; the people who are heading toward the shanty are the dwellers of this ramshackle log cabin."

Drake also thought that "They may just be innocent hunters and that they are returning back to their shack, and some Godforsaken miscreants followed Mr. Henklin other than these three fellows and shot him while these people were out. But, on second thought, if that was the case, then why didn't they take the money in the makeshift coffer that was set against one of the walls of the living room and skedaddled?" Thought Drake and made his mind up.

"It must be certain that these are the three that were the culprits for the bank robbery and the murder of the bank president." Drake thought, "I am not going to wait and find out what they are going to do with me. If I could just only get rid of these dogs, I could have a real chance to escape out of here safely, because as soon as I fire a shot, these people are going to split up and hide. That will be my real chance to bust out of here and escape, then hide. But, if the dogs were alive, they would follow my scent and reveal my hiding position, and then my corollary would not be pleasant. As a matter of fact, it might also cause my death," Drake thought.

Drake was in a quandary. He thought, "I have two options here; I either have to capitulate to these alleged nefarious miscreants and face the inevitable horrid consequences that may entail my unfortunate demise, or waste them two beautiful dogs to get away from these ostensible ruffians."

Drake pulled his .45 Caliber pistol and trained the barrel on the dogs. He waited until they were close enough. The dogs attained Drake's scent and began to bark furiously as they continued in their scamper to reach the shack.

The three men didn't make much of their barks, as if they thought the dogs were barking at a small animal, maybe a skunk or a squirrel, because they didn't suspect anyone would find this place.

Suddenly, the sound of a quick-firing of two gunshot rounds from the .45 Caliber pistol shattered the natural silence of the milieu. Both dogs suddenly executed an immediate summersault accompanied by a few rolls on one of their sides; both delivered a plangent howl and then gave up their ghosts. They laid motionless with definite expressions of agony on their visage.

The three men heard the blast. Roger extended his right arm into the air, signaling the crew to stop, and all three stopped dead in their tracks. Jeremy, he is the shortest one of the three, turned his face to Roger and said, "Oh sh** Roger—a gunfire! We are in big f***ing trouble now. We are toast, damn it! I don't know about you guys, but I don't want to go back to prison. And—and it looks like whoever it was—sh**, somebody shot your f***ing dogs. You see guys—they are not moving. I think they're dead!

They must have found us. Dog gone it! I told you guys so many f***ing times, we need to move out of here, and nooooo, you didn't want to listen. Didn't you fellows think that eventually, someone was going to find us out here and report us to the f***ing authority?" said Jeremy with a concerned look on his face.

"Shut your f***ing trap, Jeremy, or I will do it for you! We'll deal with this our way. We 're not going to run from trouble; we 're gonna get that bastard, whoever he is, whether it be a Cop or otherwise. He is not getting out of here alive—you will see," said Roger.

"Those couple of shots sounded like .45 Caliber pistol. I know my guns, and I'll bet my life on it. It is not a rifle—so right now, we must be out of his range. He is not going to shoot in our direction, and he knows it well. He is going to wait until we get close enough so that we will become his next target for his f***ing trophy just as he did with my, with---my---dogs, that son---of---a---bitch! —these were my two beautiful goddam dogs. He is going to pay for it with his dear f***ing life I promise you that.

"Whoever he is took a very good shot at my dogs. That was still some distance. He shot them both and didn't miss a single shot. Not everyone can do that as well as he or she did. I would say very few and far between. He must be an expert in handling .45-Caliber pistol. We are not dealing with an amateur here, ladies."

"Listen up; let's disperse now. He may be a Cop on our tail," said Roger.

"Don't be silly. He is not the Cop. He can't be. First, I would say, Cops don't carry .45-Caliber pistols. You both should know that by now. Second, Cops don't kill dogs. Hay Jeremy, didn't you shoot that bastard banker dead," said Ray emphatically.

"I reckon I did. You all saw that didn't you, and you all realized that he wasn't moving when we left. I think he should definitely be dead by now," said Jeremy.

"Then who is that A**hole that shot your dogs, Roger?" asked Ray Jenkin. He was the tallest of the two brothers. He stood a little over six feet in height, built well, all muscles, and not an ounce of fat on him. He must have been working out and watching his diet.

Ray usually shaves his head bald. He had a thick mustache above his lips and was in his early thirties. Again, he is an escapee, wanted by Minnesota state authorities. Ray operated a shotgun.

"You are very right—Ray. I didn't see that. He couldn't be a police officer; good observation. That is why I have you on my team. Cops don't carry .45s; they also don't kill dogs. You are right. In that case, it could be any f***ing passer-by, the banker's uncle, or his brother or his father—who gives a f***. What really matters is that he's gonna be a dead man soon.

Ok fellows, as I have said, let's disperse now and let's get that son of a bitch, whoever he is, before he escapes in this freaking wilderness. I hate to see that f***ing bastard get away, especially when he killed two of my beautiful f***ing dogs. He is gonna pay a big f***ing price for that. I assure you.

All right Jeremy you're gona take your left; Ray and I, we are gona take the right, is that clear to everyone."

They both responded with affirmative "yes."

"Ok ladies, let's go kick ass, oh—and Jeremy, please don't get shot—you hear me? I have lots of plans for you!"

"Ok, Yah, I hear you bro."

"Let's move it," said Roger.

All along, Drake was observing their moves. He knew before hand, that they were going to disperse themselves, and they were going to plan for his demise. Drake came to conclusion that now without shadow of a doubt, he is the hunted game here.

"This is not what I came here for damn it," said Drake to himself. Although this was the most opportune time for him to escape, but thought to himself, "I can't let these bastards go on doing what they are doing, committing crimes and hurting people. That is not acceptable. They must be stopped now—otherwise, they are going to cause much more mayhem in the society."

At this moment, despite his fears and concerns, it was an obvious decision for Drake. He decided to stay and fight to end their godforsaken criminal deeds. However, it wasn't going to be an easy task. Three against one and didn't have a clue as to how well they can shoot, but Drake already had his plan made.

He ran out the door like a bat out of hell and made an immediate right turn. He slipped and fell a couple of times but picked himself up quickly and continued to run.

Drake hid himself behind the shanty. Leaned against the west wall and pointed the barrel of the gun upward, and with both hands gripped tight the gun handle, and rested his finger on the trigger. He extended his head slightly forward from the corner of the wall and suddenly caught sight of Jeremy approaching fast from the east and heading in his direction just as he thought he would do.

Drake waited until Jeremy came close enough, and suddenly, he jumped right out and shot him twice in a fast sequence, one to the head and the other to the heart. The force of the shot pushed Jeremy back a few feet and threw him off balance then quickly fell flat on his back and did not move.

Drake ran fast toward Jeremy and saw most of his head wasn't there and that he was gone to meet his maker. Drake quickly took his clothes off and put on Jeremy's clothes on, but it didn't fit him that well; he also wore Jeremy's green hat. "This will do for now," he thought to himself.

Drake grabbed Jeremy by the arms and pulled him behind a large tree. He took hold of his rifle, pulled the round out of the chamber, and hid it in his own pants that were on the ground along with the rest of his clothes. He then came out into the open approximately twenty feet south of the tree and placed his .45-Caliber gun on the ground approximately four feet away from where he stood and held onto the rifle. He waited for them to come to the scene. Drake was expecting them to show up soon, and just as he thought, Roger and Ray came into view.

"You wait here Ray, and cover my ass," said Roger. They were right where Drake was behind the shack up against the west wall before he killed Jeremy.

"Is that you Jeremy," yelled Roger.

"Yah, it's me Jeremy," yelled Drake.

"Did you get him," asked Roger.

"Oh, yah you bet your ass I did, come and see, the bastard is dead as he can be," said Drake.

"Great job, Jeremy—I am coming right now. I knew I could count on you. You came a long way. I am gonna make a man out of you after all," yelled Roger. "All right, Ray, it looks like you don't have to stay here and cover my ass. We got this son of a bitch dead just as I promised, didn't I?" said Roger.

"Yes, you did," said Ray.

"Many kudos to you Jeremy," yelled Roger.

"Hey Ray, let's go, let's go see Jeremy, and we'll break out the beers and celebrate, then he will tell us everything about how he got this, whoever the f*** he was. This is what he gets for killing my dogs, my two beautiful dogs," said Roger.

Drake was still holding the rifle with both hands, pretending that he is Jeremy, and when Roger and Ray came at a shooting distance, Drake threw himself on the ground and quickly picked up his .45-Caliber pistol, rolled a few times, and before he got on his feet he shot both Roger and Ray.

The impact of the rounds pushed them both backwards, and they fell like a log on a mass of foliage and hard ground.

"You shot me Jeremy. Why the f*** did you do that for, and why in the hell did you shoot Ray?" yelled Roger. Roger's abdomen was bleeding heavily, and he was covering it with both hands.

Ray, on the other hand, was approximately fifteen feet away from Roger, and when he got shot, pieces of his brain splattered everywhere like a bevy of birds hearing the sound of gunfire and all flying at once in every direction. Ray died instantly. Most of his head was missing when he hit the ground.

Drake walked slowly toward Roger until there was about five feet of distance between them.

"What the f***! —you're aint Jeremy," said Roger.

"Well—I am sorry. I suppose the truth is out. As you see, I lied, and you are right: I am not Jeremy. Sorry to disappoint you." said Drake with a cold stare laced with a slight smirk on his face.

"What did you do to my brother, you bastard, mother f***er you! Where is he? What did you do to him?" asked Roger emphatically, and at the same time, the blood was oozing out of his mouth as he burst out in a few coughs.

"Well let's say, he is a sound asleep here. He is not looking to get up any time soon. As matter of fact, his sole is not in his body. His sole is feeling big time hot right now as matter of fact his sole is experiencing the flames. So, he is not around to give anyone anymore trouble, isn't that nice for a change?" said Drake.

"You killed him, didn't you, didn't you? He was my brother damn it. f*** you, you mother f***er," said Roger and spat on him, half blood and half saliva.

"Well, it was going to be either him or me. I thought it would be better for him rather than! Don't you think so? You understand that, don't you?" said Drake with a calm and controlled voice.

"Ray—Ray where are you," said Roger with a faint expression.

"Well, you don't want to disturb Ray right now. He is going to be asleep for a long long time like your brother is, but with half of his brain is gone, I wonder if he could still get up from his sleep," said Drake.

"You killed him too, didn't you!" said Roger.

"Welllll—did you guys give me any other choice? — noooooo. Soon, you are going to meet your friends and your brother in hell. I call it an "eternal summer" where you can bask in the hottest flames. Hello, barbeque time and you, you will never have to feel cold chills anymore as you may be feeling right now, because you are oozing lots of blood. And perhaps you will be walking naked without your balls, and the demons will have a way with you. Maybe then, you can sing soprano loud and clear, where everyone could hear your agonizing song and perhaps your cronies will be nice to you and sing a dirge or two for you. Of course, then your eyeballs will be bulging out of their sockets, and your mouth will be gaping wide for all eternity where it is, as I have said, hot and very painful always; you might even forget your name. Ouch. Oh, by the way, I didn't get your name!" asked Drake.

"My name is f*** you," said Roger vehemently. Drake let a slight smirk on his face.

"Well, nice to meet you, Mr. f***you," said Drake

While Roger laid on the ground and on his back, he swiveled his head to the left and saw his rifle a couple of feet away from where he was laying and attempted to reach for it.

"It is amazing that you still got life in you, die-hard kind, aren't you? However, I don't know from where you get your strength. I should have hit you where it counted. But I suppose I wasn't that good of a shooter, and for your information, I wouldn't do that if I were you," said Drake.

"Why don't you just f***ing shoot me right now and get it over with—you f***ing Sh** Head," said Roger.

"Do you really want me to do that?" asked Drake.

Roger managed to wrap his fingers around the rifle, but struggled to lift it off the ground. He lost lots of blood and was near his end.

"Do you need any help lifting that rifle? Apparently, you can't lift it up yourself. Here, let me help you," said Drake, and went close toward his hand that was clutching the rifle and stepped on his clutched fingers with his boots and yanked the rifle out of his hand, and Roger screamed aloud in pain.

"Well, I suppose I lied again. When am I going to quit lying? I am not going to give you your rifle back to you. I am a bad boy, but for once, I am going to be a nice guy, and I am not going to give you your rifle back to you lest you hurt yourself with it. Oh, mannnn, here I go again lying. I suppose it is a habit with me, and I can't seem to quit," said Drake.

"Why don't you just shut your mother f***ing mouth and finish me off right now, you a**hole," said Roger.

"I would like to know one thing before I finish you out, you piece of garbage. Did you kill that banker who is lying dead with the pull of blood on the floor inside your filthy rotten and stinking abode?" asked Drake. Roger broke into a derisive laugh. "No, I didn't. But I wished I did. It was my brother whom you f***ing shot, you Son of a bitch," said Roger.

"You mean that one?" said Drake and pointed his hand toward Jeremy.

"Ya that one, you f***ing a**hole," said Roger.

"Well, I hate doing this. I hate being a nice guy; you know It is hard work to be a nice guy these days, don't you think so? I tell you what I am going to do for you; I am going to remain a nice person—and have you unite with your buddies down in hell. How about that; do you like that, but only if you insist." Drake didn't wait for his answer and shot him right between the eyes, and there was no more head left on Roger's neck. Pieces of his brain and blood splattered everywhere.

"Oh boy, you really made a lot of mess here with your stinking brain parts. I wonder, who is going to clean your sh** now," said Drake. He turned around and walked rather calmly toward dead Jeremy. There was no one else who was going to give him heat. He got back in his own clothes, wore Jeremy's green baseball cap, pulled the rifle bullet from his pant pocket, glared at it for a few seconds, tossed it up about a foot in the air, then grabbed it right back and placed it back in his pant pocket.

Drake decided not to leave any evidence of his involvement here. He went around and collected his spent or fired rounds from the ground, including the lead portion that struck those three thugs and placed them in his pant pocket.

He lumbered toward the front of the shack, picked up his camping gear from the living room of the shanty, and for a few seconds, he glared at the coffer that was full of money and decided to leave it alone.

CHAPTER 18

The shanty was a scuzzy place. There were remnants of food, and lots of dried-up blood on the walls and on the floor. There were animal feculents laced with disgusting stench. Drake knew he needed to exit this environment expeditiously.

The scent of the blood plasma and the fecal matter inside the shanty would have attracted many wild, undesirable, and life–threatening animals and insects to find their way here. For Drake to fend them off, it would have been an arduous or onerous task. Drake exited through the front door and went outside to continue his camping endeavors.

The sunrays were pummeling the earth straight down and indiscriminately through the thicket, timber, and weald. A few white patchy clouds braved the blue sky and hung suspended in the air, and the ephemeral haze succumbed to the heat of the daylight radiance and then abandoned its presence from sight just as Drake thought it would happen.

Drake glanced at his wristwatch, and it registered at 11:52 AM. He felt the hunger pain was slowly rearing its head, and the physical weakness was creeping into his body. He thought it was the time for his repast.

As Drake carried on in his stride, he pulled another energy bar from his haversack and began to masticate. The thought of hunting animals and eviscerating their flash for food was not in his DNA. Drake made certain to bring enough assorted energy bars that would sustain him for at least ten days and possibly more.

Drake maintained his pace northeast direction and found a small and clear footpath with the same footprints as he had witnessed previously. *"These footprints must belong to the three deceased thugs,"* he thought and decided to follow their track to see where it would lead. After half an hour of hiking, he caught sight of frogs. They were many, and some were with their tadpoles. The frogs were everywhere: on the ground, on the tree branches; many were jumping and leaping here and there. Their noises were overwhelming. Their vocabulary consisted of one word, "Ribbit," with much reiteration. Their sizes were approximately four inches in length. They had large dark spots with pale brown borders on their backsides and legs.

He thought maybe their presence here would be indicative of water nearby and paced a few more minutes, then came to the edge of a cliff. He glanced at the great open expense that was before his eyes; he also captured the sight of the glade down below.

In the middle of the meadow, he saw a large lake called "Lake Horseshoe." Patchy green and brown grass with huge and dense Ponderosa pine trees surrounded the lake. At a distance to his northwest, there were a few mountains having their peaks covered with white and patchy clouds. Drake thought this was an ideal place to rest his weary bones and decided to camp here for the night when dusk arrived.

As Drake began to descend toward the lake, he suddenly froze his movements and trained his eyes to the sky in amazement. He hunkered instinctively for his protection, but his eyes remained wide open and never left the sight off the descending object.

Drake was in total consternation and disbelief; a meteor or an asteroid was out of the question. He noticed the object had definite features of a flying machine, such as wings, tails, and a fuselage. This object was blazing brilliantly in flight and in its appearance. The air friction must have contributed to the fiery radiance, as the craft was plunging at a breakneck speed toward Mt. Adams.

Drake realized that this flying thing had most likely never been seen by the general population except possibly by the military. It appeared extremely advanced in design and technology.

"Could this vessel be an American top-secret jet fighter and the U.S. government is conducting a secret flight test away from the general population? And if so, then I should have known about it and the question is—why wasn't I informed?" for a little while, this thought had consumed Drake's mind. *"I have a top-secret clearance from the United State government to be privy to every top-secret project the government would ever be involved with, and why I'm not aware of this vessel? On second thought, could this vessel, which just landed on Earth, be alien in its origin? If so, then this would be my first. This vessel appears very different in every aspect of a regular jet fighter, also bigger in size."*

Drake carefully descended toward the lake down below, found a flat and arid spot under a large pine tree, and decided to camp there in the eventide. He glanced straight forward, faced northeast towards Mt. Adams and thought, *"I must go now while there is still sufficient daylight and find this strange looking vessel then return back before the nightfall. This vessel can't be too far off from here"*, thought Drake.

Drake pulled a map from his backpack, ascertained his position in respect to the area he witnessed the craft that could have landed, and determined the amount of time he needed to reach his destination. According to the map in his hand, the area where he was depicted was a forest, and the forest should extend approximately two and a half more miles beyond where he was standing, but it was going to be an uphill climb. Behind the forest and Mt Adams, there should be a vast open and flat land, mostly consisting of rocks, sand, small vegetation, and small life forms, including insects and arachnoids.

The unearthly flying vessel was nearing its touchdown on a horizontal but rough lava bed that was approximately 6.5 miles north of Mt Adams. The landing spot had an elevation of approximately 4800 to 5000 feet. However, it was lower than the rest of the Mt. Adam.

There were approximately fifty feet of air space left for this vessel to make contact with the terra firma. Its short delta wing-end mounted ion propelled engines flipped upward like that of the V22 Osprey (U.S. military aircraft).

The craft's brilliantly lit ion exhaust nozzles were now pointing downward, and at the same time, three byzantine and hefty hydraulically actuated landing gears that were two under the wings and one under the canopy having circular landing pods with flat bottoms slowly extended downward for the vessel to make its touchdown.

As the craft slowly neared its descent toward the ground. The force of its engine thrusts instantly created plumes of dust and debris that hovered tumultuously in the air and obscured the craft from sight. And when the landing pods just made their contact on the ground, the engines silenced, and when the dust settled, the craft came into view and appeared to be a gunship, formidable in appearance and in size. Its fuselage was like that Of a drone beetle. This craft could seat two in tandem. Its canopy is located on the top of the craft and very front from the fuselage.

The vessel's short delta wings proceeded from the front end and extended on either side of the canopy, which ended in the middle of the fuselage. Under its wings hung the big gun turrets that spewed destructive and deadly ion-charged projectiles. The rear section of the fuselage was flat and wide; it housed two vertically extended, geometrically elaborate fins on either of its sides. When the gunship landed on its pods, there was approximately six feet of space between the ground and the bottom of the gunship.

After a little while, the hovering dust settled and moments later, the glass-like canopy slowly surged upward to allow the pilot to dislodge from the craft. Sakreg pushed a few buttons at the bottom of his flight helmet, and suddenly, evanescent gray vaper jettisoned from either side of it.

Sakreg slowly pulled his helmet off his head and placed it on his lap. He immediately felt the gentle warmth of the sun embracing the exposed parts of his body, more like his head and his neck; he felt comforted by it, thinking the temperature was just right and balmy.

Sakreg braved and took a deep breath to examine the atmosphere's influence in his lungs to determine if the air was suitable for breathing. After taking a deep breath, he felt well and energized, just as his flight computer suggested that the atmosphere would be suitable for breathing.

Sakreg didn't find the need to wear his helmet and his air supply pack. He placed them both on the floor of the cockpit, then stood up and jumped to the ground. The translucent canopy began to descend to its original closed state.

Sakreg took a few steps away, then turned around and faced his craft. He circled around it to witness if there were any damages that he may have incurred during the flight to earth and realized there was none and felt relived.

On Sakreg's wrist, there was a rectangular gadget approximately six inches long by two inches wide. This gadget was able to control the functions of his spacecraft from a remote location. He pushed a few of its buttons to locate and secure its coordinates and at the same time, he made the craft go invisible in plain sight.

Sakreg turned his head to the right and faced east. His eyes embraced the long-starched lava bed full of small and large rocks, and then he turned and faced south; he witnessed the ascending patchy snow-covered slopes of Mt Adams. His first impression was that—this planet is very similar to the planet he came from. He witnessed jagged-edged rocks, large and small, strewed everywhere and thought the absence of life on this stretch of land was somewhat disconcerting. For Sakreg, not finding a life-sustaining substance such as water anywhere nearby was a thought-provoking and fear-fomenting situation.

He hopped to witness large or small size life forms around him, possibly for food, but to his dismay, there were none. However, he was very excited in a different way, he could reach a different planet all by himself and walk on its ground where no one else of his ilk has ever gone this far—especially to a different galaxy.

Sakreg felt proud and thought, *"This could definitely be a great accomplishment in my life. I will surely have plenty to talk about my journey and my newly found planet. My peers may consider me a hero once I get back home, and that is, if I ever get back home, or maybe I will be remembered in their space-travel history books as a pioneer of intergalactic traveler who risked his life to get such unreachable information about life on a distant planet in a distant galaxy."*

Sakreg turned and faced westward direction. At approximately one hundred feet or so away from his present position, he noticed a dried up and defoliated short trees with bare branches, and just beyond them, there were boulders, rocks, and detritus.

Sakreg knelt and picked raw sun-backed earth from the ground. He glared at it for a few seconds while he pulverized it in his hand and allowed the gravel to slip from between his fingers. He thought the contents, the texture, the color of the sand and the gravel were like that of his home planet. He then went a little further and picked a few rocks approximately the size of his palm and began to examine their features, their weights, and their densities. Then he let them fall freely to the ground.

Sakreg stood for a moment and breathed a deep breath; he felt the aromatic scent of the forest nearby and allowed the feeling of nostalgia to creep into his mind. The realization of his being here in a very different world fascinated him. But this also meant that there would be a good deal of possibility that he would have to spend the rest of his life here and away from his friends and loved ones, and he felt like **a stranger under a distant sun.**

Sakreg mused about his family; this, in turn, allowed him to embrace the thoughts of good times he shared with them and cracked a slight smile. But soon, he lost his cheerfulness and thought he may never be able to witness or experience their presence, their expressions, their thoughts, their conversation ever again and allowed a few teardrops to roll down his cheeks. Sakreg didn't stop there; he allowed his mind to wonder about and reminisce the good times he had with his friends, the foods that he ate, the drinks that he drank, the laughter that he laughed at, and all the fun that he had with his colleagues. He managed to crack a gentle smile as he thought of his good times. However, moments later, he woke out of his reverie and forced himself to think a different kind of thought. Now that he was here, he decided to forget the past, put it all behind him, and begin to concentrate on the issues at hand to make the best of the situation he was in at that moment. Sakreg knew, at this moment, there was not much he could do to get himself back home.

Now that Sakreg's feet were on unfamiliar ground, the first and most important objective was to survive on this unknown and mysterious planet by finding food and life-sustaining fluids to keep him alive. Second, he must learn quickly what is harmful, what is not, what is edible, and what is not.

He glanced all around and saw no one, no movement of any life form, and the reality had set in his heart that he was all alone here. The only thing he could hear and see was the howling of the wind and the gentle swaying of the tree branches under a slight breeze. There was no one to talk to, and no one to share thoughts with or break a laugh with someone.

However, Sakreg felt that there was no eminent danger that lurked around him. For a moment, a feeling of safety embraced his mind. He gazed at the green forest up ahead that was almost all around him and decided to head toward it, which he caught sight of before he landed.

Sakreg realized the 'color' of the vegetation was very different from the planet he came from. However, on a happy note, from the temperature and the atmosphere standpoint, they were suitable to sustain him on earth.

Suddenly, Sakreg's ears captured a rattling sound. It was sufficiently loud to a point where one must heed and find its source. He gazed all around to locate its position, but couldn't, and thought that was odd. *"What could cause such a rattling sound."* Sakreg appeared perplexed and somewhat frightened, not knowing the origin of the sound.

Sakreg pulled his hand-held weapon, pointed it straight, and began to move slowly and aimlessly in many directions. At first, he thought, who or whatever is making this noise must be an invisible life form, and its intent could be to do harm.

As Sakreg moved closer toward the boulders, the sound became louder and louder. He instantly realized there must be something going on at the big rocks, and decided to get close to them, and when he arrived at the scene, his eyes beheld the sight of a large seven feet long, coiled rattlesnake laying at the bottom of one of the boulders.

The presence of the snake mesmerized Sakreg. He has never seen such a coiled life form. Furthermore, he realized this life specimen did not possess any legs or arms and thought about how the creature should mobilize itself from one place to another. He thought that, surely, this animal would not stay here for the rest of its life. This thing must be able to move somehow and find food and sustenance otherwise, it wouldn't survive.

Sakreg was intrigued by the coiled animal in its anatomy and slowly came close to it to ascertain its physiology, but the snake suddenly postured by elevating its head approximately two feet above the ground. It glared attentively at Sakreg with a slivering, forked tongue. It swayed its head back and forth and sideways to maintain its concentration on him.

Sakreg decided to get closer to the snake thinking it may not move from its present position. Suddenly the snake lunged its body forward with great speed, having its mouth agape, displaying its enormous and formidable fangs to sink them into Sakreg's body. Sakreg backed off rather swiftly to evade the snake's bite and fell on the ground—back first.

He realized this life form, whatever it was, must be jeopardous, especially after witnessing the two large frontal fangs of the snake; it truly alarmed him and brought fear into his heart, but soon he concluded that if left alone, it would not attack or cause harm to anyone. He decided to move on and thought this was not a good specimen to eat for sustenance.

Sakreg got back on his feet, placed his hand-held weapon back in its holster, and dusted his pants. The snake suddenly began to move away. Sakreg's eyes became wide open in an expression of obfuscation, thinking how this animal could conduct such motion without legs, and thought this was very, very strange. In his mind, he thought it defied the laws of nature.

Sakreg decided to move on. He chose a heading approximately 200° south, southwest direction, and thought he would surely find plenty of life forms and possibly some of them could be edible and perhaps find water to sustain him inside this thick woodland.

Sakreg gingerly ambled towards the forest up ahead. He exchanged his footsteps on a rough ground saturated with large and small jagged-edged rocks and boulders. Along the way, he noticed a few small animals, such as lizards, that were cravenly scurrying from the danger and were attempting to acquire cover under the rocks. Large hairy spiders and beetles were absconding from his sight and were seeking a hiding place under the rocks. Despite all these visual experiences, he decided not to pursue them for a meal, for they were faster than he was and were quickly disappearing from his sight. Sakreg decided to continue forward toward the forest.

CHAPTER 19

Suddenly, Sakreg heard a fast reverberating but faint sound coming from a certain distance. He turned around and faced east; low and behold—he witnessed an encapsulated metallic object with four round and black in color turning gizmos under it. It was moving slowly, and to top that, it was moving toward his direction. Sakrag glowered in perplexity, not knowing what it could be. He came to his senses and thought that this moving object could be a means of land transport, and if so, there should be an intelligent life form managing it.

The vehicle teetered and tottered as it moved over the large and small rocks. Joshua Albiino was making the wheels. Suddenly, he moved his head slightly forward to ascertain what his eyes were beholding. Joshua's orbs widened in surprise as if he were witnessing an anomaly.

Joshua locked his sight upon Sakreg for a few seconds and attempted to glean Sakerg's physical features from a distance but had trouble consummating his thoughts. He realized that the entity that he caught sight of was somewhat different from the rest of humanity. However, he had a hard time believing that there would be anyone here besides them, and at the same time, all the passengers in the car were looking out of their respective windows and were visually ascertaining the terrain and absorbing the scene in their minds that the environment provided for them.

Suddenly, Josh pressed hard on his brake peddle, and the gray Land Rover SUV came to a sudden stop. There were four people beside the driver: three in the back seat and one in the front passenger seat. They were all young and restless and were eager to find means to entertain themselves and have a good time.

As the vehicle came to a sudden stop, they all spontaneously ejected forward out of their seats and bumped at each other, knocking their heads on the ceiling of the vehicle more than a few times.

*"Why the f***! Did you do that? Why did you have to stop like that, Josh? I almost had my head go through the windshield,"* asked James Chillingham, loud and perturbed. He was sitting in front of the passenger seat. He was peering outside through the passenger window and was enjoying the rugged scenery at the time when Josh brought the vehicle to a sudden stop.

"Ya, why did you have to stop like that Josh? I bumped my head so hard on the ceiling I am seeing double now. Are there two of you?" asked Ralph Ritecliff.

"What happened Josh, did you hit something?" responded the passengers from the backseat.

"No, I didn't."

"Then what the f*** is wrong with you, Josh? Were you hallucinating?" asked James.

*"No, I wasn't hallucinating, damn it. Did you all see that f***ing thing out there!"* asked Josh excitedly but having a bewildered expression on his face as if he had seen a specter and was pointing his index finger at the front windshield.

*"What thing. What the f*** you are talking about?"* asked Ralph.

*"Tell us Josh, what were we supposed to see besides rocks and f****ing sun-baked ground,"* said Steve Mayhen.

"You guys are not going to believe what I am about to tell you. I saw this tall-looking thing, a human-like creature, walking upright about half a football field away ahead of us, and I think he hid behind that, that large rock over there, slightly on your right. Do you guys see that rock?" asked Josh excitedly.

*"Are you serious, a f***ing human-like creature? Are you serious? Was it hairy? If it was, then definitely it would have been a Sasquatch?"* asked Steve.

*"No, not even close. I kid you not. That thing looked slim and very tall, wearing a black body-hugging suit in this hot f***ing weather, mind you, and in the middle of nowhere—go figure,"* said Josh.

"This is not a joke, is it?" asked Steve.

"Come on, guys, why would I want to kid you? Trust me, that was the strangest-looking thing I ever saw," said Josh.

"Actually, I don't think any of us saw anything like what you are describing, Josh. I am beginning to worry about you," said Ralph.

*"Because none of you were paying f***ing attention to what was going on in front of you. Anyway, I would say let's all get out and find out what that thing is all about,"* said Josh.

"What! Are you crazy? What if that thing that you are talking about could kill us all, if what you allege seeing is right?" said James.

"Come on man, we are adults here and five of us here, and he is one. I believe we could take him on if we had to. Besides, we came here to have fun and adventure, didn't we?" said Josh.

"I agree with Josh. I don't think he is lying. I think he sow something rather unusual. I say let's do it. As Josh said, we are five, and that thing, whatever it is, is one. Besides, we have rifles and shotguns. What could go wrong with us, ha," said Steve.

"All right Steve, you've made your point. I would say let's do it," said Samuel Neyms. They all disembarked from the SUV, picked their rifles and shotguns from the trunk of the vehicle. Samuel yelled, *"Lock and load,"* and they all walked toward the creature slowly and apprehensively, wielding their weapons in their hands and not knowing what to expect from the unknown life form.

"I say let's open fire as soon as we see that thing," said James, who was the youngest in the group. He had a certain fearful look about him.

"Not so fast, hot-shot. I don't want you to be a trigger-happy camper, do you hear me?" said Josh.

"All right, whatever you say boss," said James in a trembling voice.

"that is more like it," said Josh.

"Where is that thing, anyway? Did anyone see him yet?" asked Ralph.

"I think that thing should be behind that big boulder Josh said. It can't be anywhere else. Otherwise, we would have seen him by now," said Steve.

*"Look, fellas that thing can be very dangerous. I would say, let's all get back in the car and get the f***! Out of here,"* said James.

"Oh James, don't be such a f***ing wuss. Have some guts, will you? We don't see this kind of thing every day," said Josh.

"I don't care if we don't see this kind of thing every day!" said James. Suddenly, everyone stopped for a moment and scowled at James's skittish attitude.

"I suppose no one is going to listen to me!" said James.

*"Shut the f***up, James. We're all in this together, like it or not. However, you can stay in the car all you want, but remember we can't be there to help you if things go wrong with you where you are. A Sasquatch may come and kick your ass, or worst, maybe it will have a way with your ass, or maybe it will be hungry and have you for lunch,"* said Steve.

"All right, all right, you've made your f***ing point. You don't need to continue!" said James with a disappointed expression.

Sakreg felt restless. His heart pounded hard in its cage, not knowing who or what these walking being were. He knew he had nowhere to run and had no choice but to face these unknown beings. Sakreg began to ruminate. *"These beings are getting very close. They must have found me, and the thing that they are carrying must be some sort of weapon, and they must be out to kill me!"* His hand went to his side to heave his hand-held weapon, but he thought again, *"Maybe if they see me unarmed, they may not shoot at me. I don't want to frighten them more than I already have,"* so he abandoned the thought of using his weapon.

"We're getting close. Let's split into two groups and surround this thing so he won't get away. Is that clear to you all," asked Josh. Everyone said, *"Yah."*

"All right then, Steve, I want you to come with me, and the rest of you go around from the north. Steve and I will take the south," said Josh

Just then, Sakreg stood up slowly and glared at them furiously, and in his mind, he was saying, *"So this is what the intelligent life looks like here on this planet. They look ugly and small. I could surely take on all of them if I had to."*

The five earthlings became flabbergasted, with expressions of horror on their faces. Everyone took a few steps back and almost lost their balance.

James lost it all together and attempted to run but fell on the ground from the fear of the alien. His heart raced. His body began to sweat. His hands began to tremble. He thought he wasn't going to make it out of here alive. However, he managed to pick himself up slowly so he wouldn't startle Sakreg in any way.

"Look here fellas he is not armed. I don't want anyone to point their weapons at him or shoot unless our lives are in danger. Is that clear to everyone," said Josh. He was the oldest in the group.

"Ya, we heard you," responded everyone.

"Good," said Josh.

"My god, that's an ugly and angry-looking alien we're looking at, as if he wants to kill us all," said James.

"Yes, I agree that's an ugly and angry and fearsome-looking son of a bitch we're looking at. But he fears us as much as we fear him," said Josh.

"I think we should kill him right now before he does anything to hurt us," said Samuel. He heaved his shotgun and pointed right at Sakreg. Sakreg pulled his weapon swiftly out of its holster, let loose a crimson-colored effulgent round, and struck Samuel's shotgun. The shotgun flew right out of Samuel's hands, and when it landed on the ground, it appeared mangled and was smoking from the excess heat. Samuel immediately lifted both his arms up in the air in a display of surrender.

*"What the f*** were you thinking? He was just about to fry your ass, Samuel. Why in the f*** did you do that when I said no one to shoot unless our lives were at stake? Your hardihood act could have killed us all!"* Sakreg placed his hand-held weapon back in its holster, thinking the threat was over, because none were pointing their weapons at him.

"As I've said before, I'll say it again: no one is to shoot him unless our lives are in danger. We don't have to act foolhardy, do you all hear me, and we don't want to frighten or niggle this behemoth. Let's see if we can communicate with him instead of killing him," said Josh.

Josh picked a protein bar from his pant pocket, unwrapped the bar, he then slowly brought it to his mouth then extended his arm back toward Sakreg to make him understand that this is a food item. Josh walked slowly toward him and Sakreg extended his arm slowly toward Josh, picked the protein bar from his hand, and then began to nibble on it.

"He is eating. You all see that, right? I am sure he will not harm us if we are nice to him," said Josh. Sakreg liked the taste of the bar and extended his arm once again toward Josh for more.

"He liked it. He wants more. Does anyone have a protein bar?" asked Josh in elation.

"I do," said Ralph and pulled one bar from his front pant pocket and unwrapped the covering; then he approached Sakreg slowly and extended his arm toward Sakreg, and Sakreg picked the bar from Ralph's hand and began to masticate.

*"I say, let's leave him alone and get the f*** out of here before he gets wild with us,"* said James.

"Shut the hell up, James. You're always the scared one, aren't you? Don't worry, we're not going to do anything like Samuel did to alarm him," said Josh.

"Hey guys, that was one hell of a gun that was in his hand. I wonder how much damage it could have done if it would have hit one of us. You all saw what it did to Samuel's shotgun?" said Steve.

"You wouldn't want to find out, and I'm glad we didn't. I want us all to get back home safely. I don't want to explain to your folks how you died," said Josh.

*"All right, what the f*** are we going to do now? You all know that we can't take him back with us, and we can't stay here all day looking at this freaking oversized Godzilla. God knows where he comes from!"* said Samuel.

"I think we should leave him alone and get back to the car and get the hell out of here now," said James.

"I know that's always what you want it anyway," said Josh.

"Do you have any bright ideas? You seem to take charge of us," said James.

"All right I agree with Samuel. We can't stay here all day, and we can't take him back with us. Imagine what the world will think. The government will be on our tail and God knows what they will do with him and with us. Imagine one thing: they will do anything to not get the word of an alien encounter out into the public, even if it came to killing us all," said Josh.

"Then, what is the answer?" asked Ralph.

"All right, we will slowly back off a few steps and then turn around and walk away toward the car and get out of here, and no one will ever talk about this incident. Is everyone in agreement," asked Josh.

"Yah, let's all do what Josh said," said James. They slowly walked backward a few steps and then turned around and walked toward their car. Just around halfway to their car, a large black bear began to charge from south, and it was heading their way.

*"Oh sh**, a huge f***ing black bear is on our tail,"* hollered Ralph from the top of his lungs, and they all began to run as fast as they could to the car, and the bear was slowly gaining on to them fast. Josh stopped for a few seconds, took aim, and discharged a couple of rounds from his rifle. It hit the bear, but he couldn't tell where the round landed. Josh was approximately less than half a football field away when he discharged his rifle. The bear kept on coming. This time, Ralph discharged a few rounds from his shotgun, and that didn't affect the bear.

Ralph, while he was running, suddenly tripped over a rock, lost his balance, and fell to the ground. Josh immediately stopped to pick him up when the bear caught on to josh and swung its huge hairy arm right at Josh's chest. Josh flew about ten feet into the air and landed on one of his sides. The bear then charged at

Ralph, and with its hefty paws, it rolled Ralph onto the ground a few times and attempted to maul him. Ralph screamed his lungs out for help while Josh remained semi-unconscious and sprawled on the ground.

James amazingly lost all his fears, walked bravely toward the bear as if he was in charge, and at the same time discharged a few rounds from his shotgun, but the bear wasn't even fazed, and it only made him more agitated. The bear stopped mauling Ralph and charged after James. Suddenly, Sakreg pulled his hand-held weapon out and fired a plasma round at the bear, and within a few seconds, the bear became pulverized.

James stood silently and glared at the comminuted bear with his mouth agape. James observed, beside the bear's head all that he witnessed was a black soot on the ground. He lifted his head, directed his sight toward Sakreg, and gave him the thumbs up.

Samuel and the rest of the group ran toward James. Steve went to attend to Josh's needs and got him back on his feet.

"James, you f***ing surprised the hell out of me. I didn't think you had it in you to fight this goliath of a bear. Many kudos to you, James. You have overcome your fears and become a man. I am very happy for you." Said Josh, and they all went back, got into their SUV, then turned around and drove in the opposite direction. This time, Steve took the wheels while Josh recuperated in the car.

CHAPTER 20

There was this sense of light-heartedness, the sense of peace that encompassed Sakreg's mind, for the very fact that the danger and the intimidation were no longer present at this moment. He began to tread toward the forest up ahead. He was hopeful that he would find a source of sustenance.

Sakreg huffed and puffed but managed to arrive within fifty feet of the timberland. However, he paused for a minute or two, elevated his head to size the trees up ahead, and ruminated about the dangers that he might be facing by going through it.

Sakreg took a deep breath. He sensed the ubiquitous scent and the aroma of the vegetation nearby; it exhilarated his sense of smell. The color of the trees, branches, and leaves amazed him. Despite the beauty and unconventionally colored forest up ahead that he witnessed, he knew there were going to be many challenges to remain extant in this unknown and rugged territory.

Sakreg felt life inside these pervasive trees could certainly house diverse life forms that could very well enchant and overwhelm him for the very fact that whatever he had witnessed so far, they were all very different from what he had observed or experienced on his own planet. He thought there was going to be much to admire, much to learn and much to dread should he enter the forest alone, but, despite, Sakreg proceeded to move forward. He felt he had no other choice, but to proceed.

The rough ground behind Sakreg certainly was a harsh place to contend with; it provided no source of comfort or sustenance; he felt he would certainly die if he had to remain there.

As Sakreg reached the fringes of the towering trees, he stopped for a moment to hear the forest. He heard the howling wind passing through the trees. He heard the loud and faint chirping of the birds and thought, *"This forest must be rife with life and was beckoning me to venture inside and face the unknown."* Sakreg realized the sounds of the forest were very different from where he came from and didn't know what to make of them. Trepidations he felt. Fear of the unknown slowly snaked into his mind. Despite the fact that he considered the challenges in life to exist, then conquering them was going to be a necessity in one's life's affairs. However, his thoughts began to tell him otherwise. *"Let's turn around, attempt to leave this beautiful but dangerous planet and go home,"* but in his heart, he couldn't accept the thought of defeat, or being conquered by his own fears.

Sakreg trained his mind to be gallant; after all, he was a soldier and a warrior at heart. He should be ready to face the challenges head-on, explore the mysteries, and experience the beauty and the perils of life that awaited him inside this forest, but in all this, to exercise God's given gumption, foresight, and acumen to win over the challenges that awaited him.

Suddenly, Sakreg heard a sound. It was profound to his ears. It was very different from the rest of the sounds he heard so far. It was a high-pitched whistling, or piping sound. He trained his eyes to the sky, and there it was, a large stout golden eagle perching on a treetop approximately sixty feet above his head.

After a moment or two, the eagle suddenly spread its huge wings, and leaped into the air, then flapped her wings a couple of times to gain balance and to remain afloat. It circled gracefully above Sakreg's head more than a few times, than began to descend.   Sakreg's eyes widened, and his mouth remained gapped, he never left the sight of the eagle as it descended to the ground. But what was so amazing in all this was that he had an uncanny peace about this animal he encountered.

The eagle landed approximately twenty feet away from Sakreg. He took a few steps back. He didn't trust his feelings as much as he should. However, he lost his balance and fell to the ground. Sakreg didn't seem to be alarmed by the presence of this bird, but was totally and pleasantly intrigued and astounded.

Sakreg thought his conviction about this flying creature was rather strange and that he shouldn't experience such peaceful feelings. Through his instinct, he determined that this flying creature must be gracefully amicable despite the fact that he had never witnessed such an animal in his life. But, at the same time, he grimaced his face in consternation not understanding the intentions of this creature that was before him.

The Eagle remained on the ground, glaring attentively at Sakreg for a duration of fifteen to twenty seconds or more. Suddenly, the eagle began to waddle slowly towards him, and just when he decided to get back on his feet and get away, the eagle jumped on his abdomen, tottered, towered over his chest, came close to his neck, then glared at him as if she desired of tell him something. Sakreg froze all his movements from sheer ambivalence. Moments passed, the eagle spread its wings across his chest in demonstration of affinity and ardor, then twisted her head to her side, at the same time lowered her neck and her body toward his chest, and quietly rested on him like a baby resting on mother's bosom.

"How strange is this incident? This is odd, very odd indeed. Nothing similar ever happened to me. This is something I can get used to," he thought.

Sakreg felt oblivious as to how to respond to such a pleasant anomaly. But the thought of the creature resting on his chest amused him greatly. Never mind it being an animal, he felt wanted, needed and loved in this strange and unknown world that he was so unfamiliar with. At least for now, he felt he had a friend; never before had he seen or felt such affection from anyone, let alone being on an alien planet and finding such passion from a very alien flying animal.

As the eagle rested on Sakreg's rib cage, he remained frozen in his position. He didn't desire to alarm the animal lest it became whimsical, changed its mind, and caused a detriment. But, at the same time, he machinated his next move. Sakreg knew that the eagle felt safe lying next to his heart, but at the same time, he knew he couldn't stay in this position for long.

Sakreg gently folded her wings, grabbed the eagle with both hands and placed her on the ground next to him. The eagle attempted to get back on his chest but suddenly Sakreg got back on his feet and dusted himself, then buckled his left elbow in an attempt to beckon the eagle to get on his forearm.

The eagle understood his beckoning. She leaped off the ground, wings wide open and flapping; she landed on his forearm. He then gingerly placed her on his broad shoulder. Sakreg felt her pressing weight and her talons clinching on his shoulder for stability, but he didn't make anything of it.

As he turned to face the large, thick growth of trees and underbrush, to his surprise, he observed a pack of gray wolves, seven in total. They were standing side by side at the brim of the forest and approximately one-hundred feet away from him. The wolves were observing him attentively but peacefully. Normally, wolves were scarce in this part of the world, but they were there anyway. Perhaps they were charting a new territory.

Sakreg realized that these carnivores were not making sounds nor making angry or frowning growling faces displaying their k-nine teeth for a meal. He thought it was strange. However, Sakreg immediately felt at ease with these wolves. There was no reason for him to resort to his weapon for his protection.

The wolves began to amble toward him slowly, and as they approached him, they all bowed before him. They were demonstrating their homage to his presence. However, the eagle suddenly flapped its wings, flew to a higher ground, and landed on the not-too-distant boulder.

Sakreg rested his fundament on the hard ground laced with clustered gravel and desired to experience the affection of the wolves, for he felt an affinity with them. A few wolves suddenly jumped on his shoulders from his backside. They extended their necks toward his head and began to stroke their tongues all over his pate, his scruff, and his face, and some jumped on his chest and began to do the same. After a few minutes of feeling the romance of the wolves, he stood erect, and within moments, the eagle once more spread its wings and descended on his shoulder. The wolves created a small circle around him for his protection, and they moved as he moved and stopped as he stopped, and as strange as it may sound, they did not even harm the eagle. Sakreg was not aware of possessing such magically calming influence over the alien animal life forms, and it pleased him greatly.

CHAPTER 21

Faint and distant choppy or thumping sounds were getting louder and louder with each passing minute. These were the sounds of three HH60W Pave Hawk helicopters coming from Fort Lewis-McCord, located approximately a little over nine miles south-southwest of Tacoma, Washington. Their squad monikers were Dragon, Teflon, and Empire.

These choppers were used for search and rescue missions by the U.S. government, but this time, they were used to locate and investigate the unidentified object that had just landed on a dried-up lava bed located slightly northwest of Mt Adams. The military called this mission "Operation Day Star."

These choppers arrived at the alien craft landing site and circled around about it a few times, but to their surprise, the pilots were unable to physically witness the alien craft anywhere in sight. They received their GPS information from NASA and military satellites. The data from these sources should have indicated that the spacecraft must be here at this specific spot. Since they couldn't locate the craft, they thought their given coordinates must have been in error.

"Mc Chord, this is operation Daystar, Dragon squad, tango Charlee, Whisky, Two Five, Niner, 6.2 miles northwest of Mt Adams, requesting verification of Daystar GPS mission coordinates over!" said Captain Sarga.

"Dragon squad, tango Charlee, Whisky, Two, Five, Niner, this is Mc Chord Airfield ATC (Air Traffic Control) tower. We read you loud and clear, and we have you on our screen. The

Daystar coordinates are 46.191 Latitude and -121.476 Longitude—over," said the ATC tower.

"Affirmative, we copy Mc Chord. Our instruments confirm your coordinates, and they are correct. The instruments on board the choppers should have also picked up the subject on our screens. However, with these coordinates, as you have indicated we should be on top of the Daystar, but we have no visual of the subject down below. There is nothing here but rocks, sand and gravel on lava bad," said Captain Sarga.

"How could this be? We have the Daystar (the alien craft) on the radar screen and we also have you on our radar, and yes, we see you as being on top of the Daystar. How is it that you have no visual of the subject on your screens especially when we have our instruments calibrated recently—over?" said the ATC tower.

"I am going to have to reiterate my statement. It's simply not here! There is no damn Daystar here. We must have false reading, or possibly instrument malfunction over!" said the Captain, and decided to search the forest instead.

Sakreg, along with his wolf friends and the eagle on his shoulder, stood silently, and all were observing the three helicopters that were at a certain distance. Sakreg couldn't decide what they were. He noticed they were enormous in size and were bulky. They hovered right above his gunship and made lots of noise. He immediately realized that these flying things were not a life form of any sort. They coruscated like a metal under the sunlight.

Sakreg determined that *"these flying things must be a mechanical apparatus of some sort, and that an intelligent life source that he had witnessed previously must have fabricated these flying contraptions, and the sole purpose of their rotors are to create a lift, and the fuselage is built to transport things,"* he thought. However, he had never observed such an awkward and strange-looking flying structure.

"Oh no, they must have located my craft. They are right above it. I wonder if they were able to see it. I must watch their next move carefully. Oh, perfect, they are now moving away from my craft and are heading toward the woods. They must not have been able to see it physically. I would reckon they are looking for me. Their instruments must have picked up my arrival here. These beings must be very intelligent. I must be careful. But if they are anything like what I saw before, then I don't have much to worry about," thought Sakreg.

The sound of the helicopter engines was getting louder and louder as they were approaching the woodland. Sakreg and his newly found wolf friends felt unsettled and apprehensive. Sakreg had no clue what these flying things were and what they were capable of accomplishing. He began to cogitate his next move, to forefend a capture and to subsist.

Without knowing a thing or two about these flying machines and their entities on board operating them, he thought for a moment, *"Should I blatantly make myself known to them and find out their true intentions concerning me? But what if they are hostile and seek my immediate demise or capture me and parade me around like a slaved animal? Or even worst yet, to have them perform dangerous experiments on me, and as a result, that would cause my demise. I didn't come out here for this purpose, and I don't intend for them to capture me.*

"On the other hand, should I secretly wait and observe them? Perhaps they are very different from what I have seen already. I

need to observe their physical characteristics to determine whether they are strong or weak, and examine their mental behavior towards each other, whether they are nettlesome, choleric, and eager to destroy, or tranquil, and mindful in keeping their peace, and have the zeal to come for each other's aid if it were necessary. Also, to determine whether they are carrying weapons, and if so, would I then have to seek my means to defend myself by resorting to my ion blaster," thought Sakreg.

As the copters entered the forest airspace, the noise level from their engines became enormous, almost to the point where it would deafen the ears. The trees and the vegetation beneath their rotors fluttered furiously. Dust and defoliated leaves hovered aimlessly in the air as they passed over the trees in unison.

The Dragon Squad arrived right above Sakreg and his wolf friends. It hovered stationary approximately twenty feet above the trees. The other two choppers, the 'Empire' and the 'Teflon,' were both relatively eighty feet apart from each other.

Sakreg hid behind the thick and small clusters of shrubs and embraced the eagle with both arms while the wolves surrounded him ever closer to the point that they were almost on top of him, protecting him and the eagle from the flying machines.

Sakreg remained surrounded by his wolf friends almost to the point where the pilots were oblivious to his presence on the ground. Sakreg freed one of his arms from the bird and pulled his ion blaster from his side to ready himself to vaporize them whirlybirds should they pose an imminent danger to his life and the life of his newly found friends. But the enormous wind pressure of the rotors that were right above his head was obscuring his sight and his aim.

"Captain—I see a pack of wolves right beneath us," said the pilot.

"Yes-yes, I see them too. But I don't think the alien is down there among the wolves, lest he wants to be their next meal. Let's get out of here. His craft must have landed somewhere in the clear zone here in the woods somewhere. We will find it soon, no doubt about it," said the Captain.

"Do you really think the alien is somewhere around here, Captain," asked the copilot.

"Why not? This is a perfect place for anyone to hide or get lost from sight," said the Captain.

"Well, if you think he is around here somewhere, don't you think these wolves might have already found him, and perhaps he became, as you have said, their next meal?" said the pilot.

"Well, that is a possibility. But if they did, then we will find his remains don't you think so?" said the Captain.

"I reckon you are right, Captain. We should find some of his remains somewhere around here," said the pilot.

Sakreg remained put in a squat position, secured the eagle on his shoulder with one arm, and pointed his blaster at the chopper with the other arm. However, before pulling the trigger, the chopper that carried the Dragon squad began to move away and continued its search for the alien, along with two other choppers following the Dragon squad.

Sakreg felt the riddance of the danger, at least for this moment and let out a big sigh of relief. He relaxed his finger from the trigger and placed his blaster right back in its housing.

"Oh great, they didn't see me. But if I am going to survive here, I must find a way to know more about these creatures who flew them flying machines," thought Sakreg to himself. He managed to stand erect, having the eagle rest on his shoulder, and began to move forward with his pack of friends further into the forest.

Sakreg planned his stay on this planet, but for now, meeting humans wasn't going to be his option. He decided to remain stealthy and hidden in the forest at least for a short period, until he could plan his next move.

CHAPTER 22

The three eggbeaters flew deeper into the forest and in tandem. The Dragon crew (the lead squad) took notice of the shanty down below and the graceful amount of clearing that was in front of the shack. All three choppers circled the cabin a few times, and then the Dragon Squads decided to land and investigate the hut and its immediate vicinity.

Captain Sarga ordered the Empire and the Teflon squad to remain afloat and to circle the cabin with the door gunner's finger on the trigger to be ready to rain blazing bullets upon the suspecting subject should there be a conflict down below. As the Dragon squad slowly began to descend—through the wake of its rotors, clouds of dust ascended into the air and hovered for a while, then the Dragon chopper slowly made its touchdown. Six heavily armed soldiers, having their instructions previously provided by their commander, Captain Sarga, all hastily dismounted from the fuselage door. Accompanied with the crew was a civilian scientist by the name of Mick Rayner, a CIA agent by the name of Sage Branston and Crew Chief Corporal Mark Jinkns.

The names of the soldiers were Captain Larry Sarga, Second Lieutenant Marvin Harsteff, Staff Sergeant Ralph Nayk, Sergeant Jeffery Hanson, Corporal Roger Sanders, and Private Travis Rayker. They were all in full battle gear, plus they were wearing gas masks and decontamination suits, having their M4 carbine assault rifles locked and loaded, and were ready to engage in case of a firefight with the alien or aliens.

In the chopper, there were three people: Warrant officer Jacob Stew the pilot, and the Warrant officer David Merhimech the copilot and the Crew Chief Sage Jinkns. The Crew chief was to inspect the flight records, maintenance schedules and ascertain possible mechanical flaws, and fixes.

Captain Sarga is the one in charge of the "Operation Daystar." He is in his early thirties, has a black hair, hazel eyes, slightly stocky in the mid-section, approximately five feet-eleven inches in height, has a crew cut hair and a small mole at his right lower cheek. Lieutenant Harstaff is second in command. He is an African American in his mid-twenties, right out of college, and muscular built. He is approximately six feet in height and has a strong handgrip that scares just about everyone who attempts to grab his hand for a handshake. No one dares to shake hands unless they desire to have their bones crushed.

Staff Sergeant Ralph Nayk, he oversees the three men: Sergeant Jeffery Hanson, Corporal Roger Sanders, and Private Travis Rayker. Staff Sergeant Nayk is a veteran in U.S. Army, and has fifteen years of service. He is also a decorated infantryman, served in many wars.

Staff Sergeant Nayk is in his late forties, about six feet two inches in height, has a slight protruding beer belly, completely shaved head, and a large scar at his lower chin. It happened during a bar fight he claims.

Captain Sarga ordered Second Lieutenant Harstaff, Corporal Sanders, and Private Rayker with hand signal to cover the rear of the shack while Captain Sarga, Staff Sergeant Nayk, and Sergeant Hanson stayed in the front. In the interim, the civilian scientist and the CIA agent remained sandwiched between the Staff Sergeant and the Captain.

At the Captain's orders, Staff Sergeant Nayk and Sergeant Hanson were to enter the shanty from the front door, Captain Sarga, the CIA agent MR. Branston, and the civilian scientist Mr. Rayner decided to stay outside and guard the front entrance of the shanty from intruders, and the animals.

Staff Sergeant Nayk and Sergeant Hanson approached the front door simultaneously and surreptitiously. They acknowledged the door was shut. Each took the left, and the right side of the door. They remained silent for a duration of ten seconds to ascertain if there were any sounds coming from inside and to witness if there would be anything or anyone exiting the door.

Staff Sergeant Nayk rendered a hand signal to Sergeant Hanson to move in. Sergeant Hanson kicked the door open with vigor and rushed inside the shanty. Rifle pointed forward, finger on the trigger as if Segeant Hanson was going to engage someone or anyone who attempted to challenge him. Soon, the Staff Sergeant Nayk followed Sergeant Hanson's path.

Both found themselves inside the Living room. They immediately experienced loathsome smell of ever-prevalent animal fecal matter and leftover food that might have been there for some time. They shook their heads in grimace and in disgust but carried on by focusing on their mission.

Nayk silently pointed his index finger toward the alcove, and beckoned Hanson to assay the room. Hanson quietly approached the room at the anteroom that led from the living room and noticed the door was slightly ajar. He slowly pushed the door open while Sargent Nayk pointed his rifle right at its door just to provide firepower in case of problem.

Suddenly Sargent Hanson jerked his head back in disgust. He discovered a lifeless body lying motionless on the floor. There was plethora of flies hovering over the carcass, and plenty of hardened blood on the ground.

"Hey Sarge, you better get over here. You got to see this," said Hanson and at the same time, he beckoned Nayk by the hand to get him over where he was.

"Why—did you find a dead alien body," asked Nayk.

"No Sarge, no such luck, but a human body. Someone is brutally murdered here," said Hanson.

"Whaaat! What----did you just say—a human body!"

"Yes Sarge. That's what I said. You have heard me right Sarge—a human body."

Nayk scurried to the room where Hanson was, and his eyes beheld the revolting sight of the human corpse rolled on one side facing north, with a big hole on his back.

*"What! -----the hell happened here. A man found in a black business suit with a huge f***ing exit hole on his back, and dead in this f***ing part of the world. Don't you think this is rather strange—ha!"* said Nayk.

"Yes Sarge, I agree, this is very strange, but could it simply be a kidnaping and a murder case, as you see his hands are tied on his back. I believe we are dealing with thugs here Sarge," said Hanson.

*"Well----yah, you could say that, but----I have my own f***ing theory. I would say this dead man must have been a government agent in pursuit of the alien we are looking for. As you know, the alien craft landed around here somewhere, and we*

are still looking for it but couldn't find it yet. I suppose the alien was here and got him first, and we must be careful. He could be roaming around here you know, and he could as well be watching us right now."

"But what about the cuffed hands on his back; be real Sergeant, the alien is not going to do this," said Hanson.

"Never mind the cuffs on his hands. I would say the alien could still have a part in this. We must be very vigilant, but for now, don't touch anything until we notify the authorities, and that's the Captain's job." The Staff Sergeant grabbed his communicator from his side and began to chat.

"Captain this is Staff Sergeant Nayk—do you copy?"

"Yes, Sergeant I copy, go right ahead," said the Captain.

"Captain as far as the alien is concerned it is all clear inside. There is no alien here. However, we have found a deceased body and it is a human. He is a male, young, possibly in his mid-thirties, dressed in black business suit, and both hands are tied in his back.

This person was callously murdered here sir. The cause of his death, a weapon of some sort struck on the chest. There is a big exit wound on his back, also plenty of blood on the ground. The time of his death seems to be a recent event. As you know sir, I am not a forensic man. But, from the looks of it, I would say, it couldn't have been more than three hours max sir," said Nayk.

"All right, Sergeant you can come out and tell me more about it. The Captain is over and out."

"You stay on your toes Sergeant Hanson while I go out to inform the Captain of this dead body we have found here. As I

said Sergeant, don't touch anything." said Sergeant Nayk and went outside to meet the Captain.

Sergeant Hanson began to traipse inside the shanty, attempting to avoid stepping on the fecal matters and at the same time scrutinizing the immediate surroundings for evidence. Suddenly he noticed a box, or a coffer pushed up against the wall of the Livingroom and was covered with twigs and blankets.

He took a few swift steps, came, and knelt before the coffer and pushed the contents that were on top off the container, and then slowly opened its lid. Suddenly his eyes bulged in wonderment and his mouth became agape. There was money—oodles of them—in freshly bundled up hundred-dollar bills.

He grabbed a few batches and glared at them in disbelief then placed them back. He also came to notice a badge with a picture on it. He grabbed the badge and read its contents stating the identification of the breathless body. He then dropped the badge back in the chest and closed the lid. Sergeant Nayk on the other end began to address the Captain Sarga of his finding in the shanty.

"Captain as we spoke little while ago, we have a victim under this roof—a dead body with pool of blood on the floor, and the cause of the man's death could be the alien we are looking for. I would suggest you to take a look at the dead body, and see what you make of it," said the Staff Sergeant. Just then, Sergeant Hanson's voice broke through sergeant Nayk's communicator.

"Sergeant Nayk, this is Sergeant Hanson, do you copy?"

"Yes! I copy, go ahead,"

"I think you should get here as soon as you can Sarge,"

"What's the matter, did you find another body inside?"

"No Sarge! I found the needed evidence about the deceased body,"

"All right I'll be there. As I've said, don't touch anything. Got it?"

"Yes Sarge,"

"Sir I am going back inside. Sergeant Hanson has informed me that there is some form of evidence about the deceased body. Would you like to accompany me sir," said Sergeant Nayk? Just then, Lieutenant and his men returned to the front of the hovel where the Captain and the Staff Sergeant Nayk were discoursing.

"Sergeant, go right ahead and see what Sergeant Hanson has to declare as evidence," said Captain Sarga.

"Yes sir!" said Sergeant Nayk, executed a firm salute, made an about face, and began to amble toward the shanty. At the meantime, the Lieutenant approached the Captain and began to explain his findings.

"Captain, we found three dead bodies lying on the ground. Two got their heads blown off, and one got it in his abdomen and his head. It looked like these men didn't have a chance to even fire their weapons," said the Lieutenant.

"Did you touch anything," asked the Captain.

"No sir. I have advised my men not to, until we figure out what had happened here," said the Lieutenant.

"Very well Lieutenant, but do you think it is the alien's work in all these carnages that we are finding here," asked the Captain.

"Well sir, I don't know what to tell you. To me, it looked like a gunshot wound, not an exotic weapon of any sort. We looked for the spent rounds, but we couldn't find any. If it was a murder by a human being, the person has really cleaned-up the evidence well. It seems that the murderer is very calculating one, and could still be roaming around here sir," said the Lieutenant.

"We haven't examined the dogs yet. They are very close by, let's go, and examine them first. I would say whoever killed these men have also killed these dogs," said the Captain. The Captain and the rest of the crew including the Scientist and the CIA agent ambled toward the two bereft-of-life dogs.

The Captain knelt and began physically inspecting the breathless hounds, while the Second Lieutenant and his crew being suspicious of their surroundings, glanced around attentively with their rifles in their hands to challenge any unusual movements that they may observe or encounter.

"It appears that these beagles had their hearts blown away, and ironically, both at the same spot, and that concluded their instant death. I would say a .45-calibar pistol did the job on these dogs and not an alien weapon of some sort.

Whoever did this, he or she must be a very, very good shooter. As matter of fact, the person is an expert shooter. I haven't seen such precision in my entire life. I wished we could all shoot like this person.

Folks, we are dealing with a professional here, don't you agree Mr. Rayner" said Captain Larry Sarga.

"Well, looking at the evidence and where they were shot at, the person must have known a thing or two about dogs. Because this person knew where the dog's heart laid and shot them

accordingly. This tells me we are dealing with a human rather than an alien. Because, the alien would have no knowledge, or even understand the anatomy of the dogs to shoot them at the right spot. So, my conclusion is that I agree with Captain. We are dealing with a human rather than an alien," said the scientist Mick Rayner.

"Why would anyone want to kill these beautiful dogs in the first place," asked the CIA agent.

"Whoever the shooter was must have felt threatened somehow, and now that I think about it, I wouldn't say these dogs were here by chance. They must have had owners, and I have a feeling that you—Lieutenant, you have already found their owners in the back of this shanty," said the Captain.

"It makes perfect sense now Captain. Whoever shot these dogs and the men we found dead at the back of the shanty is not only an excellent shooter but also a very smart one at that. I agree with you, Captain that we are dealing with a professional here," said the Lieutenant. In the interim, Sergeant Nayk entered back into the crudely built hut.

"I am glad you're here Sarge," said Sergeant Hanson

"All right, let's see what you have got here for evidence," said Staff Sergeant Nayk.

"All right, Sarge are you ready for this?" said Sergeant Hanson

"Yes, I am ready all the time. Go right ahead and tell me what you have gotten here, and stop wasting my time," said Staff Sergeant Nayk.

"All right, all right, here it is," Sergeant Hanson opened the lid of the coffer and exposed the piles of money.

*"What----the----f***,"* said Sergeant Nayk.

"Yes, isn't that nice? Don't you wish you had all this money Sarge? By the way, it gets better, this is not all," said Hanson, and pulled the badge of the deceased man and said, *"He is a banker. Somebody brought him here and murdered him. So--- what do you want to do Sarge?"*

*"All right, we have seen enough here. Close the f***ing lid now, and let's get the f*** out of here. The authorities will be here soon. We have to let them do their job. I hope you didn't stash any of that money on you, or did you!"*

"No, Sarge I didn't. I know better," said Sergeant Hanson

"All right, that is being smart. Now stand up and lift your arms up in the air. I have to frisk you," said Sergeant Nayk.

"What is the matter Sarge, you don't believe me?"

"It is not a matter of believing—It is a general routine. I must do this for your sake, so that if I must testify in court about this murder and the money, then I can tell the truth all the way through with a clear conscience. You understand me, right?"

"All right—I do see your point Sarge. Go right ahead. Do what you have to do," Sergeant Nayk padded Sergeant Hanson's body from the neck down to his feet to find money on his person, and there was none. He even made him take his shoes off for inspection.

*"All right—you're clean. Good—now close the lid, and let's get the f*** out of here,"* said Sergeant Nayk.

"Yes Sarge," said Sergeant Hanson. After closing the lid of the coffer, they both vacated the cabin and ambled toward the Captain.

"Staff Sergeant Nayk, you went back inside. What else did you find?" asked the Captain.

"Well sir, we now know that the deceased body has a name and a position. His name is Mr. Henklin, and he is a bank president. Sir we also found an unthinkable amount of money in a large coffer. Don't worry, we haven't touched anything," said Staff Sergeant Nayk.

"Is that all Sergeant," asked the Captain.

"Yes sir, that is all sir," said Staff Sergeant Nayk.

"Very well then, men, listen up; now that we are all here, we know that we are not dealing with an alien running around loose and killing people. The alien is not the cause of all this carnage. I would say let's wrap it up and give the rightful authorities a chance to deal with this bloodshed before we contaminate the evidence any further than we already have.

There is nothing more we can do here; I don't need to look at any dead bodies here to determine if it was an alien or a human that did this atrocity. As I have said, we will leave that to the authorities, which I'll soon notify.

However, either the authorities, or we will find the real killer soon. Whoever it is—can't be far from here," said the Captain Sarga.

"Captain I know you want us to get out of here fast and I know we have a mission to accomplish. But don't you think we have to

wait a while here until the authorities arrive?" asked Staff Sergeant Nayk.

"No Sergeant, I don't think so. If we do—then we will be deviating from our main objectives. We already did to some extent. We need to stay focused here. That is how we are going to achieve our objectives; otherwise, things may get out of hand. And you know very well what our main objective is here, don't you Sergeant?" asked the Captain.

"Yes sir, I do sir," said the Staff Sergeant.

"Very well then, does anyone have any question," asked the Captain

"Yes, Captain, I have a question," replied one of the team members in the group.

"Sir, this is Corporal Roger Sanders, sir. Since we are not dealing with aliens here, may we take our gas masks off sir?" asked Corporal Roger Sanders.

"Yes, you may. I don't see why we have to keep them on," said the Captain.

"Is there any other question here?" asked the Captain. After a brief hiatus, no one else responded to his proffer.

"I see that there are no further questions here—In that case, I am going to explain to the authorities what we have found here and give them the exact coordinates where we are, and I am going to tell them that we are on a special mission without disclosing our objectives, and we can't linger here for long. They will have to understand, and they will be here soon.

"All right, Lieutenant get all your men accounted for while I call the authorities. We are flying out of here in five minutes. Is that clear," asked the Captain.

"Yes sir," said the Lieutenant. They soon got into their chopper and flew out of there.

CHAPTER 23

Drake suddenly stopped in the middle of his tracks to hear a distant, low-pitched, choppy sound. He thought it belonged to more than one chopper in the air. *"These sounds must be and can only belong to Pave Hawk helicopters,"* he thought.

The cacophonous sounds were slowly getting louder with each passing second. At first, Drake didn't make much of their presence in the air and continued in his path to find the mystifying vessel that must have landed somewhere nearby.

Suddenly it dawned on Drake, thinking *that "These choppers must also be looking for the alien craft. It looks like the government must be aware of this craft descent."* Drake began to cogitate silently in his head. *"Now it looks like I have a competition brewing between the military and me as to who will find it first; otherwise, what in the world are they doing here? What are they looking for? It couldn't be anything else but the alien craft. The military must have detected its descent and sent these choppers to locate the vessel. I hope I can find this spaceship before they do."*

The Dragon, the Empire, and the Teflon squads were heading approximately forty-six degrees northeast direction, and so was Drake. He knew his heading was correct and didn't think he was far from the unknown vessel.

"Captain, at ten o'clock direction, about a quarter click away, I see movement on the ground. It looks like someone is hiking alone in the forest. He could just be a camper or a subject of interest," said the pilot Warrant officer Jacob Stew on the Comline.

"Excellent—get close to where this hiker is. We may have to go down and question whoever this person is. This hiker may know a thing or two about the shanty murders, and who knows, we may be lucky and find this person as our prime suspect for all the killings we have encountered and or knows a thing or two about the alien vessel and could direct us to the right spot if he cooperates," said Captain Larry Sarga.

"Yes sir," said the pilot and veered the chopper to the left, and assumed the heading of three-hundred- and two-degrees northwest direction. In less than a minute, the Dragon chopper reached Drake's location along with the rest of the squads. They circled in the air a couple of times, and then suddenly, the Captain blurted through the megaphone, *"Do not move. Stay where you are. I repeat, stay where you are."* Drake knew that, eventually, they were going to have to come down and question him about the alien vessel.

Trees fluttered and danced violently under the rotating rotors. They created very loud noise, a noise that can destroy anyone's eardrums.

The Dragon chopper descended and hovered just above the trees for about ten to fifteen seconds, then suddenly and rapidly, four soldiers repelled to the ground with their full military gear and weapons. They were Captain Sarga, Sergeant Jeffry Hanson, Corporal Roger Sanders, and Private Travis Rayker. They landed approximately eighty feet due East of Drake and began to trot toward him. While they trotted, they all trained the business end of their rifle barrels on Drake and were ready to shoot should there have been sudden and anomalous movements by him.

Drake began to feel apprehensive. His heart began to pelt like a drum. In his mind, he began to question, *"Why do they have their weapons pointed right at me? I wonder if it is a standard operating procedure for the military to do so or they may know a thing or two about my involvement in the shanty's incident. However, it is not looking good for me. I must cooperate lest they shoot me dead.*

"What if they have a knowledge of the carnage that went on in that stupid hovel? Will they have to blame me for it? After all, I am the only one here. So far, I haven't seen anyone else here. They are for sure to tag me as their prime suspect. Why do I feel this is going to be a long and arduous day for me? I did not come here for this." thought Drake.

"Ok Men, put your weapons down. Can't you see he is unarmed?" The three soldiers obeyed the Captain and lowered their rifles down, and the Captain turned around, faced Drake, and spoke.

"Good morning sir. I am so sorry for the inconvenience and the intrusion I am causing you at this moment. I know this is the last thing you need in your camping adventure, and I sincerely want to apologize. But we are here on a special mission sent by the government and thought that you might be of help to us therefore we would like to ask a few questions. I hope you wouldn't mind."

"No—not at all," said Drake calmly.

"Excellent, but first, let's get acquainted, shall we? My name is Captain Larry Sarga, please to meet you," the Captain extended his hand in a "handshake gesture," and Drake did the same, and they all shook hands with a slight smirk on their faces as if they were glad to see him. The captain swung his arm and said,

"These are my men, Sergeant Jeffry Hanson. Sergeant Hanson delivered a slight bow of the head in an expression of respect. And this is Corporal Roger Sanders; he also bowed his head slightly as Sergeant Hanson did. And this is Private Travis Rayker," he did not express any form of homage or respect, just glared attentively at Drake and in his mind, he already condemned Drake for the murders of the shanty.

"And your name sir," asked the Captain.

"My name is Drake Grenhr sir."

"Excellent. Now that we have become acquainted and that is out of the way, I would like to ask you for your ID, please, Mr. Grenhr, "

"What is it for?" asked Drake and delivered a concerned expression.

"I could see that you are concerned—no need to fear. This is just a standard procedure we must follow. We like to know whom we are dealing with. You understand, don't you? So now, if you don't mind, I would like to see some ID, please."

"I will give you my ID, but first, I need you to tell me who the heck are you folks, and what in the world are you doing here in the first place?" asked Drake. The Captain cracked a slight smile and replied calmly.

"If you remember as I have said before, we are here on a special mission from the government, and with all due respect, we are not allowed to discuss any details of our mission with anyone. You understand that don't you----now—the ID please," asked the Captain.

Drake hesitated for a few seconds, then pulled his wallet from the back of his pants and delivered his ID to the Captain.

"Oh! Mr. Grenhr that is you I suspect. Is everything current here?"

"Yes, sir," said Drake.

"Very well then," the Captain handed the ID back to Drake.

"Now that wasn't so bad, wasn't it?"

"No sir that wasn't bad."

"I could see that you are very far from where you live. Do you camp here often?"

"No sir," said Drake.

"Then what brings you here, Mr. Grenhr?"

"You could call me Drake, sir."

"Very well, Drake, now we are on a first-name basis."

"I am here trying to clear my mind from everything."

"Why—is there anything that is bothering you a lot lately?"

"I don't know what you are getting at, but that is a personal question sir, and I would rather not answer that."

"Very well then, Mr. Drake, I am going to cut through the chase; we don't have much time here and I don't want to waste anymore of your time either. I am going to ask you a couple of questions and it depends on how you answer them, there could be more to come. Have you seen anything strange or unusual around here lately?"

"Strange----like what, a Big Foot?"

"Don't be silly, Mr. Drake. We aren't here for a Big Foot. As I have said, anything that is different than the usual?"

"Oh—you mean like UFOs?"

"Ok, something similar to that—yes."

"No—I haven't."

"All right then, I see that question is out of the way. I am going to ask you the second question."

"Go ahead sir."

"Drake—you may have lied about the first question, but I don't want you to lie about this second question that I am about to ask you. Have you seen a hovel or a shanty around here?" Drake immediately understood that they had been there and had knowledge about the dead bodies, and now he felt he is in a deep trouble. After a brief pause, he answered.

"Yes, I have."

"Why was there a pause and a sudden change in your mood Mr. Drake? Are youuuuuuuu hiding something from us?"

"Like what?"

"I am sure you know where I am going with this question, don't you?"

"No sir I don't."

"Ohhhh, come----on Mr. Drake! Don't take us for a fool. We know what happened there. Did youuuu shoot the two----- beautiful --------beagles?"

"Welllllllllll," blurted Drake. There was a sullen pause for a moment or two.

"I knew it! Mr. Drake, if you don't mind, we are going to have to frisk you."

"Why?" asked Drake with a slight anger expression on his face.

"Come onnnnn Drake, I think you are smarter than you look. Don't disappoint us. I don't think we must explain it to you. You should already know why, Mr. Drake! —Sergeant Hanson, I want you to frisk this man now! And you Corporal Sanders, I want you to make a thorough inspection of his haversack! And you, Private Rayker, I want you to keep an eye on him at all times! Is that clear?"

"Yes sir," said all.

Sergeant Hanson began to frisk Drake, and after a short while, he blurted.

"Well, well, well—what do we have heeeere," Sergeant Hanson's eyes glued on Drake's face for few seconds, attempting to read his expression, for the very fact that he found a .45 Caliber pistol on Drake, and pulled it out of its holster and handed it over to the Captain, then he continued to frisk him further.

The Captain held the pistol with tip of his two fingers attempting to make sure not to destroy any evidence and looked around for a large leaf to rap the gun with it.

"Wow, what the hell we have here nowwww." Sergeant Hanson pulled plenty of .45 Caliber clips full of ammunition and placed them in his pant pockets.

"Just as I thought; this could be the .45 Caliber pistol that killed the dogs and the rest of the people there—and all this

*ammunition here---what the hell are you trying to do Mr. Drake—start a f***ing world war III here?" said Captain.*

"Hey Captain, there is more ammunition here in this sack," said Sanders.

"All right, don't do anything else. Put everything back. We are going to confiscate this sack—and you Mr. Drake, you don't look so innocent now, do you? I hate to tell you this, but you are under arrest and in big trouble for killing four people and two beautiful dogs. Right now, I want you to put your hands behind your head and don't move an inch until I tell you so; is that clear?"

"Yes sir," said Drake.

"Thaaaat's what I like to hear. You know, I would have had you laying on your bally and facing the ground, but in this case, I am going to be nice to you since you have been cooperating well. I am going to have you get on your knees and your hands behind your back and stay there until I tell you to move. Is that clear?"

"Yes sir. But look, I could explain everything," said Drake.

"Oh, you don't have to explain anything to us Mr. Drake. You 'll have plenty of time to do your explaining—your end of the story to the authorities because that's where we 'll be taking you right now. Sergeant Hanson! I want you to cuff him now!"

"Yes sir," said Hanson, and while Drake was on his knees and hands behind his back, Hanson placed the plastic manacle around his wrists and secured it well. Now, both of his hands are behind his back and cuffed.

"Dragon, this is Captain Sarga speaking, do you copy?" asked the Captain.

"This is Dragon, go ahead sir, I copy you loud and clear, over," said the pilot Warrant officer Jacob Stew.

"We have a passenger here who needs to be extracted. Please arrive at the extraction zone as I have specified, over."

"Roger to that Captain, I am on my way; ETA (Estimated Time of Arrival) in two minutes, over."

"Very well, the Captain is over and out."

In less than two minutes, the Dragon chopper arrived at the extraction zone along with Empire, Teflon and the Dragon. The chopper hoisted all including Drake and his belongings.

CHAPTER 24

The sun is at the twelve o'clock position. There are a few white and patchy clouds heading eastbound toward the inland by a worm and slightly gusty wind, causing the trees to sway like a dazed and drunkard person. The three choppers are now flying westbound against the wind and are in tandem. The Dragon chopper is leading the way.

"What is the ETA at the shanty?" addressed the captain to the pilot and to the copilot through his headpiece.

"Approximately four minutes sir," answered the Copilot David Merchimech.

"Very well—I am sure we will find the authorities to be there by now," said the Captain.

"Well—I hope you are right captain, but if not?" *Do you have plan B sir?"* asked the Copilot David Merchimech.

"Yes, I have—the hiker will have to come with us. Later, we will have to address his hideous crime to the local law enforcement authorities and hand him over to them. Now, we don't have much time to deal with his issue," said the captain.

"Very well sir," said Merchimech, the copilot.

Drake was sitting on his rump on a cold, hard, steely ground with his hands tied behind his back. He directly and frowningly glared at the captain's eyes, and in a loud voice laced with ire, he said, *"I am not a criminal!"* The Captain, being a few feet away from him, sitting on a bench, he turned his head and faced Drake with a piercing stare, and angry deminer he blurted, *"Like hell you're not! After killing all them people—now let's see*

Hummmmm—Heck—they may even tag the death penalty on your ass for what you have done, and I don't see you feeling a bit remorseful for what you have done. You don't go out killing people and thinking you can get away with it—you do understand that, don't you?" said the captain.

"Look here, you Mr. dimwit, you have diarrhea of the mouth and constipation of the brain, as I have said, and you don't listen—I am not a criminal!" side drake with conniption and attempted to jump on the captain. The captain immediately pulled his 9mm pistol and pointed right to his head at point-blank.

*"Go ahead and make your move, you son of a bitch. What gives you the f***ing right to take one's life, especially the life of those two beautiful dogs? You Know, I could finish you right here and right now, which I am tempted to do very much so, and no one here will speak of you to anyone. If a large hole and a splattered brain is what you want, then just continue in your mindset!"* said the captain.

"Then you would be as bad as I will, won't you? And, when the truth comes out, they will tag me innocent, and they will burn your stinking ass in jail and all your cohorts too," said Drake.

*"Shut your f***ing trap before I finish you right now, once and for all,"* said the captain.

"You can't shoot, can you Mr. so called captain!" said Drake. The captain brought the barrel of his 9mm handgun right to his head, cocked the Slide, and rested his finger on the trigger.

"Don't do it captain," said the lieutenant while Drake remained frozen in his movements, then moments later, he blurted,

"Here, I'm waiting! What's wrong? Is it perhaps a constipation of the mind, or perhaps your mother cut your balls off so you wouldn't get in trouble? Besides, you want to shoot an unarmed man with his hands tied behind his back don't you Mr. Captain? Is that what they taught you to do in the military.

You know, there Is nothing more cowardly than that—answer me Mr. so called captain. And one more thing, you know—you are a despicable and hidebound entity. You have no right to be in charge of any human being let alone you being in the rank of a captain. To whom you gave your ass to, so that you can be promoted to a rank of a captain?" said Drake.

*"You know, you are really, really pushing your f***ing luck right now, aren't you, aren't you!"* said the captain.

"Well—for your information, at least I got balls, and what is your excuse Mr. so-called –captain? You managed to condemn me and judge me without hearing my end of the story. Only barbarians and demented people like you handle this situation the way you are handling it. One more thing: you should really think about resigning as a captain. You really are unfit for military duty, Mr. Barbarian," said Drake. The Lieutenant and the soldiers around him began to chuckle. The captain stood up and in a fuming anger, he kicked Drake hard at his right flank a few times.

"That is right, mister coward! This is how you operate. You can only hurt a man when his hands are tied, and you can't do much to retaliate. Isn't that right? Why don't you fight like a man? Of course, you can't, because you don't have the balls?" said Drake.

*"Captain, please don't mind him. He may have already lost his f***ing mind. Soon, the justice will show him a lesson or two. Don't dirty your hand of his blood. Leave him alone. It will soon be over with him,"* said the lieutenant.

"Yaaaa, you are right lieutenant. He is not worth wasting a bullet on. He is a scumbag for sure," said the captain and placed his 9mm handgun back in its holster.

"Now that's batter," said the lieutenant.

There was silence for a moment or two in the chopper. Tension was thick, very thick. You can almost cut it with a knife, and everyone's eyes are glued on the captain to see if there is going to be another life-threatening situation here inside the chopper.

Suddenly, Drake blurted, *"I did what I had to do. Anyone else would have done the same!"* said Drake, glaring straight at the captain's eyes with a perplexed and serious look on his face.

*"Hay hay—Spare me the f***ing details. I don't want to hear it. You will have your f***ing chance in the court. I should have shot you just for you to shut your big f***ing mouth, but nooooo, you kept on blabbering, and you're still doing it.*

*You need to thank the lieutenant because I was just about to blow your f***ing head off. I will say it again. I want you to keep your f***ing trap shut and be quiet for a change before I really shoot your ass this time. You will have your f***ing chance to explain yourself in the court,"* said Captain Sarga.

"Captain we are approaching the landing sight. I see we are not alone here. There is a Black Hawk chopper on the ground. Your instructions sir," said the Pilot Jacob Stew.

"Very well—circle the designated area to determine if the situation is friendly or hostile and be ready to engage the target should it become necessary and inform the others to do the same," said Captain Sarga.

"Yes sir," said the Pilot.

"Captain I see people in military gear with weapons in their hands looking for something, and some are standing and looking straight at us," said the Pilot.

"How many are there?" asked the captain.

"I counted six—sir," said the pilot.

"Yes, yes. I believe it is the police I called in for; establish communication with ground crew, then find a spot to land this f***ing bird," said the captain.

"Yes sir," said the Pilot.

"This is Dragon squad, Tango, Charlee, Whisky Two Five Niner. Do you copy?" said the pilot.

"Yes, I copy you loud and clear. This is special agent Captain Tom Ransfort FBI. State your mission—over."

"This is Warrant officer Jacob stew, U.S. Army. We have been expecting you. We are here to hand over a prisoner that may have perpetrated the murders you are investigating in this vicinity—over."

"Very well, proceed with caution," said Captain Ransfort. He stood six feet four inches in height, wore dark glasses, was armed with a side arm and an assault rifle, wearing military gear and a protective vest.

The pilot gently landed the chopper next to the Black hawk. Within moments, the cabin doors opened; Captain Larry Sarga, second Lieutenant Marvin Harstaff and Staff Sergeant Ralph Nayk accompanied Drake Grenhr, the prisoner, with his belongings; they all disembarked from the chopper and rushed toward the FBI Commander Tom Ransfort, who was standing near his Black Hawk chopper and was waiting for their arrival. Captain Sarga approached Captain Ransfort and took notice of Captain Ransfort's name on his uniform.

"Greetings Captain Ransfort," said Captain Sarga, and extended his arm for a handshake. Captain Ransfort did the same, and both concluded a firm handshake.

"My name is Larry Sarga, captain in the United-state Army. I'm attached to the first brigade, 23rd Infantry Division, and am situated in Fort Lewis-Mc Cord. It is not too far from here, and these are my crew: Second Lieutenant Marvin Harstaff and Staff sergeant Ralph Nayk, who is accompanying the prisoner Mr. Drake Grenhr."

"I am also the commanding officer of the operation called Day Star. Pleased to meet you," said Captain Sarga and handed a business card to Captain Ransfort.

"We are here to hand over the suspect who perpetrated all the murders you have witnessed here so far. This is the sole reason why we are here and talking to you about it," said Captain Sarga.

"Very well, I am Captain Tom Ransfort, FBI SWAT team commander in charge of this murder investigation, and I believe you were the one who called for this incident, didn't you?" asked Captain Ransfort.

"Yes, as a matter of fact, I did, and frankly, I was expecting the sheriff to show up," said Captain Sarga.

"Yes, that was a right assumption, but they were shorthanded and asked us to take care of the matter, and we said we would be glad to handle it. However, how did you find yourself and your crew to be in this part of the country and be witnesses to such a heinous crime?" asked Captain Ransfort.

*"Your question implies what the f*** are we doing here in this no men's land in the first place. Isn't that right, captain Ransfort?"* asked Captain Sarga.

"Well, if you want to put it that way—yes something like that," said Captain Ransfort.

"As I have said before, we are working on a program called operation Day Star. It is a government-initiated program, and that is all I can divulge at this moment, and that is what led us to this part of the world sir," said Captain Sarga.

"I believe you are going to tell me it is a top-secret program, and you can't discuss the details, isn't that right?" asked Captain Ransfort.

"You are absolutely right, but look, captain we don't have much time to spend here. I am a man with a mission I have a task to accomplish.

"I am here to hand this criminal suspect over to you for further questioning, and as soon as I hand him over to you, we will be out of here, and I am sure that is clear to you, Captain Ransfort?" said Captain Sarga. He didn't wait for Captain Ransfort to respond and asked Staff Sergeant Ralph Nayk to bring Drake and hand him over to Captain Ransfort.

"Staff Sergeant Nayk heaved Drake's belongings, provided a slight nudge at his shoulder and said, *"Let's move it, Mr.,"* and Drake began to amble toward Captain Ransfort with his hands tied behind his back. As Drake stood facing Captain Ransfort, Captain Ransfort delivered an attentive glare at Drake from head to toe.

"Our job here is done, and I hope our judicial system will not disappoint us," said Captain Sarga, facing Captain Ransfort.

"Are you sure you have the right man for all these murders?" asked Captain Ransfort.

"Yes, I have no doubt. I have the right man. Don't let his looks deceive you, Mr. Ransfort. He is as guilty as sin," said Captain Sarga.

"Well, with all due respect Captain. I know a criminal when I see one, and I am a good judge of that when I see one. I have never been wrong in my judgments. He just doesn't fit the bill, Captain Sarga. But nevertheless, I will take him and question him," said Captain Ransfort.

"You do well Captain Ransfort, and I know very well that you will come to the same conclusion as I did, then you will thank me for it!" said Captain Sarga with a slightly stern voice.

"Did you witness the crime yourself, Captain?" asked Captain Ransfort.

"No, I did not," said Captain Sarga.

"Then what makes you so sure that he is the perpetrator of this crime?" asked Captain Ransfort.

"I have plenty of reasons to believe he is the one who committed all these murders, and I have questioned him about it,

and as I have said before, I am very sure that soon, you will come to the same conclusion as I did," said Captain Sarga.

"Will see to that," said Captain Ransfort, and he turned his head and faced Drake, then asked, "Son, I'm going to ask you a question, but you can plead the Fifth Amendment right now if you like, and before I arrest you, I will read your rights. Are you in agreement with this?"

"Yes captain. I have nothing to hide," said Drake.

"All right then, —did you or did you not murder all these people?" asked Captain Ransfort.

"As I've said before, I have nothing to hide Captain. To answer your question, yes, I did. I had to do what I had to do; otherwise, you would have picked my dead body instead of theirs. I am not a criminal," said Drake.

"So, it is you who killed all these people, isn't it?" asked Ransfort

"As I have said, I am not a criminal. It was totally self-defense."

"I see—son you have a lot of explaining to do, you understand that don't you?"

"Yes, I do sir, and I am ready to cooperate with the law enforcement all the way," said Drake.

"Very well—soon we will rap this investigation here, then you will come with us to the headquarters, then I'll read your rights. If you want, you could explain everything that went on here, or as I have said before, you can plead the fifth. In any case, you are going to need a lawyer son. Do you have one?" said Ransfort.

"No sir, not at this moment, but I know I am innocent of all the killings that went on here sir. However, as I have said, I will cooperate all the way sir, it will be my pleasure and my duty sir," said Drake.

"You see captain? —what did I just tell you? He confessed to you that he murdered all those people. He is as guilty as sin. Now----you may thank me," said Captain Sarga with hubris.

"Not so fast captain. You are very presumptuous and so quick to judge and condemn. I am sure that you are aware of laws that may protect his rights, and if he is telling the truth that it was a total self-defense, then he may come out innocent of all these murder charges," said Ransfort. Captain Sarga changed his expression toward anger, or frustration at first, but worked hard to maintain his cool.

"I believe we are done here, Captain Ransfort! As I have said, our task is over when it comes to handing over this prisoner. Now, we must concentrate on our real mission and why we came here in the first place. Well, it was nice meeting you, Captain Ransfort. I wish you the best in your endeavors," said Captain Sarga.

"Likewise, captain," said Ransfort and both shook hands. Captain Sarga turned around and faced his crew and said,

"All right, men let's fly this bird out of here. We have a job to do." They walked to their chopper and flew out of the area.

CHAPTER 25

Sakreg's keen sense of hearing acquired faint, distant, and unintelligible sounds as if there was an articulation between two life forms. He stopped dead in his tracks, made a slow 360° turn, and attempted to determine the direction and the location of the sounds as to where it was coming from.

Sakreg carefully followed the bearing of the ensuing conversation and closed the distance between him and the gab that he was hearing. Sakreg knew he was approaching an area where a possible intelligent life form could be evident near the vicinity because he heard two different sound patterns in a mode of communication.

"Could it be the same life form which I had witnessed when I first landed? I have a mixed feeling about their creatures. At first, they desired to kill me, and then they wanted to feed me. Or, are they the ones that flew these flying machines, and if so, then could they be hostile in nature and different from what I have already experienced?" Sakreg was intently ruminating these questions in his mind.

Suddenly, Sakreg acquired a slight apprehensive feeling that crept slowly in his mind about being captured and being dealt harshly with, but he instantly spurned the thought and embraced the reflections of feeling desired, loved, and welcomed on this planet, at least by the animal life forms that he met so far. Now, he hoped the dominant, intelligent creatures of this planet would do the same, and then his quandary would disintegrate.

Sakreg came within four bus length distance of the shanty, knelt behind the bushes, and peered through the clearing.

Suddenly his eyes widened and glared in awe. He finally witnessed two live human specimens and thought that they could possibly be the intelligent life form of this planet. He realized one of them was outfitted in warrior attire, and the other who was standing next to him was wearing simple garments and having his hands tied behind his back.

"I wonder why his hands are tied. Could it be that they are here to catch a criminally minded creature? If so, then they must have law and order in their midst, or they must be cannibals; they eat their own kind, and in this case, he is the poor soul.

These creatures look very much like the ones I saw already. They must be the dominant beings of this planet, and there may not be another," thought Sakreg.

Both Captain Rumsfeld and Drake were near the chopper that was resting on the ground, it was a little distance from the shanty. Sakreg swiftly arrived at the conclusion that the flying things he witnessed in the air previously that made a great deal of noise and wind must have housed these types of creatures. He then scrutinized their physical characteristics and their expressions.

Approximately a quarter football field away behind Sakreg, there were three FBI agents wielding assault rifles, wearing full SWAT gear and helmets. They were silently combing the forest to find more evidence of the cabin murders.

The lead agent in the rank of lieutenant said, *"Perhaps we'll be lucky should we locate the body of the possible suspect who is at large at this moment and end this f***ing investigation right now and make it a closed case,"* the other two agreed with his statement by responding, *"Yah, wouldn't that be great?"*

*"What---the---f***------lieutenant—are you seeing what I am seeing?"* asked one of the three agents in a subdued voice.   His name is Ansh Singh in the rank of Sergeant. Ansh is swarthy in complexion, approximately six feet tall, lanky, graduated from law school, in his mid-thirties, and has four years of experience being an FBI agent.

"Yah, a wolf pack facing toward the shack. Perhaps they are planning to make a meal out of the captain and the Pilot. I wouldn't want to alert them from the impending wolf attack," said Tim Remrok, an FBI agent in the rank of lieutenant. He is a Harvard graduate from the East coast, in his mid-forties, slightly stocky, five feet and ten inches in height, and has ten years of service as an FBI agent.

"That's sadistically funny, but not nice sir. I am sure you don't mean that," said Larry Hooth. He is another FBI agent in the rank of Private from the West coast, approximately six feet and two inches in height, and in his mid-twenties. He graduated from one of the prominent universities and majored in Astrophysics. He is fresh out of SWAT training, but he has been with the FBI for two years.

*"Who asked for your opinion Private? It would be better for you to keep your f***ing mouth shut and do as I say and nothing else,"* said Remrok.

"Come on, lieutenant be nice to him. He is just a private," said Ansh.

*"Yaaa! Well as I have said, he had better keep his f***ing mouth shut. F*** you all and the horse you wrote on,"* said Remrok. Ansh giggled.

Did you guys notice that there is someone in the middle of the wolf pack and is in a squat position staring at the whirlybird?" questioned Hooth.

"Private---did you say there is someone in a squat position amid the wolves?" asked Remrok.

"Yes, sir that's what I said. There is someone—Can you see that Sargent?" asked Hooth.

"Affirmative, I do witness that too. Good observation Hooth," said Ansh

"You guys are out of your f***ing minds. What am I going to do with you both? You both are hallucinating. You guys say he is in the middle of them f***ing wolves' ha!" said Remrok.

*"Wait, wait! —I'll be a f***ing dammed if I am not witnessing a person in the middle of them freaking wolf pack. You bitches are right all along!"* remarked Remrok.

"I am glad you have verified our find sir. We were beginning to worry about you, but what took you so long to see what we sow?" asked Hooth.

*"Shut the hell up Private. I don't have to answer your shit. Just concentrate on your f***ing work and do as I say. Is that clear?"* said Remrok.

"Yes sir, verrrrry clear," said Hooth.

*"Sir it is very interesting—whoever this person is, He also has a f***ing eagle on his shoulder. How could this be possible? That is stranger than a fiction. Check this out, wolves surrounding the man while the bird is perching on his shoulder. What the f***; what could be stranger than that ha? Why the*

wolves aren't devouring the bird? It is against the nature of things. Don't you think so sir?" said Ansh.

"Well, that would have a simple explanation, you moron," joked Remrok.

"Really, I 'd like to hear that!" held Ansh.

*"Ok, he must be a wolf whisperer, or he must have raised these f***ing animals right when they were little pups along with the bird,"* said Remrok.

"Well----that's a good explanation sir. Yes, it makes damn good sense. I see your point now. You know—you might be right lieutenant. All right enough of that, what's on your mind sir? You know we are not going to be here all day," observed Ansh.

"He may be the suspect we are looking for. We can't let him get away. We must proceed quietly and exercise caution. He may be armed and dangerous," said Lieutenant Remrok.

*"But what about them f***ing wolves,"* said Ansh?

"That's easy, we must distract them somehow without having our suspect get away," said Remrok.

"What if these wolves attack us first," asked Hooth?

*"Do we have any other choice ha? Well, then we'll have to blow their mother f***ing heads off don't we! But you don't have to Hooth; you should let them devour you, so that you will become their tomorrow's shit. You are a shit after all aren't you,"* said Remrok.

Hooth was just about to have a response.

Lieutenant Remrok responded on his behalf, *"Don't you ever open your f***ing mouth on me, just zip it! All right, here is the* *plan, listen well: we will discharge one or two rounds in the air. The wolves will disperse and run for safety to some distance. Then, we will charge the suspect with ferocity to the point where he will not have the opportunity to impose any harm. If he does, then we will have to exercise our shooting rights and defend ourselves, don't we?"*

"It sounds like a plan—let's do it," said Sargent Ansh. Hooth felt very offended by Remrok's previous remark, he couldn't hold it anymore and blurted, *"You know lieutenant—your response to me was very offensive. I shouldn't deserve such an insult especially coming from you as a team leader. I am one of the members of your team. You should extend respect and teamwork effort on your part. For your information, I'm doing what my job, and performing all the duties that my job calls me to do, and you are being such a big jackass, you have no respect to any human being. Heck, you don't even respect yourself let alone others. You know, you should resign from your post. You have no qualifications and the freaking right to lead or manage anyone with your stinking attitude,"* said Hooth.

*"You know, right now you're so f***ing lucky. This is not the time nor the place for me to kick your m******f***ing ass for talking back at your superior officer. However, I promise you when we get back I will I be reporting you ass for being disrespectful toward your superior officer and possibly get you fired, but now we must concentrate on the issue at hand,"* said Lieutenant Remrok.

"You know, Mr. Lieutenant, for your information, I have a very good ear and a very good memory. I remember everything well, all that you have said to me, and that is all your insults. When we get back, I will have you lose your rank and your post.

You see when they come to know about your attitude toward your team members, they will have no choice but to demote you and have you lose your post. You know one more thing if I were you, I would be very concerned now," said Hooth with a slight derisive smirk on his face.

"Are you threatening me, Private?"

"Threat or otherwise. You take it any way you want," said Hooth. Lieutenant Remrok glowered at Hooth, but reluctantly remaind silent.

The three agents having their rifles ready for action, they surreptitiously began to move toward the alien (Sakreg). The wolves acquired their scents, they instinctively turned around, faced the agents, and then they began to posture and growl.

Sakreg perceived an out of the ordinary situation was developing around him and thought, *"These animals wouldn't make such guttural sounds and expose their sharp teeth for no reason. Why did they become irked or perturbed in the first place, there must be a reason here?"*

Sakreg swiftly stood up from his squat position, turned around, and faced the same direction as the wolves were facing. He swiftly pulled his weapon out from its holster and pointed toward where the wolves were attentively glaring and growling. With the weapon in his hand, he made several 180° sweeps back and forth and at the same time attentively scanned the area for any unusual movement or activity, but to his surprise, he detected nothing that was out of the ordinary. The agents were already hidden behind large trees, but they were not too far from each other, they were in a hearing and hand signal distance from each other.

Since Sakreg couldn't locate anything unusual, he then thought he may have to face an invisible and life-threatening entity and decided to get out of his present location and run as fast as he could, lest he will alert the captain and Drake and whoever else happened to be around, and triple or quadruple the magnitude of the danger.

Sakreg ran as fast as he can into the forest with his wolf pack following him. His heading was approximately 54° northeast direction. His intent was to leave as much distance as possible between him and whatever it was pursuing him.

"Damn it—he found us. He must have realized we were following him! Let's not lose him," said Remrok through his communicator mouthpiece and the three began to pursue Sakreg.

"Sir I haven't seen anyone run so fast. His leaps are long and fast almost nonhuman, as if he is flying in the air, and did you guys take notice of his Halloween costume with some sort of facial mask that resembles some sort of amonster. I suppose he likes to emulate being space alien," said Ansh thru his mouthpiece as he was running as fast as he can to catch up with Sakreg.

"Look guys most criminals wear masks to hide their identity as if you don't know, but you all know eventually they all get caught. Come on men, we can't waste energy talking while we're running. We must conserve what we have in order to catch that son of a bitch whoever he is. We can't lose him," said Remrok.

*"Damn it, we are losing him already. He is far ahead of us. How the heck did he learn to run so f***ing fast, I wonder,"* said Ansh. As he was running, he was talking through his mouthpiece.

"Why don't you ask him when we catch him?" said Hooth, running like mad.

"He must not be far. We could still see him. We're gonna get him," said Remrok while trying to catch his breath from sheer exhaustion.

Sakreg came to an area where it was a steppe; he stopped to catch his breath and rest his weary bones. For the moment, he felt safe to be here. He was able to have 360° visual of his surroundings, and witness what was coming towards him from any given direction. However, he witnessed the tall trees round about at some distance from him and felt that there could be menacing creatures now hiding behind them trees and maybe they are glaring at his direction.

Sakreg pulled his weapon out and trained its barrel 360° and indiscriminately he paused for a few seconds along each pause to determine the direction of the sounds he was hearing. However, he didn't witness anyone, but now he for sure felt that there were eyes watching him deliberately.

As he attempted to rest his mind for a minute or so, he noticed the wolves were at it again. They were ones again becoming restless and were growling. He immediately realized the danger was right around the corner and it could manifest itself any moment now.

"Whoever or whatever is out there must be stocking me," thought Sakreg. He kept his weapon in his hand just to be ready for anything that came along his way, and attentively scrutinized the area for anything that moved.

"I'm glad he stopped. I don't know if I could have run any further. I am so out of breath right now," said Ansh, and he was panting heavily.

*"Me too—man I'm sooo out of f***ing breath,"* said Remrok and while standing, he bent over and placed both hands on his knees and breathed hard.

The pack of wolves caught the scent of the FBI agents and began to move slowly and quietly toward them. They were posturing as if they were out on a hunt for a prey.

"Hey lieutenant, are you observing this; the tall man in the costume, oh man he is freaking tall all right, taller than anyone I have ever seen! But with that costume on, he may be thinking the Halloween is not over yet," said Hooth.

"Yah, it looks like he is wearing some sort of a flight suit and probably living his childhood dreams. Probably when he was a kid, he wanted to be an astronaut or a pilot. Now that I took a better look at his uniform—that looks more like a jet fighter's uniform, somebody should inform this idiot that Halloween ended a long time ago.

*"In my book, whoever wears such costume out of the occasion, I consider that person is f***ed up in the head like you both jack asses are,"* said Remrok with a smirk on his face. Ansh chuckled and disregarded his statement, but Hooth rendered a frowning face at Remrok.

*"All right Hooth lose that f***ing expression of yours. I was just being facetious. You don't have to take it sooooo seriously you dumb f**k,"* said Remrok with a sneer on his face and acted as if he forgot his previous argument with Hooth.

*"You know lieutenant; he is crazier than anything I've ever seen so far. One more thing fellows, I see the wolves have left him and are heading our direction, but he still got that f***ing bird on his shoulder,"* said Ansh with a concern look on his face.

"I would say you are right, Ansh. The wolves got our scent and are heading our way. They know we're going to be their lunch," held Hooth.

"All right men, in a few seconds, we will execute our plan just like I have planned it before. Is that clear to everyone?" said Remrok.

"Yes sir," replied Hooth and Ansh.

*"Ok, on the count of three I will fire a couple of shots to distract and disperse them f***ing wolves and then we will charge on this guy like we always do when we conduct raids. Let's hope that will work. We have no other choice but to do this,"* said Remrok.

The lieutenant pulled his Springfield .45-caliber pistol and counted to three than rapidly fired a couple of shots in the air. The wolves immediately changed course, dispersed, and disappeared, just as he planned it, and the eagle leaped into the air and flew away. The three charged speedily forward and with their rifles trained on the alien. They all screamed loud and obstreperously.

"This is FBI—put the gun down and drop to the ground now! Get down! Get down! Get down!" exclaimed the Officers in unison and trained the business end of their rifles on Sakreg. Sakreg did not have sufficient time to neutralize the situation in his favor, especially when three assault rifles were pointing right at his head at close range.

Sakreg placed his hand-held weapon back in its holster lightning fast and attentively but silently glared at the officers as they circled round about him with their weapons still pointing right at him.

*"What the f***, didn't you hear what we have said? We told you to put the gun down—not back in its holster—dumb f**k!"* said the lieutenant.

"Get your hands out in front where we can see them and get down on the ground now, now, now!" said Remrok. There was no response from Sakreg.

*"I said get your f***ing hands where we can see them and drop your body to the ground, now!"* said the lieutenant and the rest of the agents hollered the same at slightly different intervals. There still was no response from Sakreg.

Sakreg stood erect and ascertained all their moves, including their body gestures, but he remained flummoxed as to what in the world was their intention. However, he understood one thing from their gesture, they were commanding him to lay down on the ground, and that wasn't going to happen unless he decided to give up on life all together.

"What's the matter, are you deaf or something?" said Remrok.

Suddenly, the captain spoke through the mick, *"This is the captain. I heard Shots were fired. What is the nature of them shots Lieutenant, do you copy---over?"*

"Captain, this is Lieutenant Remrok I copy you. We have a man with a gun, and I believe he is the suspect we are looking for, over."

"Do you need assistance, over?" asked the captain.

"Negative sir, everything is under control. We will handle it, over," replied the lieutenant. The captain thought there could be a real possibility that the real killer would still be out there and not Drake, and that, Drake might be covering up for someone else's murder and taking the blame on himself, because he didn't think Drake was a murdering kind of a person.

"I copy that," replied Captain Rumsfeld.

*"I said—Get your f***ing ass down on the ground now!"* said Remrok. Sakreg kept on staring and posturing, and at the same time attempting to protect himself from them by not executing sudden movements that might make them to discharge their weapons.

"Hey lieutenant, he may not understand English or what you are saying. Maybe he speaks Spanish," said Ansh.

"Al suelo ahorita! Al suelo!" exclaimed Hooth. Still there was no response from Sakreg, just a frowning glare.

*"Take that f***ing mask off now! So, we can see your face. This is not a Halloween time,"* said Remrok.

"Lieutenant-------I don't think he understands you. He doesn't look like he is from here sir," said Hooth.

"What, —is he French, or Italian, or German?" asked Remrok

"No sir, none of that sir," said Hooth.

*"Then where the f*** is he from? How are we going to make him understand!"* asked Ansh.

"As I have said, he is not from here sir," said Hooth.

*"What! What the f*** do you mean he is not from here!"* said Remrok.

"I know this is going to sound really crazy and far fetch to you sir, but I am going to say it anyway." There was a slight pause and silence. *"Sir I think he may be an alien from a different planet or galaxy sir,"* said Hooth.

"What—did—you just say Private? Did I hear you right when you said he is from a different planet or galaxy?" asked Remrok.

"Yes, sir that's what I said," said Hooth.

*"I surely didn't expect that from you Hooth. You are definitely out of your f***ing mind like you always are,"* said Remrok.

"Just as I said, I knew it was going to sound crazy to you sir," said Hooth.

"Ansh, what do you make out of Hooth's statement?" asked Remrok.

"Well siiiiir, I think he is out of his mind just like you said," said Ansh.

*"How—how could you possibly come up with such a f*** conclusion—Private Hooth? Are you really losing your f***ing mind?"* asked Remrok.

"Sir let me explain," said Hooth.

"Really, I don't want to hear it!" shouted Remrok and pulled his Taser out and shot the alien to bring him down on the ground and arrest him.

Sakreg felt the electrical jolt at the strike zone that happened to be his chest and shook his body for a few seconds and then he pulled the probe out of his chest immediately and threw them aside violently. Two more shots ensued one from Hooth and one from Ansh they both shot almost simultaneously only seconds apart and Sakreg did the same, he pulled the probes out and forcefully threw them aside.

"I don't know how we're going to take him down, lieutenant. He is not armed. Legally, we can't shoot him. I think we all have to jump on him together and take him down by force and cuff him if it had to come to that point," noted Hooth.

"We've got to at least get his mask off his face first so we can identify who we are dealing with, and maybe we will find out he is a known criminal," replied Ansh.

"I don't believe he is wearing any mask Ansh—that is his real face and when it comes to his uniform, only a jet fighter pilot wear one. That means he must have traveled in space to get here, and if so, then he must have his spaceship somewhere close by. We should attempt to find it.

"I have noticed a few more things about him. Did you men see his hand-held weapon? It's nothing like what we have seen before. I wonder what it will shoot, Laser or Ion charged projectiles, perhaps and certainly not bullets like ours. Also, take a good Look at his outfit; it is not an earthly design, is it? And did you take a notice of his hands? He has three long digits instead of five, as normal human beings have.

"This is a dead giveaway concerning the fact that he is not a human being that we are dealing with. Hay guys don't ever think he is a freak of nature, or a mutant of some kind.

"I believe we are looking at a true alien in our midst, and we have no idea as to what he can do. One more thing, guys, if I am right about this whole thing, then the government must want to

know about this alien, and it would be nice if they had him alive rather than dead. I don't think we should kill him. We may learn a thing or two from him, his culture, his language, his technology, and where he comes from," said Hooth.

Remrok shook his head in disbelief and in disdain.

*"Are you done Hooth? I have allowed you to blabber for so long, just to find out and be more conviced that you have truly lost your f***ing mind. You know, I have heard all your bullshit and all your nonsense that came out of your f***ing mouth. So far, you did not make any sense. I am greatly disappointed in you Hooth, and I say you have definitely lost your f***ing mind. I can't have this kind of thing in my team.*

"This job must be very stressful for you. I don't think you can handle it. You need to leave the force and look for something else to do, something that you can handle.

*"Your imagination has it running faster than your f***ing brain could catch up with it, and it is dangerous, I would say, very dangerous. You need to put your f***ing imagination at bay, Private, and face the f***ing reality.*

"I am beginning to think that you are on something that you shouldn't be taking. We'll have to deal with you when we get back. This is serious what you are saying, very serious, I mean it. I am going to write you up. 'Unfit for duty,'" said Remrok.

"Go ahead and write me up sir. I know I am well, and I am not on something that I shouldn't be taking. I know I am right. And if you feel brave lieutenant, then go ahead and try to arrest him instead of dancing around him cowardly, see what he will do to you? I promise you that he will break every bone in your body" said Hooth.

"You are not giving orders here, I am! You are a Private remember that, just remember that!" said Remrok.

*"Sergeant Ansh—Arrest this f***ing clown with the mask on and do it right now!"* said the Remrok.

"Yes sir!" said Ansh.

Sergeant Ansh, still wielding his rifle, approached Sakreg rather slowly and said,

"Get your hands behind your back now. You are under arrest!" still there was no response, just a serious and glowering glare from Sakreg.

*"I said, get your f***ing hands behind your back you overgrown Son of a bitch, what's the matter with you—are you deaf or pretending to be one? Can you talk—Say something! As long as we've been here, you haven't said a f***ing word. Why don't you just grab your neck firmly and pull your head out of your f***ing ass so you can hear me well, or that you might be able to say something.*

*"Did you ever wonder what life would have been like for you if you had enough oxygen at birth, and by the way, don't you need a license to be that f***ing ugly? You know, you don't have to thank me for insulting you. The pleasure is mine, all mine,"* there was no response from Sakreg.

Sakreg appeared very muscular and stood approximately two and a half feet taller than them, and perhaps he weighed approximately 300 pounds in all muscles. He would have surely clobbered any one of them should they have attempted to lay hands on him, and they knew that very well.

Ansh mustered sufficient courage, came within a foot off Sakreg, and attempted to grab his right arm to place the cuffs on it. He didn't think he could succeed but tried anyway just to follow Remrok's order. Sakreg grabbed Ansh quickly with one arm, yanked him approximately four feet off the ground and glared at him eye to eye for couple of seconds, then tossed him approximately twenty feet away like a rag doll.

*"What —the —f***! What just happened here now? Sergeant—are you all right?"* said the lieutenant.

Sakreg switched the direction of his scowling sight and focused on the lieutenant and the Private.

Ansh tumbled a few times on the ground. His rifle flung away from his hand then landed approximately twenty-five feet away from him. He laid there for a few seconds and screamed in pain.

*"Sir----I might have broken my f***ing leg and I can't move my left arm. Why don't you justdo me a favor and shoot his f***ing ass for me now sir?"* said Ansh.

*"Shut your f***ing trap. I gave you an order and you f***ed it up!"* Lieutenant Remrok picked his mike and said,

"Badger 1, this is Lieutenant Remrok, come in please; over."

"Yes, this is Badger 1 Captain speaking over,"

"Captain we have 10-33 (Emergency), requesting air Medevac. Agent Sergeant Ansh acquired a broken Leg bone. He is unable to walk or move. Full report will ensue over!"

"10-69 (Message received) will advise ETA (estimated time of arrival). What's taking you so long to arrest the suspect lieutenant? The CSI (Crime scene investigation) and the coroner have done their investigations here. We should be out of here soon. Advise if you need further assistance, over."

"Negative captain, no assistance required at this time. Everything is under control. We are about to wrap this up sir," said the lieutenant.

"10-4 (acknowledged) the Captain is over and out."

"Sergeant Ansh—Stay put. Help is on its way," said the lieutenant.

Ansh managed to drag his body slowly to reach for his rifle. At the time, he didn't think he could stand on his feet or make quick movements.

*"I feel hesitant calling the captain for backup. I will hear him say, what's the matter—among three of you, you couldn't even arrest this son of a bitch! It is not gona look good on my f***ing report, is it Private Hooth?"* said Remrok.

"No sir it will not. So, what's next sir," replied Hooth.

"Well—we can't shoot this behemoth. He is technically armed, but not flaunting any danger, by that I mean he doesn't have the gun in his hands and pointing it right at us. You understand that don't you, and in this part of the country, people usually carry some sort of weapon to protect themselves from predators. It is necessary for survival."

"We can't arrest him. He hasn't done anything that suggests murder. We can't see anything on him that ties him to the crime: such as, bloodstains on his clothes, there is none. Shoe imprints we found at the murder sight; it surely does not match his, or type of weapon used to commit the crime, such as .45-caliber pistol. His weapon is not a .45-caliber pistol. It is something else, which I can't determine now. But I would say his weapon is specially made for him. There is no probable cause, only speculation."

That is not sufficient to warrant an arrest. He could very well be a passerby, caught his attention as to what was going on around him."

"What about his appearance over all sir? Doesn't he look like an alien to you sir?" said Hooth.

"Here we go again with the word alien. I don't know what to do with you, Private Hooth. Are you in this world or somewhere else, somewhere, perhaps in a La-La land ha? Earth to Hooth, Earth to Hooth, come in, and make a touch down on planet Earth, will you."

*"OK—enough of that, welllllllll I would have to admit. He does appear to be very strange. His height, the number of fingers on his hands as you have indicated, and his face only depicts that he may be a total genetic f*** up, like you and the Sergeant are now. You both are a total f***ups. He is a freak of nature because something created him to appear like a monster, or perhaps he is a Big-Foot's cousin who knows? That is why he is here and not with the regular population living in cities or towns like normal people do, did you get it? Or, his mother must have f***ed a wild animal. Who knows—people do that kind of stupid and wild things; it has been recorded all throughout the history? You should know that by now! There are many sick people on this f***ing planet and that is why we are here to set them straight them out. But what is your f***ing excuse Private?*

"Come on sir; get off your high horse for once will you! With all due respect, sir, I don't mean to school you. Where did you leave your professionalism sir? Certainly, it is not an FBI teaching for you to be so rude and obnoxious especially toward your teammates.

"But you manage to be both at the same time. You denigrate people with whom you associate. You certainly have issues to deal with sir. And for your information, just because people may think and believe differently, especially the person who happened to be one of your teammates, it is not an excuse for you to put that person down in any case, sir. However, I still say he is not a human; he is an alien sir." said Hooth.

*"Stop that Private! You are really beginning to piss me off big time. I don't know how you got on this team in the first f***ing place. But certainly, they didn't do a good job looking at your f***ing background. Stop watching too many f***ing Sci-fi movies. That is affecting your f***ing judgment, damn it.*

"I would say you believe in UFOs too, don't you? You know— I am still going to have to write you up when we get back. I don't want to have people like you on my team. You are dangerous!"

Sergeant Ansh reached halfway to where his rifle crash-landed, then suddenly froze his movements and laid on his back glaring at Sakreg in a menacing way. There was murder in his eyes. Then he slowly moved his left arm towards his .45-caliber pistol holstered on his right thigh.

He grabbed the handle of the gun and pulled it slowly, then curled his fingers around it and anchored his index finger on the trigger.

Sakreg's attention was gravitated towards Remrok and Hooth, attempting to understand their intention, and was somewhat amused by their conversation. However, he wasn't aware of what the Sergeant was planning for him.

Sergeant Ansh elevated his left and good arm, carried the .45-caliber pistol approximately a foot above his body, took aim at

Sakreg, and pulled the trigger twice consecutively in a rapid form. First shot, he missed, but the second shot hit Sakreg in the left shoulder.

Green blood oozed from the wound and stained his upper cloths. It was a clean shot. The round passed right through the body, and unlike humans, it rendered a small hole both at the entrance and at the exit.

Sakreg instantly turned around and hauled his hand-held weapon out of its Hollister, took a quick aim, then pulled the trigger. Couple of large and effulgent red Plasma projectiles emerged from its barrel, and as soon as they struck Ansh, his whole body glowed in red for a few seconds, and then Ansh became pulverized. All that remained of him was a blackened, triturated, or comminuted grass and plants that were beneath his body.

Infuriated Remrok by the demise of his close friend Ansh, he opened fire at Sakreg and shot him in the right thigh. Sakreg lost his balance and fell to the ground then laid on his back. He began to bleed profusely. The bullet remained lodged in his thigh, and he screamed aloud in pain. The sound of his cry was something unheard of on earth.

The lieutenant and the Private ran in haste toward Sakreg and pointed their rifles at his fallen body with ire.

*"Don't you f***ing move an inch or even twitch a f***ing muscle, you son of a bitch. Otherwise, I will have you meet your maker, you ass hole. You will pay for killing one of my man,"* said Remrok and kicked him in the kidneys a couple of times.

Lieutenant Remrok did not waste any time and quickly stepped on Sakreg's wrist that was holding the hand-held blaster and applied pressure on it with his boot until Sakreg lost grip to his equalizer, and Remrok picked it up off the ground then tossed it away.

"Private Hooth, arrest this creep. We are going to charge him with first degree murder, and don't forget to read his f***ing rights!" Remrok commanded.

"Sir these cuffs are not going to do it. They are not big enough to fit his wrists," Hooth insisted.

*"Then use your f***ing plastic ribbon cuffs, damn it, do I have to tell you everything, use your f***ing head if you got one?"* Remrok ordered.

"Sir these plastic ribbon cuffs aren't strong enough to hold him. He is going to break them anyway," observed Hooth.

"Do as I say damn it. And stop questioning my decisions. You should realize you are not the one who is in charge here—I am—so get to work now."

"Badger 1 this is Lieutenant Remrok come in please; over."

"This is Badger 1, Captain speaking. Go ahead, I read you loud and clear over."

"Captain we have 10-95 (The prisoner/subject in custody). The suspect presumed to be 10-96 (Mental subject) we have a situation 10-52 (in need of ambulance). However, Disregard the Air Medivac for Sergeant Ansh, but perhaps the suspect needs to be Medevacked instead. Sergeant Ansh is no longer with us sir," said Remrok.

"10-9 that!" (Repeat), said the Captain.

"As I said—Sergeant Ansh is no longer with us, sir."

"What do you mean he is no longer with us?" asked the captain.

"Sir he is deceased sir," responded Remrok.

"Did I hear you right when you said he is deceased?"

"Affirmative sir, and it is more than that sir," said the Lieutenant.

"What now! —what do you mean it is more than that?"

"The body can't be found sir. He is completely pulverized and there is no trace of him left at all sir."

*"What—the—f*** are you talking about his body being pulverized? How could that be lieutenant? —explain!"* asked the captain.

"I will explain when you get here sir," said the lieutenant.

"All right then, I will. But I want full repot when we get back, do you hear me lieutenant?" said the captain.

"Yes sir, I hear you sir," said the lieutenant.

"What is your 10-20," (Location) asked the captain.

"About a quarter mile away from you, sir and the heading is approximately 50° north-east sir. One more thing I want to inform you sir, and that is, there is a pack of wolves at about 200 feet from where Private Hooth and I are standing sir, and they are casting angry glares at our direction. But I detect fear in their eyes, and as a result, they are not posing any immediate danger as yet sir, but it is nothing that we can't handle sir should the occasion arise."

"Very well then, we will be there shortly. The captain is over and out."

CHAPTER 26

"Sir I couldn't help but overhear the conversation between you and the lieutenant. Sir when it comes to the wounded suspect that they have shot, they certainly shot the wrong man sir. Whoever he is, had absolutely nothing to do with the killing of these men sir."

"He must have been a passer-by, and I would say your men acted very irrationally. Will they be paying for their mistake sir?" asked Drake.

"Look here young man, it is better for you to shut your trap and do not stick your nose in police or FBI business. Is that clear?" demanded the captain.

"Fine sir," said Drake.

"I am glad you understand," said the captain and paused for a second or two, then blurted again, "you see—you have absolutely no knowledge as to what transpired in their midst and what warranted the use of deadly force," said the captain.

"Well, it is same here with me sir. I was just defending myself from these crooks that you found them dead sir," said Drake.

"Well—will see. We will let the court to decide, but I don't know why for some odd reason, I find myself believing in you. I hope for your sake I am right," said the captain.

"Thanks for believing in me sir. I could see that you are a good judge of character, I am sure that comes from years of experience, but however, coming back to the wounded so-called suspect, I heard he is wounded sir, and I know I can take care of his medical needs sir. I say that because my father happened to be a surgeon and when I was a kid growing up, he taught me a lot about how to perform minor surgeries. He wanted me to be a medical doctor when I grew up. But I disappointed him. Instead, I became an engineer working for a reputable aerospace company in Salem Oregon, and I am not sorry for being an engineer. I earn a decent living, and I am very happy with what I do," said Drake.

"An engineer ha, I suppose there is more to you than meets the eye," said the captain.

"Look, captain as I said, if you allow me, I might be able to take care of his medical needs. As I have said before, I could perform minor surgeries if it came to it," said Drake.

"You are not lying to me just to have the opportunity to run away, are you?" asked the captain.

"Yes sir, I am not lying to you sir, and if you like, go ahead and accompany me every step of the way. I just don't want him to die for no reason," said Drake.

"Very well then, there are some medical tools in the chopper. They might come in handy for you. Go ahead and get them and I will follow you, just in case you decide to get a wild hair up your ass and decide to run," said the captain. Drake extended his cuffed hands forward, pointing them at the captain's face.

"What is it that you want now!" said the captain.

"Well, isn't it obvious to you that I need my hands to be freed so I can get to work sir?" said Drake. The captain froze in his place and provided a puzzled glare at Drake.

"Well, don't just stand there looking perplexed. Time is of the essence. We need to move fast; his life may depend on us.

You need to free my hands so I can get to work. You understand that don't you sir!" said Drake.

"Oh yes, yes, but," said the captain.

"I understand your concern sir, but don't worry. I am not going to run. I promise. Although I know I am innocent, I promise you I am not going to run. The court will soon exonerate me that I know. Now if you please, we will have to save that innocent life sir," said Drake.

"All right then, you have promised," said the captain.

"I tell you, if you try to run, I swear I myself will shoot your ass with no hesitation do I make myself clear to you?" said the captain emphatically as he unlocked his cuffs.

"Yes sir. You have no worries of me running away. Now let's get them medical equipment from the chopper as you have said sir," said Drake.

Captain Ransfort and Drake ran to the chopper, and as soon as Drake entered the fuselage, he couldn't help but notice his tossed belongings in a corner, but realized an FBI agent and Captain Ransfort were supervising him. In result, he couldn't get access to his rucksack. However, Drake decidedly picked the medical accouterments he needed for his patient, and a couple of agents carried the gurney, and they all scurried toward Lieutenant Remrok and Private Hooth's location.

"What—in the world is this—who do we have here—or better yet, what do we have here?" asked Captain Rumsfeld.

"He is a mutated human being sir. He should belong to the "World Guinness Book of Records," for being the ugliest man alive sir," said the lieutenant with a slight smirk on his face.

"Really---I would think a mutated human being would still have red blood in him, but what is that green substance oozing from his wound and spilling on his pants?" asked the Rumsfeld.

"I don't know, but I would think it could be algae growing from inside sir and not his blood sir."

"Are you trying to be funny, lieutenant?" queried Captain Rumsfeld.

"No sir, but don't tell me that thing is an alien being," said Remrok.

"And why not?" asked the Rumsfeld.

"Because you are going to make Private Hooth happy," said Remrok.

"Really, so he also believes this thing is an alien, right?" enquired Ransfort.

"Right sir!" said Remrok.

"Well, he is not far off by thinking like that. I to—believe he is an alien being," said Ransfort.

Drake silently agreed with Captain Rumsfeld that this life specimen was not a human being. As a matter of fact, he thought this alien must be the pilot of the craft he had seen previously that was descending silently toward earth.

Drake approached the alien cautiously, knelt right beside him, and communicated with him using his hands and body signals to assure the alien that he was there to help and protect. Some agents were still pointing their rifles at the alien to be ready to shoot in case there was a conflict.

"See—I told you lieutenant that he is not a human being, even the captain thinks so," said Hooth.

"I suppose I better shut the hell up. I'm getting ahead of myself, don't I sir," asked Remrok.

"Yes, you are!" said the captain vehemently.

"Lieutenant—where is the weapon that killed Sargent Ansh?" asked Rumsfeld. The lieutenant went and picked the alien weapon from the ground and brought it to the captain and said, "Here it is captain," and handed it over to him.

"What the hell is this thing? I have never seen anything like it," said the captain and started to examine the weapon and brandish it in the air with his hand on the grip.

"I would be very careful with that if I were you sir," said the lieutenant.

"Yes, now I am more convinced that we have an alien in our midst, and I believe these Army guys in the choppers were looking for him—and were probably sent by our government to capture him. What an interesting time we're living in now; we get to meet a live alien. How fascinating is that?

"We have a lot to learn about this guy. All right Drake, this is your chance to prove to me that you have said previously, now how is he doing?" asked the captain.

"I am almost done here sir," said Drake.

"Look son, we don't want to lose him. Do you hear me? The scientists might want to get their hands on this fellow for further study," said the captain.

"Put your guns away. You are scaring the shit out of him. Can't you see he is not in a position to hurt anyone!" said Drake.

The captain ordered everyone to put their guns away, so they did. The captain turned his head to the right, saw the scorched area on the ground, and started to amble toward it along with Lieutenant Remrok.

"Hay captain, who the heck is he anyway?" asked the lieutenant,

"Well, he is our alleged suspect, mind you. He is the one responsible for all the murders committed here," said the captain.

"What—what—the—hell —then why in the f***ing world is he loose, not cuffed, and arrested, sir?" said Lieutenant Remrok.

The captain stopped for a moment, faced the lieutenant, and said, "Hold your horses' lieutenant. No need to get emotional here. Everything is in control. You see—he knows a thing or two about medicine. His father was a surgeon and taught him a thing or two about surgeries, so now it is his opportunity to demonstrate his knowledge of medicine by treating this alien and that is why he is here—understand? Also, besides that, he claims he did all these killings for self-defense. He explained everything to me without pleading the fifth, and I tend to believe him.

"By the way, these deceased bodies were a wanted criminal. I have checked their backgrounds they are a prison-escapees and are wanted for a slew of murders, rapes, and bank robberies. They also have their pictures and mugshots everywhere. I would also say that they have shot the bank president. It surely wasn't he who shot and killed the president of the bank. If I had been in his situation, I would have handled them the same way as he did. He doesn't look the type of a man who would do such a thing and I am a good judge of human character you should know that by now."

"Well, if you say so captain. I am not going to argue with you on that," said the lieutenant.

"So, this is the area where Sergeant Ansh died, isn't it?" asked Captain Ranford as he knelt and examined the burned ground with his fingers.

"You are right. Nothing left of him. This thing must be a weapon that can do such damage. The military may want to be interested in the make of this, whatever it is called," said the captain.

"I wonder what we are going to tell his family as to how he died. They are going ask for his body, and there isn't one sir?" asked the lieutenant.

"We certainly can't tell them or tell anyone for that matter about this alien—that is clear, isn't it?" said the captain.

"Yes sir, I understand your concern. But what are we going to do if Agent Ansh's family wants to see the body as you have brought the point up?" asked the lieutenant

"We will have to think of something to say don't we?" said the captain.

Drake managed to extract the bullet that anchored in the alien's leg, then sanitized both wounds and wrapped them up with gauze. The alien elevated his head slightly and extended his left arm, then wrapped his fingers gently around Drake's right elbow. He then shut his eyes for a few seconds and opened them up again with a few teardrops running down his cheeks. He uttered a few words that were unintelligible to Drake. Drake understood that the alien was attempting to thank him for healing his wounds, and Drake said,

"You are welcome."

The captain and the lieutenant returned to where the alien was laying on the ground, and the captain said, "Is he going to make it?"

"Yes sir, as you see, the bullets are out, and his wounds are sanitized and wrapped," said Drake.

"Good job," said Captain Ransfort.

"All right men, by now you understand what we have witnessed here. In case you didn't, for the first time in human history, we have witnessed a live alien in our midst. I am going to say this, and I am going to say it once. You are not to talk to anyone about what you have seen or experienced here today. You will take this incident to the grave with you. Is that clear?" asked the captain.

They all responded, "Yes sir."

"All right then, let's wrap it up; we can't be here all day." Four officers gingerly grabbed the alien at the shoulders and at the feet, then lifted him up just enough to transfer him on the stretcher.

CHAPTER 27

The military choppers were still circling the forest in the air. They were still searching for the alien and his craft who was still at large. They decided to circle the old shanty one last time before permanently changing their direction of search.

"Hey Captain, I hear them choppers again. They are at some distance east of us, but their engine sounds are getting louder. It is them, the Army guys again. I smell trouble, captain. I believe they are heading in our direction, and I reckon they will be here soon.

Captain, once they find out that the alien is here, they will take him with them, and only God knows what they will do with him. If you don't have plans to hand the alien over to them, then I suggest we should either hide him, or get out of here real fast. What do you say captain?" asked Drake.

"All right, you have a point here. We don't know them from Adam. Not everyone can be trusted, but somehow, I believe you're not a criminal, and I feel I can trust you.

For your information, those people you have killed were wanted criminals. We found out that one of their men killed the deceased body in the hut. You might have done the taxpayers and us a great favor by getting rid of them. The community can finally rest from their mayhem, but you can't take the law into your own hands. You should have known that.

"However, in your case, I am sure that it was self-defense. I would have taken the same path as you did. Life is too precious to give up, no matter what comes your way."

"I tell you what; I trust you enough to set you free. I am not even going to arrest you for their deaths. I know what happened here at the shanty.

"However, coming back to the alien, I want you to hide him from them army rats. I will have some of my people to help you," said Captain Ranford.

"Thanks for believing in me sir. You have judged well. I will attend to the alien's need as you have requested. Oh! by the way, I would like to have my belongings back just in case I need to defend myself and who knows, I hope it doesn't have to come to that, but I might save someone's life like maybe your life sir," said Drake.

"I see your point, go right ahead son, and get your belongings from the chopper. I will inform the crew of your arrival and hurry," said the captain.

"Thank you, sir you won't regret it, I assure you," said Drake.

The three-army choppers have arrived at the scene where the FBI S.W.A.T team has concluded their murder investigation at the hut. They flew right over them, and in a short while, they all turned around and circled the air right above the agents.

While the Empire and Teflon crew remained hovering, the Dragon chopper began to descend slowly and landed approximately 60 feet away from Captain Ranford and his team.

Out came Captain Larry Sarga, second Lieutenant Marvin Harstaff, and Staff Sergeant Ralph Nayk from the Dragon chopper. They all began to amble toward Captain Rumsfeld.

"Greeting Captain, I see we meet again. I thought by now you would've concluded your investigation and you and your crew

along with your suspect, would have been long gone. But apparently, that's not the case. What's holding you back captain? Is there anything I should know about—that you are not telling me," Asked Captain Sarga.

"What is it that I am supposed to tell and that I am not telling you Captain Sarga. What are you actually looking for anyway?" Asked Captain Rumsfeld.

Captain Sarga began suspiciously glance around to find any evidence of an alien presence here.

"I will let you know in a minute," said Captain Sarga. He knelt and took notice of a green viscous substance on the foliage and sampled it with his fingers by rubbing them together and asked,

"What is this viscus thing?" Captain Sarga asked. Then he looked for more of this green semi-liquid object on the ground and found more of it. *"It looks like some kind of secretion, don't you think so, Captain Rumsfeld,"* said the captain.

"Yes—I saw that too. I don't know what to make of it, but whatever that maybe, it doesn't concern us. Our duties are to conduct law enforcement operations and not scientific investigations," said Captain Rumsfeld.

"All right Captain, I am going to cut through the chase. Have you seen anything unusual here? I mean something out of the ordinary," asked Captain Sarga.

"Like what?" asked Captain Rumsfeld.

"Come on Captain—by now, you should have an idea what I am talking about!" said Captain Sarga emphatically.

"The only thing I see unusual or, as you say, out of the ordinary is you army people being here in the middle of nowhere. Don't you folks have anything better to do than kill your time in the middle of this forest? Besides—perhaps I should hold you men accountable for being possible suspects or accomplices of the shanty murders. Normally, most criminals come to the spot where they committed their crime, and I see the same pattern here with you folks," said Captain Rumsfeld.

"I thought you were a better judge of the character as you have said, but I am beginning to have my doubts about you, and I thought we have already established the suspect of all these murders and now hopefully he is in your custody, but I don't see him anywhere. I hope you didn't let him loose by believing in his statements. I tell you what Captain Rumsfeld, you are going way-off tangent here by suspecting us to be accomplices to the crime committed here. I believe you are a reputable man, devoted to your work and very well versed in your profession I see, but please don't let your imagination take the best of you.

I will tell you why we are here. We are here on a mission from the U.S. government as I have stated before, and we are not here for the purpose of killing time as you have suggested captain. Captain Rumsfeld I want you to know that your statement offended me and the rest of my crew—I expect an apology from you!" said Captain Sarga.

"No apology will be extended, captain!" said Captain Rumsfeld.

"Fine then---You are being rude and unprofessional. A man with your caliber that you are, I wasn't expecting such an insolent remark from you."

"Get used to it captain," said Rumsfeld.

"Fine then, I don't need your apology---so, straight out, why don't you just tell me what I want to hear, you damn well know what I want, Captain Rumsfeld and don't waste my time here!" said Captain Sarga.

"Amazing assumption; all of a sudden, in your conclusion, I should know what you want to hear isn't that right? Don't you think you are being presumptuous? You see—I haven't a clue as to what you are talking about and what you want to hear! Why don't you just speak out what you have in your mind instead of fooling around, and taking my time," said Captain Rumsfeld.

"All right—then I will. What do you make of this green semi liquid stuff on the ground ha," asked Captain Sarga?

"Well, let me ask you the same question Captain. What do you think that is?" questioned Captain Rumsfeld.

"I think that is an alien substance, and I think you attest to that don't you?" asked Captain Sarga. Captain Rumsfeld broke out in a flouting chuckle.

"I think you are out of your mind Captain Sarga. I hope you are not going delusional on me. If not, then you may have seen too many sci-fi movies. For all we know, that could be an animal secretion—who knows what it is----but an alien being? You must be out of your mind for sure to think that way," said Captain Rumsfeld.

"Come on Captain! Come forward with it and come clean. I think you are hiding something that I want, and you are not telling me what I should know," said Captain Sarga.

"Look here captain—with all due respect to you and to your crew, you are really beginning to piss me off big time, do you hear me? I don't have all day to spend here and listen to your nonsense and you being delusional on me. I have my job to do, and you have yours whatever that is to do. So why don't you just go on and mind your own business before I arrest you for interfering in police business," said Captain Rumsfeld.

"Captain Sarga cracked a laugh and turned around and faced his men and said, "Did you all hear that? He is going to arrest us." They also chuckled, then Captain Sarga turned around and faced Captain Rumsfeld with a stern face and said, *"You can't give me orders here Captain. I am in charge now.*

"As a matter of fact, from this moment on, you and your men will take orders from me. I am going to tell you this—that you are interfering with the United State government operation, and I know you are hiding an alien somewhere around here and you are being uncooperative. How are you going to explain your actions to the U.S. government?"

"The alien is considered a U.S. government property. And if you don't hand him over soon, then you and your men are coming with us for further interrogation and that is not going to look good for your law-enforcement carrier. Is that clear enough for you Captain Rumsfeld?" asked Captain Sarga.

"You're not going to scare me with your tactics Mr. Captain. If I must, then I will arrest you right now for obstructing police activity, but however, if the U.S. government has sent you and your crew to find such a thing called 'alien', then I am willing to cooperate."

*"Wowwwwww! I am so impressed with you now captain. What a turn around. You really made a 180° turn. I couldn't ask for more. Excellent captain, this is what I wanted to hear from you all along. So—where is this f***ing alien that the U.S. government is so heart set in having it?"*

"He is over there, just about two hundred feet away," said Captain Rumsfeld, pointing his index finger toward 300 degrees northwest.

"Very well Captain, thank you for your cooperation. For your sake captain, I hope you are not laying to me, because I hate layers and I will deal very harshly if someone lays to me. Now I want you to gather your men right around you so that we can observe you and your crew, hoping that they will not do anything funny or stupid, do you get it? Otherwise, you see these choppers up there, pointing his index finger towards them—for your information, they are very well armed and ready to commit to action when it is necessary—you understand what I am getting at don't you?"

"Are you threatening me and my crew?" asked Captain Rumsfeld.

"Wellll Captain as you see, I am just doing what Uncle Sam pays me and instructs me to do. I take orders from my superiors just as you do. A man of your caliber should have no problem understanding the issue at hand, and the issue at hand is the alien in which the government is so interest in having it. I suppose you can take my statement any way you want to, threat or otherwise, it is your choice. I will achieve my goals whatever it takes to achieve them.

I just want to make something very clear to you Captain Rumsfeld. My men know what to do in case there is trouble from your end. I have instructed them in advance as to what to do should there be a problem from your end.

I am committed to the safety of my men, and I am sure you think the same for your men too. So, if there is no funny business from your end there will be no funny business from our end then this whole thing could go very smoothly, and no one gets hurt capisci?"

Captain Rumsfeld felt powerless, out gunned, and outnumbered. Threats from the ground and from the air loomed before his sight, and he decided to play Captain Sarga's game for now and gathered his men around about him.

CHAPTER 28

"All right lieutenant, you, and the sergeant follow me now," said Captain Sarga.

"Yes sir," replied both and the three began to run in a slow pace toward the direction where Captain Rumsfeld had pointed out. As they closed the gap to their intended destination, they hunkered ever more to be indiscrete and pointed their rifles forward position as to be ready to shoot should there be a danger imposed by the alien. They stooped low even more so and slowed their pace to almost a crawl as if a hunter is out on a hunt for a pray, ready to shoot at any given moment.

When Captain Sarga's crew arrived at their appointed destination, they took notice of the slight rustling of the shrubs and the small trees. Their eyes widened in anticipation, hearts began to beat hard in excitement, thinking this is going to be it.

Captain Sarga's mission was soon coming to an end. They were all going home with the alien in their custody. And in result, they were going to start the party, celebrating their victory, but for now, despite of all the anticipation of vanquish, the three felt the trepidation settling in their hearts and minds for not knowing what to expect from the alien.

Captain Sarga and his two teammates trained their rifles toward the area where they thought the alien could be found. But, to their surprise, a puma suddenly leaped onto a tree branch and angrily growled at the three with disgust and fear as if how dare you bother me on my turf.

"Now what captain! What do you want us to do?" asked staff sergeant Ralph Nayk emphatically.

"That son of a bitch lied to us! The alien is not here," said the captain.

"Perhaps the alien realized that we were here and took off running and God knows which direction," said the Staff Sergeant.

"Hey captain what is that green stuff on the ground and on the plants. It looks like same type of liquid that was on the ground where you and the FBI captain were talking," said Lieutenant Marvin Harstaff.

"Where?" asked the captain.

"Right here where the puma was standing," said the lieutenant. The roar of the puma became harder and fiercer as if it was ready to prance.

"The green stuff must be an alien blood. You sow the same stuff near Captain Rumsfeld didn't you sir?" said Lieutenant Harstaff.

"Yes I did," said the captain

"Then I think the alien must have been here Just as Captain Rumsfeld said. He wasn't laying sir. What we have here is a wounded alien sir, and he can't be too far from us. Puma must have followed the scent of his blood. It all makes sense now," said the Staff Sergeant.

"But then, where is the alien now?" asked the captain.

"The Sergeant is right. What we have here is a wounded alien, and he is on the run. However, he can't be far from us captain. If we allow the puma to do its job by following the scent of his blood, it will lead us to the alien sir," said the lieutenant.

"It's a great idea. Let's beck-off a little and leave puma alone to do its job and maybe it will avoid us all together thinking we are not a threat, and we'll follow the puma wherever it goes, but if it pounces on any one of us, then it is shoot-to-kill is that clear?" said the captain.

"Yes sir," replied the Staff Sergeant, for he was the closest to the puma.

The puma suddenly changed its bearing and bolted fast east direction, which had nothing to do with following the scent of the blood and disappeared into the wilderness.

"Captain I believe we have lost puma," said the Steff Sergeant.

"All right, men I could see that already. Now, we must follow the green blood trail ourselves. We must find that son of a bitch alien before dusk and make Uncle Sam happy. Tomorrow, it will be too late, and I don't intend on going back empty-handed is that understood?" said the captain

"Yes sir, we will find him soon, you will see captain," said Staff Sergeant Nayk.

The captain ordered "Dragon" chopper to circle the area to locate the alien at large. After 5 to 10 minutes have past, the Dragon chopper reported.

"Captain, this is the Dragon do you copy."

"Go ahead, Dragon, I copy you loud and clear," said the captain

I see two bodies holding each other. They are bustling as if they are attempting to get away from something, but one of them is very large and strange-looking. Oh! My God, that son of a bitch is huge. Sir—I am sure it is the alien we are looking for. He is damn huge sir, and the other one looks like a man trying to help this behemoth to get away."

"Excellent work Dragon; we are going to wrap this up soon. By the way, we can hear your engine sound. You must not be far from where we are. What is your location?" asked the captain.

"About half a klick due north-west of you captain," said the copilot.

"I want you to halt their movements or slow them down until we get there?" asked the captain.

"I will do my best sir," said the Copilot.

"Don't just do your best, no matter what, don't let them get the f*** away, understood that Dragon?" said the captain.

"Understood sir!" said the copilot.

The captain turned around and faced the lieutenant and the staff sergeant then said, "All right men, this is it, I think we have found our subject of interest. They are not too far from us. Today—we are going to have our alien and the one who is helping him to get away. This is going to be a good day after all, Helllllo promotion.

"Let's move this direction man, and let's pick up some speed along the way. We don't want them to get away," said the captain, pointing his index finger approximately two degrees north.

The Dragon chopper circled twice around Drake and the alien, then swooped down fast in attack mode and passed right over their heads just above the tree lines. The chopper crew intended to let them know that the crew is aware of their presence and connoting that both of you are a subject of interest and soon without a doubt you will be caught and dealt with.

Not much time have past, the other two choppers, the Empire and the Teflon have arrived at the scene to join the hunt. Now there were three choppers circling the subjects down below, but neither Drake nor the alien had any intention of stopping. They kept on moving forward in a slightly inclined slop toward predetermined direction appointed by the alien.

Approximately two-hundred feet away, soldiers began to repel from three choppers quickly one by one in full combat gears. Sakreg realized he was going to be in a heap of trouble if he didn't act quickly. He stopped and faced the choppers then without hesitation he pulled his handheld weapon and let loose three ionized crimson balls that struck all three choppers, and they all exploded like a fourth of July, then all three plummeted to the ground and became fully engulfed in flames.

"Oh, shit, did you all hear that?" asked Captain Sarga emphatically.

"Yes sir, it sounded like three separate explosions sir," said the Staff Sergeant Nayk.

"Dragon this is Captain Sarga. We heard explosions. What's going on out there do you copy?" asked the captain, but there was no response.

"Dragon, come in Dragon!" there was a slight pause, then the captain said, "answer me damn it!" there still was no respond.

"Teflon and Empire, do you copy!" there was no response from them also.

"What the f*** is going on here! No one is responding! The choppers must be down, that's it. My men are hurt, or may even be killed," said Captain Sarga with deep concern on his face.

"Captain, I believe the alien must have caused them explosions. That f***ing alien must be very well armed sir, and I might say we must exercise caution in handling this son of a bitch," said Lieutenant Harstaff.

"I agree. But, we must get there fast and help our injured men, then we will deal with that f***ing alien. Let's pick some speed in our steps," said the captain, and they began to scuttle through the shrubs and the thickets on an inclined terrain.

Only eight soldiers managed to rappel before the choppers went down in flame that included Lieutenant Kenten. Lieutenant Kenten took charge of the seven rappelled soldiers and decided to take five with him to save the crew from the flaming choppers, and assigned two to pursue the alien, then dispatched MEDVAC to transport the dead and the wounded to the nearest medical facilities.

Drake and Sakreg managed to hide behind a chaparral and at the same time, they kept their sight of the approaching soldiers. Drake felt weary. He witnessed the destruction of the government property and experienced the loss of many soldiers lives that caused by his alien friend, which now makes him an "accessory to the fact." Big penalties awaited him if he should be caught; Drake decided it is not going to be his choice of being caught.

The two soldiers were getting close, in fact, too close for the comfort, but they still had no clue as to the where about of Sakreg and Drake.

Sakreg slowly began to pull his weapon from its housing and was getting ready to shoot. Drake gently impeded his movement with his hand and insisted Sakreg to put his weapon aside and lay low. This was going to be Drake's fight not Sakreg.

Drake picked up a palm size rock and threw it toward southeast direction just to create a diversion. As the rock hit the ground, it made a thudding sound. As intense and alert the soldiers were, they immediately opened fire in full auto toward the fallen rock, but soon they realized it was just a diversion. They immediately replaced their empty clips with full magazines.

Drake suddenly stood up, with his .45 caliber pistol and took a very quick aim at one of the soldiers that was closest to him and pulled the trigger then set right back down. The soldier acquired the round right between the eyes and fell on his back then hit the ground fast and hard. His corpse remained on the ground motionless and breathless.

Sergeant Hoyt immediately threw himself to the ground and laid on his bally, he remained in that position for few seconds to ascertain as to what just transpired here. He slowly swiveled his head to his right shoulder, glared at the motionless body that was lying on the ground approximately fifteen feet away from him and he came to realization that Sage was indeed dead.

Hoyt couldn't believe his eyes that Corporal Sage was dead on the ground and began to mussitate by uttering these words to himself, "Damen—that could have been meeee!"

He immediately assayed the area for a nearest hideout place, at the same time attempted to ascertain the exact whereabouts of Drake and the alien. However, from the sound of the gunfire, he was able to conclude their whereabouts in respect to his location.

Sergeant Hoyt found an interim hiding place and slowly crawled to it, which was behind the thick and tall bushes that were nearby.

Captain Sarga, Lieutenant Harstaff, and Staff Sergeant Nayk heard the same shot that downed Corporal Sage, for they were approximately three-hundred-fifty feet away from the incident. The three dispersed themselves immediately and hid behind large bushes.

"This is Captain Sarga. Can anyone hear me out there—over?" said the captain in a very low voice.

"Yes sir this is Sergeant Hoyt. I hear you sir—over."

"What was that shot about sergeant?" asked the captain.

"Sir—Corporal Sage from Teflon group is down sir. Shot by the man who was assisting the alien sir. I would say he sure is a damn good shooter. He got Sage right between the eyes and half of his f***ing brain is gone sir—over," said Sergeant Hoyt with sadness in his voice.

"All right, we are dealing with a professional here. Be careful and stay low. We're coming to help you. We're going to get that son of a bitch and the f***ing alien if my life depended on it. Damn it, I see my choppers are down in flame. How the f*** did that happened over?" asked the captain.

"I don't know sir. All I know is that all of a sudden I saw three red balls of light came out of nowhere and hit all three choppers and they instantly were engulfed in flame, and then, went down quick sir—over," said Sergeant Hoyt.

"All right, what's the count? —over," asked the captain.

"I don't know how many dead or wounded we have here sir. Before the choppers went down, eight of us were able to rappel—including the Lieutenant Kenten. He was in charge of us eight and dispatched five to help rescue the soldiers from the downed choppers including himself sir and assigned Corporal Sage and me to the detail of capturing the alien and his assistant sir—over," responded Sergeant Hoyt.

"Very well, Sergeant; do you have a visual of the alien and his helper at this moment—over?" asked the captain.

"Negative sir, but I would say, from the sound of the firearm that killed Corporal Sage, it must have been a .45 caliber pistol, and I would also add the distance and the direction, that would be approximately eighty feet due North of me sir that will make approximately nine o'clock from my position sir—over," replied Sergeant Hoyt.

"All right proceed with caution! I don't want to lose another man in process do you hear me sergeant?—over," said Captain Sarga.

"Yes sir—over and out," said Sergeant Hoyt and raised his head slightly just enough to witness top of the shrubs.

"Captain, do you copy?" asked Sergeant Hoyt.

"Yes Sergeant I copy; go ahead," said the captain.

"Sir, did you see that?" asked Sergeant Hoyt.

"See what Sergeant, be specific?" asked the captain.

"Yes sir, I will, I Have just witnessed some movements behind that large Pine tree next to the smaller one. It's approximately at ten o'clock position, and one-hundred-twenty feet away from where I am, and about twelve o'clock position from where you are sir, and I would say approximately one-hundred -fifty feet away from you. It's just about the same place as I thought the alien and his friend helper would be by now and the direction of their observation is southbound. "I believe at the present time they are not moving sir. Can you see that large Pine tree sir—over?" asked Sergeant Hoyt.

"Yes, yes I see it. All right, we must move fast. Sergeant Hoyt, at my command, when I say, "let's move", you will head northbound and come from his left side, lieutenant and you Sergeant Nayk, do you copy?" asked the captain, and each responded, "Yes sir, we copy—over."

"Very well—lieutenant, you and Sergeant Nike will have to go straight forward toward that pine tree next to the small one at twelve o'clock position. Do you both see that pine tree?" asked the captain.

"Affirmative sir," responded both the lieutenant and the sergeant.

"Excellent! Then give yourselves approximately forty feet apart, and both of you will engage in a suppressive fire.

:" I will take his right and come from left side. At my command, we will proceed. If this is clear to all, there will be silence for ten seconds then I know all of you have understood my instructions. I will then give the command, just wait for my command!" said the captain. When the ten seconds were up, Captain Sarga gave the command.

"All right, let's move it. Fire at will, but be careful with your ammo, and remember—we want the alien alive if all possible!" said the captain.

They all carefully began to move forward toward their intended target as planned. Sergeant Nayk and the Lieutenant Harstaff began their shooting spree a few bursts at a time, their intended target was Drake and the alien. The shooting conducted in an alternating fashion to deprive Drake of his opportunity to use his hand-held weapon.

Drake acknowledged their motive and their movements. He thought to himself, "should my alien friend and I stay in this present location, these bastards are going to ambushed us and possibly kill us in the process." So, Drake came to a decision to move fast and head the same direction where Sakreg was leading him all along, "northeast" toward the lava bed next to the Mt. Adams. Drake had a hunch that is where he will find the spaceship, somewhere on the huge lava bed and possibly clocked.

Drake beckoned Sakreg with hand signals to get up off the ground and stay low, then move quickly toward the intended direction, "northeast". As Drake and Sakreg kept being astir, volleys of rifle rounds kept on whizzing by them like fiery darts; some were extremely close, maybe inches apart from their bodies.

Sakreg caught sight of Sergeant Hoyt charging fast and closing in on them both from southeast direction. Sergeant Hoyt's body having been fully exposed to the elements. He didn't think of any evasive maneuvers, and stormed headlong.

Sakreg immediately froze all his movements, swiveled his body quickly and faced Sergeant Hoyt. Without hesitation, he discharged his fearsome weapon. Red ball of bright plasma projectile, an inch in diameter jettisoned from its barrel, and within seconds, it engaged Sergeant Hoyt and immediately pulverized him right on the spot.

While Sakreg and Drake were fleeing the area, Drake from the corner of his eyes captured sight of Captain Sarga and noticed he was closing in on them from northwest direction. Captain Sarga on the other hand thought now he had the advantage point and halted all his movements, poised his body in a position and brought Drake in his Rifle crosshairs, and was ready to shoot at any moment.

Just before pulling the trigger, Drake made a quick summersault, and before his feet hit the ground, he discharged a round from his .45 caliber pistol and engaged Captain Sarga right between the eyes. Captain Sarga instantly fell face forward and hit the ground hard and didn't move or even execute a twitch.

"What the f***, Lieutenant, did you see that? The captain just got shot and he didn't get up. I think he is dead. I would say, we're gona need more men here, as you see, the captain is dead, so as Sergeant Hoyt, let me call for backup now sir! I don't want us to be the next in the body bag lieutenant!" said Sergeant Nayk.

"No, we are not going to be the next in the body bag sergeant! What's the matter with you? What happened to your military training and your confidence? We should be able to handle this Jackass. He thinks he is a big shot. We will show him who the big shot is! Let's split, you take your right and keep your f***ing head low. As you see, he is going to aim at your head. I will take the left, and do the same," said Lieutenant Harstaff.

Just as Lieutenant Harstaff stopped, chatting with Sergeant Nayk a .45 caliber round hit Lieutenant Harstaff right between the eyes and he fell forward to the ground like a free-falling log. He wasn't moving nor breathing.

"Ohhhh shit, now the lieutenant is dead. Damn it, I don't want to die here," said Sergeant Nayk outloud to himself. He leaped forward, landed on the ground belly first to dodge Drake's fiery rounds, and began to shake uncontrollably from his fear.

"Lieutenant Kenten this is staff sergeant Nayk, do you copy?" asked Sergeant Nayk on his communicator.

"Yes Sergeant, this is Lieutenant Kenten. I copy you, go ahead," said Lieutenant Kenten.

"I need more men lieutenant. Captain Sarga is dead, so as Lieutenant Harstaff. I am all alone here and trying to take this asshole down. I don't think I could stand a chance with the son of a bitch he is the best f***ing shooter I have ever seen in my entire f***ing life. Lieutenant I need your help now. I have a feeling, I am going to be the next to bite the f***ing dust like the rest of them did before me," said Sergeant Nayk.

"I copy you Sergeant. I understand your concern, please calm down and I will get the help you need! I will send some men in your way as soon as they are done helping the wounded," said Lieutenant Kenten.

"Well, make it fast lieutenant. I don't have much time here over!" said sergeant Nayk with fretting expression.

"As I said sergeant, the help will be there as soon as possible. Don't take many chances. Just follow them wherever they go. Keep your head low. The help will be there for you soon—over."

"Fine lieutenant; the sergeant is over and out."

"Look, I don't know who you are. I mean no harm to you or anyone else for that matter. I know it is hard for you to believe that. I am just defending the alien and me from folks like you.

You should have left us alone then you wouldn't have to be in this predicament.

"I really feel sad for the decisions you and your cohorts have made by perusing the alien and me in this God-forsaken place. You and your mischievous gang of army rats left me with no choice, but to do what I didn't want to do all along.

"Look, as I have said before—I don't have any intention of harming you or killing you, whoever you are. I just want the alien and me to leave here peacefully and go on our merry way. I promise you, our path will never have to meet again, so what do you say!" said Drake in a serious and loud voice so that Sergeant Nayk could hear.

"Nice try a**h*le! No, not a chance! Whoever the f*** you are, You know we are going to get you and your f***ing alien friend, you son of a bitch! You have caused us lots of f***ing problems and killed lots of my men, and they were all good men with families. You are going to pay for all this with your God-forsaking life, damn it, and you are not getting out of here alive, you know that, don't you! Did you hear me?" asked Sergeant Nayk loud enough so that Drake could hear.

"Ya, I heard you. I feel sad for your decision. Ok then suit yourself whoever you are! We'll see who gets out of here alive and who doesn't. But for your information Mr., I could have shot and killed all of you a lot sooner. I picked your men one at a time for a reason, for you all to understand and reconsider with whom you are dealing with. I wanted to instill God's fear in you all so that you would understand to back-off and spare your lives.

"Let me inform you, for your information, I am a professional shooter and expert in handling all sorts of weapons. I have national trophies to back my statements. I am going to say this with all humility; make no mistake, you really don't stand a chance with me I really mean it.

"Please consider my statements, move on, and spare your life. If you decide otherwise, my conscious is going to be clear, because I am going to think that I gave you the world of chance to get out of here alive, and you refused, so what do you say?" Drake yelled out aloud, but there was no response from Sergeant Nayk.

CHAPTER 29

Suddenly, there were faint and distant choppy sounds in the air. The sounds were getting stronger and louder in each passing second. They were the sounds of two Medivac choppers that were summoned by Lieutenant Kenten. Their mission was to evacuate the dead and the wounded.

Staff Sergeant Nayk gained new strength and new purpose to continue the hunt for the alien. His confidence shot to the roof thinking his help is on its way.

"Do you hear them choppers? They are here to take you in custody for all the crimes you have committed," said Staff Sergeant Nayk.

"Oh—my—goodness, I am really scared now! What do you think I should do?" asked Drake in a fearful voice but with derisive expression on his face.

*"I am glad that you are coming to your senses. Now, you should surrender to me—you, a**h*le before we install a bullet in your head and that would be ugly,"* said Sergeant Nayk.

"Surrender---what's that. I don't understand. Please tell me, is it something you eat because I am hungry?" asked Drake with a smirk on his face.

*"No dumb f***, it is you give yourself up to me, before I feed your hunger with a bullet in your head. Did you hear that?"*

"Ohhhhhhhh------soooo that's what it means. Thanks for explaining that to me. It is then I should surrender to you right?" asked Drake with a flouting expression.

*"Yes, you dumb f***, do it now before it is too late for you!"* said the sergeant.

"Now let me think, how should I do that, should I raise my arms up? Is that how it goes?" asked Drake.

"Yes, and do it now," said the sergeant. Drake let loose a guffaw.

"Don't be silly. Look here, whoever you are; you should have known that those sounds belonged to HH-60 Jayhawk choppers used for transporting the dead and the wounded. If you be stupid and challenge me, perhaps they will pick your dead body too, after I am done with you," said Drake aloud.

"How do you know that the choppers are HH-60 Jayhawks?" asked Sergeant Nayk.

"I worked on them. I designed their rotors. I know what they sound like. I'll bet you didn't know that these choppers were HH-60 Jayhawks, did you?" said Drake aloud.

There was silence for about ten seconds.

"Look, whoever you are, we are going to leave now. Do not attempt to follow us, or you will have to meet your friends in hell just like the rest of them have. I suggest that you go and help your friend soldiers who are hurt in result of your foolishness.

The HH-60 choppers are already there. Your friends are going to be very busy air lifting the dead and the wounded and they are not going to come for your aid trust me," said *Drake.* There was silence.

Drake and his alien friend Sakreg began to move same direction as they were heading before. A quarter mile left for them to exit the forest. Sakreg occasionally glanced at his wrist attachment possibly to locate his craft and to make sure his heading is accurate. Sergeant Nayk began to follow them indiscreetly leaving approximately one-hundred feet of distance between them.

Sakreg came to conclusion that he must leave this planet and go back home as soon as possible. His dreams, his expectations, and his explorations cut short and shattered. He thought how such a beautiful planet could house such a barbaric race called humans. He knew his life would be in danger should he decide to remain on this planet.

"Sergeant Nayk, this is Lieutenant Kenten. Do you copy?"

"Yes, this is Sergeant Nayk I copy you."

"What is your position, over?" asked Lieutenant Kenten.

"Less than a quarter mile and approximately three hundred degrees northwest of you, lieutenant, over," said Nayk.

"Very well Sergeant, now I am sanding some men along your way over," said Kenten.

"Great—how many?" asked Nayk.

"Seven, to be exact, over," said Kenten.

"I hope they make it here in time, they are getting away fast, over," said Nayk.

"Distract them for a little while until the men reach you. They should be there within three minutes, over," said Kenten.

"I will do my best to hold them down until they arrive lieutenant, over," said Nayk.

"Very well Sergeant, carry on. Lieutenant Kenten is over and out."

Sergeant Nayk let couple of bursts from his rifle at their direction and hid behind a large tree. Drake and Sakreg on the other hand, were just leaving the forest behind them, and were beginning to step on to the lava bed. Suddenly they stopped and turned around and faced the direction of the fire.

"Is that you again whoever you are, when I have warned you not to pursue us?" yelled Drake aloud and began to scan the area for movements.

"Ya, that's me, I am not gona let you get away. Do you hear me?" said Nayk. Nayk was feeling very secure and cocky knowing there will be help here in no time.

Drake began to think. Why all of a sudden, this man is feeling so sure of himself and cocky? He is perusing us and engaging in fire, unless there should be help coming his way soon, and perhaps any moment now. *"Let me guess, I recon, you have some help coming in your way, isn't that right?"* asked Drake.

"Ya you bet! —you are a smart cookie, aren't you? You figured it out all that by yourself. But you know something—too bad, you are not going to see tomorrow's sunlight," said Nayk.

"Really? —Should I be scared now?"

"Yes, you should be scared very scared!" said Sergeant Nayk.

"All right, if it makes you feel happy to hear that I am scared, then I dare to say I am scared now. There you go I have said it and I suppose now that makes you feel happy to hear that— right!"

"Yes, very much so!" said Nayk.

"You know, you are one sick cookie; but sorry, I hate to disappoint you Mr., I lied to you. I am not scared. Will you forgive my lie?" exclaimed Drake.

"What!" exclaimed Nayk.

"I know what you are trying to do, you are trying to stull me until your help arrives—right?" said Drake.

"You have scored one more time. Are you a mind reader?" asked Nayk.

"Weeeeell—shall we conclude that I am much smarter than you and your cohorts put together? Don't you agree?" asked Drake. There was silence.

"Well, I am moving now. I suggest you don't follow me— unless you want to die. That is my final warning to you Mr. and Hast la vista whoever you are," said Drake.

All seven men arrived surreptitiously at the prescribed location. Sergeant Nayk immediately felt emboldened and beckoned them with his hand pointing out Drake's position. They immediately took cover behind tall growths around the lava bed.

For Drake to engage his intended targets that were well hidden, he must attempt to lead them out into the open area so that he could have a clear shot at each one, but doing so, he may have to jeopardize his life. He must devise a plan otherwise he will be besieged soon from all sides and the corollary is going to look dismal.

The soldiers began to move around swiftly and silently giving hand signal commands to each other to blockade Drake and his friend the alien.

"Drop your weapons now. You and your alien friend will soon be surrounded. You don't stand a chance. You must surrender or die. Do you hear me?" said Sergeant Nayk.

"Ya, ya I heard you loud and clear. Let me be the one who decides if I have a chance or not. Besides, I should have killed you long time ago while I had the chance. I don't know why I spared your life. Now that I think of it, it wasn't worth it," said Drake aloud. Moments later, Drake signaled Sakreg to watch his left flank and Drake decided to watch his right flank and attempted to wait for the soldiers to arrive. He couldn't move anywhere, should he have moved, he would have left himself and his alien friend wide open for host of gunfire.

However, there was some distance between Drake and the incoming soldiers. For the solders to get to Drake and the alien; they had to close their distance by moving to an open space, that meant they would be exposed to Dake's deadly aim. Drake knew they didn't stand a chance to remain alive once they were exposed.

Drake had only one drawback. It was his hiding place. He was hiding behind a large fallen tree bole, which meant his exposed body parts were vulnerable to gunfire and that meant the soldiers could have still harmed him and his friend alien too, should they have desired to do so.

However, Drake occasionally reared his head to witness what was coming his way. That in turn left him and his alien friend vulnerable, but thought he had no other choice in this matter, because there was no better hiding place then the large fallen tree trunk.

The three soldiers plus Sergeant Nayk debouched and initiated their suppressive fire so that Drake wouldn't have a chance to extend his head beyond the large tree log. Two more soldiers on each flank began to move forward cautiously and surreptitiously along with the four in front including Sergeant Nayk. Bullets whizzed over Drake's and the alien's head, and occasionally the rounds struck little rocks, and made a ricocheting sound.

Drake felt trapped behind the tree log, and regardless of his gun expertise, he felt uneasy dealing with oncoming soldiers who were bent to take his life away and the life of his alien friend. The thought of death began to linger in his head. He realized that maybe venturing into this part of the world was a definite mistake on his part and now it may have to cost his life after all. Nevertheless, he was determined to handle whatever that came in his way to his last breath.

Drake thought now is the time to execute a very risky do-or-die action. Should he stay put, it will certainly cause his demise. Drake threw himself on the hard ground and quickly rolled and each time he rolled he shot a soldier right between the eyes. They fell back like a freshly cut log gravitating towards the ground. He eliminated the two that were coming from his right flank and the three from the middle flank. The bullets were still flying by and whizzing very close to his body, missing him by a few inches.

He quickly rolled right back where he was, behind the large tree log. Sakreg on the other hand shot and vaporized the two that were coming dangerously close from his left flank. The only soldier left alive was Sergeant Nayk.

Sergeant Nayk froze in his position with his rifle in his hand and appeared dumfounded, mused, and distraught, exposed, and assailable. *"This is not happening, it couldn't happen,"* he muttered to himself, *"All my men are dead except me. How could this be? Why I am not dead like the rest of them? This is not fair."* He dropped his rifle and pulled his nine-mm handgun, cocked it, and pointed it right to his head with a trembling hand.

Drake came out from behind the tree log into the open and began to walk briskly toward Sergeant Nayk and at the same time he never lost the aim of his .45 caliber pistol right at Nayk's head just in case he obtained a wild hair up his ass and changed his mind than started to shoot.

Drake came within six feet of Nayk and said, "Drop it now." Nayk ignored the instruction and continued as if he didn't hear him.

"I said, drop it now! It is not worth to be dead like the rest. Think of your precious loved ones who are waiting patiently for your return home. The good Lord must have purposed you to be alive don't waste it. Life is precious. There will be plenty of good times ahead for you and your loved ones at home. Don't shortchange them and yourself too. Drop it now, drop it I said," said Drake.

Teardrops began to roll down Nayk's cheeks. His silent cry was becoming an obvious expression on his distressed and melancholic face.

Drake approached Nayk slowly and cautiously with his gun still pointing at Nayk's head. Drake freed one of his hands and reached for Nayk's handgun and curled his fingers on its barrel, and told him, *"Let go. Let go of it now. Everything is going to be all right. Just let it go."*

Drake slowly pushed the barrel of the gun away from Nayk's head and Nayk surrendered the nine-mm handgun to Drake. He immediately took the clip off the gun and emptied the round from its chamber, also ejected the remaining bullets from the clip and gave it back to him an empty gun. Drake did the same with Nayk's rifle that was on the ground and gave it back to him.

Nayk stood still, maintained a quiet and sullen expression with teardrops still rolling down his face. Appearance of daze hunted his face with a fixated stare to the ground. Drake came closer to Nayk and read the name label off his chest, and it read Nayk Ralph.

"Now that's better Sergeant Nayk," said Drake. Nayk raised his head and glared angrily at Drake and said, *"Why didn't you shoot me Mr.!"*

"I didn't need to shoot you. You were not a threat to me at any given time, and if you want to know, I am not a killer. I don't kill for fun, maybe you do, but I don't.

I respect life in every form including the alien's life. I kill only for self-defense and for survival—mind you. You folks didn't give me much chance to go on my merryway peacefully, especially your notorious freaking Captain whatever his name was. I want to cuss him out so bad, but I knew I had to restrain myself from using colorful expressions. It is not my forte, besides, my God doesn't appreciate such language. Now it doesn't matter anyway. Sadly, your captain has made many bad choices that lead him to his demise. One thing I would say, he certainly did not deserve the rank he had, nor lead anyone. All right—enough of that. I am going to take the alien to his spaceship. It must be here somewhere close by. His craft could very well be cloaked. You know what that means right?

"No sir—not really," said Nayk.

"It means the physical object what-ever it is, with some clever technology it renders the object invisible. That is why we can't see it, and that is why your men in choppers couldn't see it. Now, I want you to go back to your men and get out of here, and I will go on my merryway—this time I reckon peacefully I hope. Can I count on that?"

"I will do you no harm sir. Yes, you can count on that," said Nayk

"Thanks. Maybe someday our paths may cross, and we will have a drink or two and talk about the events that took place here. You can tell me how it all started," said Drake.

"Yes, I would say that could be a possibility, if you don't go to prison for all that you have done sir," said Nayk.

"I don't intend to go to prison—Sergeant Nayk," said Drake.

"I didn't catch your name sir," asked Nayk with a slightly spirited expression.

"Well, if you should know — my name is Drake Grenhr, and the alien's name is Sakreg," said Drake. He turned around and continued his path as Sakreg lead the way. Sergeant Nayk made the move to go back to his men, but after taking few steps, he suddenly stopped in his tracks and changed his mind to stay around and witness what was about to transpire right before his eyes: the revelation of the alien craft, and the alien's departure from this planet.

Sergeant Nayk surmised Drake would leave with the alien because he didn't have anything else going for him but a heap of trouble with the law enforcement and the military too. He couldn't afford to remain here and face the judicial system.

Drake and Sakreg gingerly walked eastbound attempting to avoid sharp edged rocks and broken beer bottles from the previous visitors. Sakreg began to monitor his wrist gadget and pushed few of its buttons and there it was in fullness of its glory: the giant alien spacecraft that has come to life from nothingness.

There was no craft like it on this planet. It appeared foreboding, redoubtable, ominous, and commanding. Nayk stood in total amazement and raised a quizzical eyebrow. He quickly pulled his smart phone from one of his pockets and took a picture of it that included the alien and the Drake from their backside.

Sakreg and Drake neared the gap between them and the spacecraft until they were standing right next to it. Drake couldn't help but gaze at it for few seconds in total astonishment. He remained speechless and admired its graceful but aggressive design and the amount of technology that went into producing such an amazing craft. He moved all around this flying beast, felt its material and its texture with the tip of his fingers, and realized the material was not the kind of material that one could find on earth. There were slight electrical discharges every time when his fingers encountered the exterior of the craft.

Sakreg pushed few buttons, the canopy began to ascend, and the boarding ladder began to descend toward the ground. He stepped up the ladder, entered the canopy, and beckoned Drake to get on board his craft.

Drake glared attentively at Sakreg. He was utterly surprised at Sakreg's gesture, and thought, *"what should this beckoning really mean? Does it mean that I am to leave this God blessed earth for good and never to see it again in my entire life, and go on to an unknown world, which it could be fraught with danger, and take my chances along the way? How dare I, how dare I leave my son, my friends, my job, my house, my treacherous wife and leave without announcement.*

I came here to make my mind up about my marriage, yet the result was short of my decision. Also, should I venture into the unknown with such a strange looking alien, which I have some clue about his character, his attributes, and his behavior. I still don't know much about him and his culture and nothing about his planet, is it dark and gloomy and foreboding, or pleasant to the point where I may not desire to return home?

If I should go to his planet, could he provide for my protection from rest of his kind, deliver ease of mind, and make me forget about everything that I cherished here on earth. Could that be possible, or will I be bereft of earth and pine for it for the rest of my living years?

On the other hand, how am I going to explain to the judge and to the jury of all the killings I have done? Self-defense I may protest, but that will be very difficult for me to prove especially when the military is attempting to destroy me. If I should stay here, someone may have to sign my death certificate soon, or I may have to be incarcerated to life in prison with rest of the imprisoned miscreants. Life in the prison is not going to be a walk in the park. I must always be watchful of the prisoners lest they stab me in the back at any given moment, and that I must always sleep with one eye open." These were the thoughts that blasted through his mind.

Sakreg pointed at his wrist gadget, then beckoned him again to come on board hurry up the type of thing. Apparently, for Sakreg, the time was running short, and Drake was wasting

Sakreg's time thinking about his own plans and attempting to determine his destiny within few moments that he had.

Suddenly many troops egressed the timberland to come to Nayk's succor and began to run towards the ship and shoot at the same time. Bullets whizzed near Sakreg and Drake and some struck the spacecraft but didn't cause any damage.

This was not the time for Drake to display mettle as he did before. He knew, if he didn't get out of here with Sakreg in time, he would be knocking at the death's doors, because there was nowhere for him to run or hide and take any action to defend himself. He was standing on a hard and open dried up lava ground.

Drake now must surrender to the troops if he wished to remain alive, but then the court litigations should occupy most of his time and the corollary wasn't going to be to in his advantage.

Drake hauled his duffel bag scurried toward the ladder while the bullets were still flying by him. He stepped into the canopy with all his belonging. Sakreg sat him on the copilot seat that was right behind the pilot seat, arranged for Drake's comfort, attached the life support system on him, went and sat on the pilot seat, and started the engines.

Suddenly there were plumes of dust in the air. The craft slowly began to lift off the ground, and when it reached sixty feet up into the air, it made 180° turn toward east, then suddenly accelerated with great speed, ascended toward space, and then vanished from sight.

CHAPTER 30

Sakreg was a "lone fighter," the co-piolt's chair remained empty while arriving to the planet earth. The empty chair had all the adjustable safety accommodations including a breathing apparatus. With one push of a button, all the accessories and the life support equipment would have attached themselves automatically on the body whoever was sitting on the chair.

This spacecraft was designed primarily for Eponans. However, because of all the extreme computerized adjustments that could be performed on the devises and mechanisms that were attached to the chair, it also functioned well on humans.

Drake rested motionless on the co-pilot seat. The cabin was pressurized by the Planet Eranduh's atmosphere, and as soon as Drake inhaled one breath of its atmospheric gases, he started to cough and wheeze violently. He felt lightheaded, eyes became red and watery, and his nose began to drip mucus. His attires became drenched in sweat, as if he was having a very severe cold. His condition persisted approximately twenty minutes, and then lost consciousness.

Suddenly Drake opened his eyes. He had no idea how long he has been out and unconscious. He appeared bewildered and somewhat out of touch with his enviernment.

Drake peered through the glass of the apparatus that was hooked on his head. His sight embraced the canopy's gadgets and flickering light dots. He shifted his eyes toward the windows of the canopy and acknowledged the blackness of the space that was peppered with distant bright coruscating lights, which he thought they must be stars. Suddenly it dawned on him that he wasn't on earth any longer, and that he must be somewhere in space, but didn't know where and how far he was in the space.

Drake moved his eyes toward the pilot and noticed the pilot's fingers were tweaking the gadgets on the console. Drake was not aware of time. However, he felt no more wheezing, coughing, feeling of lightheadedness, and no more sweating.

Drake gained his sanse of cohearance and thought the thought of leaving the earth all together was becaming a haunting reality for him. He felt, *"This is it. This is my destiny now. And I am to be venturing beyond the stars. No more earth, and no more turning back. A new chapter in my life wheather I survive it or not".*

A few teardrops rolled down Drake's checks and felt that he had already missed earth and his loved ones; furthermore, he was in a strange spaceship, accompanied by a strange being that he can't communicate verbally with, share thoughts, or even express emotions. Despite of the alien pilot piloting this craft, he felt powerless to change his fate and felt all alone in the space.

Drake had no feelings of motion. He felt as if he stopped in the middle of the vest expense of darkness that was full of distant speckling stars, but he knew that the spaceship, must be moving in a great speed in which he had no clue as to how fast it was moving through the space.

He shut his eyes and dived into a deep muse. He thought, there was going to be no more treacherous wife, no more son that he love much, no more friends that he hobnobbed with in ritzy cafes, no more highway traffic that he had to be bogged down for sometime, no more work and schedules that he had to meet, no more home that he had to take care of, no more coffee that he had to cherish the taste of, no more earth's sunlight that he had to witness, no more snow-capped mountains, hills, and valleys, and no more vegetation and people.

Drake decided to disembark from his seat knowing that he was strapped down very well. There were plethora of hoses and devises attached on him and around him; but took a moment and reassessed his thoughts. He acknowledged that these attachments must be crucial for his survival out here in space and decided not to precede with his decision, he made his mind to sit back and enjoy the ride however the length of time it took to reach Sakreg's destination.

Drake glanced at the counsel and took notice of the elaborate gadgets having buttons with flickering lights: some red, some green, some yellow and some white and devices having levered handles and large revolving knobs and in the middle of the cockpit, there he was, Sakreg wide awake sitting on a huge chair, and operating the flight counsel.

Suddenly at a distance, a planet came into a view with a pale lit atmosphere. Drake immediately knew that it was the planet Mars because he had seen its recent photos back on earth. He noticed the red crust, the great-canyons, and its craters. The planet appeared just like the photos he had seen and couldn't believe his eyes that he was embracing the sight of the planet Mars, and that, he was near it—just above its atmosphere.

The spaceship passed the planet Mars with great speed. Sakreg turned his face around and glanced at Drake. Drake couldn't tell wheather Sakreg was perturbed or calm. Suddenly Sakreg made an up and down motion with his hand attempting to tell him to be calm, and do not move.

Drake remembered the photos of the solar system he observed in his science books and realized that there must be an asteroid belt that they were nearing to—and that it was the sole reason why he was being beckoned by Sakreg to stay calm and not to move. A few hours later, they have arrived at the asteroid belt.

Drake noticed there were countless amounts of rocks of all sizes; some were large, some were as big as the huge mountains on Earth, and some were as big as a large American sedan, tumbling and moving with no specific direction. Some were striking at each other and splitting into many pieces and in result, disturbing their normal paths. Drake felt this was where he and his alien friend would die. His heart began to pelt fast, eyes remained wide open in terror, mouth-hung agape in sheer astonishment and fear, his body became riveted motionless on his seat, hoping, and praying that they will come out of this alarming situation alive and unscathed. Sakreg gingerly, attentively, and deftly maneuvered through them without an incident, and moved toward the planet Jupiter.

He soon reached the outer atmosphere of the planet Jupiter and was very careful not to be absorbed right into it through its intense gravitational pull. Sakreg also realized the large rock shaped spaceship that he escaped from, was no longer in the same vicinity that he experienced previously. It simply wasn't there anymore, and he didn't care, but remembered the events that took place inside the big rock like spaceship.

Drake on the other end, he was much fascinated by the Jupiter's mass and its fast-moving swaths of colorful but turbulent clouds in its atmosphere. He never thought for a moment that he would have such a privilege and opportunity to witness God's creation of the vast universe and its ornaments at firsthand and especially this close. He took a moment and praised God for it.

Drake came to realize that he was very, very far from earth, and lost all hopes of returning home once again. However, he thought that this was a hard thing to swallow, the thought of losing everything that he worked for and cherished. He also wasn't so sure that he was going to survive the trip that he was in at this moment, especially not knowing where in the universe he was destined to go.

Suddenly there it was a huge whirling phenomenon, few hundred miles ahead of his ship at ten o'clock position. Sakreg realized that this wormhole must be the same wormhole that he came out off while ago, and now he must go through it again to get home. Within few minutes, he entered right through it.

The background space, including the planets and the stars, vanished from sight. There was nothing but ink-black space, and I felt no movement whatsoever. It was as if the spaceship stood still in total blackness and had no sensation of time, but, two earth years have lapsed.

Suddenly an overwhelming light penetrated the canopy of the spaceship; Sakreg's star fighter had just exited the Wormhole with ferocity and faced the star that shed light and warmth to the planet down below. There it was all alone, a colorful planet possibly at a size that matched earth. Sakreg turned around and faced Drake with elation and excited expression. He blurted Eranduh, pointing his finger toward the planet.

Drake could swear he detected a smile and some form of excitement on Sakreg's face when he said Eranduh, and then Sakreg turned right back to manage the flight. Right than Drake knew that this planet was Sakreg's home. Soon, this planet was also going to be Drake's home. He was going to spend the rest of his life here on this planet called Eranduh.

Drake couldn't take his eyes off this prismatic orb called Erandue. He felt mesmerized by its brilliance, and intrigued by all its hues and thought that just maybe I can get use to this planet after all. Sakreg on the other hand, broke a happy smile knowing he will soon be meeting his friends and family members that he left behind for such a long time, especially his newly born son, whom he missed being with all this time.

After a short time, Sakreg suddenly lost his cheerful expression. He realized everyone might be thinking of him as being dead or lost in space, and when it came to his military duty, how was he going to explain to his superiors his absence from his military service, especially for him being away for such a long time, and that he has been alive all this time.

Sakreg entered the planet's atmosphere with great speed. A few moments have passed then suddenly his left engine began to spew bellowing black smoke, and soon after, the engine began to burst inflames throwing ambers into the air. Drake knew right then that Sakrag lost his left engine. Now, the thought of crash landing this vessel was becoming very real in Drake's mind, but the thought of having another engine to depend on had eased his mind to some extent. Soon after, the other engine followed the same suite as the first one did. It too burst into flames and generated huge amount of smoke trail from its engine. Now Sakrag had no other choice but to safely crash land this craft, and somehow avoids the population centers all together and land this bird in a rural area.

Sakreg appeared distressed and so did Drake. Sakrag kept turning his head back toward Drake beckoning him to stay calm. With great struggle and legerity, Sakreg maintained the course of his star craft but the black smoke from both engines trailed the craft like a contrail.

Sakreg attempted to engage his landing gears but was not able to do so, for it was not functional. Suddenly his eyes bulged, his mouth gaped in sheer horror as he descended toward the tera-ferma, and soon he made a crash landing without the landing gears being activated. The craft slid, scrapped, destroyed small trees, and shrubs, and just before it came to a full stop, it hit a large tree stem and broke the right wing then stopped.

The flames from the engins were becoming ever more prominent. Sakreg quickly disengaged all the connections that were attached on his flight-suite and got off his seat rather speedly and decoupled Drake's attachments frantically then yanked him off his reclined seat and broke the flight deck windshield with a blunt insturmant that he pulled from one of the compartments in the cockpit. Drake heaved all his belongings specially his backpack that was full of ammos and tossed it off the spaceship then they both jumped out in unison to the ground, rolled a few times, then they got on their feet. Drake picked his belongings and Sakrag helped to carry some of drake's belongings and they both ran away into the field as fast as they can. As they were running, parts of the craft exploded into million pieces. The exploded parts catapulted like a shrapnel and its ambers flew all over the field. The pressure of the explosion pinned them to the ground.

As the further threats of explosions diminished, they both looked at each other having perplexed expressions on their faces, but soon both quickly got back on their feet, extricated themselves of dirt and plant life that leached on to their clothing, then turned around and glared at the downed burning craft in dismay.

Drake heaved his haversack, secured it on his back, and slowly turned 360° around. He scanned the area for anything that moved or was out of the ordinary, but found none. However, he noticed the different colored vegetation all around him. Purple grass, purple tree leaves on the blood red boles and branches.

Drake raised his head to the sky and realized the sun appeared larger than that of the earth, and that it was hovering at the Southern hemisphere instead of the East. He kept on forgetting that he was standing on a totally different and unfamiliar ground. It was a sobering thought for Drake to think that he was standing on a planet other than the earth. He elevated both his arms to the sky gave thanks and praises to God, and said, "Dear God, you are an awesome God you are. Where-ever I find my self at, I find your amazing and precious and glorious handy works that never cease to amaze me. To you be the glory and honor and praise and worship forever. Amen." Then he lowered his arms down and turned around then faced Sakreg. Sakreg stood alone and was silently glaring at Drake, wondering to whom Drake was talking to.

Sakreg realized the crash of his craft happened approximately a thousand miles due southeast of the military base that he served from. There was nothing else but dense timber, tall trees, grass, and shrubs everywhere around the vicinity of the crash site and beautiful rolling purple hills and knolls at a near distance from where they stood. They both felt all alone in this vast wilderness, but at least they had each other for help and comfort despite their language and race differences.

Suddenly, Sakreg heard a distant humming sound that was coming from the eastern hemisphere (earth south). He knew immediately that this sound belonged to a flying war-craft that is trapezoid in design.

This flying vessel was approximately three buses long and housed fiercely hostile and aggressive Darkan civilian militia groups that were the denizens of the Eroom tribe. This tribe utilized advanced technology whenever they could get their hands on it. They plundered other tribes in their wealth and preyed on the effete.

There was some thick bramble, saplings, and a few tall trees with large trunks in the area as both Drake and Sakreg ventured further away from the crash sight. Sakreg swiftly beckoned Drake to hide behind a large tree that had a huge block with hefty branches that were located approximately five buses' length in the distance due earth south from where they were standing so that he became invisible to the flying intruders, and so did Sakreg the same approximately two buses in length away from where Drake hid himself.

The craft flew low, right above Drak's and Sakerg's heads, with a heavy more of its engines that shook the ground as it crossed over to the crash site; then the vessel came right above the destroyed spacecraft, hovered approximately one hundred feet in the air for a minute or two, and then moved to a landing spot and landed on the grassy ground not too distant from the crash sight. But, before the crew had disembarked from the craft, their leader, Vobak, turned around and faced all his teammates, then blurted, *"Look here all of you, before we get out of this ship, I have something to say to you all. I know I haven't told you where we are going until now. I wanted it to be a surprise to every one of you. But I thought now is the best time to tell you where we are heading, but first, I want to say —we have a little time to spend here. Whatever we do, we are going to do it fast. Second: We have an important appointment to attend to. Our Eponan soldier friend by the name of Dnak has buried ten handheld weapons that we must retrieve. They are at some distance from their military base. I have the right coordinates. With these ten devastating weapons, we could kill hundreds in one shot."*

"Really chief, we can kill hundreds?" said one of the crewmembers by the name of Angue with an excited expression.

"Yes really. These weapons are very powerful and are powered by new technology. They spit out an enormous amount of plasma balls. If one of these plasma balls hits anyone, they will immediately disintegrate. We must have them. With these weapons, we will be invincible. No one will mess with us, and we'll do what we want and when we want it," said Vobak, the chieftain of his six henchmen.

"Chief, can we trust this Eponan soldier called Dnak. Don't you think it could also be a trap? You know chief, they'll do anything to capture you and us. They know how much mischief you have caused to Eponans in all these years, and you know they have been after you to capture you for such a long time?" said one of the crewmembers by the name of Toshar.

"Yes, yes, I know, and you don't have to rub it on my face, but you have a point there Toshar. However, I want you to know that I am aware of their schemes, and I am not a fool to fall into their traps. I know this Eponan soldier. I have been working with him and studying his behavior for some time now, and I find him sympathetic toward our cause.

"I have initiated the location for the weapons where I want them to be buried. He is also going to be there at the hidden weapon's site, and we are going to pick him up and all the guns too. He will be one of our team members. I want you all to work

with him and treat him like one of our own, is that clear to you all?"

"Yes, chief," replied all.

"Excellent then, that's what I want to hear. After we pick him up we are going to collect our precious commodity—the Munar (gold). I hope Chief Gnokn will not disappoint us this time.

"If he disappoints us this time, I'll personally kill him myself," said Lanbeh, one of Vobak's henchmen.

"I like your enthusiasm Lanbeh, but I hope it doesn't have to come to that. If everything goes according to our plan, then it is going to make us rich, all of us very rich. So, now let's find out what went on here and let's do it fast, but be thorough. Is that clear to everyone?" said Vobak

"Yes sir," replied all.

Seven heavily armed Darkan militiamen disembarked from the craft, including Vobak, their leader, and began to move expeditiously toward the crash site with weapons in their hands, fingers on the trigger, they were ready to engage at anything that moved in front of their orbs. When the crew reached the burning site, Vobak suddenly blurted. *"This is an Eponan craft! What is it doing here in this hemisphere? They have no business of being here. They must be in pursuit of us. Search for the crew now! Let's hope we find them dead, and if they are not, then shoot them dead. They must be killed!"*

The crew began to comb the area to locate the pilot. They collected broken debris from the downed craft for some undisclosed reasons. One of the henchmen by the name of Gaaet, being extra sensitive to his surroundings, sensed a presence, decided to search the area in his own way, and began to deviate alone from the rest of the group.

Gaaet moved slowly in a hunkered-down position as if he was out in hunting mode and was crushing leaves and broken branches right under his boots and wasn't concerned about making noise. As Gaaet moved, he brandished his large blaster in every direction but straight.

Gaaet came really close to where Drake and Sakreg hid themselves. Drake's heart began to beat fast in trepidation. He felt at any moment now, he or his friend Sakreg would be discovered and would be dealt with severely or possibly be killed right on the spot.

Drake felt ambivalent about weather to attack or remain silent. However, for now, he hoped that Gaaet would leave without an incident, but for now, both Drake and Sakreg remained hunkered down in their hidden places. Drake had his fingers wrapped around the handle of his K-bar (military knife) and was ready to strike.

Gaaet came within ten feet of Drake then stopped and his eyes went into search mode. He sensed a presence here and began to move very slowly and carefully by closing the distance between him and Drake evermore.

As Gaaet came closer and closer, Drake moved slowly around the thick stem of the tree to remain hidden from Gaaet's sight. Drake felt now was the right time to attack, and he must do it without a sound just to be careful not to alert the others.

Gaaet was dressed lightly because of the balmy weather. He had a thin animal skin on his upper body that was covering his back, shoulders, and arms, but his abdomen was wide open. He wore short pants made from animal skin.

Suddenly, Drake came out into the open. Gaaet's eyes widened in surprise, and in horror; without hesitation, Drake swung his left arm horizontally, and with ferocity, he struck Gaaet's right arm. Gaaet's blaster flung from his hand into the air, and with the right arm, Drake swiftly swung the K-bar and slid Gaaet's abdomen wide open. Blood and guts gushed out, and Gaaet fell to the ground, screamed loud once and then gave up the ghost. The crew heard Gaaet's loud cry for it was loud.

"Chief, did you hear that? That could have been a cry of death, and it is one of our crew. I believe it came from down there," said Toshar, pointing his hand south toward where Sakreg and Drake were hiding.

"Yes, I heard that loud and clear. Who is missing from us?" asked Vobak.

"I believe Gaaet sir. I saw him go down where Toshar was pointing at," said one of the crewmembers.

"All right Toshar, take two with you and find out what happened to Gaaet, and if you see anything out of the ordinary, don't hesitate to shoot," said Vobak by having a concerned look on his face.

"Yes sir, don't worry sir, it could just be an animal, a vicious animal at that, and it got Gaaet by surprise. We'll kill the animal, and if Gaaet is still alive, we will bring him back with us. We won't leave him there sir, and let's hope he is still alive," said Toshar, and he took two crew members with him and began to head down toward Sakreg and Drake's hiding place.

Drake realized there were three more well-armed beings like the one he just killed heading his way. *"Now what; what am I supposed to do?"* said Drake quietly to himself, and within seconds, he came to a decision to hide behind the tall bushes located approximately six buses in length due west from where he was hiding.

Toshar and two of his helpers, Oree and Nakor, arrived at the general area where Gaaet was lying motionless on the ground. *"Sir this was the area where I saw Gaaet last. He must not be far from here,"* said Nakor.

"All right then, let's be very watchful. Whatever it hurt him, it could still be around here, and it could also hurt us, so let's be extra careful," said Toshar.

"Let's hope we find him alive," said Oree.

"Yes, that will be nice. He is one of my coolest friends. I ever had. I wouldn't want to see him dead," said Nakor, and they continued their search.

After roaming around for a few minutes, Oree blurted, *"Sir, what's that shiny stuff on the ground in two o'clock direction? It looks like a metal of some sort; can you see that sir?"* Oree pointed his finger toward the shiny material on the ground.

"Yes, yes, I could see that too. It's worthwhile to check it out. Let's head that way," said Toshar, and they all began to head toward the shiny object with a pep in their steps. As they abridged the distance between them and the coruscating metal on the ground, Nakor placed more zest in his steps than the others and got there faster than the rest. He stood right above the object on the ground.

"Toshar, it is Gaaet's rifle on the ground!" said Nakor in a slightly elevated tone and within moments, he swiveled his head to the left, and suddenly, his eyes caught sight of Gaaet's feet, for his body was well hidden in the bushes. Nakor exchanged slow steps toward Gaaet's body then suddenly, his eyes widened in

terror. He grimaced his face in total disgust and obfuscation. Nakor froze his movements for a few seconds and attempted to absorb the reality of what he had just witnessed, and what he viewed was Gaaet's body with his blood guts out and totally exposed to the elements.

Toshar and Oree closed their distance from where Nakor was standing, and before Nakor could open his mouth, they too have witnessed the horror that embodied Gaaet, and they too have expressed their feelings of nausea and grisly disgust.

"What kind of animal would do this by spilling the viscera of the victim out into the open? As you all see, he had a straight and clean cut from his lower abdomen to his chest, as if, a very sharp object did it. And one more thing, all animals eat the flash that they kill, but this one was left all intact. Nothing was eaten from his body. That is very strange.

We have no idea what we're dealing with here. I suggest we all get out of here fast, lest we will become its next victim. One more thing I want to add: he didn't have a chance to shoot. His rifle was flung approximately twenty-five feet away from his body. What we're dealing with here is that—this animal must be very large and intelligent and very strong to do this kind of mayhem, but this animal doesn't eat the flash it kills. What a strange phenomenon. As I have said, let's get out of here fast." Said Toshar with apprehension.

"What about the Gaaet's body Toshar? Aren't we going to take it back with us?" asked Nakor.

"How are we going to do that when his guts are everywhere? I believe we must leave him here and move on without him. Besides, it will only slow us getting back to the ship. Come on, let's get out of here now before we will be the next. I don't want

to create another victim here," said Toshar with reluctance. Everyone pulled a devise and recorded a video of Gaaet's mutilated body before they all left the scene to meet Vobak and the rest of the crew.

"Where is Gaaet? Why is he not with you?" asked Vobak.

"He is dead sir. We had to leave him there. We couldn't bring him back," said Toshar

"What! —you mean he is dead?" asked Vobak.

"Yes sir, that's what I said. He is dead sir, and in a very strange way, I would say. I have never read in the history of this planet, heard, or even seen anyone die this way. This is the first of its kind and it is brutal," said Toshar with a sullen tone and expression.

"Then why didn't you bring him back with you if he was dead?" asked Vobak.

"Sir, his guts, and his blood were all over the ground. None of us wanted to touch him sir. We were much-disgusted sir. However, we took video of his remains. I warn you chief, this video is very graphic, and is disturbing, would you like to see it?" asked Toshar.

"All right, let's see the video?" asked Vobak. Toshar pushed a few buttons on his hand-held device, and there it was, the lifeless body of Gaaet with a clean-cut abdomen and his viscera out into the open.

Suddenly, Vobak's eyes widened in horror, and as soon as he witnessed the mayhem, he was taken aback in disgust. *"I have never seen anything like this in my entire life. What kind of animal could do this mutilation?"* asked Vobak.

"That's exactly what I had to ask to myself Vobak," said Toshar.

"I wonder if we are dealing with a new kind of specie here, and science hasn't recognized it as yet?" said Vobak.

"That is entirely possible sir," said Toshar.

"All right I have seen and heard enough. I am very saddened that we are getting out of here without Gaaet. However, we need to get out of here now. We're running late as we are by lingering around here, plus I had to lose one of my teammates in process," said Vobak.

"Sir, did anyone find the body of the pilot?" asked Toshar.

"No, no one has it yet. We looked everywhere for his body, and it was nowhere to be found. I think he must be alive and afoot. I am very sure of that. However, He can't be far. Eather we or somebody from nearby tribe will find him, and will kill him, or perhaps, the same animal who killed Gaaet will also kill the pilot soon. But now, let's get out of here and get our new weapons and our precious treasure," said Vobak, and they all went into their craft and left the scene.

CHAPTER 31

Sakreg and Drake came out from their hiding places and met where Gaaet was slain. Sakreg glared at Gaaet's body and grimaced his face in revulsion for he had never seen such a gruesome death in his entire life. This was his first. Sakreg wondered, *"What kind of an alien I am accompanying at this moment that would kill in such a gruesome manner."* However, on the other thought, Sakreg had already established a complete trust on Drake. Despite of such horrid death that Drake had caused to Sakreg's enemy; Sakrag thought Drake was still a trustworthy, a sensible entity, and a friend throughout the life.

Sakreg delivered an uneasy glance toward Drake that lasted a moment or two; he was displaying his displeasure of Drake's method of kill, then Sakreg pointed with his hand the direction that they must go, and both began to move east bound on an open field full of purple grass. After roaming the field for a few minutes, he bent his elbow horizontally and pulled his hand toward his abdomen then pushed a few buttons on his wrist gadget.

Suddenly a conical light beam emanated from the devise toward his head. The beam encompassed his entire head and his upper chest that lasted approximately three seconds, and then his wrist gadget made a strident and reverberating noise for a duration of two seconds and stopped. The beam of light suddenly disappeared. Drake believed Sakreg just sent a beacon home for the authorities to track his whereabouts every moment of the day, so that they can find him and come for his rescue.

Approximately a thousand miles away the military emergency respond team received the signal sent by Sakreg. They verified his location, his face, and his frequency on the computer screen. The computer operator figured out to whom this frequency and the face belonged to, because the screen had his picture and blurted out in writing Sakreg's name, rank, and his complete military history. The computer considered Sakreg was lost, dead, or killed in action.

"Sir Mraveh, you have got to see this!" exclaimed Emoch, the female operator.

"What you've got there?" asked Mraveh.

"Sir, tell me if this is possible? The computer stated Sakreg was to be considered lost, or dead two years ago at the event of the war with Grolz. We had to notify his family that he was missing in action. You do remember that event and the war don't you sir?" said Emoch.

"Yes, I do remember it very well. How could I forge it? As a matter of fact, I lost my father in that war. The Grolz went door to door, killing the residents inside their abodes. When I came to rescue my father, it was already too late. I saw his lifeless body and his splattered blood everywhere. I still grieve to this day about his death and the way he died. He didn't deserve that at all," said Mraveh

"I am so sorry to hear that sir. I am sure he meant a lot to you," said Emoch.

"Yes, he did," said Mraveh.

"But coming back to this signal we have just received sir. This signal was registered to Sakreg, and his face confirms it. Tell me, how could this be possible?" asked Emoch?

"Yes, yes I could see your point. You are right. This is rather strange in fact very strange. What was he doing, and where was

he all this time? He has a lot of explaining to do to the military committee. However, I want you to galvanize a search party. We are going to rescue him. He must be in trouble; otherwise, he wouldn't send us this emergency signal. But why now, why not two years ago?" asked Mraveh.

The military pin-pointed his location with exact coordinates and prepared a four-crew member search party that included the pilot to rescue Sakreg. Within ten minutes or less, the crew got on board the rescue plane and flew. They were on their way to rescue Sakreg.

Drake for a moment couldn't believe his eyes that he really was on a very different planet and perhaps in a different galaxy all together! No one on earth had such a privilege, and yet, he was the first to experience this moment in time.

The thought of feeling free again occupied Drake's mind for the second time; *"no more military choppers perusing me, no more murder accusations, no more a guilty verdict, and no more army personal attempting to kill me."* Drake felt relieved of fear and anxiety for a change, but at the same time he felt ambivalent about this unknown planet as much as he enjoyed the beauty of it, he didn't know the challenges that awaited him: wild beasts, poisonous insects and plants, barbaric tribesmen, severe weather and much, much more and to top it all, he would have to face them possibly alone.

Drake slowly turned his body 360°, examined the terrane with his naked eyes. He took a notice of the rolling hills and the distand purple trees. He took a deep breath sampling the atmosphere that he became use to in Sakreg's craft. He shifted his sight to the ground, observed the vegetation, and considered that it was very different in color and structure from earth's plants. He then lifted his head toward the sky and there was plenty of sunlight, but had no clue as to the time of the day that was on this planet. He then fixated his eyes again to the ground, noticed the thick and meaty blades of the purple grass that shot about four inches off the ground, and that encompassed all over the land.

Drake stooped down, broke one of the blades of the grass then raised it to his nose and smelled it. He felt the sweet aroma embodied his nostrils and displayed his audacity by taking a small bite out of it.

Drake masticated the plant for a little while than swallowed it. Sakreg, on the other end, fixated his sight on him with concern and at the same time with amazement. He couldn't bring to himself the very thought that Drake had sampled the grass. He admired his fortitude and waited for a few minutes concentrating his sight on Drake to see if there was going to be an adverse reaction with him, but to his surprise, Drake seemed fine. However, the grass was a poison for Sakreg and the denizens of this planet. But apparently it was not the case for Drake.

The taste of the grass in Drake's mouth seemed nothing like he had ever experienced on earth. The grass was full of flavors. It had the taste of salt, sugar, citrus, piquant, tart and many more all mixed. This plant tantalized his taste buds in a very positive way and thought it was very palatable for consumption also possibly salubrious to his health.

Drake heaved his rucksack and all his belongings then both began to move toward "Earth's" east direction, which is considered north on this planet. Drake and Sakreg were afoot not knowing what they will encounter or experience in their way.

CHAPTER 32

There was plenty of sun light in the air. No clouds in sight. It appeared as if it was at nine AM in the morning—earth time. Drake had no clue how long the day would be on this planet, or whether the sun would ever go down.

Drake glared at his watch and thought that his wristwatch and his cell phone must be bootless here, but his grandfather's compass must still be serving its purpose on this planet despite of the fact that it was (indicating the planet's north, which was earth's east). However, he decided to keep his wristwatch and his cell phone as souvenirs and a reminder of earth's technology—but nothing more than that.

The weather in this sector of the planet felt balmy with temperatures perhaps between seventy to seventy-five degrees Fahrenheit. A gentle breeze was blowing from the planet's south (indicating earth's west) and Drake was feeling fine, and enjoying the sight of the distant rolling purple hills.

Suddenly Drake's lost his joyious expression and his serenity and changed his countenance to consternation as he felt the daylight abruptly and noticeably become dimmer. Shadows began to form on the ground. He elevated his head and caught sight of the long and narrow swaths of scattered clouds. Some were gray hued, and some were white, they just materialized out of nowhere and hung suspended to an approximate height of a kite that one fly's; but some white clouds coruscated like diamonds and thought that was strange.

Cold wind began to blow strong. Drake's clothes fluttered violently.   The distant trees and the grass bowed to the overwhelming sweep of the wind. The tree branches and their leaves danced vigorously and incessantly begging for the wind to stop. Many leaves detached themselves from the tree branches and littered the air with their presence.

Sakreg began to shiver so as Drake, for the weather had become extremely cold. It felt like ten degrees below zero. Sakrag immediately dropped to the ground, laid on his stomach while maintaining his shivering. He feared that the wind would jettison him into the air, for it had occurred in the past where the wind was sufficiently strong that swept heavy life forms off their feet into the air. Sakreg backend Drake to do the same, that Drake is to drop to the ground lest he will be swept by his feet and be carried away wherever the wind may take him.

Ten to fifteen minutes have passed. The clouds suddenly changed their color and became chromatic. They snaked and danced like the northern lights on earth and the atmosphere formed many large but horizontal tornado like phenomenon; however, they didn't touch the ground; they moved slowly and silently in a northerly direction (earth east).

This whole weather anomaly lasted a short while perhaps an hour or less, and then the weather came back to normal to what it was before: a sunny and cloudless morning with ambient temperature. Drake had plethora of questions to ask Sakreg about life here on this planet: the day and the weather cycle including seasons and their durations. What star is this planet revolving around, and how many planets there are in this solar system etc., but knew not how to express his thought to glean the answers he was looking for.

Sakrag and Drake got back on their feet, dusted their clothes, and began to traipse for a little while. They unexpectedly came across an acephalous corpse, a quadruped lying motionless on the purple grass and surrounded by a pool of green blood.

The animal measured approximately the size of a donkey, adorned with colorful concave stripes on its flanks that stretched from its runt to the bottom of its belly. The rest of its body was covered with shiny sky blue short-stubbed hair.

Sakreg stopped dead in his track and so did Drake. They both glared at each other at first then concentrated their sight on the deceased animal. The death of this zoological life form didn't seem to bother Sakreg; he displayed an insouciance expression on his face. His response was as if it was a normal occurrence. On the other end, Drake's visage appeared perturbed. A silent rage danced in his mind. He grimaced his face in a total disgust. He took a walk around the animal, paused a few times in the way to take a mental note of the quadruped. An interrogating thought invaded his mind, *"Who would do such a horrendous thing— killing a beautiful creature by cutting its head off then leaving the rest of the body to rot on the ground. There must be real time barbarians living on this planet that I am not aware of yet, and I am afraid I will have to meet them eventually and get acquainted with their baleful intents and perhaps I will have to greet them by putting my life on the line."*

Sakreg pointed at the critter with his long finger then turned around and faced Drake and blurted the word Alera. Drake thought, apparently "Alera" was the name given to this animal by the denizens. Drake pointed his index finger toward the beast and recited back to Sakreg and said "Alera."

Sakreg cracked a slight and brief smile at Drake's retort, but within moments, Sakreg froze all his movements, lost his harmony and his momentary grin, then switched the direction of his sight from Drake and silently and patiently attempted to be in tune with his immediate surroundings as if he was attempting to hear an uncanny sound that only he can hear, or that he sensed a movement of some kind that he may have attributed to an unseen preacence and that, it may have disturbed his psych. But it was evident that Sakreg had no idea where this haunting element of obscurity was coming from, whether it was a sound, or it was a feeling of movement or both.

Sakreg attentively surveyed his surroundings with his disquieted eyes but couldn't detect anything that was unusual, or a situation that could foment menace and conclude a peril. As for Drake, he began to ruminate and ask questions in his head, *"What was Sakreg's concerning element in this part of the planet that made him to appear so attentive and apprehensive. What was he expecting, or what was he afraid of?"* There was nothing that was unusual in occurrence that would make Sakreg to be alarmed.

Sakreg felt responsible for Drake's safety. Drake, in many ways, saved Sakreg's life from certain deaths on earth and desired to remunerate the favor.

Suddenly the ground shook, soon the crust broke open, and within the radius of a basketball court length, the dirt and the grass shot ten feet into the air in sporadic locations from every direction; it was like a volcano throwing its contents violently into the air. From the exploding ground, out came the creatures. Drake and Sakrag found themselves right in the middle of all the creatures. They experienced total dread and obfuscation.

Drake and Sakreg had no idea what was happening around them and couldn't decide which way to turn or run to save their lives. These creatures were many and some were whizzing right by their feet in a great speed, but they were not attacking Drake nor Sakreg. They all had one single mind: get to the breathless animal that was laying on the ground for their meal.

Suddenly the ground where Drake stood exploded beneath his feet. He immediately became airborne to the height of a tall man, and while he was in the midair, he made a quick summersault and at the same time a creature jetted out of the explosion then it scurried toward the cadaver. Drake landed on his feet, but staggered a few times, then found his equilibrium and stood erect.

Drake literally shook in his boots. His eyes opened wide in consternation and obfuscation. He decided to pull his forty-five-caliber pistol out to shoot at least some of them creatures and deal with the rest with his long machete, but Sakreg understood Drake's intention and signaled him by hand not to shoot these creatures and that he is to remain calm, and continue to stand still and not to move a muscle. Drake understood Sakreg's gestures rendered by hands and took his advice

These creatures numbered more than hundred. They were like a segmented worm, and were approximately four feet in length. Their heads measured just about eight inches in diameter; that resembled a head of an anaconda. Their bodies housed shiny azure blue scales. They had perhaps hundred or more little legs on each side of their bodies. Their feet were like that of a centipede, but at their ends, they had sharp and curved nails. These creatures had two large all black hued, almond shape eyes located in front of their faces. Their mouths split open from side to side, and it housed many large, needle sharp fangs on their top and bottom jaws, and accompanied a long tongue, sharp at its end.

However, in the interim, Drake noticed these esurient creatures have already gravitated around the fallen animal, and violently began to rive its flesh; some have fought each other to acquire a morsel of meat from the cadaver. Drake and Sakreg slowly reversed their steps, left some distance between them and the creatures, and felt safe to run as fast as they can to leave even greater distance between them and the creatures.

Sakreg had no idea what these creatures were. He had never seen or heard about them. However, this event was not Sakreg's main concern; he sensed in his heart that there was something more menacing and more sinister than these creatures coming their way. He stopped for a moment and pulled a cylindrical, black colored metallic object from one of his pant pockets that measured approximately one human hand in length and approximately two fingers wide in diameter. He held the devise in the palm of his hand, extended his arm forward then slowly swung his body three-hundred and sixty degrees. His intention was to scan the area for life. Their initial heading was twenty-five degrees planet's east-south (equivalent to twenty-five degrees earth's south, south-west).

When Sakreg turned his arm and his body at planet's south (equivalent to earth's west direction), suddenly, a red pulsating light emanated from the devise that he was holding. He stopped dead in his tracks, and pushed another button. Suddenly a holographic image opened right before his eyes. What Sakreg witnessed, it must have been a very disturbing view.

Sakreg's eyes bulged in sheer terror, his mind accompanied a sudden and overwhelming fear, he swiftly turned the devise off, then placed it right back in his pant pocket and blurted "Yojies"!, out loud. He looked around for a hiding place but there was none.

The Yojies were riding on their Irdnies; Sakreg and Drake needed a place to hide rather quickly; otherwise, there demise was going to be eminent, thought Sakreg.

In the holographic image, Sakreg noticed there were little more than a dozen Yojies were trotting toward their direction. They were approximately half a mile away from where Sakreg and Drake were standing.

Yojies are the denizens of this planet and are one of the many Darkan tribes. They are bellicose and fierce barbarians. They express no mercy nor compassion for strangers and especially for the occupying force of this planet that meant Sakreg. Their natural habitat is in the rural region located in the southern hemisphere.

The Irdnies are the animals Yojies use to commute from one location to the next. These animals are much like equine. However, they defer in color and in some features. Irdnies have light green and shiny furs, and a giraffe like brown patches large and small all over their bodies. Their necks are elongated and curved, and their heads are thinner with smaller face then a regular horse.

Irdnies have elephant-like ears, one on each side of their heads, which measure approximately human palm size, including exophthalmic eyes on either side of their face. They are slightly larger than regular-sized horses, with a short and pointed tail and four legs with three-toed hoofs on each leg.

The riders of the Irdnies appeared ominous in their continence. They had painted faces to engender fear in the eyes of the beholder. Their chieftain by the name of Soarp wore the skull of a freshly slain Alera on his noggin and was the only one who had the right to ware it.

Soarp wore colorful garments made from animal skins. His body had variety of piercings and was adorned by animal bones. His henchmen and he carried variety of weapons on their bodies, stolen or otherwise.

Soarp and his cohorts were returning from a burial ceremony conducted by Enob tribe. The young leader of the Enob tribe, by the name of Drash was married to Soarp's sister. Drash experienced a sudden paroxysm of pain in his chest then fell to the ground and wallowed few times as he attempted to breath but couldn't. He gave up his ghost within a minute or two.

However, for Drash's interment ceremony, the tribal women were not authorized to participate. The burial ceremony is considered sacred; only male gender was authorized to participate.

When the burial ceremony had ended, Yojies embarked on their Irdnies and began to head toward their village. Along the way, they came across the downed and destroyed star fighter that still was fraught with bellowing smoke. Soarp thought this must be of a recent event. If the pilots are dead then we will be able to find their bodies here, but if they are alive, then they must not be too far from this incident.

Soarp beckoned his coterie by his arm to come to a full stop. He summoned two of his best warriors to search the area for the downed pilots that may have been dead or were hiding in nearby vicinity, and that, these two warriors were to ravage what they can find from the downed craft in hope of finding articles that are useful by the tribe.

The warriors went by the name of Vardue and Ongar. Despite the valor they have achieved in their miscreant deeds, they entered the thickets with apprehension and were on foot, having their long rifle-like weapons pointing forward in a ready-to-shoot position. There was no feeling of ease in their minds because they felt being an open target. They moved cautiously forward toward the downed spaceship. Aside from the downed spaceship and its pilots, the two warriors had no clue as to what was waiting for them in the environment that they were in. However, there were large trees, and tall shrubs that encompassed all around them.

Unbeknownst to Vardue and Ongar, a pair of eyes was following every move these two were making. The pair of orbs belonged to an insect or a creature called Croot. The Yojy tribe has heard about this creature but never seen the creature face to face. This critter measured approximately two and a half feet long and it resembled a praying mantis.

Croots have two—one food long and pointed feather like antlers. They are located right above their heads one on each side. These antlers are for sensing heat and movements. They can point these antlers at any direction and bend them in any angle at will. They also have two protruding compound eyes, one on each side of their pileous noggins. Their Mouths are fierce. They house long and curved menacing fangs and small but sharp-edged teeth alongside of their jaws.

Croots have the capability to blend themselves with the nature that surrounds them, like chameleons on Earth.

This well camouflaged Croot was perching on a tree branch, waiting for the arrival of the two warriors: Vardue and Ongar so it can make a meal out of them.

Vardue and Ongar have heard of Croots. They also know the discription of its physical features, so as the rest of the tribe, but they haven't seen this animal in this part of the planet. They only heard about them.

As the two Sorarp's henchmen came within the range of the Croot's attack zone, suddenly and in a lightning-fast manor, a clear lump of jelly like substance jettisoned out from Croot's mouth and struck Vardue on his bare chest. It instantly paralyzed Vardue of all his movements. He attempted to scream for help but couldn't. Even his vocal cords were rendered useless. Vardue fell on strewed twigs and leaves that were on the ground. Suddenly Vardue began to convulse uncontrollably having his mouth agape and gasping for air or possibly attempting to give up the ghost.

The Croot didn't waste any time and within two seconds, it landed on Vardue, and then with a rapid succession it began to take deep chunks of flash from his chest, his neck, and his arms. Suddenly a pulsating Green blood began to shoot into the air from the areas of its bite. It was apparent that it had cut a few arteries.

Ongar spun, aimed, and pulled the trigger of his hand-held weapon, and a red plasma ball struck Croot and immediately pulverized the creature. However, Vardue lost a great deal of blood, and within less than a minute, he gave up his ghost. Ongar knelt beside Vardue and displayed his emotionally charged loud rueful scream knowing that his best friend was no longer extant.

Soarp heard Ongar's loud cry and realized there must have been a problem. He summoned four more of his teammates to ascertain the reason for the squall. The four disembarked from their Irdnies, drew their hand-held weapons, and proceeded to enter the coppice having solicitous expressions on their faces.

Ongar caught sight of the four that were coming toward his direction; he made a motion with his arm, signaling them to his corner.

The four accelerated their steps, and when they arrived next to Ongar, they placed their hand-held weapons back into their holsters and knelt beside Vardue then they commiserated with Ongar for the loss of Vardue. Suddenly, they stood up erect from their knelt positions; Tokra and Arshue carried Vardue's body to be placed on his Irdny so that they would have him back to the village and give him a proper burial.

Soarp saw the team that was coming out of the forest with the deceased body in their midst, he became perplexed and suddenly disembarked from his Irdny. Soarp placed zest in his steps and reached the party that was coming out from the forest.

"What happened here? Is he dead!" asked Soarp.

"Yes sir, he is dead sir. Croot got him sir, but I got the Croot sir. I pulverized the damn critter. However, it was too late. It only took a few seconds to inflict such a great deal of damage to Vardue sir. As you see, his chest, his neck and his shoulders are mutilated. He lost most of his blood and died in result sir," said Ongar.

"Croots—here?" asked Soarp.

"Yes sir," said Ongar.

"Did you see any more of them?" asked Soarp.

"No sir I didn't, but that doesn't mean Croots aren't around. They could be hiding anywhere here sir," said Ongar.

"But this is not their natural habitat as you know it sir. They are much more down south and far, far away from this location," said Soarp.

"Well sir they must have found a way to get here. Do you think we must notify the clan about the Croots that we found here?" asked Tokra.

"I wouldn't want to alarm them, but in this case, we have no choice, we must. All right let's put Vardue on his Irdny and secure him well. We still have some distance to reach the village," said Soarp.

"Yes sir, that was our intention sir, right from the start," said Arshue.

"Very well, then proceed," said Soarp.

Soarp ordered everyone to search for the scattered debris of anything that brings value, also to locate the dead or the wounded pilots of the downed and destroyed craft, and to be careful of the Croots. If they should find any Croot, they are to shoot and kill immediately. Soarp also ordered two of his henchmen to remain with the deceased body that was strapped on the Irdny.

After a scrutiny of the downed craft, Soarp's team salvaged what they could from it, they also realized this space plane is a two-seater type of craft, therefore, it must have housed a pilot and a copilot to fly it. However, they couldn't locate their bodies anywhere, and they found no more Croot. But, they found bunch of torn metals, shards, a broken wing, and a tail. The writings on the shards and the tail revealed the ownership of this disfigured and burning craft and it belonged to "Eponans."

Soarp screamed aloud in demonstration of fear and ire. *"Eponans are here again! We've got rid of them at least from this part of the world, but now they 're back again! They just don't want to leave us alone! What do they want from us now! They have taken our land, our planet, and our resources. They have destroyed our villages and murdered our people. We can't allow that to happen anymore! We must fight them to death! We are tired of having them in our midst.*

The pilots of this craft must be alive since we haven't found their bodies here. They must be somewhere close by. Let's do our best to find them and then exterminate them before they become destructive. Increase the search parameters now!" said Soarp having an angry disposition. His henchmen did as they were commanded by Soarp. They enlarged their search circle, but still their efforts availed no result. Soarp concluded the Eponans must be afoot and thought they couldn't be far from the wreckage since it is a recent event. The craft was still bellowing smoke.

Yojies were Sakreg's greatest fear. He has lost a few of his best friends in this part of the planet, and didn't desire to be the Yojies next victim, but felt somewhat relieved having his human expert shooter, and gunslinging friend next to him.

Drake witnessed the holographic image Sakreg was viewing and thought *"these entities in the holographic image sure do appear much different then Sakreg, could there be another race that I don't know about, and that soon I will have to content with them whatever they are."* Drake also thought trouble must have been brewing up ahead since Sakreg's disposition have changed to fear and confusion after viewing the holographic image. And that the Yojies were heading their way. Soon, Sakreg and Drake will have to contend with Yojies face to face. Drake had no clue as to what the Yojies were capable of, and had no knowledge of their way of life.

"Not now and not here dear God. I am done with conflicts, but why do I feel my strife is not over yet? Now that I am here, I must also deal with this planet's contentions. Dear lord, when am I going to have some peace and tranquility for a change?" thought Drake silently to himself.

Yojies have established new mission, or new directive, find the "Eponan pilots," no matter what the cost! The search party already has carefully inspected the grounds for any vestige the pilots may have left on the ground to determine the direction of their movements.

The search team has located footprints that belonged to Sakreg, but were greatly nonplussed when they discovered Drake's imprints. They have never seen such an impression on the ground in their entire lives and couldn't figure it out what type of animal could produce such an imprint. Nevertheless, Soarp directed his team of henchman to move forward and locate the pilot and the animal with a bizarre foot tracks next to Sakreg's footprint.

Sakreg and Drake had nowhere to hide. There were only a few short trees and some shrubs on the hilltop. Purple grass and occasional bare ground occupied most of the hill.

Sakreg and Drake knew eventually that they had to confront the Yojies face to face. It would be a matter of time before these brutal barbarians will catch up with them and do with them as they pleased.

Death was chasing Sakreg and Drake from a distance. Yojies on their Irdnies were trotting down their direction following their footprints and crushed grass until Soarp espied them both running on the grass like fugitives running from a crime scene. Soarp became excited. Soon the trot of his Irdny became a gallop, and so the rest of his gang did the same.

The running figures became larger and larger in Soarp's sight as Soarp closed the distance between them. Currently, it was not feasible for the two to engage in a firefight with Soarp and his cohorts for they were many and were carrying assorted weapons on their persons, such as spears, swords, knives, hand-held guns, and rifles that shoot ionized projectiles.

Sakreg thought it was futile for them two to run anymore. They both stopped in their tracks to catch their breath and gain their strength to deal with oncoming Yojies head on. They both turned around and faced the dreaded barbarians knowing both of their situation was a dire one, and it may have to include their deaths. With less than a minute, Soarp and his company surrounded Sakreg and Drake.

Suddenly all eyes became glued on Drake. Yojies were very astonished by Drake's appearance for they have never been acquainted with such a life form in their entire lives. They have witnessed hair and a Vandyke; only animals will have hair, the color of his skin not being like their own, and hands with five fingers instead of three like theirs and many more.

Now, the count was clear. Drake counted fifteen alive and well Yojies on their Irdnies. However, one appeared dead and was strapped on his own Irdny; plus, he witnessed a Yojy wearing a slain Alera's skull on his head, riding in front of everyone, and wearing colorful ornaments wrapped around his body.

Drake verified the differences in Yojies appearance verses Sakreg's that he previously witnessed in the holographic image. He wondered again thinking, is there only two different races on this planet, or is there more to come that he may have to contend with soon should they both come out of this encounter alive.

At first, in a brief synoptic moment, Sakreg entertained the thought of engaging the Yojies in a firefight, but then quickly changed his mind. He thought if he had pursued his decision, it would have caused his and his newly found earthly friend's demise. Sakreg also thought that he and his friend might have a better chance to survive should they cooperate and negotiate with Yojies and possibly participate in a firefight in some other day if it deemed necessary.

Sakreg and Drake with their fierce continance began to turn their bodies to the direction of the circaling Yojies as the Yojies had them surrounded. Yojies were too many to contend with; they also had their weapons drawn and trained on them both. Despite of this blatant danger that Sakreg and Drake had now encountered, Sakreg stood erect and resolute, ready to face the challenges at hand, but underneath it all he felt solid fear but didn't desire to express it. Sakrag Knew that the Yojies being a barbarian tribe and they have no sense of remorse in killing anything and anyone, Sakreg's thought that he and his earthly friend will be dead today and that it will happen in this place.

Drake knew he and his friend Sakreg were in a great danger of facing these brutal Yojies but Unlike Sakreg, Drake felt uncannily halcyon, just maybe because he thought he could handle them all, or perhaps he was still feeling enraptured by the newly found unearthly adventures.

Soarp feeling cocksure that he is going to have the victory in killing the invader of his planet and get many more accolades from the chief of the tribe. He disembarked rather swiftly from his Irdny and sauntered toward Sakreg. Despite of the fact that he was very intrigued by the presence of Drake for he hasn't seen anything like him anywhere, but he thought at first, I must disarm the Eponan and then I will deal with his partner the animal. When Soarp approached Sakreg, he didn't lose sight of Sakreg as he turned 360° around him and then blurted,

"You are an Eponan I see. You are the invader of our planet! The murderer of our people, and the destroyer of our resources! What—are you doing here on my land where you shouldn't be, and that you already know the consiquences of you being here?"

"I had not an ill intend. My spaceship caught on fire and I had no choice but to land and crash here," said Sakreg.

"Don't lie to me! Don't tell me that you had not an ill intend! Your mission was, I suppose to create further destruction and mayhem to our people—wasn't that right, now don't lie", said Soarp.

"No—not at all. Don't conjure up vain imaginations. As I have said, I had no ill intend of being here," said Sakreg.

"Then why are you here in this part of the planet, knowing that we are one of your fiercest enemies?" asked Soarp.

"My instruments failed me, and I didn't know where I was. I have lost my direction, and soon my craft's engins caught on fire and I don't know how. I had no choice but to land and crash here," said Sakreg.

"So, that burning downed craft, which is a little distance from here, is your war machine, isn't it?" asked Soarp.

"Yes, it is—unfortunately. I really didn't want to be here," said Sakreg. Soarp approached Sakreg from behind and said, *"Don't you ever make sudden moves; just do as I say and nothing else. Now, put your arms apart where I can see them and away from your weapon,"* Sakreg did as was instructed. Soarp pulled Sakreg's weapon from its glove and examined it with his hands, then tossed it in the air, far from his reach, and away from everyone. He then turned around and faced Sakreg with glaring eyes and full of fierce countenance, then said.

"You know, I didn't believe a word you have said, and I would say you have come here to destroy us with your war machine, now don't lie to me!" said Soarp. Suddenly all his cohorts raised their weapons and readied themselves to discharge their fiery rounds. A few hollered by saying,

"Let's do away with him now. Let's shoot him now." Soarp extended his arm out toward his henchmen and immediately beckoned them not to shoot yet.

"No—that is not true. As matter of fact you may not believe what I am about to say. It is that, I care about your people and I have somewhat developed an affinity towards your tribe. If I had my rather, I really wanted to work with you all to better your lives," said Sakreg.

"Did you fellows hear that? He says He carrrrrres about us, and we should believe that don't we? Isn't that right Eponan?" said Soarp.

"Yes, that is right. I am telling you the truth. I can't help what my forefathers have done to your people. I wasn't there, and that was not my decision to make. I hope I don't have to pay the price for their mistakes," said Sakreg.

"Oh! You are going to pay for it all right," said Soarp.

"Look, I want to tell you this for your own good and for the good of your tribe. Right after I crash-landed, I sent a beacon to my military headquarters, so that they come and rescue my companion and me. I believe they are on their way here. I have received their conformation that they are on their way. My rescue team should be here soon. If they find me dead then it is not going to look good for your tribe. They will investigate the source of my death and when they determine that you folks were the culprit, then, they will kill every one of you even your children. There will be nothing left of you or your tribe. I hope you understand the gravity of your decision that you will be making here today. I personally wouldn't want that for you and for your tribe," said Sakreg.

"Is that so?" said Soarp.

"Yes, and I wouldn't want to lie to you either," said Sakreg.

"Unfortunately, there is a new rule in the village. Consider yourself veeeery lucky right now. You get to live little longer How about that. The chief must execute judgement to the intruders of our land; otherwise, you would have been dead by now, by my hands alone." Soarp shifted his head and glanced at Drake.

"What kind of an animal did you bring with you? I presume it is your pet, and where did you find that creepy looking pet of yours standing on its two feet? Oh yes, it must be one of the animals you brought here from your planet. I have to say, you have clothed your pet very well, and I see the footprints that were next to yours, it surely belongs to this animal."

"He is not an animal, and I didn't bring him from my planet," said Sakreg.

"Really—then where did you find this creature at, and are there any more like it?" asked Soarp. Sakreg remained silent.

"Did you hear what I have just said?

"Yes—I did," said Sakreg.

"Then answer me!" said Soarp.

"All right then, he is called human," said Sakreg.

"A human—what is a human! There is no such animal that we have ever seen or heard of on this planet, and you tell me it is not from the planet that you come from, then where did you find this animal called human?" asked Soarp.

"He is not an animal. He is a very intelligent being, maybe more intelligent than you are," said Sakreg.

"Reeeeally—then why we haven't located such an intelligent animal called human anywhere?" asked Soarp.

"As I have said—he is not an animal. He is a very intelligent being, and if I were you, I would be very careful with him," said Sakreg.

"Why—does it bite?" asked Soarp. His gang broke out in laughter.

"Worst then a bite—he can kill all of you rather quickly if you should make him mad, which I think he is getting there right now. Don't let his size and his calmness fool you. I suggest you best to leave him and me alone, mind your own business, and move on. We don't mean harm to anyone of you and soon we'll be out of here and no one will be the wiser," said Sakreg.

"Reeeeeally!" said Soarp.

"Yes really," said Sakreg. Everyone laughed hard except Sakreg and Drake.

"From the previous statement you have made I should really be scared now. Should I run?" asked Soarp.

"Well it is up to you. Suit yourself, but as I've said, you should leave him alone," said Sakreg.

"All right—so you say it is an intelligent being. Does it have a name?" asked Soarp.

"Yes, he does. He calls himself Drake," said Sakreg.

"Drake—what kind of a name is Drake!" asked Soarp.

"I don't know. He calls himself Drake," said Sakreg.

"I suppose it can speak, and it calls its name Drake," said Soarp.

"Yes." said Sakreg.

"Does it speak our language?" asked Soarp.

"No not yet—he doesn't," said Sakreg.

"Is there any more like this freaking animal here?" asked Soarp.

"I told you many times, he is not an animal! He is a very intelligent being. His race is called human, and no, there aren't any more like him here on this planet," said Sakreg.

"What happened, did its kind become extinct, and we didn't know about it?"

"No." said Sakreg.

"But then there should be more of these animals around. We must find them and maybe they become useful to us?" said Soarp.

"I have told you, he is the only one on this planet," said Sakreg.

"This is fascinating, indeed very fascinating," said Soarp, and walked toward Drake, and Drake was about two bus length away from Sakreg. Soarp began to examine Drake from ten feet away, tilting his head to the left and to the right while turning three-hundred and sixty degrees around him, and attempting to ascertain this human life form. Soarp thought that the rest of the animal world do not carry weapons in their possessions; he didn't think that this one could be armed with a weapon of any sort. Soarp approached Drake and extended one of his fingers slowly toward Drake's face to touch him, but Drake took a few steps back,

"All right, you need to back off Mr. I am not your toy to play around with, or touch my face, so back off!" said Drake in English language, also used hand gesture. Soarp froze in his movements and glared at Drake for few seconds in a total amazement, and with mixed elation. Soarp turned then faced Sakreg and said, *"It can talk. An animal can talk. This has never happened, or ever been heard being heard of. I am impressed, very impressed indeed. I am going to take this animal to town with me. There is much money to be made here,"* said Soarp and ordered two of his henchman to detain these two entities.

Two Yojies disembarked from their Irdnies, one approached Sakreg, pulled both his arms back, and tied his hands, and the other walked towards Drake to tie his hands behind his back just like Sakreg. As the Yojy was walking towards Drake, Drake reached for his gun and clasped his hand around the handle of his forty-five-caliber pistol that was tucked under his jacket, and with the other arm, he beckoned the Yojy not to come any closer.

"Stay right there. Don't get any closer," blurted Drake, but the Yojy kept on coming towards him, and Drake kept on backing away from him and kept on signaling him with his arm not to get any closer.

"I told you to stop, or I am going to have you to meet your maker soon, you big freaking lout!" said Drake. As the Yojy attempted to lay hands on him, Drake pulled his forty-five-caliber pistol and fired at the Yojy. The bullet struck right between his eyes, the brain splattered every direction, and then, he fell backward. His body hit the ground rather hard.

Drake anticipated a reprisal from the rest of the gang and immediately jumped on the downed Yojy, then grabbed him and turned him around. This time he was on the ground and the dead Yojy was on top of him.

Quickly a few bursts of ionized rounds ensued from Sorrp's henchmen hand- held weapons to kill Drake but instead it hit the dead Yojy. However, it didn't pulverize him. Perhaps the setting on their weapons were set just to terminate and not to pulverize. The Yojy that tied Sakreg's hands was also taking an aim at Drake so as Soarp was doing the same.

Drake's forty-five pistol carried thirty rounds with an extended magazine. It was a new design in handguns. The rounds were smaller but deadlier. Drake acknowledged the situation and shot the Yojy that tied Sakrag's hands. He shot him right between the eyes and his brain splattered in many pieces then fell to the ground instantly. Drake then shot Soarp once on each leg and he fell on his back yelling and screaming in pain.

Drake left the Yojy that was on his top, began to roll rather fast on the ground, and began to shoot as many as he could in a very rapid fashion. He afflicted them right between their eyes, and the same was the result, they all fell off their Irdnies, kissed the purple grass on the ground, and were dead on arrival, but those that were still alive they kept firing the ionized rounds but were missing him all together. Two Yojies left alive beside Soarp and they ran away leaving Soarp wallowing on the ground in pain. The dead Yoji that was strapped on his own Irdny had no choice to make. The Irdny ran with the dead body on its back in a different direction and disappeared.

Drake quickly got on his feet, ran toward Sakreg, and freed his tied hands loose. Sakreg and Drake walked towards Soarp, and as they approached him, Soarp extended his arm in the air and brandished his hand-held weapon at them, Drake quickly shot at the weapon that was in Soarp's hand, and it flew right out of his palm and landed about five feet away from him.

Sakreg faced Soarp and said, *"Do you remember when I have told you don't make him mad and that if you do he will kill all of you—well, I wasn't laying wasn't I? Now you see—most of your gang is dead and gone because of your stupid decision. You should have believed me while you had the chance, and now, you wouldn't have to be in this predicament, would you?*

"I want you to know that he didn't kill you for a purpose; if he had, then your head would have been splattered just like the rest of them. You get it, don't you? Oh—and one more thing, —now you know that he is an intelligent being and not an animal right? You get it, don't you? Do you have anything to say for yourself?" asked Sakreg.

"Yes, where did you find this animal? I want more like this animal whatever it is called. I want this animal to be on my team," said Soarp.

"You never learn, do you? Just for you to know, for you to get more of his kind, you should go to a planet called earth. That is where you find more of his kind, and that planet is far, very, very far from here and its inhabitants are not very friendly like he is. However, you have no chance of getting there yourself anyway," said Sakreg.

"Earth, you said!" asked Soarp while lying on the ground and wallowing in pain.

"Yes, earth. It is a beautiful planet like ours," said Sakreg.

Drake took few steps away from them and grabbed Sakreg's gun in one hand, and grabbed his rucksack with the other hand and dragged it on the ground and brought it near Soarp. He pulled a few medical tools from it, and sterilized them by ointment he had in his medical bag.

"What is this animal doing with that sharp object? Is it going to kill me now like it killed many of my people?" asked Soarp with concerned eyes.

"No—relax he is going to operate on you," said Sakreg.

"What did you just say; operate on me? That aaaaanimal is going to operate on me? —Never!" said Soarp.

"Well, do you want to live or die? Make your choice. You know, we don't have all day. We'll have to leave you here and we must move on, and who knows just maybe a vicious animal may find you and make a meal out of you. I'll bet that will hurt more then what he is going to do to heal you."

"All right, All right—you've made your point."

"Good choice. Now, it is going to hurt a little. He is going to pull the thing from your legs," said Sakreg.

"What thing!" said Soarp.

"That thing that came out of his weapon; you will see it soon. He knows what he is doing. Don't worry. He is going to make you feel better. He has done the same for me, and see, I am well again, you will also be well again," said Sakreg.

"Why are you being so nice to me, when all I wanted to do is kill you?" asked Soarp.

"Well, it is because as I have told you before, I have affinity toward your people. I feel your struggle and your pain, and I want to be part of the solution and not the problem. I also have conditioned my mind not to resort to violence unless if I had to," said Sakreg.

"You know? —despite of our differences, you have gained my respect. I can see we are going to be friends not just an acquaintance, because you have proved to me that you really care for my people and me. I know you could have hurt me or even kill me while I was down on the ground, but you chose not to, and here you are talking with me, and helping me to get better instead of killing me. Thank you for your kindness. I have a lot to learn yet. I have never seen such kindness in my entire life. All I have seen is violence. Since my childhood, I was taught to find solutions through violence. I thought that was the way of life, and that it should be that way. But you have proved me otherwise. Thank you. Oh, by the way—I didn't get your name?" asked Soarp.

"My name is Sakreg, and you are welcome."

Drake operated on Soarp with difficulty because the pain was unbearable for Soarp, but he managed to pull the two bullets out of Soarp's upper thighs then he gave them to him for keeps. Now, all he must do is get well. Drake sanitized and wrapped the wounds well so that an infection wouldn't set in.

Drake cut a few large branches from nearby short trees and made a gurney from it, then Sakreg and Drake placed Soarp on top of it, and both carried him along as they ambled towards where Soarp was heading previously. All their personal Irdnies ran in different directions and disappeared.

CHAPTER 33

"We are getting close, real close. The signal is getting stronger. I am activating the close-proximity, signal-tracking monitor (CPSTM)—oh — there, he is! The dot indicates five Fethong away (approximately eight miles). Wait a minute, now I see three dots. Is this right?" said a very young female flight engineer on her first assignment by the name of Eewo in the rank of lieutenant.

"Well, it is the same signal we have been tracking all along, and definitely, it belongs to a star pilot by the name of Sakreg. When you turn the (CPSTM) on, it will pick up everything around the signal you are attempting to pursue. This monitor is an upgraded version of what we had before. Now we know that he is not alone and that he has company. Well, as long as he is all right, that's what matters," said the pilot Captain Enuj.

"Ok, good to know that. I am almost sure that you were aware that I was on sick leave for three weeks. I had no idea that they have changed or upgraded the (CPSTM), I never knew the changes were coming, and no one has told me about it," said Eewo.

"I understand that. Your unit supervisor should have informed you of the changes. It is their bad, but now you know," said Captain Enuj.

"Yes, I do know now—and thanks! By the way, you know—when it comes to Sakreg, if we take him to the headquarters, he will have lots of explaining to do about his disappearance from the military for such a long time. I hope, for his sake, he will not get in trouble, because that could spell the death penalty for him if he should be convicted of being AWL (absent without leave).

"Sakreg was a good soldier. I checked his record. He has many accolades and certificates of achievement from the unit. What happened to him that he had to disappear for such a long time? I don't think such a good soldier could suddenly turn rogue. Anyway, I hope he has a good explanation for the board," said Lieutenant Eewo

"I suppose you are right. When we pick him up, we will then ask him the question of him being AWL, and I hope as you have said, he has a good answer, otherwise you are right, it doesn't look good for him," said Captain Enuj.

"Captain, are you witnessing that sky-high smoke up ahead?" asked Lieutenant Eewo.

"Yes, as a matter of fact, I do see it," said Captain Enuj.

"What do you say, captain if we briefly explore the source of that smoke—Is it ok with you?" said Lieutenant Eewo.

"Yes, yes, it is ok with me. That might be a good idea. We'll circle around it at least twice. Heck, it could be one of our people in trouble and in need of rescuing," said the captain. The bellowing smoke loomed larger before their eyes as they came closer to it.

"There it is—what—it looks like one of our star-fighter craft Lumo class, said Captain Enuj, by the way Sakrag was flying the same kind of space-fighter wasn't he?"

"Yes he was. You are right. However, that don't mean it is his space-fighter. But what is one of our space-fighters doing down here and completely destroyed?" asked Lieutenant Eewo.

"It looks like it might have been shot down by Darkan people, and I believe it must have been a recent event; otherwise, we wouldn't have to detect any smoke, would we?" observed Captain Enuj.

"You are right captain. But I wonder if there are any casualties, and if so, they would have to be one of ours and we must take the bodies back to the unit for identification. I say, we should go down and investigate sir don't you agree?" asked Lieutenant Eewo.

"I think you are right in your assumption. Now that we know this craft belongs to one of our pilots, we will have no choice but to go down and investigate. It is our duty to do so, but do you know that this area is a very hostile area. It is Yojies territory. When we go down we must be armed, and whatever we do down there we must do it fast and get out of there, is that clear?" said Captain Enuj.

"Yes sir," replied Eewo the lieutenant and the rest of the search crew. Captain Enuj vertically landed the craft at an open spot and four Eponan rescue soldiers armed with handheld weapons disembarked from its fuselage. Their names were Captain Enuj, the pilot, Lieutenant Eewo, encharge of the two rescue soldiers, Corporal Larue, and Corporal Lenute. They cautiously ambled toward the fallen craft.

"What in the world is one of our star-craft doing down here in the first place. We were all instructed not to fly this zone?" said the captain.

"I suppose someone didn't want to obey the given command, and we will know soon who it was," said the Lieutenant.

Corporal Lenute uttered, "Sir—you've got to see this!"

"What you've got their corporal?" asked Captain Enuj.

"Sir, I see pairs of Eponan footprints heading that way, but I can't explain these pairs of foot prints that is following the Eponan's footprints close, real close as if they were moving as a team. This is strange very strange to me. Have you ever seen anything like this sir?" asked Corporal Lenute. They all congregated around the footprint, and glared at it in amazement.

"Lieutenant Eewo, please take some photos. We'll have the experts to analyze these footprints. These footprints are indeed strange, very strange. Good job, corporal," said Captain Enuj.

"All right now, we can't waste much more of our time here. Let's look for the bodies, examine shards, take some more photos, and move out of here. We have a mission to accomplish. Let's get going," said Captain Enuj. They picked some remains of the craft having some information on them for evidence; they also took some photos of the scattered shards of the craft and searched for the dead or scorched bodies, but they couldn't find any.

"I wonder what had happened to the pilots of this craft. There are no dead bodies here sir, but I see a trail of Darkan blood here," said Lieutenant Eewo.

"I would think perhaps there was a conflict here between the Yojies and the pilot of this craft. The pilot probably was taken as a prisoner because we didn't find a dead body here but only Darkan blood," said Captain Enuj.

"Wait a minute; I see we have a complete flight serial number on the tail. Lieutenant Eewo, would you run this serial number through your computer. This way, we will know to whom this craft was assigned to," said the captain.

"Captain that is a brilliant idea; I shall get on it right away," said Eewo. Lieutenant Eewo ran her fingers on her hand-held computer keyboard and out came the information and the photo of the pilot, and the information revealed the pilot was Sakreg.

"What in the world! —hey captain, this is very strangely interesting, you probably won't believe this!" said the lieutenant.

"What! what've you got their lieutenant?" asked Captain Enuj.

"Would you believe this craft was assigned to Sakreg. The one we are here to rescue sir?" asked Eewo.

"It can't be. Are you sure?" asked the captain.

"Yes sir, I am damn sure. That is what my computer data is saying. The computers don't lie sir," said the lieutenant.

"Yes, I know, I know, computers don't lie, but how could this be? It's freaking me out. We've searched and scanned the whole planet every square foot of it a few times over, and couldn't find him or his craft anywhere, but now you are telling me that this craft belonged to Sakreg?" said Captain Enuj.

"Yes sir, that is what I'm saying. And now we find it here and crash? How could this be right? I don't understand it. But this also means that he is not taken as a hostage because we have his signal and we did see him in our onboard scanner," said Lieutenant Eewo.

"Yes, you are right. Once we rescue him, he is going to have looooots of explaining to do for sure," said Captain Enuj.

"Sir come to think of it, when it comes to this crash, as you know, previously we have come to a conclusion that it must have been a recent event because it is still smoking and burning. That means sir, he wasn't here all this time, that is the reason we couldn't find him anywhere sir, but then, where was he all this time?" asked the lieutenant.

"Well, I am very positive that Sakreg could answer that question alone; we'll find the underlying cause of all this mystery soon. All right, we can't stay here any longer. Let's go let's get out of here before we become victims of Yojies. We've got enough evidence here; now, let's get out of here before the Yojies find us here in their territory," said the captain. They all got on board and took off in search of Sakreg.

CHAPTER 34

The rescue craft was up in the air, approximately as high as the "Statue of Liberty," when the captain saw many lifeless and strewed bodies lying motionless on the purple grass.

"Captain, I see bodies lying on the ground down below. There is no movement. I believe they are dead. What do you make of it?" asked the lieutenant.

"Yes! —I see them too. Something terrible must have taken place here and it looks like it is also a recent event. I believe these bodies do belong to Yojy tribe. I know them from the way they adorn themselves. I don't know if you had any dealings with the tribe called Yojy. If you did, then you would know that they are fierce barbarians, and they hate us the most," said the captain.

"No sir I haven't had any dealings with them. However, I have heard of Yojies. You are right sir; many people have also told me the same—that they are terribly barbarians in nature. So, in this case, I must believe what they are telling me," said Lieutenant Eewo.

"Something caused their demise. I don't see a tribal war here. I got a feeling the answer would still lay with Sakreg. Once we get him on board, he will tell us all that we want to know about what had transpired here. However, now we don't have much time to fool around and attempt to ascertain the reason for their deaths. As we all know that we have a mission to accomplish and let's just do that and hopefully get back home safely to our units," said the captain.

"All right sir, I am totally in agreement with you, let's just do that, and not waste any more time," said the lieutenant. After a few minutes of flight, the lieutenant blurted out,

"Here they are, down there. She pointed with her fingers. Do you see them captain? They are at the two o'clock position."

"Yes, yes, I see them too. Also, the signal matches that of Sakreg's, but he has a company, as we detected while ago. I suppose the instruments didn't lie after all. Let's get this bird down and pick him up," said the captain.

Sakreg gazed at the descending craft in elation and realized his rescue team has just arrived and was about to land approximately four buses in length away, at ten o'clock position from where he was standing. He suddenly burst into a joyful laughter knowing right then that his rescue is just about to take place.

Sakreg swiftly imagined his problems melting away. He is going home and being with his family that he missed so much. Also, perhaps he was thinking of continuing his military endeavor.

As the rescue craft landed on the ground, the lieutenant pulled her binoculars out and gazed through the window, the only side window in the fuselage of the craft, she aimed her sight at Sakreg and his company. She noticed an upright standing creature (Drake) standing next to Sakreg approximately fifteen feet away from him and glaring at the craft in amazement. She noticed the creature's physical appearance was uncanny and became greatly perplexed, for she has never seen his likeness anywhere. She also noticed a Yojy laying on a makeshift gurney that was set on the ground, and silently wallowing in pain. He appeared to be wounded in both legs and possibly unable to walk. She handed the binoculars to the captain and he began to gaze right through them.

"Captain, did you see that strange-looking creature?" asked the lieutenant.

"If you are referring to that strange-looking and upright standing whatever that is which is next to Sakreg, then the answer is yes, I did see that," said the captain.

"Captain, why is it that we haven't seen or heard of such a creature before? Could this be a new discovery by Sakreg?" asked the lieutenant.

"Well, when we pick him up, I am sure he will tell us all about this mysterious creature or an alien standing next to him. However, the creature doesn't seem to be harmful. It feels like this thing next to him is an intelligent looking creature. I wonder where he found this thing whatever it is, and are there more of this creature around," asked the captain.

"Captain, please be careful when you open the door. The upright-standing creature may cause harm despite it looking harmless. We may have to draw our weapons before we go down just to protect ourselves in case the creature decides to attack us. We have no idea of its capabilities, don't you agree?" said the lieutenant.

"I agree, you make good sense—we should be careful. Let's do it," said the captain.

"All right crew, you have heard the captain. Draw your weapons out, and be ready to strike in case the creature decides to attack, but don't shoot unless it attacks. Is that clear to everyone?" asked the lieutenant.

"Yes ma'am," said the crew and readied their rifles. The door slowly lifted high at an angle, and out came the crew from the rescue craft. They moved swiftly, silently and in unison toward Sakreg with their weapons pointed toward Drake. Sakreg suddenly lost his gleefulness and acquired a concerned look on his face, and as the crew came within twenty feet of him, he blurted.

"What's the meaning of this? Are you here to cause harm, or are you here to rescue?" asked Sakreg with a stern voice.

"Sir, before we get into a heated argument here, we need to clear one thing first. Are you the one who called for the rescue, and are you in some kind of danger?" asked the captain.

"Yes, I was the one who called for the rescue, and no, I am not in some kind of danger," said Sakreg.

"Great, in that case, you must be the Lieutenant Sakreg. Am I right to assume that?" asked the captain.

"Yes sir, I am Sakreg."

"Wonderful—in that case, we are here to rescue you, but we have to be careful of this creature standing upright next to you," said the captain.

Drake felt his life was in danger because of the approaching crew pointing their rifles right at him. He slowly brought his hand close to his chest and tucked it under his jacket, then grabbed the handle of his handgun, but didn't pull it out into the open yet.

"Look captain, he is not going to cause any harm to you or to anyone of you, so just put your weapons away," said Sakreg.

They all looked at each other as if they were confused and didn't know whether to believe Sakreg or ignore him altogether.

Suddenly the captain blurted, "Lieutenant Sakreg, that creature appears to be very strange in appearance. We haven't seen anything like it before. We don't know if it is really safe to be around it or not."

"Yes, I can see the concern on your faces, but I say it again: you all need to put away your rifles. Trust me, he doesn't mean any harm to any of you. However, if he feels provoked then and only then he becomes dangerous, very dangerous indeed.

Don't let his size fool you. Now, I would say that you are threatening him with your weapons pointed right at him and trust me, he is astutely aware of your actions. Please put your weapons down before he kills every one of you right now, and believe me, he can and he will.

I have seen him in action. He is incredibly fast as matter of fact, lightning fast. There is no doubt, he can take every one of you out before you even know what had happened to you," said Sakreg. They all lowered their rifles slowly toward the ground.

"Now that's better. He will appreciate that," said Sakreg. The lieutenant approached Drake to within a safe distance and slowly circled around him.

"Lieutenant, what are you doing? Don't you know that, that thing can be very dangerous?" asked the captain.

"Captain, if you don't mind, I feel just fine. I have a good feeling that, this thing is not going to harm me, so please allow me to ascertain this creature up close for a minute. That's all I ask of you," said the lieutenant. The captain paused for a few seconds in consternation, then blurted, "Fine—just be careful please!"

"Yes sir I will, and thank you. Captain I will be careful," said the lieutenant.

She briefly stopped in her tracks. Her eyes met his, and she glared intently at his face as if with a passion that lasted for approximately seven to ten seconds. She admired his looks, his black hair, and his Vandyke beard, and then she rendered an unexpected smile at him and he returned the smile back at her.

Drake realized she is interested in him and that she is not going to pose any harm. He loosened the grip on the handle of his gun and dropped his arm down in a relaxed position. She then approached him and slowly extended her arm toward his face then touched his hair. She grabbed a few strands of his hair and rubbed them between her fingers just to feel its texture, she then slid her fingers gently down his cheeks and stroked his Vandyke a few times and thought the creature was amazing.

Suddenly, Drake raised his hands, extended toward her face, and gently caressed her cheeks. She closed her eyes, feeling overwhelmed by the sensation of his touch, and then he moved his fingers gently across her moist lips. Shortly her body began to convulse, feeling amative.

"Lieutenant Eewo, what is the meaning of your action? Get away from the creature now. That's an order!" blurted the captain loud and clear. Her amorous enchantment was cut short, and she experienced the reality at hand. She left and went back to her position where she was standing.

"What was that all about, lieutenant? You are not falling for that animal, are you?" asked the captain.

"How could you think something like that, captain?" asked the lieutenant.

The captain decided to ignore her question; he swiveled his head and faced Sakreg, then said, "All right, coming back to you, Lieutenant Sakreg, we were elated and greatly surprised at the same time when we picked up your transmission. We thought you were killed during the war with Grolz, or you were lost in space permanently—as you know, it has been approximately four years since the advent of the Grolz war, but surprisingly, here you are in person as if you came back from the dead. I must say, I am very glad to see you alive. But, at first, we thought we were only going to rescue Lieutenant Sakreg, the starfighter pilot, but now I see you have company: the wounded Yojy and this animal, whatever it is, and by the way, where did you find this thing, this creature?"

"Here I go again, explaining. He is not an animal. He is an intelligent being, and he is not from this planet and neither ours where we came from," said Sakreg.

"Then—where is he from?" asked the lieutenant with an astonished look on her face as if she couldn't wait to get the answer.

"He is from a planet called Earth. That is where I was all this time," said Sakreg.

"What! —did I hear you say you were on a different planet?" asked Captain Enuj.

"Yes, not only a different planet, but also a different galaxy together; I got there through a wormhole," said Sakreg.

"So, let me get this straight. You are telling me that you have traveled to a different galaxy through a wormhole and landed on a planet called Earth, and you picked this alien thing and then brought him here with you to be on this planet. Is that right?" asked Lieutenant Eewo.

"Yes, that is right what I said!" said Sakreg.

"What you are telling us is incredible, unbelievable at best. You are either insane and have lost your freaking mind, or you are telling us the hard-to-accept the truth. I don't know what to believe in. Anyway, you are going to have plenty of explaining to do to us, to the military, and to our society. This is indeed very strange. If your story is true, then this is going to be in the history books, and our scientists are going to have a field day with you and with that thing you brought with you," said the captain.

"It is the truth, captain! I have him as my evidence, plus I have captured photos and made camcorder recordings of the planet Earth when I was entering its atmosphere. I also made recordings of its land mass, its oceans, its occupants, and some of their technology," said Sakreg.

"Well, all that is good. You are going to need all the evidence to prove yourself to the military committee; otherwise, I believe you will be in big trouble being away for such a long time from your unit that you were assigned to," said the captain.

"Yes, I know that, and the reason he is with me is because he saved my life many times over, and as a result, I befriended him. He is my friend for life. I am sure you have found a destroyed star-fighter craft and many dead Yojies along the way here, haven't you?" asked Sakreg.

"Yes—yes, as a matter of fact, we did," said the captain.

"Well—that star-fighter belonged to me," said Sakreg.

"Yes, we know that. We have checked the craft's tail number in the computer, and it came out your name," said the captain.

"You see, I crash-landed there when I exited the wormhole. However, I am very glad that I got back here in one piece. You see, my engines caught on fire when I entered the atmosphere. I don't know why. You have also detected the dead bodies of Yojies on the way here, didn't you?" asked Sakreg.

"Yes, as a matter of fact, we did," said the lieutenant.

"Well—he is the reason why I am still alive because he finished them all by himself just to rescue me from them Yojies, and this wounded one is their Chief. You see him wounded, don't you?" said Sakreg.

"Yes, as a matter of fact, he is wounded. All right," said the captain.

"Well—You see, he was going to take my life away, and he (Drake) struck him on both legs so that he wouldn't be able to get back on his feet and kill me as a result. He could have easily killed him just like the rest, but decided not to, and I don't know why. However, I want to say this one thing. He is coming with us. I want him to be transported to his village for better treatment and for the rest that he needs to recuperate," said Sakreg.

"Do you know what you are asking us to do? Do you know the consequences of your decision? Don't you know that they are barbarians and that they might just kill us all, including your so-called alien friend? I think he is nothing else but a freak of nature, not an alien?" I have a very hard time believing everything you have said so far," said the captain.

"I want you to be informed; he is not a freak of nature. He has his own language and culture, as I have indicated before, and that, we must take this chance to get this Yojy to his tribe and maybe by doing so, we may create a permanent or lasting friendship with them.

"I want you to know that I am not leaving him here alone! Don't you know that he might die here without help, especially when he is wounded on both legs and can't walk at all? God knows what kinds of beasts lurk around here! He could easily become their next meal. I am sure you wouldn't want that on your conscious, would you?" said Sakreg.

"How did all this hoopla begin anyway?" asked the lieutenant. Sakreg landed a brief glare at Drake, but then immediately changed the direction of his sight back to the lieutenant.

"It is a long story Ma'am. As I have said before, it was a matter of life and death. That is all I will say for now. I will explain all the details when the command questions me, but now, as I have said before, we must transfer this Yojy to his tribe, and that is clear to you all, I hope. His village is not too far from here. He will guide us to his home," said Sakreg.

"All right, all right—we have heard enough. We will have it your way lieutenant, but I want you to know that we are risking our lives for you and for your friend, the Yojy and your so-called the only alibi you have—the so-called alien you are claiming to be your friend," said the captain.

"Yes, I do know that you are risking your lives here for us, and I know I am taking a great deal of chance and possibly jeopardizing everyone's life here. I am sorry for that, but I want you to know that I am very much obliged and grateful to you all for coming out here to my aid. I want to also thank you from the bottom of my heart for all your services," said Sakreg.

"Look, I can see your point lieutenant Sakreg as you have indicated that there is a possibility in making a lasting friendship with this tribe by taking their leader back to their village alive. I hope that they will understand our motive that we don't want any conflict and that we strive for a lasting peace with this tribe. All right then, let's not waste any more time, let's get on board, and get out of here, and may God help us," said the captain. They all got on board the craft and became airborne.

CHAPTER 35

The rescue crew apportioned Drake to the rear of the fuselage, and away from the rest of the crew. He set quietly in a crouched position with his arms wrapped around his elevated knees and his butt rested on a hard metal chassis of the rescue craft.

Drake felt all alone despite of the presence of the rescue crew that was sitting twenty feet away from him. The tension was high within the crew. A few were spatting among themselves and during their altercation; they were pointing their fingers toward him. One of the crewmembers was silently casting a strange and ominous glare at his direction—as if Drake was an invader or a monster that wanted to destroy everyone in the plane, and another two were expressing an astonished look thinking that Drake must be a freak of nature as if how could something like this ever exist? It surely made Drake feel uncomfortable and unwelcomed here in their midst.

Drake soon concluded that he was the subject of their discussion, contention, and obfuscation. He felt like dirt and was abashed being in their midst. He wished he could have understood every word they parted from their lips, and at the same time he desired to provide a few of his own back to them, having them to understand that he is an intelligent being and has no plans to harm any crew member here.

Drake decided to ignore them all together, and began to introspect and reminisce the events he had experienced prior coming to this planet just to subdue the mundane. He thought about his marriage with his unfaithful wife and re-lived the emotional pain she imposed on him. He felt the anger, the rage that surge from deep inside but at the same time, he knew he had to put his choleric feelings at bay. He then shifted his thoughts toward his unfinished work projects and toward his friends that he hobnobbed with in fancy restaurants and cafes, but he also realized that if he should have stayed on earth, his life would have been a nightmare for sure because of all the killings that took place with his own hands. However, the most painful of them all he felt was the thought of how in the world was he going to see his beloved son and his daughter again. Drake knew that going back was going to be an impossible task and that he was going to spend the rest of his life on this newly found and unknown planet, and that he was going to be away from all the humanity, and everything that he had touched and felt on the planet earth.

Drake's lachrymose eyes gave away to his tristful expression, soon A few teardrops rolled slowly down his cheeks, and with some effort, he managed to suppress his in-felt torrent of emotions where if he wouldn't, it would have been a fully blown peroxisome of emotional outburst. Adding insult to injury, he didn't feel the comfort he needed in this craft to put his weary body at rest.

This craft had no windows near where he sat. Drake desired to have them so that he could at lease gaze right through them and see the world that he barely came to be familiar with, and in the interim, to create his own dreams and fantasies to escape the doldrums and the emotional pain he was experiencing at this moment.   However, he was able to witness everyone's expression and every nook and cranny around him so that he could be ready for any unexpected and life-threatening situation that may loom before his very own eyes. However, the constant but mild revving engine noise and the rattling hull of the craft was more profound and annoying then the heated stare of the crew.

The rescue-craft was like that of the U.S. made military Osprey V-22, but had a shorter wingspan with a tilt Ion jet engine mounted at the ends of the wing tips and was devoid of vertical and horizontal stabilizers at the tail end. The craft had a cylindrical fuselage with hydraulically actuated circular landing pods attached at the belly of the craft: two under the wings, and one under the canopy. It also had a gate at the tail end with a ladder to egress and ingress.

Drake was oblivious of their plans that they had for him. "Where are they taking me now?" he questioned this issue in his mind ever since he got on board this craft and in result it discomforted him a great deal, but despite, he thought he would be ready to take on any challenge that they may impose on him.

At the front end of the fuselage, they laid Soarp the wounded Yojy. He was still agonizing and was wallowing in pain, and was creating a ruckus while being on a stretcher. Lieutenant Eewo compelled to create a tranquilizing cocktail, and with the help of her crew she managed to inject the anodyne concoction with some elaborate gizmo and within thirty seconds or so, he was out and unconscious.

The lieutenant took advantage of the tranquil Yojy and began to examine the material of the gauze with her fingers that Drake wrapped around Soarp's wounds. She appeared intrigued by it for she had never seen anything like it.

Suddenly she turned around and faced Drake. She got off her seat, she didn't lose sight of him and slowly walked toward him while everyone else gravitated their sight on her and they quietly monitored her every move. She came and stood within three feet of Drake and gazed down at him while he raised his head up and eyes were met and were locked in an intense glare. Drake could swear that this unusual stare from Lieutenant Eewo could only portray nothing less than an amorous gawk that was burgeoning inside her ever since she met him.

Lieutenant Eewo had never witnessed so much hair on anyone's head, especially the five o'clock shadow that was beginning to develop on Drake's face, and she took fancy of it. She demonstrated her admiration toward Drake by delivering a slight smile on her face and letting him know that I am desirous of having you to myself.

The lieutenant suddenly blurted aloud so that everyone could hear, "I want to keep him as my pet. He could become useful for me. I will teach him our language, our culture, and our ways. I will make him a productive part of our society."

"Ma'am, you should know that you can't keep him yet. He has to be quarantined at first, and you know that is going to take a few months, and once the government knows that he is an alien, they will have to perform various experiments on him, and just maybe he will not survive them," said Sakreg.

"Yes, I am very familiar with government protocols. Therefore, I have decided that he will not be quarantined, nor will the government know anything about him, at least not yet. I will break the news about this alien to the world rather slowly and as I see it fit, but I need your total silence and your cooperation about this so-called alien. Could I count on every one of you?" asked the lieutenant.

She received "yes" answer from everyone except Sakreg.

"Ma'am, do you have any idea as to what you are talking about when you say the government will not know anything about him; what about my alibi? Did you forget that he is my only live and convincible alibi to save my life from definite execution?

"You should know that as soon as I present him to the command, there goes the shroud of secrecy out the door. The media will be all over him and me. Otherwise—you should know that you would be signing my death certificate if I don't come up with a different and significant alibi other than Drake, the alien.

"Therefore, if I should remain alive, then your plan must be revised or rendered null and ineffective for now," said Sakreg.

"You have a point there Sakreg. Sorry, I for a moment didn't think about the situation you were in; I was only thinking about my endeavors. Before we land this craft at the command post, I will revise my plans concerning this alien," said the lieutenant with a sad expression, and then she turned around and gawked at Drake in a mesmerizing way.

Then, Captain Enuj suddenly announced, "Lieutenant, we are approaching the Ireban village. That is where we will hand over this wounded Yojy. ETA in ten minutes, advise your crew," said Captain Enuj, the pilot, through his mouthpiece.

"All right, you heard the captain. We are going to land soon, and we might anticipate some trouble ahead. You all know that we are going to land in a hostile territory. The Yojies, I have been told, and as you know, they are our archenemy. They are considered barbaric in nature, but soon, they will realize that we have come in peace.

"However, should they fail to understand our peace gesture— you be ready and be alert to engage! Now lock, load, and energize your weapons. I promise we are not going to stay there for long.

"I anticipate every one of us will get out alive and hopefully without an incident. Is that clear to everyone?" asked Lieutenant Eewo.

"Yes Ma'am," said all, and began to lock, load, and energize their weapons while they cracked jocks and laughed and told brief synoptic and profound events of their lives to each other while sitting and working on their weapons. After few more minutes of flight, the captain announced, "Two minutes to touchdown!"

Drake realized that these entities were reading their weapons, but for what reason he asked silently to himself. Soon he concluded that he was going to experience some sort of a firefight and that he was going to be right in the middle of it. He felt apprehensive and thought that this planet is a hostile planet and worked out mentally to be ready for anything that came his way.

The Ireban village was now visible to the pilot in a plane sight. Soon, the rescue team with Soarp arrived over the communal farm area a little distance from the settlement area, and then they began to circle around in the air. They witnessed plethora of thatch type huts with conically tipped roofs. These huts were raised ten feet above the ground for their protection from natural elements and feral beasts. The hovels had wide interconnect walkways used for commuting from one hut to the next.

The Ireban village had three amphitheaters: one for court disputes, one for sports, and another for entertainment. They were not large. However, each could accommodate approximately six hundred Yojies.

The village itself is comprised of approximately a thousand and two hundred Yojy families plus their children. There are plethora of security and military personal located in strategic locations. Chief Gnokn is the residing gerent of the tribe.

At the time of the rescue craft's arrival in the Ireban airspace, Chief Gnokn was conducting the trial of the two-chained and inculpated Yojies who managed to escape Soarp's group when they besieged Drake and Sakreg. There was also passel of crowd gathered in the amphitheater to witness the trial of the two convicted Yojies.

The alleged story was circling among the villagers and the governing bodies that the two escapees from Soarp's henchmen team were the culprit in killing Soarp and most of his miscreant teammates. The villagers have reached to that conclusion because Soarp and his thugs have never returned home except them two and there were no witnesses to collaborate the statements of the two accused Yojies.

Suddenly the trial was interrupted, and everyone's eyes became fixated on the rescue craft that was circling in the air. Moments later, the plane slowly began to descend to the ground sending dust and gravel up in the air. The denizens were puzzled. There were expressions of fear and unrest among the villagers. They were thinking as to what in the world an Eponan flying craft is doing out here? Are they here to destroy us, which were the thoughts and the sentiments of the many Yojy spectators?

When the rescue craft landed, the security personal immediately surrounded the craft with their weapons; they were ready to engage in a conflict should it have started. Soon the families with their children have arrived at the scene. They also surrounded the craft, each raising their fists in the air demanding them to leave. The crowd began to haler unintelligible sounds that meant to create fear in the hearts of the invaders; with this action, they displayed their readiness to take part in a battle should it have become necessary.

Chief Gnokn stood proudly at the front line to meet the Eponan visitors at first hand. He glared ominously at the craft, and waited patiently for the crew to disembark. He felt safe and was cocksure that his security personal could handle any situation that may have risen here.

The chief was draped with long and colorful attires that were embellished with assorted ornaments, and fashionable chains circled around his wrists and his waist. There was plethora of colorful necklaces around his neck and a large ornate belt around his waist.

The lieutenant and the captain took a few moments discussing among themselves as to who should go down to greet the crowed. They both agreed that if a female gender greeted them they will not be as frightened, and they will most likely not engage in a fray.

Minute or two have passed where suddenly the gate opened at the tail end of the craft. A ladder descended slowly to the ground. Lieutenant Eewo stepped down slowly from the ladder dressed in a regular Eponan military attire, holding no weapon of any sort in her hands.

The masses suddenly became quiet as she ambled proudly and fearlessly toward the chief. She stood approximately five feet away from him in confidence as if she is in command.

"Greetings to you and your people sir," said the lieutenant and delivered a brief kowtow, so did the chief the same, he returned a kowtow.

"You must be very brave to land in our territory, I admire your tenacity. However, what brings you here risking your life in the process. It must be very important that you are here. Otherwise, what business do you have coming here other than starting trouble?" asked the Chief Gnokn.

"Yes sir, I see you have a very good foresight, and it is very important that we should be here today sir, and the reason for my visit is not to create trouble as you have insinuated. But first, please allow me to introduce myself," said the lieutenant.

"Yes, you may—precede," said Chief Gnokn.

"I thank you sir—It would be my pleasure. My name is Eewo. I am a lieutenant in the rank, and I am attached to the Eponan's rescue command center," said the lieutenant.

"A rescue center—you didn't come here to rescue us, did you?" asked Chief Gnokn, and everyone began to laugh.

"No sir, I don't see that you need any rescuing sir," said the lieutenant.

"Thank God for that!" said the chief.

"My crew and I have come in peace. We don't mean harm to any of your people."

"Well, that is a first," said the chief.

"I see you have some doubts about the statement I have made, but it is true, I do come in peace, so please instruct your people to put their weapons down. You have no need for them at this moment and for any moment to come and hopefully never have to in the future," said the lieutenant.

"I will instruct my people to put their weapons down when I deem it is safe to do so. However, if your statement is true about coming here in peace, then I would consider that it is a noble gesture on your part, but your kind may not agree with your decision," said the chief.

"I do understand your concern sir. You have the right to think in such manner, but my crew and I will do everything in our power to convince the committee to provide a lasting and peaceful cohabitation between us," said the lieutenant.

"Well, we'll see. However, you may address me as Chief Gnokn. I am the leader of this village. These are my people," said Chief Gnokn, swinging his arm toward the people.

"Fine, as you wish, Chief Gnokn. In that case, I will state the reason for my visit here. In which, you are all anticipating hearing what I have to say, and I will be brief. We have rescued one of your people who was gravely wounded in the field. He calls himself Soarp," said the lieutenant.

Soarp! Did you say Soarp? Shouldn't he be dead?" asked the Chief. Eyes widened in excitement when he heard the name Soarp and that he was still alive.

"Well—he would have died if we would have left him in the field. He incurred physical wounds on his legs and couldn't stand up straight or even walk. However, let me make this clear to you, Chief Gnokn. When it comes to his injury, we had nothing to do with it. However, at this moment, it appears to be not a life-threatening situation with Soarp.

"We treated his wound where he was lying on the ground and brought him here with us. He is in this plane. All he needs now is rest and he will recover soon. I repeat, we come in peace, and we don't mean harm to anyone here. We hope that our goodwill gesture will create a lasting peace and friendship among your culture and ours," said the lieutenant.

"Well, I would say that is a very pleasant and compassionate gesture coming from your people by saving one of my own people, in which, I was fully surprised and was not expecting from the Eponans. However, we will put your peace gesture under advisement. We do want the carnage and the hostility to end and your people to leave our planet.

But coming back to Soarp, how did he incur this deathly injury on his legs? The two who are on trial now for the murder of their commander Soarp, have told us that an animal, a bizarre-looking animal that is unknown to us, has killed Soarp. They attempted to describe this animal. They have said unbelievable statements about this animal, which we have no record of its existence on this planet, and we knew that they were telling us a lie. You are not affiliated with them two who are on trial now, are you—and that, you are attempting to cast doubt on their murder charges just to rescue them are you?" asked the Chief.

"No chief Gnokn, I don't even know them, and I have never seen them before. As I have said, he is not dead because, our people have rescued him, and according to the story I have heard from Soarp himself, as to what had transpired, your two people who are now in custody, had nothing to do with his injury neither the death of his comrades," said the lieutenant.

"Is that so, Lieutenant Eewo," asked the chief.

"Yes, Chief Gnokn. I will command my people to bring Soarp down from the plane and he will explain everything to you as to how he incurred his injuries," said the lieutenant.

"Very well then—how many are you in this craft?" asked the Chief.

"A total of six, including the injured Soarp—Chief Gnokn," said the lieutenant. She purposely left out Drake.

"I want everyone down from this plane and no weapons in their possessions. This is for our safety, you understand. I don't like surprises. Is that clear?" asked the Chief.

"Yes, Chief Gnokn, that is quite reasonable and understandable. I feel your concern. I will arrange for your demand. But first, I want to say it again: I want you to advise your people to put their weapons down for my people's safety. I am sure you understand that, don't you, Chief Gnokn?" said the lieutenant.

"All right, that is fare. You have made your point—Yojies, put your weapons down. I don't anticipate any trouble here," said the Chief. But no one listened.

"I said put your weapons down!" said the Chief one more time but this time, he uttered vehemently, and they all looked at each other in disagreement, but reluctantly placed their weapons on the ground.

"Thank you for your cooperation, Chief Gnokn. Now, I will contact my captain and inform him of your request."

"Captain come in, please. Can you hear me?" asked the lieutenant.

"Yes, lieutenant, I hear you loud and clear," said the captain.

"Excellent. The Chief is requesting that everyone disembark from the plane unarmed for their security. Please be advised, and if you should know, everything is fine and is under control down here. I don't anticipate trouble of any kind from anyone."

"Roger to that. We are coming down, lieutenant. The captain is over and out."

"All right people listen up. We are going down to meet the Chief of the Yojy tribe. I was informed that it is the request of the Chief that we all come down with no weapons in our possession. We will transfer this patient down with us and hand him over to the Chief. But the alien must stay here. Is that clear to everyone?" asked the captain.

"Yes sir," replied all.

"Sakreg—since the so-called alien is your friend, I want you to hide him in this craft and don't let them find him. Is that clear to you?" asked the captain.

"Yes sir, I will take care of that myself sir," said Sakreg.

"Lieutenant, come in please," asked the captain.

"Yes captain, I read you loud and clear. Go head. What are your orders?" asked the lieutenant.

"We will come down in two minutes. Hold your position over," said the captain.

"Yes sir, I will inform the Chief of your decision. The lieutenant is over and out." The Lieutenant informed the Chief as to what the captain had decided to do.

CHAPTER 36

After two short minutes, two Eponan rescue personnel, Corporal Larue and Corporal Lenute, carefully carried the stretcher down the ladder from the rear of the craft. On it was laid Soarp and him having a composed and alert disposition. The pain at his injury site subsided to a minimal level, but he was still hesitant to stand on his feet. There was this certain and special sparkle in his eyes, knowing that he was home at last and soon to meet his loving family and that the danger of becoming forlorn and dying in the wilderness alone was no longer an option.

The rescue crew carried the gurney and laid it on the ground right in front of Chief Gnokn. Everyone was silently observing this unfolding scene, and before the chief had the opportunity to open his mouth to say anything, Soarp's wife and his two boys rushed through the field; his boys were yelling, "Dad, dad, you are alive, you are alive." Soarp saw his loving wife and his family running with purpose in their minds, coming and kneeling next to him, having elated expressions on their faces, embracing him, kissing him on his cheeks and on his hands many times over, and welcoming him home with tears of joy that were rolling down their cheeks.

Everyone froze in their positions, observed the unification of Soarp's family, and couldn't hold their joyful tears, the chief wasn't immune from it all; there were some tears rolling from his lachrymose eyes. The chief extended his arm toward Soarp and attempted to raise him up off the ground. Soarp did the same. He extended his arm toward the chief, hands clasped together, the chief pulled him up off the ground, and Soarp stood up on his feet for the first time and gained more confidence that he was on the road to recovery. Everyone cheered and hollered words of joy.

The chief embraced him, and at the same time, he said: "Son, it is good to see you back home—and alive. We all thought you were dead, but I am so glad that you are here and alive and standing next to your family and next to all of us. At the same time, I am saddened because I can't say the same for your crew. What happened son."

"I will explain everything to you soon, honorable Chief Gnokn. But now I want to thank you and thank everyone here for honoring me with your visit. However, if it wasn't for them, I certainly wouldn't be here and standing before your eyes," said Soarp.

He turned around, embraced the Eponan Lieutenant Eewo, and thanked her for all that she did. Soon, Captain Enuj and Lieutenant Sakreg came down the ladder, and both ambled with brisk steps toward the lieutenant.

"Did we miss anything here?" asked the captain.

"Yes sir, a lot, especially an emotional moment that I will explain later," said the lieutenant.

"Chief Gnokn, please allow me to introduce my crew."

"You may proceed," said the chief.

"Thank you, Chief Gnokn. This is Captain Enuj the pilot of this rescue craft, and Lieutenant Sakreg, the starfighter pilot. He was involved in rescuing this planet from Grolz. These two are Corporal Larue and Lenute. They are my medical technicians." They all kowtowed before the Chief in a demonstration of respect and honor.

"It has been our pleasure to have met you, Chief Gnokn, and I hate to say goodbye, but our mission here is accomplished, and we must return home," said Captain Enuj.

"I understand. Thank you and your crew for all your kindness and especially for taking care of my right hand Yojy. He is very precious to us all. He is the pillar of our society. We can't lose him. This day will go on in our history. You and your crew are welcome here at any time and acquire our protection if it needs to be. You will receive our utmost hospitality for your good deeds," said Chief Gnokn.

"Thank you, Chief Gnokn. We are honored, and we will not disappoint you," said the captain. The rescue crew each delivered an Eponan military salute and made an about-face, including Sakreg being in the middle of the captain and the lieutenant, and the two corporals followed right behind them. They all began to walk toward the craft to leave the area for home.

Suddenly, the two accused Yojies that were on trial and were in chains, yelled from a near distance saying, "You who are in the middle, wearing a black uniform, you are the killer who killed all our teammates, and now you are attempting to get away and get out of here like you haven't done anything wrong. You should be on trial, not us, for all the killings you have done, especially your animal friend." The crew stopped dead in their track and turned around then faced the crowd.

"Yes—yes, you're the one in the middle with the black uniform," said the two that were on trial for the murder of Soarp. They were pointing at Lieutenant Sakreg.

"What is it that I am hearing about you and your friend, the so-called animal? Did you have anything to do with the killings of Soarp's team, as they have said?" asked the Chief.

"No sir, I did not kill his team Chief Gnokn! They are totally mistaken," said Sakreg.

"Then what are they talking about? Either you or they are telling me lies, and lies will be dealt with very severely here. So, which is it, and while we are at this, who is your friend, the animal that they are referring to, and is the animal in your plane now?" asked the Chief.

"Chief, we don't have anyone else in the plane, and we have spent much of our time here already. We must really be going now. Our command post expecting us at a certain time, and we must answer for being late," said the captain.

"Is that all you can do—really, captain—what are you running from? We were about to execute the two that were on trial, but now, allegedly, we find them to be innocent of the crime, but I am not too sure about that myself.

"However, at the same time, we find one of your crewmembers with his animal friend are at fault for killing Soarp's people. Soarp's people are my people, and you want us to let you depart without understanding the full story! You must understand one thing, and that is we must find the real culpable one and deliver the condign punishment for all the murders committed.

"I must say this to you captain; —there is no need for any of you to be offended by my decision. I have decided that no one is to leave here until I find the underlying cause of this heinous story of murder that is allegedly perpetrated by one or two of your members. I will have to punish the ones that committed this horrible crime against my people.

"For that reason, we must search your craft to see if anyone else is hiding inside, just to verify your statement stating: 'There is no one else in this craft." I am referring to the so-called "animal friend' you understand that, don't you captain," said the Chief.

"Well yes, certainly, Chief Gnokn, your point is well taken. You do have to verify my statement to see whether it is true or falls. I would have done the same. No offense taken, Chief Gnokn," said the captain.

"Very well then, it is good that we do understand each other captain," said the Chief.

"For your information, Chief Gnokn—I did not kill or murder any of Soarp's crewmembers!" said Sakreg with a concerned expression.

"I agree Chief, he wasn't the one. It was his friend, the animal; I am a witness to that, but…..," said Soarp. He couldn't finish his statement.

"Stop there, Soarp. I must find this so-called strange-looking animal that I have been hearing about all this time and kill it, lest it harms more of our people in the future. However, you Sakreg, now that we know who the real killer is, it appears that you are off the hook for now. Thanks for Soarp's statement," said the Chief and summoned four of his security personnel to go inside the rescue craft to conduct a thorough search for the animal (the human called Drake).

Four security personnel ambled toward the craft with their weapons drawn. Anxiety, consternation, and apprehension surely was evident in their expressions. They had no knowledge of what they will be expecting from the so-called animal. However, they surreptitiously ascended the airstair and cautiously entered inside the fuselage with their head-banded flashlights turned on. Although there was plenty of sunlight outside inside, the craft was dark as midnight, humid, and laced with a stale odor.

Drake realized four armed Yojies just entered the craft with their headlamps and weapons drawn and were slowly and cautiously trading toward the front of the craft. They were searching every nook and cranny for the animal (the human). They had no idea of the animal's size, shape, or strength.

Drake slowly and quietly stood up, leaned against one of the framed structures in the back, and glared attentively at their every move. His heart felt the dread. The butterflies churned in his stomach. He knew his end was near. He felt the chills and the sweat of the thoughts of death.

Drake's eyes were used to the darkness that existed inside the craft. However, he was able to have a clear visual of Yojes that had entered the craft and begun to move slowly toward the front of the fuselage. He thought of hiding, but really, there was nowhere that he was able to make his body disappear from their sight inside this craft, no recesses nor especial compartments that were sufficiently large enough to hide his body.

"It wouldn't be long before they will find me and capture me. Perhaps this is where I will die," thought Drake. "How about if I Sneak out of this craft while the Yojies are busy and are attentively looking for me in front of this craft? It would be a real chance, or an option for me to escape," he thought. He placed his thinking into action and took a few careful steps down the airstair just to have a visual of the outside environment and to assess the type of people and how many were out there. After acknowledging a large crowd waiting for him outside and that there were soldiers or security guards surrounding the craft, he thought, "I have no chance to escape; the weapon-toting security personnel, who are out there, are probably anticipating and waiting for me to come out and attempt to escape from this craft. In that case, they wouldn't hesitate to shoot me, and if they decide not to shoot, then they may have to chase me to capture me like a fugitive, and who knows what they will do with me, knowing that I am very different in appearance from them. The merit for saving Soarp will have to go right out of the window." He thought this plan wasn't going to be a good plan for escape.

So, he abandoned the course of his action, went back up the airstair silently and cautiously, and hid himself in the same place as he was before.

"It wasn't going to be long before the four who are inside this craft—find me and arrest me. If I should shoot these four, there will be more of them attempting to get in, and perhaps if they can't get to me, they will blow this plane into smithereens, and I will be destroyed in it. I may have a better chance of staying alive by being caught by these four who have entered this plane. After all, I did save the Yoji's life. I am sure that should count for something to them—I hope. Heck—they might even count me as being a hero", thought Drake.

The security detail began to turn around and face the tail end of the craft. They were on their way to the exit. Suddenly, one of the security personnel shined a light in Drake's direction and noticed a slight movement at the corner of the craft. The Yojy shouted in his language unintelligible words to the rest of the crew; soon, they all shined their lights in Drake's direction, took a few steps back and almost fell to the ground from sheer fear laced with obfuscation and amazement.

Horror and trepidation consumed their faces as if to say, "What in the world are we looking at." They palavered among themselves for approximately ten to twenty seconds and trained their weapons directly at him, anticipating an attack from Drake at any moment, but that didn't materialize. His inaction pleasantly surprised them, and they thought this would take some intelligence for him to react this way.

The light from their headlamp was very bright; in fact, it was blinding him. He hid his face with his arm, and right at that moment, he knew he didn't have much of a chance to escape. He couldn't bribe them so that they will turn the blind eye; but bribe them with what he thought?

He had seen the overwhelming crowd outside. He realized there was nowhere for him to run. He felt his fate was now sealed with uncertain consequences.

Drake signaled using both arms, telling them to back off and give me some room to move around, then he gave them another hand signal, telling them to let's all get out of here by going down this airstair into the open air. They understood his intentions.

When Drake began to move toward the airstair to exit the craft, the leader of the security detail appointed two of his members to go down first to meet him on the ground, so that they would restrain him from running. The other two, including the Yoji in charge, decided to follow him from behind, lest Drake change his mind and instead decide to stay inside the craft.

Drake moved toward the airstair. He balked for a moment or two and gazed down the steps, then began to think. "What am I going to experience next? Am I going to die here? I didn't come here for this, oh lord. Please keep me safe from these beasts," he prayed silently. Just then, the head of the security goaded Drake from his back by the barrel of his hand-held weapon and prompted him to go down the steps.

"All right, all right, I am going. Just take it easy, and no one will get hurt," said Drake. They glared at each other, having a confounded look on their faces. They both decided that this animal could talk and had a language of his own that they didn't understand. Besides, they also took notice of his attire and the shoes he wore and thought this animal was not an ordinary animal. How could this ever be considered an animal when he is wrapped in technology?

Drake took slow steps as he descended from the flight ladder. Soon, he reached the ground and stopped for a few seconds. He took a deep breath, thinking this could be his last minutes being alive and delivered an ominous glare at the two security personnel that was on the ground waiting for him to come down as they took a few steps back from Drake for their safety, and soon the other two followed him from behind, then they all ambled toward Chief Gnokn.

Drake noticed the gathering of the huddled crowds and thought silently, "They all must have come just to witness my presence and my eminent death. I wouldn't blame them. They have never seen anyone like me here on this planet."

The flabbergasted crowd that was in the front row took a few steps back in fear of him. They were amazed at his appearance. They began to chatter aloud among themselves and think how unusual of a creature this entity is and what must be that is standing here before us now.

The Chief swung his arm in an arc, signaling the crowd to be quiet, and suddenly, there was not even a whisper to be heard. He then turned his head toward Drake with his eyes open wider then normal, consumed in utter amazement, and his hand resting on the butt of his holstered weapon, and said, "That is truly a strange-looking animal standing upright on two feet instead of four like the rest of the animals are. I wonder what powers this thing possesses that made it possible to kill most of the Soarp's team?" thought Chief Gnokn and began to walk toward Drake with fear in his eyes as he signaled his henchmen to be ready to shoot and kill should this animal begin to attack.

The towering Chief Gnokn came within five feet of him and began to circle around him quietly and slowly having a very puzzled expression on his face. The looks of Drake fully mesmerized the chief: his full set of hair on his head, his Vandyke beard on his face, the color of his skin, and the attire that he wore. The Chief desired to study him a little further before he shot him for the murders that he committed. Drake also slowly swiveled his body three-hundred and sixty degrees so that he would never break his glowering eye contact between him and the chief.

"Chief Gnokn, your excellence, I must caution you, for your safety, please do not get any closer to him. He is extremely dangerous. He could take your life away right now if he decided to do so. I know that he can and please keep your distance and do not provoke him please," said Sakreg.

"Is that so, Eponan soldier?" said the Chief

"Yes sir, it is so, and that is the truth sir. Stay away and spare your life, Chief Gnokn," said Sakreg.

"Is there any more like this animal roaming in this part of the land that we are not aware of?" asked the Chief.

"First of all, Chief Gnokn, he is not an animal. Second, there are no more of his kind here on this planet," said Sakreg.

"Are you sure about this, Lieutenant Sakreg?" asked the Chief Gnokn.

"Yes, Chief Gnokn, I am very sure of that," said Sakreg.

"If this thing is not an animal as you say, then what is it?" asked the chief.

"He is a very intelligent being sir. They call themselves human. He is not from this planet. He is from a different planet. He calls it Earth. The humans are from different galaxies all to gather, and they call their galaxies the "Milky Way," said Sakreg.

"I am nettled by your frivolous statements, Lieutenant Sakreg, and with all due respect, I have heard enough of your nonsense. A different planet, a different galaxy. Do you have me for a fool!" asked the Chief vehemently.

"No sir—you have my utmost respect for you sir," said Sakreg.

"Very well then, Captain Enuj, you must contain your people carefully; this one is becoming delusional," said the chief.

"I will, sir. I will take that under advisement," said Captain Enuj. Sakreg approached Captain Enuj (the pilot) and said in a muttered word, "Captain, I don't want him to be killed. He is my only alibi," said Sakreg.

"I understand that, but right now, there is not much we can do here. We are greatly outnumbered and are in grave danger. We must play our cards right. Otherwise, we are not going home. We will either be prisoners here, or dead. Let's hope things will turn out in our favor and that we get out of here alive. Thanks for all the trouble you have caused us all," said the captain sarcastically that was laced with a slight anger in his expression.

"In that case, captain—I have one request. If he should die here, then I ask that you leave me here and go on to tell the command that Sakreg must be dead and that we couldn't find his remains anywhere. You should know that if I should return and attempt to explain my story to the command without my one and only alibi, they will not believe me, and therefore, I will be executed, and—I am not planning to die yet. As a matter of fact, I would have a better chance to survive here by living amongst the Yojies than going back without my Drake," said Sakreg.

"I understand your predicament perfectly Sakreg. Let's take it easy and see how our situation is going to turn out, then we will decide our next step—your fate. Remember that you got us in this situation in the first place, so at least let's play it cool, and there will be a good chance that every one of us will get out of here alive. Is that understood, Sakreg?" asked the captain.

"Yes sir I do sir," said Sakreg.

The Chief went back to where he stood before, and announced to the crowd aloud, "Today we will have justice rendered. Now we finally know the killer of Soarp's covey, and it is here—you are looking at it. This animal killed Soarp's league; now this animal is in our custody, and it must be killed, and that will be its condign punishment, so then it will not harm anyone of us anymore.

"I am prepared to take this action upon myself to accomplish it. I don't want anyone to pull the trigger to silence this animal. It is now my responsibility to do so," said Chief Gnokn.

Drake began to feel something dreadful soon to take place, and it must involve him. He began to recite out loud the bible in Psalms 23, verse 4: "YEA, THOUGH I WALK THROUGH THE VALLEY OF THE SHADOW OF DEATH, I WILL FEAR NO EVIL: FOR THOU ART WITH ME; THY ROD AND THY STAFF THEY COMFORT ME."

"This animal can talk," said the Chief.

"Chief, he might be preparing to attack you. Please shoot him now before he harms you," said one of the soldiers that was standing in near proximity to the chief.

"I will choose when it is deemed necessary to kill this beast, not you. Is that understood?" said the chief.

"Yes, Chief Gnokn?"

Drake thought silently, "If my lord is going to allow me to die here, then I am surely going to take all that I can with me, especially this one, the thrasonically hick, whoever he is," Drake was thinking of Chief Gnokn.

Chief Gnokn swiveled his body and faced Drake. He pulled his hand-held weapon from his belt, and slowly leveled it and pointed at Drake, thinking there is nothing that this animal will be able to do to stop him; he aimed at his chest, and just before an attempt made to pull the trigger, Drake swiftly pulled his forty-five-caliber semiautomatic pistol and pulled the trigger. The Chief's hand-held weapon flew right out of his hand and landed on the hard ground approximately twenty feet away from Chief Gnokn. Drake swiftly but spasmodically rotated his body three-hundred and sixty degrees and pointed his pistol right at the security personnel that brought him down from the craft and noticed that they were frozen in their positions. Their mouths were gaped, their eyes were filled with horror, and they were speechless.

The Chief immediately yelled aloud to everyone, "Do not shoot this animal or whatever it is. It doesn't pose any danger. Put your weapons down." The chief realized that Drake's intention was only self-defense and that Drake had no intention to kill anyone. Drake realized the danger was over and placed his pistol back in its sleeve then turned around and faced the chief.

"You see Chief—if he wanted to kill you, he would have already done so. He kills only in self-defense. Chief, this is what I was attempting to tell you, but you stopped me. My people and I harassed him and put his life in danger. I saw how, in a matter of seconds, he blew their heads off one by one, and he was sooooo quick that no one knew what was going on, except they were falling with their heads being blown off. I was very afraid that he would do the same to you. He could have done so very easily, but he decided not to," said Soarp.

The Chief was amazed at Drake's accuracy and was dumbstruck at his speed and his decision. He couldn't believe his eyes that an animal could tote and use a weapon and be so accurate in doing so, and at the same time be so decisive as in— to kill or maim or to disable.

The Chief froze all his movements and glared at Drake for a few seconds, displaying a bug-eye and befuddled expression, thinking about what had just transpired here, especially Drake's unbelievable feat in which it was very difficult to be duplicated by the Yojies. He thought, just maybe the Eponan (Sakreg) was telling the truth about Drake's background after all.

CHAPTER 37

The day was still young. It appeared as if it was approximately eleven AM Earth time, but Drake had no clue as to how the day was cycled here. There were no visible clouds to dim the light of the blazing sun, or to cast shadows on the ground. The sun rays were freely and incessantly pounding the land and worming everything in sight, and the Yojy community was feeling the heat of the day.

Suddenly, the spectators shifted the direction of their sight from Drake and focused their attention on a spaceship that had just emerged from behind the rugged mountain chain that was located due west (earth north) from where the Yojie crowd was gathered.

The craft appeared trapezoid, approximately fifty feet long, twenty-five feet wide at the rear, and fifteen feet wide at the front. It had an oval contour that led to a flat bottom and was powered by four ion propulsion engines.

The spacecraft was heading toward where the chief and the crowds were standing. Soon, the craft arrived right above the multitude and slowly and vertically descended by spitting sporadic ion jets from either side of the craft and from the bottom just to bring the vessel to a horizontal level while it attempted to make a touchdown.

The spaceship finally landed and rested on its three landing pods two were in the back and one in the front. Moments later, a door opened at the end of the fuselage and out came the airstair that slowly swang vertically toward the ground and made a thudding sound as it made a toucheddown.

Chief Gnokn, having firsthand knowledge about the occupants of this craft and the purpose of their arrival here, suddenly scowled and then acquired a saturnine and worrisome disposition. He patiently but undesirably waited for the crew to disembark from the craft and had no choice but to meet them face to face.

A Darkan by the name of Vobak; he is from the Eroom tribe, which is located approximately a hundred miles southwest of Ireban village. Vobak slowly stepped down the airstair, wielding his cherished weapon in his right hand and pointing the barrel up toward the sky. He didn't lose sight of the crowd in each step that he took going down and had a surly appearance on his continence as if he was very angry at everyone.

Vobak acquired this devastating weapon from a secret designated area with the help of an Eponan soldier friend by the name of Dnak, and Dnak filched the weapons from one of the Eponan command posts.

Most of the security personnel in this village, including the chief Gnokn were aware of this weapon and its abilities. They feared this weapon dearly, because, with one burst from this rifle, it could kill hundreds of lives at once by just pointing in the direction of the kill.

Moments passed by, and six more of his henchmen, including the Eponan soldier Dnak, disembarked from the craft to join Vobak, their leader. These six Vobak's cohorts were also brandishing the same devastating weapon in their hands. Eponans used this weapon against the Grolz, and that is how the Grolz lost the second invasion.

"What! Isn't that Dnak who cooked nice meals for us all in the base? What is he doing here with Darkans and holding one of our prized weapons in his hands?" asked Lieutenant Eewo to Captain Enuj quietly while everyone else's attention was on Vobak and his henchmen.

"He must have stolen the weapons from the armory, and he is sure in trouble, as a matter of fact, in big trouble. We will report him to the command as soon as we get back and sand investigators to hunt him down and arrest his ass for good, and you know darn well what the military will do, right?" said the captain.

"Yah, a death penalty for sure," said the lieutenant sadly. Dnak concentrated his sight on the Eponan visitors and thought, what in the world are they doing here in hostile territory, and what is that thing, whatever it is (the human), doing in their midst?

"Greeting Chief Gnokn, at last, we meet again, and right on schedule, I might say. I am sure you were expecting us today, weren't you," asked Vobak.

"Yes, as a matter of fact, I was expecting you sometime today," said Gnokn.

"Very well, then, do you remember last time—you disappointed my crew and me? As you remember, we went back empty-handed, but we went back with a warning, didn't we?"

"Yes, I remember that warning," said Chief Gnokn with a concerned expression.

"Very well then, as you know, today is the day I have come to collect the Munar (Gold) that you promised us would be ready for today's visit. I hope for your sake and the sake of your people, you have good news for us today," said Vobak with a firm and serious expression.

"What is the meaning of this weapon in your hands and in the hands of your crew? Do you come in peace or make war with my people," asked Gnokn.

"Well----let me say this---it will all depend on your answer, Chief Gnokn. By the way, why are you folks gathered here in the first place? Oh yes I see, you were all expecting my arrival, and that you are all here to greet me, isn't that right?" asked Vobak, but there was no response from Chief Gnokn.

Vobak suddenly swiveled his head and faced the Eponan crew Drake then said, "What are these Eponans doing here? Are you conducting business behind my back and especially with our enemy!" asked Vobak. Not waiting for an answer, from the corner of his eyes, he descried Drake's presence and swiveled his head toward him. Suddenly, his eyes opened wider in disbelief he turned and faced Gnokn and said, "What in the world is that. I have never seen any life form as such. Is it a new animal species or a mutant of some kind?" asked Vobak.

"Why don't you ask the Eponans? They brought that thing here with them. That thing already hurt some of my people and it has been said by the Eponan crew here, that this creature is very dangerous, and I believe them," said Gnokn.

"Is that right?" asked Vobak, facing the Eponans.

"Yes, this creature is very dangerous sir. I wouldn't advise you to get near it or provoke it in any way," said Lieutenant Sakreg.

"Really—you arc telling mc that I should be scared now," asked Vobak, and he let a big guffaw, so as did his henchmen.

"You say that this little dweeb, whatever it is, is very dangerous? Let me guess, it spits poison, and I'll melt all over and die right on the spot?"

"It is worse than that; you will have a very violent death when he strikes. It wouldn't let you take another gasp of air to breathe. You see this thing, you call it a creature, but he is a very intelligent being," said Sakreg.

As Vobak was ambling toward Drake, halfway through his destination, he became entirely captivated by the strange looks of Drake and forgot the reason for him being here in the first place. Suddenly, Lieutenant Sakreg uttered, "Please don't get any closer; he will kill you before you even blink."

"You shut your mouth Eponan. I don't need some advice from my enemies, you filthy intruders! Before we leave here today with our prized item, none of you will be going back alive, and anyone else that interferes with our operation here, that is a promise.

I don't do business with my enemies. I should kill all you Eponans that I will be doing soon anyway," and Vovbak gave orders to his henchmen to be ready to shoot them when he called for it. He knew the Eponans were unarmed and couldn't do much but yield to his command.

"They come in peace Vobak. Leave them alone. Your quarrel is with us, not with them. They saved one of my people's lives from eminent death, which is why they are here. They want to leave in peace. Don't hurt them, please!" said Gnokn.

"Shot up, you old Yojy. I don't care for your answers. You just deliver what I came here for, or you and your Yojies are in big trouble with me," said Vobak.

Vobak turned and faced Drake and proceeded to move toward him. From seven feet away, he circled around him in sheer amazement, and so as Drake; he never left sight of Vobak and glared at him menacingly. Drake knew that the thing that was circling around him was boisterous and a troublemaker for everyone there.

Vobak stopped dead in his tracks. Drake realized that he was up to something. Drake reached for his forty-five tucked under his jacket, but decided not to pull it out into the open yet. His hand on the grip and his finger on the trigger he was ready to act at any given moment.

Just when Vobak extended his arm to grab Drake by his shoulder, Drake pulled his gun out and shot Vobak in his upper arm that wielded the weapon. His arm entirely tore away from his body and fell to the ground, and the fingers were still on the trigger. Vobak let loose a loud scream. He was in great pain. Right at his shoulder, blood began to squirt out from his torn arteries, and when the bullet met his body, it propelled him back a few feet. Drake switched his sight from Vobak, threw himself to the ground and rolled, and at each roll that he made, he shot Vobak's crew one by one, including Dnak the Eponan and blew their heads off before they even knew what was happening, then he stood up and turned around then faced Vobak and pointed his gun right at his head.

"You see, I told you he is dangerous, but you didn't listen to me, did you? Now you stand there powerless against that thing and us. Your days are over. Your threats no longer mean anything to us. You are finished here today. You are not getting out of here alive. If that thing doesn't finish you, then we will. It is enough that you have bullied us with your destructive weapons and stole our precise commodity over and over and over again," said Gnokn.

"Pleeeeease let me leave here in peace. I will never bother you again. I promise. I don't want to die, and please tell this creature to get out of my face," asked Vobak while he was in agony. By now, he lost his strength. He was barely standing on his feet, for he had lost a great deal of blood.

"I don't know how to tell him that. We don't speak its language, and it doesn't understand ours," said Gnokn. Drake suddenly pulled the trigger and blew Vobak's head off. He didn't want to see him suffer any longer, and Vobak fell hard on the ground and remained motionless. Vobak was dead as it can be.

Everyone screamed in joy at Drake's saving feat; for once and for all, their lives had been saved from the bullies. No more harassment and no more threats. Gnokn walked toward Drake. He came within seven feet of him and kowtowed before him in an expression of homage.

Drake extends his arm in a gesture of a handshake. Gnokn stood in confusion and attempted to understand Drake's motive. Drake jolted his hand once in the middle of the air to cue him to do the same. Gnokn extended his hand slowly and emulated Drake. Hands met in a tight grip and Drake brokered a smile on his face, and they shook hands vehemently. Suddenly, all Yojy tribes did the same with each other; the Eponans did the same, as if they had learned something new in their lives.

Gnokn turned and faced the Eponans, then said, "Today, we have peace and salvation extended to us by your alien friend, and friendship has been established between our race and yours. Go in peace and take your alien friend with you. We are ever more grateful to all of you and your alien friend too. As I have said, he literally saved our lives. This day will go on in history. Our children and their children will know about this day as to what had transpired here," and Gnokn delivered a kowtow.

"Chief Gnokn, thank you for believing in us. We feel the same toward your race. May there be a permanent peace between us forever. Now it is the time for us to depart to our command, but first, we must acquire the weapons that were in their hands. These weapons were stolen from our headquarters. We must return them back to the command," said Captain Enuj.

"Take what belongs to you, captain, and one more thing," Chief Gnokn pulled one of his necklaces' from his neck, then placed it upon Captain Enuj's neck, and said, "This is a token of my appreciation to you and to your crew. Depart in peace and may God be with you and your crew always," said Chief Gnokn.

The Eponan crew gathered the weapons and stood in line, then all rendered a kowtow to the Chief Gnokn, executed an about-face and marched toward the craft in unison. They got on board the craft, including Drake, and flew away into the blue sky.

The End.

About The Author

George Orchanian is an accomplished design drafter in the aerospace industry with a deep passion for writing. Born in Iraq and having moved to the United States in 1969, George draws inspiration from a diverse cultural background and rich life experiences. A former U.S Army servicemember, George served from 1976 to 1979, bringing an authentic military perspective to their writing. With a family heritage of writers, including an uncle who was a minister and an aunt and mother who were both writers, storytelling runs in their blood. This book is a testament to George's lifelong dream and dedication to creating realistic science fiction narratives. He explores themes of communication, resilience, and the wonders of science, reflecting their deep interest in the cosmos and the human spirit's unyielding quest for knowledge. Outside of writing, George enjoys studying space and technology, always seeking to expand his understanding of the universe.